REFLECTIONS IN THE NILE

REFLECTIONS IN THE NILE

J. SUZANNE FRANK

WARNER BOOKS

A Time Warner Company

This book is a work of fiction. Names, characters, places and incidents are either the product of the author's imagination or are used fictitiously, and any resemblance to actual persons, living or dead, events, or locales is entirely coincidental.

Copyright © 1997 by J. Suzanne Frank 11|16|00
All rights reserved.

Warner Books, Inc., 1271 Avenue of the Americas, New York, NY 10020

 A Time Warner Company

Printed in the United States of America

ISBN 0-446-52089-6

Book design and composition by L & G McRee

*To my parents
who never said "you can't," who never doubted I could, and who always loved me,
regardless.*

Thank you.

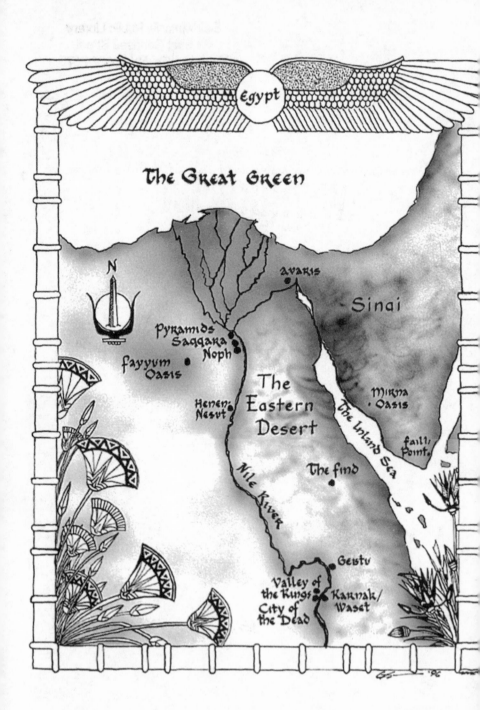

GLOSSARY

ab—ancient Egyptian for heart

ankh—the Egyptian key of life; a loop-headed cross

AnkhemNesrt—name of the goddess of the eighth hour of night; HatHor priestess eight o'clock

anu—a wanderer

Apiru—the enslaved races in Egypt, Israelites among them

Apis—a sacred bull

atmu—twilight

ba—the psyche and soul of a person

bukra—tomorrow

calèche—a horse-drawn carriage

cartouche—the ring surrounding and protecting a pharaoh's name

Chaos—creation

corvée—slaves or serfs attached to the land

crook—a symbol of Pharaoh's power in the shape of a shepherd's crook

cubit—measurement from elbow to fingers, approximately eighteen to twenty-two inches

decans—the twenty-four designations of night and day; charted by the stars

Deir El-Bahri—Arabic name for Hatshepsut's mortuary temple; called the-Most-Splendid in her reign

djellaba—a traditional Egyptian garment

electrum—a blend of gold and silver, used for plating statuary and walls

Elohim—Hebrew word for Lord

emmer—a cheaper grade of grain

erpa-ha—a hereditary title in ancient Egypt

fellahin—Arabic for common workers

felucca—a Nile boat

Gerchet—a personification of the night; HatHor priestess ten o'clock

hemu neter—first physician-priest

henhet crown—one of Pharaoh's crowns, covering the head and ears

henti—Egyptian measurement of distance

Herit-tchatcha-ah—name of the goddess of the seventh hour of night; HatHor priestess seven o'clock

Hyksos—the conquerors of Egypt in the Middle Kingdom; vanquished at the beginning of the eighteenth dynasty

hypostyle—the Greek term for a hall of columns

Inshallah—Arabic for "As God wills it"

inundation—the annual flooding of the Nile valley; used to count the years

jinn(s)—Arabic for demon(s)

ka—a person's individual and spiritual power

khaibit—a bloodsucking shadow

khamsim—a killing windstorm from the desert that brings extreme heat and sometimes sand tornadoes

kheft—enemy, opponent

khetu—an Egyptian measurement of water weight

magus, magi—magician(s)

Meret Seger—name of the mountain at the mouth of the Valley of the Kings

natron—natural salt; main ingredient in mummification

nome—the districts that Egypt was divided into

neter—a priest

Neter—the beginning, the creator, the unknown

Osiris—resurrected king of the netherworld

ostraca—pieces of stone used for everyday writing

RaAfu—means "night form of Ra"; HatHor priestess nine o'clock

RaEmhetep—means "a lunar form of Ra"; HatHor priestess eleven o'clock

rekkit—common people; common language (as in "low" Egyptian)

ReShera—means "the little sun"; HatHor priestess five o'clock

Ruha-et—means "evening"; HatHor priestess six o'clock

sa'a—"son of the heart" (beloved son)

Sekhmet—lion-headed goddess of vengeance

sem-**priest**—the first rung of priesthood

senet—an ancient Egyptian board game

shadoof—an irrigation tool used as far back as 2000 B.C.E.

shenti—a calf-length Egyptian kilt

shesh-besh—Arabic for backgammon

Shores of Night—euphemism for Hades

sistrum—stringed instrument used in worship

souq—Arabic for marketplace

tef-tef—a kind of plant

tenemos—the mud-brick walls surrounding every temple complex, symbolically making it the original mound of earth from which creation began

ushabti—figurines placed inside the tomb; in the event the deceased was called to a task in the afterlife, they served as the deceased's proxies

wadi—Arabic for canyon/valley

Wadjet/Udjet—names of the cobra and vulture who were supposed to protect Pharaoh from his enemies; hence their presence on the crown

web-priest—the lowest-rung of the priesthood

w'rer-priest—the second rung of the priesthood

THE MAJOR GODS AND GODDESSES

Amun—god of Thebes; his name means "Hidden or Unknowable One"

Amun-Ra—synthesis of Amun and Ra; king of the gods

Anubis—jackal-headed god of the dead and embalming

Aten—god of the sun disk, raised to monotheism by Ankhenaten

Atum—the creation god of Heliopolis; a form of Ra

Bastet—cat goddess; a personification of Sekhmet

Bes—child-protecting dwarf-god

Hapy—god of the fruitful Nile; shown with man's body and woman's breasts

HatHor—goddess of love and music; often represented as a cow

Heqet—frog goddess of fertility

Horus—falcon god; son of Isis and Osiris; the animation of the present pharaoh

Imhotep—builder of the step Pyramid, later deified

Isis—wife of Osiris; divine mourner

Khepri—Ra in the form of a scarab beetle

Khnum—ram-headed god of creating man

Khonsu—creator god associated with the moon; child of Amun and Mut

Ma'at—representation of justice and universal balance; the dead's heart was weighed against her "feather" of truth

Min—ithyphallic fertility god

Mut—wife of Amun

Nuit—goddess of the sky; said to swallow and give birth to Ra every night and day; wife of Geb, personification god of the earth

Nun—the personification of primordial chaos

Osiris—god of the dead and the afterlife; always shown as green-skinned mummy

Ptah—creator god of craftsmen; temple in Noph

Ra—the great sun god

Sekhmet—goddess of vengeance, war, and terror; wife of Ptah; shown as lioness or lion headed

Set—murderer of Osiris; Horus' rival
Shu—god of the air
Sobek—crocodile-headed god
Thoth—god of writing and knowledge; shown with an ibis-head

LOCATIONS

All Names Are Ancient Egyptian

Abdo—modern Abydos, a town in Lower Egypt on the Nile
Aiyut—town in Lower Egypt
Avaris—capital of Lower Egypt in the delta
Aztlan—empire in the Aegean
Canaan—modern Israel, Jordan area
Fayyum—an oasis in the western desert
Gebtu—an Upper Egyptian town; doorway to the eastern desert
Goshen—Lower Egypt's fertile plains
Hatti—modern Turkey
Kallistae—the island of Santorini; center of Aztlan empire
Keftiu—Crete
Kemt—what the Egyptians called Egypt
Kush/Kushite—country/countryman of modern-day Sudan
Midian—modern Arabia
Noph—classical Memphis
On—classical Heliopolis
Pi-Ramessa—literally "House of Ramessa"; building project in Lower Egypt
Punt—modern Somaliland
Retenu—modern Syria, Lebanon area
Waset—modern Luxor (classical Thebes)
Zarub—RaEmhetepet's hometown

FOREWORD

There is a fissure in time—a channel through which, by certain combinations of astronomy, location, and identity, it is possible to leave the present. The person who travels is not an observer but steps into the body and mind of another, a shadowed reflection . . . and fulfills another destiny. Like a ripple in a pond, each switch alters the present and the past. Sometimes the changes are miracles. Other times they are nightmares. History comprises both. Which people are the key to the combination? Who intrudes in our world, observing from another century, hidden in the flesh of another, hidden behind our expectations? Hidden because, ultimately, we see only what we expect to see.

PART I

CHAPTER 1

Egypt was gorgeous. Lapis sky, green palms, sands the color of pale gold. The artist in me could appreciate the beauty, never mind that my feet were swollen and my eyes bleary and that I felt as though I'd left my soul about two thousand miles back. It had been a long trip, flying from Dallas to Cairo via New York and Brussels, then taking an overnight train to Luxor, which at one stop had thrown me violently from my bunk to the floor. It went with the territory. I had spent some time growing up in the Middle East, so I knew what to expect and was familiar with the three ruling concepts, namely *Inshallah*—as God wills it; *bukra*—tomorrow; and an ever-present, incomprehensible hospitality.

Unfortunately, said hospitality didn't extend to someone helping me with my backpack as I stepped onto the platform at Luxor station. It was a heady moment as the city enveloped me. I had forgotten how the Middle East smelled. I had left in 1987, off to university at age seventeen. The odors drowned me now: spices, incense, unwashed bodies, and urine. They combined into a potent mix that caught me between gagging and smiling. And the noise! The shouts of reuniting families, the babble of tourists, the cacophony of radio stations, and, above us, the Muslim call to prayer. I pushed past the hawkers offering me "very best price, lady," on cheap hotels, because I knew cheap equaled no door, no closet, and many multilegged sleeping companions. This was Christmas and my birthday, and I had left behind the cool glitter of the Galleria, spiked eggnog, and crackling fires. No way was I staying in some sleazy, doorless hotel.

My sister, Cammy, short for Camille—believe me, I know it's confusing, her Camille, me Chloe—stood across the way. You'd never guess we were sisters, since I'm tall and lean, with copper penny–colored hair, green eyes, and pale skin, as opposed to Cammy, who looks exotic. She's not as tall, but she's statuesque, with chestnut hair and eyes the color of new Levi's. Indigo blue—sometimes they almost look purple. All that and she's brilliant, too. I was here to celebrate her receiving her doctorate in Egyptology. I love Camille; she's been my idol all my life, despite the fact she cursed me with a goofy nickname—kitten.

"Chloe! Hello, sis!" she said, looking into my face, her smile bright against her tan.

"Dr. Kingsley, I presume?"

Cammy threw back her head and laughed, a low throaty sound that garnered more than one appreciative male glance. "I'll bet you've been waiting all day to say that!"

"Actually, I've been waiting most of your life to say it. Is all the toil and sweat worth it? Now that you're finished you've got to find a real job."

"Not a problem. I believe I'll be employed sufficiently for quite a few years," she said with a smile Mona Lisa would have envied. She took my daypack and headed to the taxi queue. Further conversation was drowned out by the cries of "Baksheesh!" from a pack of children, their large dark eyes dancing with excitement as they played their game with tourists. Baksheesh was not begging, it was more like a tip. A tip for them being alive, if nothing else.

"Did you bring those pens I wanted?" she asked.

"In the pack."

Cammy pulled out a handful of cheap, almost worthless ballpoint pens, and the children oohed in awe. With admonishments in Arabic to leave us alone, Cammy distributed the pens, and the children scattered. "You've just bought yourself a handful of helpers," she said triumphantly.

"All for a few ballpoint pens?"

"Yes. Now when they go to school they will have something with which to write. Keep the pens with you—they're good for reducing the price of anything in bargaining."

She knew how truly dreadful I was at bargaining. "Cool," I said.

As I shouldered my bags a taxi screeched to a halt before us, and I climbed in next to Cammy. She gesticulated and argued with the driver before we took off, as he tried to push the ancient machine from zero to thirty-five in something under a half hour. We headed south on the main road, parallel to the river.

Luxor is two cities, one a modern reflection of the other. While the "touristic" part has hotels, restaurants, shops, and a few nightclubs surrounding the ancient sites of Luxor Temple and Karnak Temple, the "native" part consists of ramshackle houses, mosques, and tangled, narrow streets filled with small barefoot soccer players. We charged past several horse-drawn calèches clip-clopping along the waterfront, turned a few streets away from the *souq*, and drove through the twisting lanes until we finally lurched to a stop before a dilapidated inn with a fluorescent cartouche on the awning.

I couldn't believe it.

Dingy didn't even begin to describe this place. However, exhaustion was taking over, and I cared less about where we were going to stay than when I could rinse my face and lie down. We were settling for "native" versus "touristic," but at this point I would have slept on a camel if it was still long enough. I hauled my bags out of the taxi and waited while Cammy paid.

I arched my brow. "We're staying here?"

Cammy smiled. "Yes. It's a fun place. It has a rooftop garden with a wonderful reproduction of a statue of Ramses . . ."

Yep. I was back in the Middle East. "Do the doors lock?" I asked.

Cammy continued extolling its nonluxurious, nonamenable virtues. I held up my hand. "Okay, okay. I'll stay here while you're in town, but as soon as you hop that bus to your desert outpost, I am heading to the nicest four-star available!"

She opened the door with a smile and a flourish. "I didn't expect any different, my civilized little sister."

A nap revived me. We changed clothes, locked the flimsy door that a halfhearted kick from a six-year-old would have popped right open, and headed into the Egyptian night.

The sky had deepened. Golden fingers wove purple, magenta, fuchsia, and rose pink into a tapestry, bleeding to midnight blue with silver stars. I huddled into my jean jacket against the breeze, since the temperature had dropped. We rode in a calèche down to the waterfront, where countless cruise ships moored, casting myriad lights onto the dark water. Immediately upon arriving at the hotel restaurant, we were shown to a table and we ordered one of everything with double the olives. I raised my gaze and looked expectantly at my agitated sister.

"You're about to pop. Excitement is almost an aura around you. What's going on? Anything to do with that cryptic statement about having a long-term job?"

Cammy's eyes widened. "Me? Excited?" Unlike mine, Cammy's face was an open book. Mom and Father never told her about Christmas or birthday gifts because she couldn't keep a secret longer than ten minutes.

"Yep," I said around an olive.

"You should be excited, you are about to be related to a very famous person." Her navy eyes were sparkling.

"Did you find another King Tut's tomb?" I asked carelessly.

"Maybe," she said smugly. She ate a piece of pita, watching me. She had always been overly dramatic.

"Are you going to tell me or just let the curiosity kill me, Cammy?"

"It's weird."

"Weirder than your monkey?" Her first find had been a small clay monkey from around the time of Ankhenaton, now lost in the vaults of the Egyptian Museum. It was anatomically correct and *strategically* painted blue. She was still teased about it.

"No," she said firmly. "It's not like the monkey." She sighed. "I really can't describe it."

Oh, great, twenty questions. "Is it animal, vegetable, or mineral?"

"It's papyrus."

"And . . . ?" I prompted. Really, she had learned too much discretion.

"Well, let me start with the initial hypothesis. The religious artifacts found at the temple—"

I cut her off. "English, dear sister. Plain, everyday English. No references, no footnotes, no mentioning names like Carter, Petrie, Mariette, nobody. What have you found?"

Cammy opened her mouth, then shut it again. "No references?"

"None."

She tapped her fingers, thinking. "Right. It is possible there are some undiscovered tombs in the eastern desert. We—" She stumbled, and I knew she was rephrasing. "The university . . . is excavating out there. It's almost a joke, which is why we have mostly grad students working on it. Then we found this subterranean cavern. It looks like it was inhabited at least once.

We found several huge earthenware water jugs leaning against one wall."

"How big is huge?" I asked between bites of baba ghanouj. I love eggplant.

"About five feet tall."

"Cool."

"They reminded me of the jars found in Qumran. Do you remember?"

Yep, I remembered. Summertime by the Dead Sea. It had been around one hundred and twenty degrees in the shade and smelled like a rotten egg farm. We'd hiked all over the wadi, with Mom and Cammy commenting and comparing theories about the dig and the find while Father and I followed, sunburned, peeling, and dehydrated. "Go on," I said.

"Well, these jars we found are filled with papyri. We brought them back to Luxor to unfold. . . ." Her eyes gleamed fanatically. "It's completely amazing, because according to all our tests, the papyri are from about 1450 B.C.E. That's around the time of Thutmosis the Third," she said to me, the Egyptologically impaired one. She leaned closer and whispered, "What's so unusual and baffling is that they are depictions like nothing the Egyptians have ever been known to do!"

Citrus and incense teased my nose for just a second.

"They are illustrations," she continued, with enthusiasm. "However, they are so perfect and so detailed that they look almost like photographs." She leaned back abruptly. "Then there are the lions."

I choked on an olive. "Lions?"

Cammy shrugged. "The entire site appears to be where the lions came to die. There are hundreds of bones; generations and generations of lions died there." Her voice again dropped to a whisper. "I had the eerie sensation they were still watching us." She shivered.

I took a sip of my bottled water. "Let me get this straight. This is such a marvelous find because you have found photographic-quality illustrations of ancient Egypt?"

"Yes. I think we have, anyway."

"Are the colors bright? Do they have writing on them, or are they easy to identify as everyday scenes or what?"

Cammy thought for a moment. "We've only unrolled a few. One is a scene of daily life, done in bright colors; another is . . . well, just unexplainable. Another is a masterpiece of ink and charcoal."

I felt professional artistic curiosity rise in me. "May I see them?"

Cammy bit her lip, looking at me. "Well, they are kept in high-security cases."

"But you have the keys?"

"Yeeesss," she said reluctantly.

"I won't touch them. I'm just curious to see them since I've been drawing Egyptian-style pictures for you since we were kids. Do you realize even your paper dolls were ancient Egyptian?"

Cammy laughed. "So I was a little obsessive. It runs in the family."

"What am I obsessed with?" I asked foolishly.

"Roots," she said.

I agreed.

Roots that had kept me connected even while I grew up in alien and foreign lands. Roots that gave me pride in my European heritage and southern family. Roots that consisted of an iron-filled, camellia soft grandmother, Mimi, who had been my best friend and anchor, until her death six months ago.

• • •

I woke, not quite rested, my mind still clouded with disturbing dreams. Ancient dreams. Dreams of death, passion, possession. Not my normal fare. I'm more likely to dream about rewriting Cadillac ads and having dinner parties with Monet and Michelangelo. Or better yet, running a Coca-Cola campaign. But the feeling stayed with me. A definite Middle Eastern ambience, exotic, fragrant, and sensual. I shook my head. Apparently fries and chick-pea dip before bed was a really bad idea.

The day passed in a jet-lag blur, but I managed to jot off a few post-cards, eat a couple of times, and work halfway through Agatha Christie's ancient Egyptian murder mystery. Then Cammy cracked her whip and the tourist bit began in earnest. She had me walking through the Valley of the Kings by seven in the morning, followed by an extensive tour of Deir El-Bahri, the mortuary temple of Queen Hatshepsut. However, as Camille said, you were either pharaoh, which translated literally to "great house," or consort. Since there was no word referring to queen as an absolute monarch, every reference to Hatshepsut was masculine. Therefore she was usually depicted as a man.

Camille had taken on her lecturing voice. "No one knows what happened to cause her temple, her obelisks, and her other monuments to be symbolically destroyed—"

I interrupted, "Symbolically destroyed?"

"Yes. You see, her name is obliterated. If she had no name, she would have no part of the afterlife; to destroy her presence here would be to destroy her also in the hereafter. Names were of great consequence; even the gods' true names were kept secret to protect them. For instance, the name 'Amun' literally means 'Unknowable One,' which is partially the reason he had such awesome power. So to eradicate Hatshepsut's name would be to make her an unknown, wandering throughout time and eternity."

I fingered the chipped-away cartouche. "How malicious! I thought pharaoh, regardless of sex, was revered as the incarnation of god on earth? Who would have the authority?"

As I spoke, my stomach churned. I felt a widening around me, a feeling of space, as if I were suspended over a precipice; suddenly I smelled incense and citrus. I blinked rapidly, reaching out to touch the brilliant white stone walls, trying to steady the fuzzy reflections.

I turned to Cammy. "What?"

"I said, 'You've picked up a lot more about Egypt than you realize, sis,'" Cammy repeated.

"What did you say before that?"

She frowned, apparently confused. "Before?"

"Yeah. You called me something, it began with an 'R'; a word I haven't heard before. Ray-something? Or maybe it was Ra . . . ?"

Cammy eyed me askance. "Hatshepsut's ghost must be getting to you, Chloe, because I didn't call you anything. Are you feeling well? Do you need to get in out of the sun?"

I looked across the columned porch. "No, I'm fine. I must have heard the wind or something."

"Probably. It can whip through this site pretty fiercely sometimes." She caught her blowing hair in one hand, twisted it deftly into a knot, and secured it with her pencil. "To answer your question, most historians and archaeologists suppose that Thutmosis the Third defaced Hat's things out of spite, since she effectively usurped his throne for twenty-something years. It's really a gray area in Egyptology. No one knows and no records exist except what's been left standing."

In silence we observed the graceful ramps and columns that merged into the craggy rock behind, highlighting the delicacy of the structure and the strength of the cliff. It was a perfect artistic statement. I snapped off some photos, trying different angles and wishing I had sprung for a wide-angle lens before I'd left Dallas.

The temple was a monument to an aberration in Egyptian history, a triumph of art over human desire, because Hatshepsut, despite the best efforts of her descendants, lived on in this architectural masterpiece. This was her immortality.

Cammy wandered through the sunlit porticoes and practiced reading the faded hieroglyphs, while I crouched in the dust and made thumbnail sketches of the soaring columns with their carved female faces. What had I heard before? It had been a soft word, which still whispered, undefined, on the edges of my consciousness. Just the wind, I told myself with a mental shake, and turned back to my notepad.

We were quiet the rest of the visit, each absorbed in her own thoughts.

That afternoon Cammy had to help with some translations at the university. I walked to the Nile and looked out toward Karnak Temple, imagining it in ancient times, garnished with embroidered flags hanging from the vibrantly painted pylons.

As the sun cast a golden-and-rose glow over the city, I caught a taxi back to the inn. Dinner was my treat tonight, since Cammy had treated last.

We met in the darkened hallway to go out. "Do we have time to see your find?" I asked, still curious.

Cammy glanced at her watch. "Well, there is a Christmas party tonight, so I guess I can sneak you in."

She wasn't overly enthusiastic, but then I had always been the one who got us in trouble. She had more than a healthy respect for the rules. Ironic that I was the one with a military rank and serial number, since I had always been the one willing to bend the rules.

However, officer's candidacy school for this spoiled daughter of an American diplomat had been more than enough to curb me. Not only had I been different from the other officer trainees—definitely more foreign than American—I was also younger. As a twenty-year-old with a degree in art, I had a hard time making friends. I proved to be a whiz, however, at emergency management, my reservist assignment. Whatever the situation, the Kingsley pride kept me going. Kingsleys never gave up, I'd been told, so I persevered.

Military service had actually been my brother's "duty," but he'd been the black sheep for so long, his name not even spoken, that it was unlikely he'd follow through. My father's family had served since the War Between the States, known to the rest of the country as the Civil War, and it was time for the next generation. I'm not sure my joining the air force reserves was what Mimi had had in mind when she'd told me stories of glory about my southern heritage, however.

At any rate, here I was leading Cammy astray . . . again. Maybe I wasn't as curbed as I thought.

A few minutes later we stepped into the foyer of her university's dorm and research facility, known as Chicago House. A scraggly artificial Christmas tree stood in the dimly lit room, decorated with glass balls and cut-out cardboard hieroglyphs. Fortunately the place was deserted.

Cammy pulled a hefty ring of keys from her daypack and stepped up to a metal door. She unlocked it, and we walked into the lab. After turning on the light and unlocking another room, Cammy went to a wall-length cabinet, passed an ID card through a scanner, unlocked the door, passed the card again, and entered a code. Finally she opened the door and pulled out a long metal drawer. I helped her set the huge thing on the table.

"This place is tighter than Fort Knox!" I exclaimed. "Is the papyrus plated in gold?"

Camille unlocked the drawer, her hands trembling faintly. "What we have found is far more valuable than gold. It's knowledge. Though, as yet, we have no explanation for what is in these boxes," she said, gesturing to the drawer. "At the very least, we must protect it." She opened the top. "The papyri we have unwrapped are lying between sheets of glass. It's a prolific find—we estimate there are more than fifty scrolls altogether." We stood in semidarkness. "I have a feeling that these scrolls will be as significant as the Dead Sea scrolls," she murmured as she turned on the specialized overhead light.

They *were* startlingly un-Egyptian.

I shivered suddenly and reached for my silver ankh necklace, letting its heat seep into my chilled blood. The papyrus scroll was about two feet by three and a half feet. The paper had aged to a pale honey color, the edges curled and ripped.

It was a sketch of a mud-brick village. Instead of the two-dimensional profile paintings typical of Egyptian work, this was rendered in a realistic perspective. The people were not dressed in djellabas, as if it had been drawn today, but wore the kilts and sheaths of ancient Egypt.

Cammy moved the plates, and I stared at painstakingly detailed botanical drawings of pomegranates, figs, grapes, lotus, palm, and several other plants I couldn't immediately identify. Under each was what I assumed to be the name in hieroglyphs. I looked into Cammy's face, stunned.

"Cammy, are you sure these are not modern practical jokes?"

She shrugged. "The papyrus is ancient. I don't know how to explain the content. This next one is the pièce de résistance; it was pieced together and wrapped on the outside, probably because it is more fragile than the rest."

I stared at the huge unrolled scroll. Unlike the others, it was about five feet long by five feet deep and the entirety was dense with detailed illustration—there was no other word. A broad avenue was filled with people, possessions, and animals. In the distance stood a huge archway, silhouetted against the delicately shaded sky. I looked closely. Unlike a lot of drawings of multitudes, many faces were visible, and each was distinct. A mother and child talked over a gaggle of geese, the woman bent under the weight of an infant on her back, the girl's tousled hair banded with a cloth around her forehead. An old man, his beard halfway down his chest, leaned heavily on his walking stick, surrounded by sheep. To the right of the artist's perspective was a man.

He was frozen in time, looking over his shoulder as if sharing a joke with the artist. His face was lean, with high cheekbones that accentuated his long-lashed eyes and thick brows extended by Egyptian makeup. His profile was clean, the straight blade of his nose leading to full lips and a squared jawline. Black hair touched his neck and ear, framing a gorgeous jeweled earring.

I was awed. It was a masterpiece. *He was so real.* Tiny marks embossed my fingertips as I clenched my necklace. Stubble darkened his chin and cheek, and there were lines around his mouth and eyes. He looked as though at any moment he would share the punch line.

"I can almost hear his laughter," I whispered.

Camille agreed. "The strangest thing is that although this appears to be a depiction of some Egyptian city, and they are headed to the border of Egypt, symbolized by the gate with the cobra and vulture, not many of the people appear to be ancient Egyptians."

Cammy laid the others on top of it.

"Is this all you have?"

"Yes," Cammy said. "There are many other scrolls, but they have not been unrolled yet. It's very painstaking and time-consuming work." I watched her hide all traces of our unauthorized visit.

"What do you think is the explanation?" I asked when we were back on the street.

"I don't know what to think. There are no records of a mass exodus during the time of Thut the Third—that was in Rameses the Great's time—if it happened. We know that Thut the Third was a conqueror, spending a lot of time outside Egypt, subjugating other peoples. Even if we're wrong on the approximate dates, there are no records from his predecessor Hatshepsut's rule and just basic information from his progeny's rule."

We turned onto the main thoroughfare. Sounds from the cruise ships along the dock wafted up to us: male and female laughter, piano music, and the ever-present Arabic radio. We walked in companionable silence as I mulled over what I had seen. "Could you be wrong about the dynasty? Could they be from another pharaoh?"

"The papyri date to Thut's reign. There is just no explanation for the work and the way it's done. Is there an aspect of Egypt we are unaware of? Even the most naturalistic art is still two-dimensional." She sighed, then chuckled. "It makes the science of Egyptology seem like nothing more than educated guesses when we find something like this."

I spoke without thinking. "That's all it is anyway."

Cammy sighed in the darkness. "That's your opinion. Our guesses are becoming *more* educated. We're able to state things with more certainty. There are facts."

"Like . . . ?" I prompted, intrigued despite myself.

"Like Senmut. He was a grand vizier in Hatshepsut's court. Five years before the end of her reign, there are no more records of him. His picture is both inscribed in and removed from her temple at Deir El-Bahri. His body has never been found. In those last five years there is some hint that Egypt went through internal turmoil, but we don't know what or why. We also know that Hatshepsut died, but we don't know how. She was succeeded by Thut the Third in 1458 B.C.E. Those are facts."

I looked at my sister, the light from the river reflected in our similar features. "What happens if you discover that Senmut changed his name and continued to live for years? Or that Hatshepsut was banished and became the wife of some foreign king? What you are calling facts just seem like unsubstantiated theory to me. They can't be proved or disproved. My idea of a fact is . . ." I searched for an example from my world. "Red and blue make purple. No matter how many times, under how many circumstances or ways, if you mix red and blue, you will come up with some shade of purple. Every time."

Cammy turned to me, exasperated. "Look, Chloe, no one is ever going to know for absolute certain about anything. We can't prove a god exists. We can't prove he or she doesn't. No one will ever come from ancient Egypt and tell us we are right or wrong about the timeline of the pharaohs. Every little bit we learn, whether or not it is *your* definition of a fact, make us, in our knowledge, more human."

Impulsively I hugged her. "I miss you, Cammy."

"I miss you, too."

We continued walking, arms linked, staring at the stars stretched out across the Nile and the treasure-laden desert beyond. Cammy spoke, her voice dreamy. "One of the reasons I got into Egyptology was because of the feeling of connectedness it gives me. I get chills when I think that four thousand years ago, two sisters very likely walked along this same path, feeling the same love for each other."

My throat tightened and I squeezed Cammy's arm as we walked along, our images reflected in the dark Nile waters.

That's how the days passed. We talked a little about Mimi, though with her death only six months before, it was painful, especially for Cammy. She had been in the middle of her dissertation and unable to get away. We viewed the sights and relaxed, enjoying the days together. It had been too many years since we had just hung out. Then Cammy had to go, boarding the hot, dusty train for the eastern desert the day before my birthday. We hugged briefly on the platform, and she shoved a small package into my hands. "Happy twenty-fourth, Chloe," she said, and I waved until she was out of sight.

I immediately checked into the Winter Palace Hotel. It was straight out of *Death on the Nile*, complete with potted palms, layered silk rugs, and brass samovars. A page out of time.

At dinner I was joined by a guy who was good-looking in a rugged, studious way. He had a lean build, dark tan, and intelligent gray eyes. He was older, maybe late thirties, to judge by the streaks of gray in his longish brown hair.

He was so charming, though. He kissed my hand when we were introduced and proceeded to tell me that he visited Egypt at least once a year—it was in his blood. So I told him about my sister and how Egypt was in her blood, too. Dr. Anton Zeeman was his name; I guessed from his accent that he was Dutch. We chatted through dinner, laughing at the tourist couple at the next table who unwittingly ordered sheep's stomach (the chef was Greek) and insisted it was what they wanted when the server tried to explain. We watched the belly dancer, and I felt Anton's stare, questioning, on me more than once. Over coffee he offered me a cigarette. I usually smoke only when under extreme stress, but when in Rome . . . I staggered up to my room about two A.M., hoping all my fun would send me straight to sleepy-bye land with no dreams.

It did.

I was haunting the *souq* the next day after lunch—since it was the only thing still open—enjoying the mixture of cumin, saffron, turmeric, and cinnamon that scented the air. I managed to purchase a sackful of saffron for ten dollars and two ballpoint pens. I would auction it off to my friends when I got home.

Tambourine and drums blasted me from every radio station as I stepped into a shop. Racks of postcards filled the front, and I began looking through them. I collect postcards, use them for all personal correspondence, so I try to keep a lot of interesting ones on hand. These were of an Egypt many years ago, swamped by sand and virtually deserted. The representations were intriguing, the detail work impressive. They were a snapshot in time.

Feeling someone behind me, I turned just as a faintly accented voice spoke. "They are David Roberts's works," Anton said.

"I recognize his style. I've seen his work," I replied. "I don't know anything about him, though." I scrutinized the meticulous artistry. "Who was he?"

"One of the many who came to Egypt in the early to mid-1800s," Anton said. "It became quite a popular destination following the war. France began the trend in 1798 when Napoleon sent a huge cortege over to catalog Egypt's monuments. Tradition claims they are the ones who shot the nose off the Sphinx." He grinned at me as he stepped back. "Not that you can see it now."

I gathered up all of David Roberts's postcards. "Really? Where can I learn more? I didn't know Napoleon took artists with him."

"At the Luxor Museum bookstore," he said. "It was quite a famous expedition. It awakened interest in Egypt. In the next years those who would create the field of Egyptology visited here." He ticked off a list that would have been familiar to Cammy but left me clueless. Vivant Denon? August Mariette? Gaston Maspero? Richard Lepsius? Jean-François Champollion? Giovanni Belzoni? Ippolito Rosselini?

The rediscovery of ancient Egypt had all begun with Napoleon's expedition, he said. Interest was heightened by the paintings of David Roberts and others. Anton turned toward a low display of alabaster statuettes, changing the subject. "Have you been to an alabaster factory yet? These are quite good reproductions."

I looked at the shelf, covered with white, rose, blue, and gray figurines, and reached for one of a seated woman with the head of a cow, a disk between her horns.

"I see you pick the goddess HatHor."

"What was she the goddess of?" I asked. "Dairy foods?"

Anton grinned. "Well, most writings will say she was like Aphrodite. The goddess of love, childbirth, dance, et cetera. No one knows for sure. Very little is absolutely certain in Egyptology."

"Yep. My sister says almost everything is subject to debate, though there are a few facts."

Anton nodded. "That being the case, HatHor could be goddess of anything."

As I gripped the statue, a cold foreboding rushed through me. For a few seconds I heard a high-pitched keening and the jangling of cymbals. I glanced around in confusion: the dimly lit room seemed to be full of spinning bodies, with long black hair and white robes whipping around them as they twirled like tops. Then, in an instant, the impression was gone.

With suddenly shaky hands I put the statue back among the others: human bodies with the heads of animals. Anton watched me. "Are you unwell?" he asked.

"No, no, I'm fine. It was just a surrealistic mind flash," I said with a wavering smile. Another weird experience, I thought. Still mystified and wobbly, I crossed the shop to admire the vibrant textiles that decorated the back wall. Nervously I fingered my ankh.

"You want to buy, lady?"

I turned and saw a young boy with a silver tray bearing small Arabic tea glasses. I paid him for the postcards and hurried into the sunlit street.

Anton followed me. "Are you okay?" he asked, concern apparent on his sharp features.

My fingers trembled as I unzipped my daypack and slipped in the postcards. Anton offered me a cigarette, which he lit with a courtly gesture and a gold lighter. No ordinary backpacker, this, I thought momentarily. Then I remembered. The images had been so intense, so real. I had felt a . . . a displacement of some sort . . . through to my bones. I was slightly nauseated. I inhaled deeply and enjoyed the sting of the aromatic tobacco as it singed my lungs and probably took another year off my life.

"Yep, I'm okay. It just felt as if time froze for a moment, and I could feel past and present—a window open to another world. . . ." I trailed off, my memory of the twisting and swirling bodies fading rapidly in the bright Egyptian afternoon, filled with the squawk of radios and the honks of car horns. I stubbed out my cigarette, feeling stupid for rambling. "I'm sorry. I sound crazy." I turned away from Anton.

"Come, I will buy you a coffee and pastry," he offered.

"Thanks," I said, and set off with him, trying to shake off the otherworldly feelings.

After spending the afternoon in the Luxor Museum, I bought the *Rediscovery of Ancient Egypt*, slathered myself with SPF 50, and slipped a CD into my Discman. I sat out by the beautifully sculpted pool to read about Egypt during the French empire, pages about people whose names I'd heard from Cammy most of my life. Old portraits and detailed reproduction artwork filled the chapters. However, I was restless and began playing around with a logo on my sketch pad. It mixed the hieroglyphs for cat into a strangely attractive design. Not quite right, but I was getting there. Kitten, Cammy's nickname for me as a kid, was one of those things you learn to hate. However, the glyphs for it were interesting, so I ignored their meaning. I couldn't spell in ancient Egyptian anyway, but the shapes were great.

The setting sun brought me back to reality.

This close to the equator, the brilliant sunset illuminated the sky for only a few minutes, but the colors were vibrant—pinks, violets, and golds merging for a brief but exquisite moment. Then it was dark, a soft blue-blackness that felt like an engulfing blanket, gleaming with the silver of the first stars. I reluctantly went inside to the artificially cold interior of the hotel. Sleep would be a welcome refuge tonight.

•••

December 23, my birthday. By the time the sun rose I had been up for an hour. I'd breakfasted on the hotel's terrace and made quick sketches of the graceful feluccas racing from shore to shore, their triangular white sails achingly bright in the sunshine.

Anton did not make an appearance at breakfast, not that I was surprised after our coffee the day before. I hadn't said two words—which was strange in itself—and after several attempts at conversation, he had given up. He'd finally excused himself to go visit a mosque, and I had turned down the invitation to join him.

Yesterday had been disturbing.

After my third cup of Turkish coffee, however, I felt ready to face anything, even another day of playing tourist. I donned my espadrilles.

The temple at Karnak was amazing. When I'd gone through it with Camille, she had wandered off in the middle of her explanation to stand in awe of the largest temple in the world. I had wanted to return alone. So far I had dodged all the "helpful" tour guides by bribing some kids with my trusty ballpoint pens to protect my privacy. Before being besieged by a group of Italian tourists, I had captured some great sketches of various walls. Snaking my way through the columns and up to the inner sanctum, I found three rooms.

Feeling like Goldilocks avoiding furry carnivores, I poked into them all. Cammy had said they were for the resident gods, the holy family of Luxor: Amun-Ra, the sun god; Mut, his consort; and Khonsu, their child. I tuned out after that, the intricacies of Egyptian religion confusing and alien to me. When we were kids Cammy tried to explain how the different gods and myths all fit together, even as they directly contradicted each other. She would explain at length how people became priests and priestesses because of family connection, not because of any personal devotion to the gold-covered gods. I hadn't cared.

All three rooms were small. In ancient times the god-statue resided there on a barque, an Egyptian papyrus-sheaf boat that angled upward at both ends. The first two rooms were empty, the reliefs on the walls faded to almost nothing, the gold that had once accented them picked off thousands of years before by greedy nonbelievers.

I stepped into the third room. Also like the Goldilocks tale, the third room seemed to fit, why I couldn't say. Wisps of peace, acceptance, and desire wrapped around me. I grabbed the ankh around my throat and rubbed it across my chin. As I looked out the broken window, I realized some amazing pictures could be taken from here. *A beautiful sunrise*, my mind whispered. One of the many turbaned guards stepped in and told me to leave, but I was determined to return and get those shots.

Still burning inwardly from the feeling of the third room, I left the temple grounds in search of lunch. I saw a small boat restaurant offering the "bestest food in ancient Lucqsur" and ordered the specialty of the house, fish stuffed with figs and pomegranates, my favorite fruits. It seemed fitting to celebrate with an expensive meal. After all, a girl turned twenty-four years old only once. I savored a honey-coated pastry and heavy coffee for dessert as I watched boats race from shore to shore, the whole world bleached by the power of the sun. No wonder the ancient Egyptians had worshipped it as Amun-Ra.

After eating, I sat on one of the many benches that lined the Nile and watched the procession of tour boats, tourists, and Egyptians. Idly I sketched, capturing on paper the sparse waterfowl and the hands of the sailors.

I heard steps behind me.

"Chloe?" he said. "How are you today? Feeling better, I hope?"

"Hello, Anton," I said with a smile. "I'm much better, thanks. Where are you off to?"

"Nowhere, I think. I am tired," he said, wiping sweat from his brow. He stepped out of his Birkenstocks and laughed. "So much sand." He shook his head ruefully. "I think I will go swimming this afternoon and then to the Son et Lumière tonight."

"Oh?" I said, curious. Cammy had recommended going, but not alone, under any circumstances. "The Sound and Light show? I've heard it's supposed to be wonderful, but what exactly is it?" I gestured for him to join me.

He sat gracefully, stretching his leanly muscled tanned legs before him and laying his backpack on the ground. "It is in Karnak. After dark they lead one through the temple, while describing what it was like to be an ancient Egyptian worshiper, yes? Then it ends by the Sacred Lake about half after ten."

I grinned inwardly. It was tonight, huh? Maybe my wish to explore that third room was not quite so impossible. Or the sunrise photos . . . ? Hmmm . . . did I have the right lenses?

He continued, "It is quite expensive, very crowded, and gets cold, but it is also amazing and should not be missed. It is not Christmas church services, but it promises to be memorable."

"It sounds great," I mused. "I think I'll go, too."

Anton looked at me through his dark sunglasses. "And your sister? Maybe you will both go with me and after we could get a coffee?"

I smiled. I was actually surprised he would give me a second thought since I had been such a doorknob yesterday, but it was a great opportunity. I hedged, since I'd told him Cammy was in town. It wasn't smart to travel alone, being female. "Cammy has been before. It would probably bore her. If the invitation is open to just me, I'd really like to go."

Anton smiled widely. "I am very pleased." He looked over my shoulder at my pencil sketches. "You are quite talented."

One of the curses of being a redhead is that when I blush, the whole world knows it. "Thank you," I said with wildly rosy cheeks.

He held out his lean hand for the sketchbook. "May I see?" After a second's hesitation I handed him the book. He flipped through exacting renderings of buildings, trees, flowers, and hands, then gave it back. "You have a very strong hand," he said. "You are obviously an artist."

I nodded. "Advertising. I created the TacoLitos spokes-iguana." This obviously meant nothing to him. If one didn't live in the southwest part of the United States, my spokes-iguana was unknown.

"Why are there no people in your drawings? Only structures and plants?"

"I don't do people." I said, a little embarrassed.

"Why not?"

"I can't capture their essence, their personality or spirit. They come out very flat, lifeless. Like cartoon characters." It would have been too much to say I didn't have enough depth as a human being to interpret others' faces accurately.

"I see." He lit a cigarette. "I love comics and cartoons."

I laughed. In silence we watched a boat debark tourists from every nation, fanning their faces rapidly and drinking bottled water. There were Aussies, having escaped their scalding winter on the other end of the planet; German students in shorts and backpacks, thrilling in the sun; American retirees in hats, sunglasses, and cameras; and packs of Asians, immaculately dressed and videotaping madly. I fiddled with my necklace. Anton glanced over.

"What is this necklace you are always touching? Is it for good luck?"

I flushed. "No. I've had it a long time and play with it. It's just a habit."

He picked up the silver chain and brought the ankh close, looking at the hieroglyphs etched into the silver. "From where did it come?"

"Cairo."

"So you have been here before?"

"No. Not Luxor. Just Cairo. My father traveled through Egypt when I was about eight and my sister twelve. Lizza, our au pair, took care of us while my parents traveled on diplomatic missions. We were in the *souq* with Lizza when this woman stepped forward."

I could see it all as if it were yesterday. The dirty, dusty street, our correct au pair behind us, Cammy and I holding hands, cringing as a wrinkled shop woman, who looked for all the world like a character from the Brothers Grimm, came forward, calling out to us, her bright black eyes acknowledging our foreign coloring. She hustled us into a small shop and looked back and forth between us, as if making a decision. Then she held out the silver ankh necklace. Cammy, after a moment, reached for it. The woman screeched and snatched it back. Frightened, Cammy started tugging on my arm, but the woman placed the long silver chain around my neck and started laughing.

We were both terrified. Leaving Lizza to pay whatever the old woman wanted, we ran through the crowded streets, searching for a way out of the bewildering and smelly market.

"Do you know what it says?" Anton asked, breaking into my memory.

"No. Cammy has never wanted to touch it; she claims it burned her as a child," I scoffed. "She regards the whole thing superstitiously. However, she's the only one I know who reads hieroglyphs."

His angular face was close to mine now, his brow creased in concentration, dark glasses hiding his eyes. "I read hieroglyphs," he said, releasing the necklace but not moving away. I looked at the expanse of tinted glass two inches from my nose . . . and felt my breath check. Anton licked his lips. "Would you like to know what it says?" he asked softly.

Time stood still, a frisson making me shiver, suddenly cold on this Egyptian afternoon. I felt rather than heard a still, small voice in my head say this was where the road divided. What road? Was Anton going to kiss me and change my life? Not likely.

"Tell me," I said, equally softly.

Anton leaned back and took off his sunglasses, his pupils becoming pinpoints of black in the intensity of the sun. "It is a time."

"A time?" I blurted out, disappointed.

"Yes. A certain designation of time, and the name of that time. It has to do with Egyptian astrology. Maybe your sister can illuminate it for you." His gaze was intent on my face.

I looked away. A time? An astrological time? As an imaginative child and even as a young teenager, I had fantasized that it was a secret message, a hidden identity. *Something.* "A time" was definitely anticlimactic.

Anton rose to his feet, stubbing out his cigarette. "I shall see you later? Yes? Maybe we will walk together?"

"Walk together?"

"To the Son et Lumière?"

"Oh. Yeah," I said, my disappointment about my necklace having knocked everything else out of my mind. "That would be cool."

Anton picked up his backpack and leaned toward me. I lifted my head, and he kissed my forehead. Just a gentle peck, like a brother. Then he left, the breeze blowing his faded green T-shirt against his lean body. I sat there, a bit dazed. I didn't want to admit even to myself that I was disappointed. I'm not easy, but who can resist a holiday romance? He was almost across the street when I shouted, "Anton?"

He turned back to me, glasses on and his hand shading his face.

"What was the time?"

He put a hand to his ear and I cupped my hands, ignoring the looks I received. "The time? The astrological time?"

I heard his response as if I were listening underwater. "The RaEmhetep," he shouted. "The name for the eleventh hour of the night."

Waving absently, I walked back to my bench. Bizarre! I looked down at the necklace, at the tiny inscription on the one side. The writing was just as clear as it had been sixteen years ago. The silver had not worn at all, despite the fact I couldn't remember ever having taken it off. I mused, staring across the Nile.

The RaEmhetep.

Dismissing it from my mind, along with the ruggedly handsome man who had chosen *not* to kiss me, I put away my notepad and pencils and started to walk toward Luxor Temple, making my plans for the night.

•••

The mirror was foggy from the steam of my shower, but I could see enough to know I looked striking. With a long nose and squared jaw, my features have always seemed too strong for my coloring, but what could I do?

I had bought the long black skirt, tank, and crocheted tunic less than six hours before my flight. It was from my favorite trendy boutique, an example of impulse shopping at its most dangerous. I put on some copper lipstick and pinched my cheeks. The dry air did wonders for my hair. It swung smoothly from my crown to just below my chin, the bright color reflecting gold and bronze highlights. The contrast of the black outfit and my rosy skin made my angled eyes look even greener and more catlike. I ran a tongue over my freshly brushed teeth and stepped into my sandals.

I made an appropriately dramatic entrance to the lobby and choked back surprise that the charming backpacker now wore linen trousers and a cashmere sweater. And glasses. He kissed me on the cheek and gave me a white flower, then we left on foot.

"So, do you travel for fun or pleasure?" I asked.

He laughed as we dodged a group of begging children, ignoring their cries of "Baksheesh! Baksheesh!"

He looked at me intently for a moment. "Pleasure," he said. "I am a biochemist, and my specialty is hematology. It is very, um, how do you say, intense? So each year I have several months of holiday and travel."

"Several months! Wow! You better keep that job," I said. "I've never heard of a company giving months off at a time. Do you, uh, enjoy working with blood?" The whole idea grossed me out.

Anton chuckled. "Yes, yes." Enthusiasm filled his voice. "Blood is amazing. It is the essence of who we are as creatures, and it is what we need to live, yet we are quite unknowing about the effects modifying it can have on live beings. Life is in the blood." He must have seen my involuntary shudder at his words, because he asked what I did.

"I work free-lance, and fortunately the company I am contracting with now is run by a traditional Italian family who basically close down from December fifteenth to January fifteenth."

A cool breeze blew off the Nile as the first glitter of stars appeared low on the horizon.

"How is it that you travel with no group? Americans always travel in groups, yet you are alone? Especially at this time of year?"

"My sister is here," I interjected.

"Ahhh, yes, your sister," he said glibly.

"I'm, I mean, we're, a little bit different from your average American family. My mom is an English archaeologist and my dad is with the State Department. He's originally from Texas and used to be in uniform. He was stationed all over the world, so I've traveled alone to meet my parents since I was a kid. We've lived mostly in Moslem countries; consequently, Christmas has never been that big a deal, unless we were going home. None of us felt like going home this year."

I looked down the rapidly darkening street, the muffled voices in a variety of languages floating out to meet us. "I guess because I've lived so many different places, when I travel I like to stay longer—really absorb the atmosphere and culture. That's almost impossible to do when you see five countries in three days."

We laughed together.

"As for my being here . . . my sister just got her doctorate and suggested I meet her to celebrate."

"Where are your parents now?"

"Brussels, I think. Their schedule is hard to follow," I said with a laugh. "We'll meet for the New Year in Greece. My parents have a house there, since that's where they met and married. Aren't you going to miss Christmas with your family?" I asked.

Anton smiled, a little sadly, I thought. "My family is somewhat scattered. I am divorced."

"Do you have any children?" I was embarrassed at bringing up such an obviously painful topic.

"No. My wife is also a scientist. It worked well for us. At least I thought it did, until she asked for a divorce. She came out of the, um, cupboard, and no longer wanted to be married."

"The cupboard?" I asked, confused.

"Yes. She has a woman she loves."

"Oh. I see. You mean she came out of the *closet*. That must have been very difficult for you." Talk about your awkward conversations!

"The most difficult part is that I did not know why she no longer wanted to be married," he said. "We spent almost two years going to counselors, taking romantic vacations; I did not want a divorce." I felt his shrug. "However, in the end, my wishes were secondary. There were other things about me she also could not live with." He paused, as if he had revealed too much, then spoke in a rush. "However, she is happy now, and we still work well together." We turned toward the temple and joined the groups of people lining up before the Tourist Police gates in front of Karnak. I was relieved for the change of subject.

Despite, or perhaps because of, the multicultural ragtag gathering before it, Karnak was one of the most impressive places I had ever seen, especially at night. Lights illuminated the lengthy Avenue of Rams, and the whole temple seemed an embodiment of the mysterious and occult. I fingered my ankh and felt a companion chill to the one from the *souq* run down my spine; just for a moment I questioned the wisdom of my evening's plan. Only for a moment, though. I wasn't planning on stealing or defacing anything, I just wanted some unusual shots of the place. Perhaps I could even sell them and make up for some of the cost of this trip.

"Tonight is in French," Anton said. "I hope that is not a problem for you?"

I smiled. "No, French is my second language, though my accent is definitely not Parisian."

A sounding boom indicated the "show" was about to start, and we joined the throng in buying tickets and moving through the gates. Suddenly we were plunged into darkness . . . then a smattering of lights spotlighted the foreboding stone pylons.

A sensual feminine voice spoke against a background of dissonant music. *"May the breath of Shu soothe your brow, O weary sojourner."* A male voice joined in. *"Walk now in the steps of the imperial family of Thebes, entering into the House of the God, a house built for two thousand years for the god, his human family and priesthood, alone. Listen to the whispered response of the all-knowing, all-being Creator. Stride forth, O mortal, and behold the hidden glory of the Unknowable Ones."*

Anton took my hand in a warm, dry clasp and we moved forward with the crowd. The light from the moon was hidden as we passed through the inner courtyard, before an enormous statue of Rameses the Great and into the columned porch.

I suddenly became aware of how alien Egypt really was to our modern world, with animal-headed gods, intermarrying brothers and sisters, and everyone walking around half-naked. It seemed so far removed from our Western mind-set. I felt chilled by the strangeness of this place. Not only was it foreign ground, but it all seemed so vividly, disconcertingly, different.

The voice continued to speak over the hushed crowd. *"All of the majesty of the dynasties is represented here at Karnak. I am the* neter: *the father of all, the mother who birthed the fountainhead of all life. I am the sun of day and the defender of the night."* The voices spoke together: *"I create that which is, from Chaos. I walk before, so that men should have a path of life. Come, worship the eternal."*

For the next hour or so I imagined the temple in all its glory: shaven-headed priests clad in leopard skins scurrying to and fro to meet the golden god's every imagined need; the never-ending construction as each pharaoh sought to make an everlasting impression on the place; the wealth of gold and jewels that was supposed to have adorned the temple. When the lights came up around the Sacred Lake, I realized I'd better move quickly if I wanted to stay the night and catch the sunrise from Karnak Temple.

We were caught up in the crowd, being ushered through the temple by Tourist Police with polite but firm gestures. Anton put his arm around my waist so I wouldn't get crushed. As we left the ancient temple, still within the modern gates, I saw my chance.

"Anton, I see a ladies' room. Please excuse me."

He looked baffled. "You mean the toilet? I never understand these American euphemisms for basic necessities," he muttered. "You go on, and I will wait."

Initiating plan two. "Don't be silly. Look, there is a café just outside the gates. You go wait for me there and I will be out in a minute," I said. He looked at me quizzically, but I decided it was just my guilty conscience for lying to such a nice guy.

He shrugged, gave my waist a quick squeeze, and walked away. I struggled upstream through the people and finally pulled aside to the revolting, overused facilities. Gagging from the stench, I walked away and sat down behind a pillar, upwind of the toilets.

I could see the café, where Anton had selected a table facing the front gate. I swore softly. Time to implement the backup measure.

After scanning the Arab children around me, I picked out a raga-muffin boy and gestured to him. Giving him a note and a ballpoint pen in payment, I instructed him to deliver the folded piece of paper to Anton. The attractive *doktor* had been drawn into a game of *shesh-besh*, and for a few minutes I wondered if I should join him. He had been wonderful and entertaining, and he was definitely good-looking in a rugged, intellectual kind of way. Camille would love him, I thought abstractly.

The boy had already reached him, and I watched Anton read my note informing him that I had run into my sister and an old friend and we had gone to my friend's hotel and I would see him for breakfast in the morning. He shrugged, then handed the boy some gum, mussed his hair, and rejoined the game.

I watched as the last of the tourists were escorted out of the gate, and I melted farther back into the shadows, keeping my eyes on the many caretakers milling about the grounds. They shouted back and forth to each other, bidding good night with wide gestures and laughter in their voices.

Satisfied the grounds were empty of tourists, they began to file out, joining the group at the café. The moon had risen high, and feeling safer from discovery now, I stepped into the light and checked my watch: 10:53. I sat quietly, waiting until the lights of the café went out and its doors were also locked.

I felt a moment of trepidation; what had seemed like a childhood prank would *not* be very funny if I were found out now. I stayed as silent as one of the stone sphinxes.

Finally, all was dark and the only sounds drifted in from the river. I let out a breath I'd been unaware of holding. Certain there must be more guards, I knew I'd have to be cautious.

I passed quickly through the Great Court, its statues given an eerie life in the stillness. Moonlight streamed over my shoulder as I paused in the Hypostyle Hall, not daring to breathe, waiting for sounds of pursuit. Had I been discovered? Not a sound. I could hear guards in other parts of Karnak Temple, calling out to one another to be careful of the jinn, the night demons, as they went home after another long, tourist-filled day. They would not be pleased to find me.

I dodged from column to column and crossed an ancient hallway until I found myself beside Queen Hatshepsut's partially blockaded obelisks. With reverent fingers I touched the hieroglyphs and was jolted by an almost physical sensation. Stars sparkled above in the sky, visible through the broken roof. I held my watch up to the moonlight. Although it read 11:20, my military upbringing translated it to 23:20. Dizziness swept over me and I touched the cool stone, controlling the fear and anticipation that raced through my veins and steadying myself. Something else prickled my scalp . . . déjà vu? Since I'd been here before, I ignored it. I mean, I was in an ancient Egyptian temple, late at night, on my birthday, doing something really stupid. Of course I would feel a little creepy! I also felt compelled.

I shifted my daypack. The bag was really heavy, and I briefly reconsidered my pack-rat traveling habits. Switching it to my left shoulder, I took a left at the cross-passage. Almost immediately I found myself at the "Do Not Enter" ropes that barred these three chambers of Karnak. With another backward glance, I stepped over the ropes and passed two of the small rooms in favor of the third.

Again, compulsion overwhelmed me.

The room was dark, lit only with the spotlight brightness of the moon. I sat on a carved stone table, directly in its path. By dawn I would have some awesome pictures of this place, both sketches and photos. I sat quietly, absorbing the atmosphere and wondering what would happen if I got busted for being in here. Like a ghost story, it was both scary and exciting. A breeze blew over me, laden with the same citrus and incense that had followed me since I'd arrived in Luxor.

The shadows of profiled figures were barely visible on the wall; traces of black paint pocked the drawing like scars in the moonlight. As I looked about the room, my eye caught a glitter of metal on the floor. The smell of incense grew stronger as I knelt on one knee, stretching my left hand toward the metal. This action caused my overloaded backpack to shift, and I reached across my chest with my right hand to catch it.

Then it happened—instantly and without warning. My sensations snapped and I was caught in a whirlpool of energy, spinning with so much force that I could taste sound and hear smell. I was being pulled down rapidly. Nausea rose in my throat and pressure built in my head, until my ears popped. Through flashes of indescribable color that I could feel, I saw a woman. Dark and elegant, she hurtled toward me from below. In panic I reached out to stop her, seeking the solidity of another body, but I screamed as she passed right through me, through my flesh, my bones, severing me from my body in a bloodless surgery. The last thing I saw before darkness was her mouth, open in the terror of a soundless scream.

PART II

CHAPTER 2

Silence. Seeping coldness. Chloe lay still, trying to overcome the nausea and pain that had racked her body in those last few seconds before thankful oblivion. Once her senses were sorted, she did a mental review of all major appendages and body parts. She could feel very little, and the parts she did feel hurt like hell; she wished they were numb, too. She tried opening her eyes, and after an effort that caused sweat to bead her upper lip, she managed it. Slowly her vision focused.

Egypt. White walls with life-size figures in colors so bright, they hurt.

The floor on which she was lying was cold and getting colder. Chloe attempted to sit up, only to fall back onto the stone, boneless as a rag doll. She looked around again, a feeling of horror and disbelief growing in her.

Something was wrong.

Was she dreaming? But dreams should not be filled with cloying odors. She should not hear singsong voices from beyond this room. She should not be able to taste the blood from a cut on her lip. She should not feel bruised and battered.

Something was terribly, horribly, unfathomably wrong.

Before her was a cleaner version of the last room she had seen. It was in good repair, fresh and colorful. The parading gods and goddesses were painted brilliantly and seemed almost to move in the still air. The room was filled with a muggy odor she couldn't quite place, the star-painted ceiling hazy through the fog of smoke. There was also an acrid smell, a frightening smell . . . very recognizable, but she couldn't recall it now. Chloe turned around and looked up at the granite table. Her pulse trebled.

A silver statue stood on the table, a perfectly formed female with a horns-and-disk headdress. Before the statue were silver bowls of incense and a large plate with bread, dates, and what looked like a whole roasted bird, complete with head and feet. Several silver goblets were beside it. Chloe looked hard at the statue and felt something in her mind stretch, grasp, and miss. She *knew* she knew who it was and what it meant; she just couldn't reach it now.

She turned back to the window. Dawn was breaking, sending slivers of pink and rose into the misty silver of the sky, invading the black shroud of night.

As she mentally shrugged away sluggishness, her mind suggested and rejected possibilities for her position. Another indigestion-induced nightmare? Delusion? Serious drugs? Insanity?

Shakily, clutching at what she called an altar, she drew herself to her feet—and promptly fell down again.

Someone rushed to her side. "My lady, my lady? By the gods, what has happened?"

Chloe's fogged mind perceived a girl about fifteen years old, with a heavy black wig and black-ringed eyes, wearing a white dress that exposed one tanned breast, kneeling at her side, holding her hand, and chattering in a voice and words that came and went like a car phone just out of range. Chloe heard rushed footsteps in the corridor, and the girl leaned close to her, her face full of concern, awe, and more than a little fear.

Two men entered the room, dark skinned, wiry, and bald. They were wearing dresses! That was a new twist, even in her sometimes wild dreams. Where in the bloody universe was she supposed to be? She reached for the silver ankh that hung around her neck; her stained fingers gripped it . . . funny, it hung much lower than usual. She looked down and saw her body, with only a few scraps of white cloth hanging from a belt at her waist and streaks of fresh red *what* on her skin. Her hands were also coated with it.

What the hell was going on? Chloe's head felt as though it weighed a ton. It kept flopping around as she tried to see the girl and understand what she was saying. The girl spoke rapidly, her hands flying as she talked to the men. Chloe heard the frustration and fear in her voice but had no idea why she was so upset.

The concept Chloe refused to acknowledge pinched, poked, and prodded her consciousness, giving her no choice but to pass out and hope that when she came to, it would be in a ruined temple, helped by somebody named Mohammed carrying a Diet Coke.

No such luck.

Instead a terrible itching woke her and she started, fully expecting large portions of her body to be covered with fire ants. She writhed and whimpered but was unable to tell why she itched so badly.

Suddenly it was over, the burning itching replaced by strong awareness and feeling. Once more she could move her body and feel something besides her face. Her fingers touched the smooth painted wood of her bed and traced the raised design on its edge. She felt the roughness of a linen sheet on her knees, belly, and breasts. Chloe looked around her. The room was all white, with a cloth-covered doorway and a small alcove off to her right. It could be any room, any time, any where.

An insane asylum, she thought. That must be it. Where was her straitjacket? In a movie, when one woke up in a room like this, it was always in a straitjacket.

As her mind cleared, the possibilities and impossibilities crowded in on her. The only rational conclusion was that she had been kidnapped and was on some strong mind-expanding drug. It was understandable she would dream of Egypt, since that was what she had ingested mentally for the past month.

She'd heard rumors of kidnapping and white slavery. Despite government policy against it, it was still practiced in Egypt and the Middle East. Chloe had felt fairly safe, however, since she was the antithesis of what the Middle Eastern mind considered attractive. According to Cammy, the ancient Egyptians had always considered their Satan to be a redhead, and uneducated Egyptians still feared light-colored eyes and red hair. So she'd doubted they'd go for her.

Not to mention she was too tall and too lean for most Egyptian tastes.

Her musings were interrupted when the door curtain was pulled back and the same girl from the temple entered—at least Chloe *thought* she was the same.

Seeing Chloe awake, she crossed her breast with her forearm and knelt. When Chloe just stared at her, she rose and came toward the bed.

"My sister, are you faring better?" She glanced nervously away from Chloe's eyes and made a small gesture that some part of Chloe's mind identified as a sign against the Evil Eye. Chloe understood the girl, but the words didn't feel familiar. It was as if something were interpreting in her head before the words actually got to her brain, making her very dizzy. That smoke . . . an incense . . . where had she smelled it before?

The black-haired girl pulled back the sheet, and Chloe saw that her body was clean and naked. Well, she *thought* it was her body . . . but the freckles that were the plague of redheads were gone, and her skin was a rich café latte. The girl reached out and felt the pulse at Chloe's throat and then touched the juncture of her thigh.

Chloe tried to jerk away from the familiarity of the touch, but her muscles did not respond. The girl watched Chloe carefully with her black-circled eyes. Pulling the sheet back up, she spoke in a gentle, singsong voice.

"The Sisterhood has been most concerned for you, my lady. To sleep for so many days is quite unhealthy. Even My Most Gracious Majesty has inquired after you. She is sending a foremost magus to heal you. The priestesses have offered special intercession to HatHor for you also. The goddess will not allow her favorite to be sick." As she spoke she gathered a washbasin, assembled a tray of food, and emptied several jugs of water into the bath in the alcove.

Chloe raised her hands to her head. What was this girl talking about? What sisterhood? Which majesty? A magus? What the hell was that? What did they all have to do with her, and where in the *bloody universe* was she?

She who was no longer the same color.

Chloe decided she had endured this patiently and the time to speak was now. She would have answers. If this was a dream, some pointed questions should wake her up. If this wasn't . . . She ignored any possibilities and opened her mouth to speak. Only a strange gurgling came out, though, shocking Chloe and scaring the girl so badly that she yelped.

"Hush now, my lady," she said in a wavery voice that belied her familiar words. "Please, rest now, and perhaps the *hemu neter* will drive this *kheft* from you. Please, eat now." She placed a tray of breads, figs, and a flagon of milk in front of Chloe. Her stomach rumbled in response. The girl laughed, the first unguarded moment Chloe had seen since she'd opened her eyes.

"Perhaps a *kheft* has your tongue and so your stomach speaks for you, my lady," the girl said teasingly. With a strength Chloe would not have thought the girl's body capable of, she eased Chloe into a sitting position. Basha handed her the milk. . . . Wait, *where* did that thought come from? Suddenly, in a drowning wave, rushed in thoughts of where and who and why she was, with little order or sense to them.

She knew Basha was her serving girl, and she, *Chloe*, was actually RaEmhetepet, one of the priestesses to HatHor; that they were in a small room beneath the Karnak Temple compound; that for the Great House to send a magus she must be extremely ill. . . .

What was going on? Where was she getting this information? Was she being hypnotized? Brainwashed? What was this? Chloe punched the bed in frustration, and Basha bolted to the other side of the room. Something told Chloe she would not see Anton at breakfast.

The quaking Basha retrieved her tray and escaped out the curtained door, glancing warily behind her at RaEm . . . no, Chloe. I am Chloe.

No, the "other" said.

I am, Chloe told the "other."

Agreed, said the voice, mildly. You are both.

Both?

Both.

How could she be RaEmhetepet and still be Chloe? What had happened to her in the sea of confusion between arriving here, in an altar room, and leaving there, an old temple? She had not changed her physical location, yet somehow she had been sucked back into time.

Chloe almost slapped herself for that stupid thought. *No bloody way.*

That was something out of Cammy's *Star Trek*, not what happened to single tourists on their birthdays. She could understand the language— and it definitely was not English, French, Arabic, or Italian. She couldn't separate her mind long enough from itself to analyze the words. This was too exceedingly strange; there *must* be another explanation. Could she be going mad?

The insanity theory was looking better and better.

Chloe looked toward the door, if you could call a white sheet a door. No one was there. Grabbing the skin on the back of her hand, she pinched and twisted, digging her nails into her flesh. Her eyes watered and angry half-moon marks showed on her hands. She was awake.

Yanking back the sheet, she looked carefully at her body. There was the scar from Cammy's motorcycle accident on her knee, the countless faint discolorations on her feet from blisters, mosquito bites, and small cuts. She held out a hand. It was the same—long elegant fingers that were hopeless at any keyboard except a computer, short oval nails, and a faint scar on her palm from a long-ago dog bite.

Yet the skin was not fair, not freckled. Cautiously she reached up and tugged some hair away from the band at her nape. It felt the same: thick, coarse, and board straight. It was the same length, but instead of copper, it was black, so black as to shine faintly blue. Chloe dropped her trembling hand.

Oh my God.

Before she had time to compose herself, Basha came back through the door with two dark-eyed men. Chloe searched the memories that flooded her mind, trying to place things in some semblance of order, sorting through the "other" mind that was also in her head.

No luck.

One man walked to her side.

"RaEm," he said, his look taking in her body, "what is this illness that has befallen you?" He sat on the bed beside her and grasped her hand. His words were polite but distant. He was young and handsome, a white kilt wrapped around his waist and his upper body impressively muscled. To one-half of her mind he was familiar, his presence comforting but surprising.

The other half of her mind was reeling from the heavy eye makeup and gorgeous jewelry he was wearing, not to mention his elaborate hairstyle. Was he wearing a wig? The other man was older but dressed in the same skirt, his wide shoulders covered in a gold-and-leather collar. He looked on, no expression readable on his fleshy bronze features.

Basha laid a gentle hand on the seated man's shoulder. "My Lord Makab, your sister will be healthy again. She will be singing and dancing before the goddess once more. Do not trouble yourself. She will be well."

A bolt slid into place. This was her older brother, Makab, a young noble who lived in the country. In accordance with Egyptian custom, she had inherited all the property when their parents died years ago.

Hesitantly she returned the pressure of his handclasp. He turned from Basha and focused on Chloe's hand. "You know me, then?" Her affirmative nod brought his glance to her face. Then, startled, he drew back, dropping her hand as though it were a scorpion as he traced ankhs into the air. "Holy Osiris! Your eyes!"

From the corridor came the sounds of many feet. A squat man walked in, torchlight shining onto his bald head. "Make way for the noble Hapuseneb! High Priest of the Great God Amun, who rules Upper and Lower Egypt! Father of Pharaoh Hatshepsut, living forever!" So saying, he banged his staff on the floor and stood back. A taller, older man, clad in a leopard skin and an ankle-length kilt, came into the room.

Everyone stood back and bowed: Chloe sat dumbfounded. She'd always known she had a lot of imagination, but the details in this particular flight of fantasy were incredible.

"My lady," he said in a low, beautiful voice, "the *khefts* have left you. This is good." He stepped closer to her and Chloe dropped her gaze, some instinct warning her that if her "brother" was frightened by her eyes, this priest of Amun might feel even more strongly. Provided he even existed outside her own mind, her left brain railed.

"The Great House is concerned about her defensive priestess. Please tell us what happened."

Basha stepped forward and made a motion. "Your Eminence, the lady has not regained her voice."

Hapuseneb gazed thoughtfully at her for a second and then away, back to Chloe. "When you are well, then, we will receive you." He came closer and Chloe looked intently at his chest, hoping her eyes were lowered enough. Apparently they were. He inclined his head and left the room. An uncomfortable silence filled the chamber, and one by one the ornately dressed and made-up well-wishers bade Chloe a good rest and left.

WASET

THE GOLDEN CHARIOT RACED through the eastern desert, eating up the *henti* under the benevolent winter sun. Pharaoh held the reins tightly in her red-gloved hands, the ends wrapped around her gold-belted waist. Senmut, her grand vizier, held on to the side, watching not the sands before them but the slender body of the woman who had given him the world. He glanced behind them; two chariots were following, slowly enough to give Pharaoh the illusion of privacy, just as they had camped out of sight last night in the desert. He looked over Pharaoh's head as they left the trail and raced across a series of rising dunes. A ridge of mountainous desert framed the horizon. Hatshepsut slowed her speed; her newest toy might lose a wheel in the depths of the warm sand.

A rock face rose rapidly before them, its shade carving a bluish shadow in the sand. Hat secured the horses and jumped down, wiping dust from her face with the back of her gloved hand. Senmut stepped down beside her, his architect's eye taking in the sandstone block that jutted out of the ground, reaching toward the sun. A gods-made obelisk. Hat watched him as he mentally measured.

"Beloved architect," she said after they had walked around its large base twice, "you have built for me the most splendid of all mortuary temples in the western crescent."

"It is a minute tribute to your own beauty, Pharaoh," he replied as they stood in the shadows. She flashed a brief smile.

"However, I fear it would be unwise for me to make it my resting place for all eternity." Senmut opened his mouth to protest, but she held up a hand in silence. "My nephew Thutmosis hates me. I will not speak ill of him, for he is born of the god and of the royal bed and has my father's sacred blood in his veins. I should just feel safer if I knew my tomb would be undisturbed because it would be unfound."

Senmut looked at the rocks around him. "You would wish to be buried on the east bank of the Nile?" His tone was dubious. Death was synonymous with the west bank, as life was with the east bank. "What if, in future dynasties, they build cities out here? Egypt is growing, and if the irrigation systems are improved, who is to say this could not be arable?"

"I am to say!" she commanded. "I am Egypt!" She turned from him, running her hand across the gritty stone. "Please, precious brother, build a chamber deep under the earth, covered by this rock, so that our rest will be undisturbed."

Senmut halted a few cubits away, staring at her in shock. Her wide lips, lips he knew so well, spread into a smile.

"We shall be together for all eternity," she said.

"We?" his staggered thoughts questioned: *"We?"* He ran to her and fell

to his knees, grasping her around the waist, his body trembling with emotion. To be buried with the god-goddess he loved; for all eternity to look at her golden perfection, to serve her . . . Senmut looked up into her face, her lips parted now in sensual anticipation.

He stood up and pulled off her red leather *henhet* crown, freeing her long ebony hair to fall about her face. After wrestling with his belt, he left both it and his kilt in the sand and advanced on Hat. She took a step farther back, so she was standing against the stone, her eyes large and dark in her wrenchingly beautiful face. He kissed her face, savoring their mutual hunger, taunting and twisting her gold-dusted breasts until they jutted into his chest. He ran a hand underneath her boy's kilt and found the warm welcome that still shook him with desire.

She moaned and leaned back against the stone, her breath hot pockets in the cool shade. He raised her off her feet as she wrapped her legs tightly around his waist. They began the give-and-take of any man and woman, forgetting for a while the pressures and intrigues of her royal status. She pulled him deeper, and Senmut braced his legs as they began to shudder with release. Her body shook with her suppressed cries, his in delighted surrender. They fell to the ground slowly, still intimately entwined.

When Hat could speak again, she said, "You will build for us, my amazing architect." It was a statement.

"Aye, My Pharaoh," he said, and held her close.

They spent another few hours in the sun, the royal architect and his Majesty, pacing around, analyzing how to tunnel far beneath the earth. Hat did not want any outward marker, any temple. She wanted everything underground. The rock itself would be enough of an indicator to any future worshiper. No one would know. It would be their secret.

They coupled again in the sand, slowly and completely, then slept until their tent of shade was broken by the traveling of Ra's barque. Hat gave Senmut the reins, and he headed them back to the Nile, the sand streaked with red and gold as Ra lost his strength at the hour of *atmu*.

CHEFTU REINED IN HIS HORSES and threw the lead to the waiting slave. He leapt lightly to the ground, then set off quickly to the Great House. Pharaoh had called a meeting, and the messenger had caught Cheftu as he was returning from the house of a dying friend. Cheftu cursed himself as he had been doing since Alemelek's death.

How could he not have known? How could he have been so obtuse? At least the package from the man was safe . . . for the time being. He passed a quick hand over his headcloth, collar, and earrings as he walked through the palace's empty torchlit corridors. Most of the Egyptian guards had been replaced with Kushites, further indications of how far Pharaoh's paranoia for her throne had gone. He paused before the beaten-gold doors that led to Pharaoh's private audience chamber while his titles were intoned.

"His High Lord Cheftu, *Erpa-ha, Hemu neter* in the House of Life, Seer of the Two Lands, Healer of Illnesses, Proclaimer of the Future, He Who Speaks in Amun's Ear, Beloved of Ptah, Befriended of Thoth." With the bang of the chamberlain's staff, Cheftu entered the room.

It looked like a council of war. Pharaoh Hatshepsut, living forever! stalked impatiently across the room, clad in a filmy evening robe of silver cloth, the vulture and cobra of her office firmly upon her brow.

High Priest Hapuseneb sat on a stool, one leg swinging in time to Hat's pacing. His shaved head gleamed in the lamplight, catching a glint of gold in the eyes of the dead leopard that was his badge of office.

His High Chief Steward and Grand Vizier to the King, Senmut, was glaring at some documentation, his strong peasant's back turned to Pharaoh and Cheftu.

Two "royal reporters," as spies were now called, were eating in the company of another vizier. Hat spun round and faced Cheftu. *"Haii,* good my Lord Cheftu." She extended a hand, over which he bowed with a perfunctory kiss.

"My Majesty, living forever! Life! Health! Prosperity! How may I serve?"

Hatshepsut gestured to a silver-gilded chair, and Cheftu seated himself. "I hear you have just lost a dear friend." Cheftu looked down. "My condolences, physician. May he dance in the fields of the afterworld. Has he been taken to the House of the Dead yet?"

Cheftu, nervous and suspicious, replied with a modicum of his usual aplomb. "Nay, My Majesty. He was from the East and wanted to be buried in the ways of his forefathers."

Hatshepsut's lips pressed together in an Egyptian distaste for any barbarian custom. "Very well, my lord."

Cheftu smiled. "My Majesty shows great favor in asking about the details of my poor life. Although I am sure that is not why I was called here."

Hatshepsut answered with a smile. "Indeed not, my lord. My high priestess of HatHor," Pharaoh said, and Cheftu felt his stomach knot, "has taken ill in some strange circumstances. Enlighten him, Hapuseneb."

The high priest sat straight in his chair. "She was serving the goddess, and for all intents and purposes seems to have . . ." His voice trailed off, the last words spoken quietly: "I know not what."

Cheftu forced his voice to be even. "Forbidden contact?"

"Only the gods know, *Hemu neter.*"

"Was she hurt?"

Hapuseneb exchanged a quick glance with his pharaoh. "She was bruised," he murmured. "Not wounded."

"She is recovering? Can she tell us who . . . who is responsible?"

"Aye, she is recovering, but strangely enough, she has no voice to convey what happened."

"That is a simple enough matter. Hand her papyrus and ink. She is educated and can write her account."

Hapuseneb glanced at Hat. "I fear it is more complex. My lady seems to be a *kheft*-maiden."

In spite of his calm demeanor, Cheftu's grip on the chair's arm intensified for a few moments. "I beg an explanation, Your Eminence."

"She seems lost and confused. Reports have come to me that she did not recognize her own brother, her serving girl from childhood, or Lord Nesbek, her betrothed. She seems to have forgotten the simplest details of life. It is very strange."

Cheftu calmed a little. "That is of little account, Your Eminence. In my travels I have seen people who receive a blow to the head and cannot remember their own name and nationality, let alone anyone else's. In time it will return. Has the lady been examined?"

"I too have heard of memory sickness," Hapuseneb said with a grim smile. "But I have never heard of it changing the color of a person's eyes."

Cheftu's gut clenched. Was this some trick? Calmly he said, "Eye color?"

Hapuseneb leaned forward, forearms resting on his knees. "I believe you are aware of the appearance of Lady RaEmhetepet?"

Cheftu colored slightly but answered, "I am."

"Then you are aware her eyes are, or *were*, of the darkest brown."

"Aye."

"Well, they no longer are. They are as green as malachite from Canaan."

"I see."

Pharaoh turned to him. "You may not see now, favorite, but you will. We need you to go to the priestess. To examine her and see what you can find. It is simple enough; whether her needs are solely physical or if she also needs to have *khefts* cast from her, you can heal her."

"Demons? My Majesty . . ."

"I know it will be awkward, given your past associations, but since she is once again betrothed, it will be a simple fact-finding mission. Makab is also here, visiting."

Cheftu bowed his head in acquiescence. He had no choice. This was one of the joys of being the king's favorite seer. However, it would be good to see Makab. It had been many Inundations. He assumed he was dismissed and began to back to the door. No one turned their back on Pharaoh, living forever!

"Cheftu!" Hat called.

"My Majesty?"

"Do the signs declare anything unusual, my seer?"

Cheftu thought for a moment. "Ancient prophecy is about to be fulfilled in the destiny of Kallistae, in the Great Green."

"The Keftiu? The same who trade here in Waset and Avaris? What prophecy concerns them?"

"The Aztlan empire has been nearly destroyed twice since Chaos, My Majesty. This time the destruction will be complete. I fear its repercussions not only in the Great Green, but even to Egypt. Perhaps these are the unusual portents you speak of?"

Hatshepsut stared at him for a moment, then her gaze darted to Hapuseneb. "No miraculous births?"

"Births, My Majesty?" Cheftu looked at her in slight confusion. "None that are foretold." His gaze dropped to Hat's concealed waist and then to the floor. She laughed delightedly.

"Have you never erred since I made you Proclaimer of the Future?"

"By the grace of the gods, I have been correct, My Majesty."

A secret and triumphant smile played around the edges of Hat's wide mouth. "That is well, favorite. I grant the god's discernment and wisdom in your quest."

Well and truly dismissed, Cheftu crossed his chest in obeisance and left. Once outside he drew his cloak of office around him as a shield against the cool night air. He leapt into his chariot and took the reins, starting up the wide sycamore-shaded avenue to his house, swearing fluently, all thoughts of the priestess gone.

CHLOE WAS AWAKENED AND TAKEN TO HER BATH, where after being soaked, exfoliated, shaved, and massaged she was wrapped in a long white sheath and seated before a makeup table. When they approached her with sandals, Chloe realized she was wearing a dress, not a robe.

What about underwear?

Realizing all the slaves were watching her with more than a little fear, Chloe tried unobtrusively to look at her body in the sheath. The linen was so fine, one could see right through it. She blushed. No wonder they shaved so carefully.

She looked down at the delicate sandals presented to her—and gulped. Size nine was not huge in her day and time—she knew quite a few women with size ten and above—but the way everyone was staring at her long narrow feet, she guessed they were the size of a soldier's today. A male soldier's.

With a weak smile she shoved in her long toes, grasping the thong. Her feet pushed into the upper curve, squished out the sides, and hung out the back. She'd be lucky if she could walk without falling.

She waddled over to the trunk where Basha had pulled out her clothes and opened it. There was nothing except more flimsy, see-through, white wrap dresses. She looked at Basha; you could see every line of her young body through her one-strap dress. And Irit, her slave girl, wore only a short shift with beads around her hips.

Apparently, in this hallucination, she was to be an exhibitionist with an enormous podiatry bill.

Sighing, she seated herself at the dressing table and motioned to Irit. Once the girl tore her stare away from Chloe's enormous feet, she painted long black lines of kohl around Chloe's eyes for protection against the sun.

After Chloe's chin-length black hair had dried, Irit plaited strands, periodically winding the ends with silver bands. She reached behind her for a small woven trunk and opened it, revealing a jewelry collection the Louvre would kill for. It was all silver. The "other" admonished her; priestesses of HatHor never wore gold. Bravely Chloe reached for a bracelet and ring.

"Would my lady select a collar?" Irit asked, a little bewildered, Chloe thought. The choice was incredible. She picked a silver filigree collar with enameled lotuses and birds. Irit fastened it around her neck, adding a beautiful falcon pectoral under it, so it rested heavily beneath Chloe's skimpily covered breasts, covering her own ankh necklace. Chloe stood, trying to see her reflection in the polished bronze that passed for a mirror.

This was *too* unbelievable. The jewelry, the clothing details, the faint odor of myrrh that hung over the place, the dissonant chanting that could be heard from time to time . . . now this. Chloe was not seeing herself. A tomb painting stared back. The fitted white dress, the black drawn-on eyes and brows. Only the reflection of her slanted green eyes was familiar. Chloe looked behind her, sensing she was being watched.

The dark-eyed man from yesterday, Nesbek, the "other" mind suggested, came forward.

He was squat and broad, obviously middle-aged and dressed in a wealth of gold . . . collar, armbands, bracelets, and rings. His eyes were small and deep-set, filled with some emotion that Chloe couldn't read. The room cleared as if by invisible command.

"RaEmhetepet," he said, approaching her, "I trust you remember me?" He took a step forward, leering at Chloe's appearance, frowning at her sandals. "It would be a pity for me to have to remind you. . . ."

His tone shifted between teasing and threatening, and Chloe took a shaky step back.

He smiled, revealing blinding gold teeth. "I must leave for my estate in Goshen, but once I have disciplined my Apiru, I will return for my bride." He glanced around as he pulled up his kilt. "Will you give me something now? A *token* to remember you by?"

Chloe averted her eyes, not even wanting to know what this was about. Was she a real sicko in this hallucination? He made her skin crawl, the way he looked at what her transparent clothing revealed. Instinctively she crossed her arms over her breasts and wished for a robe.

"*Aiii*, I can see it is a shock." He dropped his kilt, straightening the pleats with fat, manicured hands. "A pity that you have forgotten such a"—he paused—"passionate and beneficial relationship. I will take pleasure in reminding you." He reached for her and was halted only by a velvety, razor-edged voice.

"The lady is still in her serving time, when she must be unknown to any man. If you touch her, the Sisterhood will reprimand you, as will the goddess HatHor, for defiling one of her favorite maidens."

Chloe's and Nesbek's attention jerked to the doorway, in which a tall Egyptian stood in silhouette. He stepped into the room and Chloe saw him fully, from his floor-length robe to his red-and-gold-striped headcovering. It ran straight across his forehead and fell to his shoulders, framing his strong, bronze features, which even heavy earrings did not diminish.

"My Lord Cheftu," Nesbek ground out slowly. He turned back to Chloe. "I will await our marriage, my lady." He walked to the doorway, where the cloaked Egyptian inclined his head. "Life, health, and prosperity to you, Lord Nesbek," the man said, the words sounding like a curse.

Chloe tensed her muscles, trying to stop their trembling. Nesbek was gone, but this arrogant Lord Cheftu still stood in the room, glowering at her. She met his gaze and was shaken by the animosity in it. "So, my lady," he said in a deep, chilling tone, "we meet again. Health, prosperity, and life to you. My felicitations on your betrothal. I trust you will attend this time?" Chloe stared at him. He tried again, a cold smile showing white, even teeth. "Are you looking forward to it?"

Chloe shook her head violently.

He arched a painted eyebrow. "Then, if not to your marriage accounts, perhaps to your married bed? With whoever else is invited to join you?"

Chloe gritted her teeth against his comments. This hallucinogenic drug was not agreeing with her at all. The belief that this was a drug-induced episode was growing dimmer every moment. The details were too sharp, the sensory impact too real. What other alternatives were there?

None that were within the realm of sanity.

Cheftu sighed. "I am not here because I enjoy rescuing you from the embrace of your betrothed. My Majesty Hatshepsut, living forever! asked me to examine you, so please, come forward and sit at the table." So saying, he took off his gold-embroidered cloak. With a clap of his hands he summoned two others, *w'rer*-priests, both about twelve. Their heads were shaved, save their youthlocks, and they wore simple kilts fastened with plain leather belts. One carried a large woven trunk, the other carefully laid aside Cheftu's staff and cloak.

Chloe could only stare. She was still adjusting to the elaborate costuming everyone wore, and Lord Cheftu looked like every depiction she'd seen of an ancient Egyptian—and every fantasy. He was broad shouldered, long legged, and glittering with gold, from the wide collar across his chest, the armbands that hugged his beautifully sculpted upper arms, a tiger's eye-and-gold scarab ring, to his black-encircled eyes, dusted with gold powder.

Except that his weren't the dark eyes she'd seen and come to expect on everyone. They were amber, topaz, and gold swirled together and bordered by thick black lashes that accentuated his long, straight nose.

She dropped her gaze and searched through the "other" mind for some clue about this man. When she got it, her head snapped up in surprise and she tried not to gape. He was closer now, opening his basket and pulling out metal instruments.

"First we must do an examination." Without meeting her gaze, he called over his shoulder, "Keonkh! Take down our comments." One of the boys settled himself on the floor, crossed his legs, and smoothed his kilt over them tightly, forming a table of sorts. The other boy busily added water to a black pad and twisted his brush tip into a fine point.

"We are ready, *Hemu neter* Cheftu," said the boy called Keonkh, his voice cracking.

"Very good," Cheftu said with a warm glance at the boy. "Now, Batu," he addressed the other, "what is our first point in examination?"

The boy came forward and looked at Chloe, who was seated silently on her night couch. "Health, prosperity, and life to you, great priestess," he said. Turning to Cheftu, he answered, "First we examine her color, then the secretions from her nose, eyes, ears, of the neck, belly, limbs, looking for any swelling, shaking, broken veins, sweating, or stiffness."

"Very good." Cheftu walked behind Chloe, staring over her head. "Tell me of her color." The boy observed her skin carefully, and when she met his perusal he blushed faintly.

"Please extend your arms, my lady," he requested, and Chloe stuck them straight out as he carefully went over every inch of her newly browned skin. *"Hemu neter,"* he said, "the lady's color is perfection.

There are no abrasions, no swelling, no odors, and no discoloring."

Cheftu came around, staring at her blankly, like an exhibit, which Chloe supposed she was. Keonkh was furiously taking down every word Cheftu and the boy spoke. "Send the girl Basha for the lady's morning removal," Cheftu said, and the boy left, music from the main temple audible when he opened the heavy curtain.

Cheftu asked Chloe to open her mouth. He examined her ears, pressed down on her nostrils, and checked her neck. *"Assst,"* he mused as he finished his search and tilted her head back to look full into her face.

"Try to speak," he said.

The sounds that issued from her mouth were garbled and painful to them both.

"Haii. That is enough at present." He stepped back and she looked away. "Have you had any secretions, my lady?" he said as he counted her pulse, his fingers warm and tingly on her cool flesh.

Chloe shook her head.

Keonkh went for water. Then Cheftu tilted her head forward and placed his hands on either side of her head, his long fingers probing in her carefully arranged hair. "My lady, did you fall?"

She shrugged.

"Did you dream of grapes? Or figs?"

Was he weird? What kind of bizarre question was that? Then the "other" reminded her that those dreams were warnings from the gods of an upcoming illness. She shook her head no. No fruit-filled dreams.

Basha entered the room with Batu, carrying a large pot. Chloe recognized it as the chamber pot she'd stumbled to this morning. Cheftu had it set on the floor, and then he and Batu bent over it, discussing the contents in quiet tones.

The physician turned to her, and Chloe felt the breath catch in her throat. This couldn't be real. It must be a dream, a hallucination. He looked familiar, so apparently he was someone she'd liked and so had given him a role in her Egyptian fantasy—just as the *Wizard of Oz* was populated with Dorothy's friends and enemies. She dropped her gaze to his hands.

They were beautiful—the hands of an artist or scholar—with long fingers, squarely trimmed nails; not rough, but not soft, either. Hands to create and heal.

Her thoughts were interrupted as both boys returned to their places: Keonkh rapidly writing, Batu assisting Cheftu. From an alcove beside the door Cheftu removed a cow-headed statuette and replaced it with a jackal-headed obsidian statue. He then lit a dish of incense before it.

She searched her memory, trying to place the god's face and name. Cheftu withdrew a small papyrus from his basket and handed it to Chloe. "Since the problem is within your mouth, we shall speak to the god of your lips." Chloe took the scroll in her hands and looked at it. It was written in hieratic, a shorthand version of hieroglyphs.

Batu handed Cheftu the water, and Chloe watched as he poured some of it in a black alabaster cup decorated with carvings of the jackal-headed god. He poured the remainder in a cup he'd brought. Chloe watched in trepidation as he pulled small jars out of his basket. His broadly muscled back hid his actions, but she could hear him murmuring while he worked. He turned back to her with a cup of yellow green water. "Drink, my lady."

Chloe sniffed the water and tried to hide her smirk. This great ancient Egyptian physician had fixed her herbal tea! She sipped gratefully, honey easing the ache in her throat. He watched, his arms crossed over his chest. Closed body language if ever she'd seen it.

"Have you been relieved, my lady?"

Chloe met his look. His eyes were as emotionless as the stone on his finger and as exquisitely colored. He reminded her of a cat, watching, carelessly and coldly. Hesitantly, because she didn't know what he was talking about, she shook her head.

Cheftu's lips twisted in a cold smile. "Shall I call a slave, or would my lady prefer a sister?" Chloe shrugged. His eyes twinkled maliciously. "Batu, fetch the lady's slave!" Irit came in a few minutes later, crossing her breast.

"Life, health, and prosperity to you, *Hemu neter*," she said. "My lady."

Cheftu acknowledged her with a nod. They walked toward Chloe, and Batu handed Cheftu an instrument, narrow and long, no wider than a number eight paintbrush. Irit looked offended, but they both stared at Chloe. Her mind raced, consulting the "other," who remained suspiciously quiet. Even Keonkh caught up in his dictation.

Cheftu's eyes darkened. "Does my lady need assistance?" he inquired icily. Chloe shook her head, and Cheftu handed Batu the instrument. He stared at Chloe, as if weighing a decision. Before she knew what hit her, she was turned over on her chair, her gown around her waist, and *something was being pushed up her . . .*

Chloe tried to squeal and squirm, but a large, hairy knee was pressed into the small of her back. "Relax!" Cheftu commanded. "You are making it difficult for Irit." Chloe forced herself still and looked over her shoulder, trying to see what was going on. Then she felt it, water pushing through her system. An ancient enema.

I don't believe this! her subconscious screamed. Irit's face was mahogany from the exertion of blowing water into Chloe's bowels. No wonder she looked offended, Chloe thought. Then it was over. The long instrument was removed and Cheftu dropped her narrow skirt over her bare bottom, removing his knee.

She stood haughtily, pulling her frail gown straight. Cheftu was turned away, and Irit had already escaped, giving Chloe a moment to calm herself. She hated enemas! Mimi had administered them regularly when she and Cammy were children, believing them to be a cure-all. Chloe seated herself, trying to ignore the squishy feeling in her body.

Cheftu asked over his shoulder, "Can you write yet, my lady?"

They had been handing her writing utensils for days now, and as her other memory supplied, she was able to understand and remember more of someone else's life. But it was only facts, figures, chants, languages. She had no idea how she had related to her family, her friends, the mysterious Sisterhood everyone spoke of . . . *no emotional memories at all.*

However, she knew enough fact to know she previously had been betrothed to the tall, straight-limbed man before her and could fathom no reason why anyone would have exchanged him for that pig Nesbek.

She watched his long-legged body move across the room, pouring water from the alabaster cup over the statuette of . . . Anubis, the "other" mind provided. The god not only of embalming, but also of her lips and ability to speak. Cheftu caught the water in a cup as it poured off the figure, and he brought it back to Chloe. "Since you are unable to invoke the god, I will speak for you, lady." His voice became singsong, rich, and hypnotic.

"Hail to you, Anubis, god of the West, speaker of the desert, he who protects the voice. I come to you, I prize your beauty, your sharp talons, which take illness from this priestess's side. Your teeth, which with mystery and justice tear apart the kheft *which prevents the priestess speaking your worship. . . ."* Then he threw the water in Chloe's face. She flinched in surprise and saw Basha step farther away, clutching at the Eye of Horus pectoral she wore.

Cheftu stood before Chloe, watching her face. "Basha," he called over his shoulder. "The lady must take the water from Anubis' power four times a day for four days. You must recite the prayer for her, until she can speak for herself." Chloe dropped her gaze, feeling the water drip down her face and dress, making it transparent. She crossed her breasts with her arms. Cheftu noted her movements and gave a hollow bark of laughter as he walked away.

He left to mix some herbs, taking the others with him. Chloe sat in her chair; she had serious doubts about the success of the medical care she had just received. Hadn't Cammy said the Egyptians were far advanced medically? Enemas and herbal tea? She sighed. Apparently the lean Egyptian was not a graduate of Johns Hopkins, Wasetian style. Now that she didn't have an audience, she wiped the water off her face.

It had been fourteen days since she had awakened in this white room. Fourteen days of hearing she was in ancient Egypt during the peaceful reign of the Great House, King Hatshepsut . . . called pharaoh in Chloe's time.

Fourteen days of inhabiting her own body in the skin of another. Fourteen days of seeking an explanation between the alternatives of drugs, insanity, Technicolor dream . . . or reality. During her time here, she'd grudgingly acknowledged that just as she had merged, *if she had merged*, with RaEmhetepet's body, she also had access to RaEmhetepet's mind. How and why—and sometimes even *if*—it had happened, she did not know and did not know whom or how to ask.

She had been regaining her strength and wondering how to get back to her own life—provided she could. She decided to sneak out of her room later tonight and run back to the altar where she'd been found, hoping that some combination of time and position would throw her back into her own century. If, indeed, she had time-traveled at all.

If that was a possibility.

Meanwhile people kept showing up, threatening, cajoling, and speaking of incidents and stories that were apparently a part of the emotional memory she did not have, like the hooded figure who had stood beside her bed in the middle of the night and recited charms over her, her face hidden by her cloak. Chloe had remained immobile, turned on her side, head resting on her arm. The visitor obviously had not expected her to awaken, and when Chloe heard the threats she was making, Chloe didn't want to. Something about revenging her family, the *ka* of her brother finally resting.

Everyone was trying to prompt her memory; what they did not realize was that she had the wrong memory. Whatever else RaEmhetepet might have been, she had associated with some real slimeballs and was walking on the edge of something dangerous.

Cheftu's cold voice brought her out of her reverie, ". . . to dream about your happy future." He placed an alabaster jar on the table before her and turned to go. The boys were cleaning up the supplies. Chloe reached out, grabbing his forearm.

He turned to her, his golden eyes angry, his voice bitter and disinterested. "Leave me be, RaEm. I am no longer interested in your plotting and games. I cannot imagine why you are not speaking and what magic you have used to change your eyes, but I am beyond caring. The past is gone— only for the sake of your position am I here. Take your talons from me."

Even as he finished the angry words that apparently RaEm would have understood, Chloe could sense him softening as he looked into her eyes.

SWEET ISIS, CHEFTU THOUGHT. Somehow RaEm did not know what to do or where to go. Though nothing was physically wrong that he could find, her memory seemed genuinely incomplete. If so, she was at a distinct disadvantage. She didn't seem to know that Hat and Hapuseneb were stalking her, trying to ascertain if she had broken her vows, gauging how to find out and rid themselves of this unknown factor. Cool and calculating RaEm, for once *she* was under the blade.

Cheftu felt no surge of power or sweet taste of revenge as he saw the faint lines of strain in her forehead and around her full lips. Had he forgiven her? He certainly had not forgotten.

She snatched back her hand and clasped it so tightly in her lap that white showed around the knuckles.

"RaEm," Cheftu said, wondering at himself, "there are those who will not betray you. Tell them your tale. Maybe they can help you; these are uncertain times. Though we have hated each other these past years, still do not forget we once were close. For the sake of your family, and my esteem for Makab, tell me for whom to send. You can trust my discretion."

She did not look up.

Cheftu stood, anticipating for a moment, then cursing his own hopeful stupidity. With a curt word he and the two *w'rer*-priests left. She didn't move, but Cheftu felt her gaze as he walked down the cool, dark hallway away from her.

CHAPTER 3

Chloe slipped out of her room. It was dark, and she knew Basha was gone. Drawing a thick white cloak around her, she stepped outside her door, alone for the first time since waking in this fantasy world.

The heavy odor of myrrh floated in the air. It was Amun's favorite, so Pharaoh had sent to Punt and brought back myrrh trees. The temple was filled with their fragrance at all times.

The cloying smell made Chloe gag. She hurried down the corridor, following the mental map of the temple she had gotten from the "other." Soon she should be entering one of the main chambers.

She did.

Chloe felt her heart jump into her throat. The room was so far beyond what she had ever even conceived. Every word in *both* of her vocabularies failed to express the splendor before her. She could only stand in the flickering torchlight and stare.

She was in a hypostyle hall. Not the one she had seen in the twentieth century, however. This hall eclipsed it in grace, in beauty, and in majesty. She passed a shaking hand over her dry lips.

It was true; *my God, she* was *in ancient Egypt.*

She leaned against the wall, and slowly slid to the floor, her trembling legs unable to support her. She couldn't take it all in. Total sensory overload. She tried to unscramble the jumble of images, focusing on one thing at a time.

She looked at the floor, tracing the lotus border with one long finger. It seemed to glow and shine simultaneously. It was alabaster! She touched one lotus bud. It was inlaid lapis, held in place with gold. Gold? On the floor? She swallowed.

The rising and falling of voices that was always in the background seemed to be growing stronger. Straining, she began to make out the words.

"Thou createst the Nile in the otherworld, and bringest it forth to give life to mankind. Even createst thou men for thyself, to serve and worship thee. Lord of them all, who art weary because of them! Lord of all lands, who risest because of them! Disk of the day and conqueror of the night! How perfect thou counsels are, O Lord of Eternity! Thou art lifetime thyself, and thus we worship thee. Rest in thy barque, O Amun-Ra, ruler of the world. Speakest to the . . ." Of course, her "other" mind called out, they were putting the golden god to bed. Chloe hunched closer to the floor.

They would pass through the columned walkway; she could see the light. It licked flame across the chamber, animating the brilliantly painted images that covered every column, every bit of roof. She jumped involuntarily when the grotesquely huge shadows of the priests flickered against the walls. Even the multitudes of torches did not penetrate the dark, oppressive space above her. The columns seemed to reach into the heavens. Chloe craned her neck. She could barely see the glint of gold- and silver-painted stars shooting across the midnight ceiling.

Barefoot and shaven headed, the men progressed through the passage. From her position they walked in a relief, a tomb painting come to life. Their voices rose and fell dissonantly, at once eerie and ecclesiastical.

Another line of priests appeared. The torchlight illuminated their white, stiff kilts and lent an amber sheen to the cloths draped across their bodies. More priests, these covered in leopard-skin badges of office. Still more priests. Their chanting echoed back and forth in the chamber, their hundred voices multiplied into thousands.

Next was a group holding the saffron standard of Amun-Ra, the great golden god of Waset. The incarnation of the sun itself. The heavenly father of Pharaoh. Chloe's breath caught in her throat as her gaze sharpened. These priests carried on their shoulders an ebony-inlaid barque inhabited by a gold-covered statue.

All of this for a statue?

Her Egyptian mind and her Western mind warred. To part of her, this was God. He was offered food, his clothes were changed, he went on visits to other temples and other gods. He was the balance of life and justice embodied in a wooden, gold-covered statue.

To her Western mind this was an exquisite museum piece. The concept of having to care for a "god" as if he were an invalid relative was ludicrous. God, by definition, should be the end-all and be-all. He should not have to be carried from his bath to his sleeping chamber.

To her superstitious mind, the long black eyes of Amun-Ra seemed to wink in the fading torchlight, almost as if he could perceive her unholy thoughts in this most mysterious and sacred of places. Then the linen-clad, gold-covered back was to her, and she slowly let out her breath. The procession was almost finished.

Next came a line of priests swinging incense censors in the already myrrh-filled air. Chloe stifled a cough. She counted another seven lines of priests, singing and praising this gold statue.

Then, just like the red caboose in the children's song, came a solitary priest with a brush and ancient dustpan to clean their tracks from the alabaster floors. He was even wearing a red sash. Chloe smiled broadly into the newfound darkness.

She was alone once more.

Relying again on RaEm's memory, she slipped through the multitudes of towering columns and magnificent halls until she reached the small chamber set aside for HatHor. She was not the main goddess at Karnak, but the HatHor chamber had been built by a royal consort who had tried for many Inundations to get pregnant. When she finally gave birth, the child was stillborn, rumor said. Nevertheless she claimed to have had a son, one of the many offspring of Thutmosis I.

Years later that son had killed one of Pharaoh's viziers while he was overseeing a building project. Thutmosis I's anger had known no restraint. He had searched in vain for his son, finally giving up and striking his name from all official records.

Chloe reached the metal-plated doors that led to HatHor's Silver Chamber and slowly pushed one open. The room was as she remembered it . . . sort of. The walls were painted with stories about helping the queen to conceive and give birth to a healthy male child.

Blood pounded through her head with the dual excitement of being able to read the hieroglyphs on the walls as if they were yesterday's *Ad News Weekly* and the anticipation of returning home.

She had no watch, but it seemed to be late. She would re-create the situation that brought her here, as best she could, in hopes that it would return her. Cammy hadn't forced her to watch *Star Trek* for nothing! Chloe approached the altar with its elegant silver-and-electrum statue of HatHor in her most bovine form. She turned toward the window, its clerestory gap showing sky as dark as ink. Slowly, so slowly, she knelt down.

Nothing.

She tried kneeling quickly.

Nothing.

After an hour of different configurations, different speeds, different mind-sets, she was still here. Ancient Egypt. With black hair and brown skin.

Alone.

So hideously, frighteningly, alone.

Even more alone than standing in that graveyard six months ago, the loneliest she thought she'd ever be. Oh, Mimi! she cried in her heart, aching for the comforting softness of her family. But they were not here.

Exhausted, she stood up, glanced wearily at the brightening sky, and began to make her way to her room.

The sun god Ra was approaching, and a trace of light could be seen everywhere, giving a startling life to the colored paintings, warming the alabaster and gold beneath her feet, reflecting off the enormous gold-and-silver doors that hung everywhere, blinding her with the light. Marking her an alien.

Discouraged and more than a little sick to her stomach, Chloe lay down in the simple whitewashed room on the hard wooden couch and stared up at the ceiling blankly.

What to do?

CHEFTU RECLINED, enjoying Ehuru's expert shave. Birdsong wafted in through the clerestory windows, easing his mind as he lay beneath steaming linen facecloths. The day was free—only a report to make to Pharaoh about the bewildered priestess, then glorious decans to himself. He had traded his instruction time at the House of Life with another physician and could go hunting, or taste his newest wines while he read, or even go visit the wealthy Kallistaen widow.

Ehuru removed the linens. The morning breeze cooled Cheftu's smooth cheeks and jaw. His manservant plucked Cheftu's brows, then drew heavy kohl across his eyelids and extended his brows. Cheftu sat up. "Do you go to court this morning, my lord?"

"Only for a brief time, Ehuru."

"*Haii!* Is this to be a fortunate day for the yellow-haired widow?"

Cheftu looked into the older man's snapping black scrutiny. "I have not seen her horoscope, so I do not know how the gods will treat her today," he said dryly.

Ehuru's gaze fell, and he exhaled loudly. "My lord, who is going to take care of your House of Eternity unless you beget children? All of these travels are well and good, but they will not warm a man in the night! If you had a woman, your belly would not trouble you so!"

Cheftu waved him away. "I know, Ehuru, I know. If I do not have a son, I will starve forever after, and if I do not have a daughter, the priests will inherit my lands. Without a wife, you say, I am likely to lose my member to the freezing Egyptian nights!" He laughed. "I am yet unwilling to give up my comfortable life at this point. I have enjoyed my travels. Only for the past season have I been back in Egypt." Cheftu arched a brow. "And, old father, as I am a *hemu neter*, I can medicate my belly, *haii?*"

Ehuru shuffled out. "Very well, my lord. However, even your friends will marry and you will be alone, drinking and gaming your life away, inflaming your innards because you have no wife." Cheftu smiled at Ehuru's back. He was like a father, servant, scribe, and housekeeper in one person, and as illogical as the four combined.

He raced up to the second floor, calling for servants, then stood as they wrapped him in a heavily pleated kilt and fastened the long, fringed sash of the Oryx Nome, his family's district, around his trim waist. They settled an ibis-headed pectoral of lapis and tiger's eye on his chest. He added a simple red leather collar and headcloth, strapped on sandals, and sent them to prepare his horses and chariot.

Exiting his house through the side garden, he strode through the sweet-smelling flowers just beginning to bud, predicting a return of life to the red and black lands of Kemt. He took the reins, turned his chariot onto the wide, sycamore-shaded avenue, and headed up Nobleman's Way to the palace and Karnak complex.

Hatshepsut's antechamber was full of petitioners, so Cheftu stepped into one of the long, dark hallways leading to the resting room of Pharaoh. The guards nodded to him, several flashing smiles when they recognized their fellow veteran of the Punt trip and other expeditions. The red wood doors were closed and Nehesi, Hatshepsut's trusted Leader of Ten of Ten Thousand, announced him. Cheftu entered, bowing immediately.

Hatshepsut was to one side, Senmut the other, but even her heady myrrh perfume could not cover the musky scent of the room; they had not been resting. He hid a smile, waiting to be acknowledged. *"Hemu neter,"* she said, her voice rigidly controlled.

"Pharaoh, living forever! Life! Health! Prosperity!"

"How is my priestess? I have received disturbing reports from the Sisterhood, reports of incidents even before this last. Seat yourself."

Cheftu sat on one of the leopard-covered stools in the room and looked fully at his pharaoh and friend. She was dressed for the archery range in white kilt and blue leather collar, shin guards, sandals, helmet, and gloves. Her gem-studded flail and crook lay on another stool, her white-and-gold-embroidered cloak cushioning them. He met her lapis-circled gaze and, as always, was slightly stunned by her personal power and almost masculine command.

"There is no physical reason she cannot speak. For four days she has been administered the waters of Anubis by *w'rer* Batu and servant Basha. I will examine her again tomorrow, see if there is improvement."

Hat looked away from him, her gaze meeting Senmut's across the room. "What will be your next prescription?"

"The spittle of HatHor's *ka.*"

Hatshepsut nodded.

"If that is unsuccessful," Cheftu continued, "I suggest either the sacred baths of Isis or Ptah. My only other consideration is that sometimes when a person sees something so far beyond their normal experiences, it steals his voice." Hatshepsut glanced at Senmut, and Cheftu explained. "I was treating a slave some years ago who was unable to speak. After countless and pointless treatments we took him back to where he had lost his voice." He licked his lips as his stomach clenched.

"Hemu neter?" Senmut inquired a moment later.

Cheftu shrugged. "It was a slave that one of my students was treating. Suffice it to say he had seen the death of his son, and once we took him to the place where it happened, he regained his voice." Cheftu could still hear the old man. He and his son had been fishing in the deep water of the Great Green. They had been teasing and drinking when the son fell overboard. The man had laughed; his son was as agile as a fish. Suddenly the waters stirred, violently, and he heard the stricken cries of his son as he was torn apart by creatures he swore were half man and half fish. Cheftu restrained a shudder.

"Did he recover?" Senmut asked, his modulated tone unable to hide his *rekkit* roots.

"Aye, my lord," Cheftu said. "He was able to speak." Cheftu did not add that the man's grief had led to self-destruction.

"So there is a possibility that RaEm has seen something so magnificent or so horrible that she cannot speak of it?" Senmut clarified.

"A possibility."

"Could Set's magic be at work here?" Hat asked.

Cheftu looked down at his kilt, straightening the folds. Should he share what he knew of RaEm? Her strange proclivities, the people with whom she associated?

Hat took his lack of response for an affirmative answer. "We have some problems, magus." His gaze met hers. "RaEm is our most powerful defensive priestess. Just recently has one been weaned to take her place." Hat snorted in derision. "In this country filled with children there is not one female chosen by her birth of the twenty-third power in all its degrees who is now old enough to embrace the full priestesshood. RaEm must be healed! There are no alternatives at present." Hat's voice was strong. "We have also heard other rumors, ones that chill my *ab* when I consider the level of betrayal they insist upon."

"My Majesty?" Cheftu inquired.

"Nay. I shall not give them the power of being named," she said in dismissal of her fears. "Keep me informed of all that transpires. I am sad to see a friend attacked to this magnitude. Should she be taken back to the chamber of the goddess? See if she regains her voice?"

Cheftu frowned. "She has tried that herself. Basha observed her go into the Silver Chamber and pray. She moved many times, but not in any ritual recognizable to Basha. Of course, they could be rites from deeper initiations into the priesthood. Since there are no priestesses outside of the Sisterhood more powerful, it would be hard to know what she was doing."

"Agreed." Hat rose to her feet, accepting her cloak and symbols of office from Senmut. "We will dine tonight at *atmu.* Join us, *Hemu neter.*" Cheftu bowed, and she turned back, a wide smile on her lovely face. "Cheftu?"

"Aye, Majesty?"

"Bring a woman!" She walked out laughing, and Cheftu stared at the floor. He didn't recall anything in his horoscope today about nagging friends, but that seemed to be his lot. He left the room, lighthearted. It was good to be home.

•••

The night was beautiful, the stars spangling on the goddess Nuit's body above them, shining brilliant whiteness on the world below. Cheftu extended his arm to his companion as they walked under the shadowed portico and into the grand hall leading to Hat's feast. The sounds of laughter reached out to them, and his companion's steps hastened into the gilded room. Columns reached high, garlanded with flowers from the royal gardens, while slave girls dressed only in beads and flowers placed perfume cones on their heads. He noted his companion's long black eyes taking in every jeweled noble in the room.

He sighed. So avaricious. Was there a woman alive who did not covet gold? She extended her hand, heavy with rings, to him, and he helped her into a seat on the opposite side of a small table. Pharaoh had not yet appeared, so he took a cup of honeyed, spiced wine and sipped as he looked over those assembled. After years in foreign courts on missions for Hatshepsut, he was startled to see the racial homogeneity of the group. Just the home crowd tonight.

An impressive crowd—the gold-hung sons of the many nomes of Egypt and the Flowers of Egypt, those beautiful young women who would inherit their mother's wealth and take husbands as suited them—mingled around him. A touch at his elbow gained his attention, and he turned to see a slave girl. From her tattooed upper arm he knew she was a sworn body servant of Pharaoh. "Come with me, my lord."

He rose, kissing his lovely companion's wrist, and saw her gazing across the room. Smiling wryly, he left, going through one of Pharaoh's private passages. The darkness was illuminated only by the soldiers standing guard, halting them each time. At every stop Cheftu showed the scarab ring of his house, and the slave girl showed her tattoo. They followed the twisting and turning passageway until they stood at a side entrance to Hat's apartments. The girl opened the gold-plated door, and he stepped inside.

The party was small, no more than twenty, but all men whom Cheftu knew—the most powerful nobles in the land. Those who were most loyal to the golden woman on the throne. Hat herself approached him, and he bowed, waiting for her to speak.

"I am glad you obey my commands, *Hemu neter*," she said, extending her hand to him. He kissed the unlined back of it and looked into her black eyes, filled with laughter.

He smiled. "I live only to serve you, My Majesty. Health! Life! Prosperity!" She laughed, a low throaty sound, and linked her arm in his. He accepted a cup of wine from one of the attendants and allowed her to lead him into the garden. The growing season was yet upon them, and it was chill outside, yet the trembling he felt in Pharaoh was more of a suppressed excitement.

They stood together, Pharaoh staring up at the sky, Cheftu admiring the strength in her body and spirit—a strength he had not seen in another woman. She could be fierce, possessive, and single-minded, but she had a passion that drew men to her and an intelligence that was unheard of in a female.

"How goes the work on your tomb, Cheftu?"

He stared at her for a moment, mind racing. "I assume it is going well; I have not been there since before I left for Retenu."

"Two Inundations, Cheftu?"

"Aye, My Majesty."

"You did not return when your father died?"

"Nay, My Majesty. He was buried before I even heard of his passing."

"Where is his tomb?"

Now Cheftu turned to her, openly. "Your father invited his nobles to join him in the same valley where Thutmosis-Osiris the First is buried. The Valley of the Kings. I do not presume, I trust, but why the questions?"

She looked up at him, her eyes shining with excitement. *"Haii!* Cheftu! I could never keep a secret from you, my silent one. I suppose the gods already know, so what is the harm in sharing with you?"

Cheftu waited.

"My tomb," she said excitedly. "I am building my House of Eternity. It is so beautiful, so worthy of My Majesty!"

"I thought that Senmut had built your tomb underneath the mortuary temple he created for you at the-Most-Splendid on the western crescent?"

Hat shrugged. "It is a temple indeed, where I can be worshiped with my father, Amun-Ra, and HatHor for all eternity. This tomb I speak of, however, is private; a home for love." She bit off the last word.

Cheftu stood, stunned. Pharaoh? Building for love? "I take it you will not be alone?"

She looked at him, and in the shadows Cheftu could not see the fine network of lines around her eyes and mouth, brought on by years of conniving, manipulating, and enduring. Yet in these twilight years she had found the love of her life . . . Senmut. Now she was building a place where they could be together.

He felt her intent gaze. "I think it wonderful to be united for all time."

"Wonderful," she said, "but forbidden." She darted a quick glance at him. "The priests do not dare say such a thing, for I am Pharaoh, living forever!, but husbands and wives of royalty have always been buried separately." They stood quietly as she said, "Marriage has been denied us, but eternity shall not be." With deft fingers she twisted her gold and electrum rings. "Already I have moved my treasure there. It is so secret that there is no temple, nothing except a natural marker." Cheftu stood in the darkness, watching her mobile lips twist. "I shall have to kill you for what you know, magus," she said with a laugh.

He waited, smiling at what he knew was a jest.

"Cheftu, you know I will not. There are no secrets between us, and I ask you to swear that this is your most precious secret. Swear it by what you hold dearest. Would that be Ma'at, the Feather of Truth?"

"Always, My Majesty, although you have told me nothing. I could walk through the Valley tomorrow and not know."

"Not in the Valley—in the desert." Her words were deliberate. "The eastern desert." They stood in silence as the knowledge penetrated Cheftu's brain. "Swear, magician. Swear!"

Cheftu fell to his knees, his guts wrenching and stomach burning. Hatshepsut, living forever! pharaoh, had told him the location of her tomb! He would die for this knowledge! "I swear on the Feather of Truth, Pharaoh, living forever! I will not betray your secret!" He could feel Hat's smile in the darkness.

"Very well, my silent one. There are no secrets now between us?"

"Never," he agreed emphatically.

"Then join the others. I understand your companion has already left on the arm of a younger son. I imagine she felt abandoned."

Cheftu got to his feet, shrugging. "It is no matter, Majesty. I would rather enjoy your company than any gilded Flower in these gardens."

"Did the Retenuian women excite you, Cheftu?"

He flushed in the darkness. He hated his private life to be so public. "I confess they are overlarge for my tastes, Majesty. They wear loud clothing and do not often bathe."

Hat laughed out loud. "So only an Egyptian woman for my Cheftu! *Haii-aii!* Then go into the hall and take whoever pleases you most, my favorite. I will explain. Go now."

He crossed his chest and backed away into the brightness of the chamber. Hatshepsut had covered the mudbrick walls with life-size depictions of herself embossed on beaten gold. He knew that should he look carefully, he would find a small illustration of himself, his Thoth-headed stick in hand, the Feather of Truth on his head.

The same picture would reveal the graceful figure of a woman wearing the horns and disk of HatHor. He swore quietly as he followed the slave through the winding hallways and back into the feasting hall. Without another thought he walked up to one of the resting performers, her black hair hanging down her back and shoulders, her body damp and warm from dancing, and brought his lips down onto hers in a hard kiss.

THE DAYS SETTLED INTO A PATTERN.

Chloe learned that since she was ill, thus imperfect, she could not attend the goddess. However, since she had become ill *while* on attendance, she also could not leave the temple complex.

Cheftu showed up every few days or so, his two priests in attendance as they made Chloe swallow hideous concoctions, tie amulets of shell and bone and hair around her neck, and undergo countless enemas.

She'd never been so regular in her life.

Cheftu hadn't said one more personal thing, and the one time he and Makab had come together they had ignored her thoroughly, making wagers on which of the nobles would come home with a lion carcass from their hunting trip with Pharaoh, bloody living forever.

She spent the mild days of winter wandering through the temple in its glory—a glory that made even Hollywood on hallucinogens look like black and white.

Everywhere was the glitter of precious and semiprecious stones. She had learned that each of the eyes represented in the hypostyle hall was inlaid with onyx. Each representation of the god Amun was studded with lapis, carnelian, and feldspar. The ithyphallic god Min sported a gold-plated condom.

To the Egyptians, these were re-creations of the gods and goddesses, each endowed with life through magic. The same magic was wrought on the dead through the Opening of the Mouth ceremony, making it possible for them to see, smell, hear, eat, and move, even make love, just as in life.

One day Chloe wandered down the colonnade leading to Thutmosis I's special temple—still within years of being finished, though he had flown to Osiris almost forty Inundations ago—when she saw a flash of brilliance. Pharaoh Hatshepsut, living forever! was having her obelisks set there and covered in electrum, an expensive blend of gold and precious silver. Because the obelisks had towered above the roof of the temple, the roof had been torn off, letting the metal-covered pyramidions pierce the turquoise sky.

The place was overrun with sweating dark Egyptians whose long eyes flicked away from Hat as she paced up and down like a caged animal. With a combination of ropes, pulleys, and brute strength they straightened the obelisks in their sanded pits. Chloe tried to make herself invisible as she watched, but the black eyes of Senmut, architect and grand vizier, found her, and she was politely asked to leave—for her safety, of course.

For days after, the court gossiped about how the army would receive no new breastplates so Pharaoh could erect more monuments to commemorate her holy conception, birth, and life. From what Chloe overheard, the army had not received anything new in many months because Pharaoh was more interested in beautifying deserted temples than in enlarging Egypt's empire, more than half the reason that Thutmosis III, her nephew, was straining at Hat's leash. He wanted to conquer new lands and bring new tributes into Egypt as pharaoh.

Apparently Hatshepsut had given Egypt a lifetime of peace, but the people wanted war. With every passing day Hatshepsut grew more paranoid about the young man in Avaris who would one day sit on her throne. It was commonly thought that if Thut III had been her son, Hat would have taken her place as consort many years ago. But her hatred for Thut II and her even greater hatred for his lowborn wife, Isis, had forced her to press on, determined to be pharaoh until she died.

Only Basha attended Chloe. She kept to her tasks and spent little time with her mistress. Chloe rested, read, and practiced writing, something her memory did provide for her. As a last resort, she tried embroidery. Apparently only Cammy had a gene for that.

Chloe made a sketch pad to capture some of the wonder around her, but Basha had been so shocked to see Chloe's drawings that she drew only covertly. She was scared they would discover her secret. Not knowing the consequences made it scarier.

Fear nauseated her; usually it was most intense in the morning. Later in the day she could pack away roasted fowl, fish, bread, fresh fruit, and vegetables, whatever was offered her. Time travel had given her quite an appetite—not that it had been delicate before. Cheftu had once watched her eat lunch, his expression one of polite horror. Apparently the "Flowers" of Egypt were supposed to be delicate. What else was there to do? Chloe had no way to exercise, wasn't allowed to pass beyond the *tenemos* walls, was sick of the smell of myrrh, and was bored to distraction.

Still she could not speak.

When Hatshepsut's royal summons came, she was reclining in the shade of a sycamore, reading some even more ancient poetry, munching from a bowl of figs and dates. She felt exhausted and couldn't imagine why. She certainly hadn't exerted any energy.

Basha rushed ahead of the courier, her brown face alight with excitement. "The Great House calls you, my lady!"

Chloe stood. Pharaoh wanted to see her? After receiving the summons scarab from the guard who would wait to escort her back, she and Basha hurried through the gardens and hallways. What to wear?

CHAPTER 4

GOSHEN

The audience chamber in Avaris was filled: red-and-white-clad soldiers, Retenu in long gold-shot robes, Kallistaens and Kefti with their many-layered garments and elaborately curled hair, and Kushites in exotic furs and feathers. It was easier to deal with foreigners at this far northern outpost than to bring them to Waset on the Nile. Everywhere Apiru slaves darted back and forth with drinks, food, and fans as they sought to keep the visitors comfortable.

At the far end stood Thutmosis III, Horus-in-the-Nest, Rising Ra, Child of the Dawn, impatience inscribed on his florid face and affirmed in the tap of his golden sandals on the polished stone floor. Faintly the sounds of flowing water and other conversations drifted in from the rooms surrounding the chamber.

He scowled.

The palace and audience chamber were not separated, as in a civilized land. No, his darling viper aunt-mother had seen to it that even the smallest courtesies were denied him. Here he was, in the mud and marsh of Goshen, forced to oversee disputes among commoners and foreigners. His blood surged at the gall of his aunt-mother, Pharaoh Hatshepsut. Gritting his teeth, he sat down on the stool—*stool*, not chair—and motioned to the chamberlain.

As Thut's titles were intoned, the painted doors opened and a band of Apiru entered, a motley selection from among the many enslaved races that kept Egypt building and beautiful. He knew from their distinctive one-shouldered garments that this particular party was composed of Israelites. Thut glanced to the wall where his "appointed" counselors and seers stood at the ready.

He turned back to observe the petitioners. There were about ten. They always traveled in packs, like scavengers, he thought. The man at the front of the group was tall, head and shoulders above most men in Egypt, bespeaking a diet rich in meat: not the usual Apiru fare. He wore the shirt and kilt of an Egyptian but covered it with an Israelite cloak, and he had a filthy Israelite beard, once black, now streaked with white. His heavy brows were straight gashes over deep-set dark eyes, whose depths spoke of great love and great loss. The soldiers behind them pushed the Apiru to their knees, for no one gave full obeisance except to the Great House. The soldiers looked to Thut solemnly.

Thut shifted his scrutiny to the man on the leader's right side. He was a faded reflection of the taller man, with the same face shape and features but lacking his power and vitality. Although unshaven and bedraggled like his companion, he had at least fixed his warm brown gaze appropriately on the ground. Thut motioned absently for a scribe to begin the audience.

"Who calls on the mighty Horus-in-the-Nest?"

The assistant replied in a pleasant baritone, "We are but two of Pharaoh's, living forever! servants, residing here in the two lands since before the time of your illustrious grandfather, Thutmosis the First, may he fly with Osiris! Life! Health! Prosperity! We seek the pleasure of Horus-in-the-Nest."

The scribe translated for Thut, who, though he knew the language of the Apiru, feigned ignorance, a wise choice at times. "Your Majesty," the scribe whispered, "this man is one of the leaders of the Apiru. He sits on their council. He is an important man."

Thut glowered at the scribe. "He is of no importance. He is only a slave. As we are not barbarians, though, I will hear his request."

"Horus grants you to speak," the scribe said.

The leader began speaking. Rather than the rough speech of a slave, however, court Egyptian haltingly emerged. His words were uncertain and his phraseology slightly antiquated, as if he had not spoken high Egyptian in many Inundations, but no translation was necessary. As the man searched for words, it became embarrassing to see his struggle. "My

Lord of the two lands, upon whom your god Amun-Ra shines, my people worship Elohim. We beg your exalted favor to take a leave of three days and worship him in the desert."

Although the words were appropriately humble, the expression in his dark eyes was not. This man's request was a challenge, flung at Thut's feet.

Horus-in-the-Nest was affronted. Pushing aside his flustered scribe, he rose and walked down the steps, his irritation growing the closer he drew to the man. "Old man, though you may have the speech of a courtier, you are nothing but a slave! Your pleas to meet with your desert god have fallen on unwilling ears. Three days! Also one day to travel there and another to travel back? That is almost half a week! You people have multiplied like vermin, and I have no doubt that if you took your hundreds and thousands of tribe members into the desert, you would not return! Are not the gods of Egypt enough for you?" Thut asked in disgust. "Or perhaps they are too noble, too gracious, and too civilized for you, living in these marshy lands, with sheep and goats for family? If you cannot worship your god here, then perhaps he is not worth worshiping at all?"

A low rumbling passed through the audience, and the supplicants flushed, except for the leader, who stood straight backed and unflustered.

"Our God commands you to let us go," he said.

Thut, on his way back to his stool, turned and stared. Did these Apiru not know they were supposed to wait for his dismissal or continuance? "Commands me?" Thut could not believe his ears. He was the prince regent; Horus-in-the-Nest; only Hatshepsut, living forever! reigned higher. He repeated, "Commands me?" The arrogant words of the old slave finally penetrated. "*Commands me?* No one commands me. *No one!*" His face purpled with rage. "I do not know your god, and I will not let you go!"

The leader persisted, undaunted. "The God of the Israelites has met with us. Let us make this journey or he may strike with plagues or the sword."

Thut advanced on the leader, halting close enough that his infuriated whisper could be heard. "What is your name, slave? You dare to threaten me with your puny god? Get you and your people back to work." With a gesture he dismissed them and climbed up to the dais to his stool.

While the Apiru were still within hearing he called out, "Scribe, send this message to all of my overseers and architects, effective upon receipt. Write, 'Apparently the tribes have too much time on their hands if they can be planning festivals and sacrifices. From this time on, the people who have,' "—he consulted the papyrus scrap his chamberlain handed him—" 'Aharon and Ramoses for leaders from among the Apiru must collect straw on their own to make the bricks required of the Great House. The production quotas will remain the same.' "

Under his breath he muttered, "Lazy, insolent wretches. That is why they want to go into the desert. Give a foreigner enough to do and he won't listen to lies or dream ridiculous dreams."

Thut had the satisfaction of seeing the assistant's shoulders slump in defeat. But the leader stood tall, his brown hand gripping his twisted and knobby staff. Teach them to cross the son of Thutmosis! he thought. He sat down and called for beer. It was turning out to be a pleasant day after all.

WASET

AS SHE RECLINED IN THE TRAVELING CHAIR, Chloe stared out in amazement. She was in ancient Egypt, about to see the pharaoh. What Camille wouldn't give to spend just one day here! The thought of her sister in this environment, her mouth wide open and her indigo eyes bulging, made Chloe almost laugh aloud. She turned it into a cough under the curious gaze of Basha. Chloe's eyes pricked with tears as she remembered her losses. Temporary losses, she thought fiercely.

Though the guards looked at her open curtains with disapproval, she could not bear to shut them. Karnak sat on the riverbank, with a wide avenue leading into ancient Thebes, now called Waset, and another leading to the noblemen's houses and the palace. Her conveyance jogged along while Chloe looked back and forth, taking in the rich green border to the Nile's lapis blue. Trees arched over the roadway, lending patches of shade from the winter sun overhead. The noblemen's mud-brick houses were flat roofed and whitewashed, enclosing, she knew, peaceful courtyards, cool reflecting pools, and whole families of Apiru slaves. Only the gods in Egypt had permanent stone housing.

They jogged through the palace gates and stopped. Chloe alighted with help and new sandals and was led through a series of painted-and-gilded courtyards and hallways until they came to Hat's audience chamber. With a shaking hand Chloe smoothed her wig as she heard her titles announced for the first time.

"The Lady RaEmhetepet, Beloved of the Night, Servant of Ra in Silver, Speaker of the Sisterhood and Priestess of HatHor. Favored of the Great House." The chamberlain banged his staff and Chloe walked into the long, narrow room, letting the "other" control her. Gold-and-white-clad courtiers and glittering ladies lined the room in an elegant gauntlet. She noted a few heads inclining in acknowledgment as she walked past.

At the far end was a raised dais, holding one of the most controversial women in all history. She, the "Great House," sat stiffly on a golden chair, her feet in gilded, curved toe sandals planted firmly on a leopard stool, her arms folded with the symbols of her office clasped tightly in beringed fingers. As Chloe drew closer she saw that Hatshepsut was indeed dressed like a man in only a kilt and collar, which further accented the decided femininity of her heavy breasts and long lacquered fingernails. Her broad forehead was smooth above unmoving, wide-set black eyes, framed by weighty gold earrings set with precious stones. Her wide mouth was dusted with gold, and the pharaonic artificial beard of lapis and gold was fixed onto her pointed chin.

Chloe prostrated herself before the dais. Minutes passed before she was bidden to rise. The "other" told her this was a bad sign. Finally she was bade to look into Hat's black eyes. Chloe felt fear, respect, and wonder. This woman had maintained peace for her entire solitary reign of fifteen years.

"My Lady RaEmhetepet, My Majesty is saddened you still cannot greet me with your own tongue. As the sage Ptah-Hotep said, 'Confine thy heart to what is good and be silent, for silence is more important than the *tef-tef* plant.' Is your heart confined to that which is good, my lady? Waset is filled with disturbing rumors concerning a strange visitor you had while serving the goddess HatHor."

Pharaoh's voice was low and throaty, with the unmistakable tone of command. Chloe blushed when Hat's glance flickered to her feet. Had Basha told everyone about her feet? Chloe kept her face carefully blank, wondering where this was leading. "Perhaps after such esteemed company the rest of us are not worthy of your brilliant conversation?" This caustic remark sent a twitter of comment around the room. Chloe smiled ruefully and drew the papyrus note she had prepared from her sash. After handing it to the scribe, she perused the front of the room while he passed it to Hat to read.

The court was living artwork, from Kushite slave boys wielding huge iridescent peacock feather fans above Hat's head to the black-ringed eyes and obsidian bodies of her royal guard, dressed in red and gold, their oiled bodies gleaming in the filtered sunlight. Chloe unconsciously searched for one face, spotting it off to the right.

Lord Cheftu leaned casually on his ibis-headed staff of office, his face dark against his red-and-gold-striped headcloth and heavy gold collar. Chloe jerked her gaze away as Hat looked up with a grim smile. " 'The lady begs My Majesty's pardon for appearing while she is still unable to speak, and begs my tolerance as she recuperates,' " she read. Hat fixed her fathomless black stare on Chloe. "I have also heard my lady is unwell in the mornings?"

Chloe blanched, and the tension level in the audience chamber rose.

"Perhaps her ladyship needs *more* than rest?"

Chloe smiled uncertainly in response. She didn't need the "other" to tell her that things were not going well.

"In My Majesty's graciousness," Hat said, "I have decided you should have complete privacy and total attention until you are able to tell me yourself that you are well. We cannot let the RaEmhetep priestess of HatHor go unattended." She paused for effect. "I think perhaps the green of the delta will do you good. The palace," she said with a smirk, "shall be at your lady's disposal. As shall"—she looked to her group of magi, physicians, and seers—"my private physician and *Hemu neter*, Lord Cheftu." She smiled at him and he inclined his head, his expression inscrutable.

What began as a murmur became an uproar. Chloe knew this was as good as being banished. What had she—*correction*, what had RaEmhetepet done to incur such wrath?

"I wish my lady . . . to be *delivered* . . . with perfect haste," Hat said in a ringing, biting tone, and then laughed.

Chloe backed from the room, her face on fire and her mind in a whirl. She walked hurriedly through the hallways and climbed into the traveling litter, pulling the curtains tight around her. Basha could find her own way.

She took several deep breaths, calming herself. She had few choices. Despite her best efforts it seemed she was unable to return to her time right now, so she must make a life here for herself until she found a way to go home. Life here wouldn't be too unbearable if she only knew what she was up against. Cammy would probably really profit from her experience. She must remember details for Camille.

After arriving back at Karnak, she rushed to her room and threw herself on the couch in a pique of frustration.

"Whatever have we done to be thrown from My Majesty, living forever's presence and made to consort with the pretender?"

Chloe rolled over and saw Cheftu seated at her vanity. The light glinted off his jewel-studded collar and the stones in his sandals and rings. His rugged face was taut and his saffron gaze deprecatory. "You do understand, do you not? The golden one suspects you of being unfaithful to your vows," he said in a velvety voice. He walked toward her, disdain in every line of his body. "Have you been?"

Chloe, uncertain as to which part of her lengthy vows he was referring, shrugged, forced herself to remain calm. What had she done?

Cheftu sat on the couch next to her and grabbed her shoulders roughly. "Do not be flippant, Moonlight; to break your vows is dangerous and sometimes deadly. I know you spread your legs easily enough when you are not serving. Perhaps you lost track of the time?"

The sarcasm fell like acid rain on Chloe's abraded nerves and feelings.

Cheftu ranted on, his voice rising in angered frustration. "Have you or have you not?"

She looked at him, suddenly weary and even more confused. What the bloody hell was wrong now?

His voice rose with incredulity. "How can you not know if you have been with a man this season? If his seed is growing inside you? Was your visitor god or man?" She jerked away, shaking her head in denial, then stopped.

She didn't have access to any information that would confirm or deny his accusation. Chloe put her head in her hands. This was ridiculous! Her nausea and tiredness were because she wasn't the same person in the same body. They were side effects from her unbelievable trip through time. It was impossible for her—for Chloe—to be pregnant, but, she thought sinkingly, it was very possible for RaEmhetepet. Her body sagged and she felt Cheftu's hand on her shoulder.

"If what is suspected is true, do not confirm it with anyone," he said in an undertone. "These should help." He pressed a small papyrus-wrapped package into her hand. "Do you know where Phaemon is?" He stared at her blank face for a moment, then rose and spoke normally. "We leave for Avaris and Prince Thutmosis' palace in two days. We shall stay for the rest of the season." He gave her another searching look, his golden eyes translucent in the light. "Life, health, and prosperity to you, priestess."

He stepped through the curtain and was gone, leaving Chloe to contemplate the newest hairpin curve in her once well-ordered life.

THE NIGHT WAS DARK, the House of the Dead unlocked because locks were unnecessary. No Egyptian would defile such a sacred place. The man stepped lightly from the shadows, motioning to the bearded servant who helped him. The room was long and narrow, with bodies laid in rows, each in a different stage of embalming, the stone beds set apart, allowing room for priests. They would move around the body, removing organs: first the brain, then make an incision in the abdomen and remove all the viscera except the *ab*, the heart.

The smell of incense and bitumen was hideous, and the man wondered if it would forever burn in his nostrils and chest. The bearded servant followed closely, his religion forbidding him to touch a dead body. They had no choices. A sudden deathbed promise had ensured that.

The body should not be in here; they walked on, passing into another room. The smell of natron hit them, and the man tasted his lunch from many hours ago. Deep boxes filled with the expensive dry salt stood close together, entirely covering the bodies in them, drying the flesh, toughening it.

He walked quickly to the wrapping room.

The body should be here, with all the organs intact yet having spent some time in the natron to stunt the natural rot of human flesh. He turned aside, lighting his torch, shining it on the hieratic designation for each inhabitant of this mummified world. He stopped. The body *was* here. Muttering prayers underneath his breath, he and the bearded servant lifted the corpse and carried it to the closest door, which opened onto an alleyway.

They hurried now to the front, to retrieve the remains of an unnamed peasant who would enjoy the hereafter as a wealthy tradesman. The man held up the torch—he had done a good job of wrapping the peasant's body, so no questions should be asked. Since the viscera hadn't been removed, the priests would expect its rotten odor.

He extinguished the light and they ran from the place of death, carrying the body up the wadi, past the City of the Dead, into the realm of Meret Seger: "she who loves silence," the guardian of the Valley of the Kings.

After hours of hiking they entered a short cave, a hole in the ground. Swiftly they laid the body in the earth, covering it with dirt and ostraca. The bearded man watched as his companion made motions over the grave, speaking in a language so foreign that he had never heard it or its like. In his heart he prayed for the soul of his deceased master. When the man was through he motioned the slave to exit the tomb first. In the last reflection of the torch, the man pulled out an ankh, its upper loop broken, forming a cross, and nestled it among the ostraca.

"Memento, homo quia pulvis es, et in pulverem revertis. Allez avec Dieu, mon ami." He crossed himself and left the dark tomb, an Egyptian once more.

THE GIRL LEFT THE BED OF HER LOVER, retreating from the gaze in which she'd seen such passion. The time had come for separation. The girl bit her lip, trying to hold back tears. Her earliest memories were of the two priestesses: one kind, one cruel. For all her life she had served the one in terror and followed the other in love. Her sister-of-the-heart had guided and instructed her. She had rescued her, and to her the girl owed her life.

So the minute sacrifice she was making was for the greatest glory to Egypt. Terrible catastrophes were foretold. Her heart-sister said only purifying the priesthood and the throne would avert them. The girl, born on a less sacred day, would actually be part of the cycle of prevention. For what greater blessing could she ask? She swallowed, furtively wiping beneath her eyes as she completed her ablutions.

"You understand, do you not?" her lover said as she watched the girl. "She is chosen by HatHor. But if she has forsaken her vows and carries the spawn of a demon, become Sekhmet! It must be destroyed, at any cost! We must save our people through her death! Else the price the goddess demands will be our lives!"

The girl finished tying the simple sash of her gown and stepped into her sandals. "She is so powerful, beloved," she said, her voice trembling with fear of her task. "Will Amun-Ra be safe without her protection?"

The woman on the couch rose, anger flaring in her eyes, her perfect body naked in the filtered moonlight. Her voice was steady. "Is Amun-Ra aided when her prayers are profane? When the very limbs she uses in sacred dance are used with the unclean in mating?" She shrugged. "It is only for a little while. The Great House is seeing to the training of another."

The girl cowered at the poison in her lover's voice. "I cannot hope to understand, but I shall do as I am bid, my lady. I seek only your continued pleasure and satisfaction with me." She prostrated herself until she felt a gentle hand on her head, caressing her hair.

"Stand, my precious. Do not tremble. She no longer has power over you. Should she hurt you again, tell me and I will deal with her." The girl nodded, shaking. "Now, Ra has not yet risen, we have many hours left to love." Before the woman lowered her lips to the girl's she said, "We must protect the priestesshood at all costs, my sister. Nothing is too precious to sacrifice. Each sacrifice is an offering to HatHor. We must be Sekhmet, we must be Sekhmet!" The girl stifled a cry as the high priestess of the Sisterhood ravaged her mouth with sharp, angry kisses. Her sash was torn as she lifted a hand to her mouth.

Blood.

CHEFTU PACED HIS PALACE APARTMENTS. He had closed his house and embossed the wax on the doors with his family's seal. Ehuru had moved him, packed his belongings, prepared his dinner, and set out a fine wine, yet Cheftu could not settle. It was well into the descending decans, and still he felt tension in his neck and shoulders. He had secreted away Alemelek's scrolls. He had kept his promises, all of them. He was prepared to leave. Cheftu paused as he heard approaching footsteps along the corridor, then a muffled rap on the door.

Cheftu glanced into the next room. Ehuru snored peacefully in the darkness. After tightening his kilt sash, Cheftu opened the door. One of Hat's Kushite guards greeted him.

"The golden one requests you." Cheftu motioned for the guard to wait while he dressed and shaved. "Do not bother with a toilette," the guard said. "She will see you this moment." Cursing Hat for her lack of courtesy, and trying to hide his shaking hands, Cheftu followed. Another guard marched behind him.

They wound through torchlit-painted hallways until they came to the one leading from the palace to Karnak. They entered the wide walkway, where the guards extinguished the existing torches and opened a panel in the inlaid floor.

Cheftu descended into utter darkness, his sandaled foot reaching tentatively for each step. The guards clanked on, seemingly unconcerned about the lack of light. Once they were on level ground again, he heard the trapdoor shut and the torches were relit. Where in the name of Osiris were they taking him? Had the scene with RaEm just been a ruse—would they now steal his secrets from beneath his very skin? Acid burned his throat and Cheftu admonished himself to calm down.

They were in a narrow passageway. Cheftu's stomach knotted—this was not a good omen. Silently they marched through the twisting and turning tunnels beneath the palace and temple complex, until Cheftu was all but lost. His muddled sense of direction suggested they were close to the Sacred Lake, but he was not certain.

The guard rapped on a plain wooden door and Cheftu heard Senmut's response. As the door opened he saw Pharaoh, Senmut, and Hapuseneb in the flickering light of the room.

"Greetings of the night," Senmut said, as if it were not the fourth decan in the morning and as if meeting under the Great Temple were an everyday occurrence.

Cheftu bowed to Hat and took the proffered chair and glass of wine. "Life, health, and prosperity to you, Count Senmut; Your Eminence, Hapuseneb; Pharaoh, living forever!"

"There is more you must know before leaving with the Priestess RaEmhetepet for Avaris," Hatshepsut said abruptly, pinning him with her black gaze. "You have been selected for a special medical assignment. It is of the utmost importance and secrecy to Egypt."

Cheftu felt his guts twist. There could be only one such assignment. Hat spoke. "When RaEm was found, she was covered in blood.

Whose blood we do not know, for it was not hers and there was no evidence of anyone else in the chamber. That same night, Phaemon, guard of the Ten Thousand, disappeared. The priestess ReShera is only now coming out of mourning for her brother. Since there is no body, he cannot be mourned for the forty days his position demands." A packet was placed in Cheftu's hands. Hatshepsut looked at him with wide black eyes, eyes that darted from side to side with barely restrained paranoia.

"Do what must be done, silent one."

GOSHEN

THUT ENTERED THE AUDIENCE CHAMBER. An awed silence fell—a silence he, as commander of the army and soon-to-be pharaoh, well deserved. He seated himself slowly on his stool and motioned to the chamberlain to admit the petitioners. He glanced toward the magi on his right. Some of Egypt's finest wonder workers were in his court. Yet he could not help but tighten his jaw in apprehension when the chamberlain announced the Israelite trouble-mongering brothers, Ramoses and Aharon.

There was something disturbingly familiar about Ramoses . . . the set of his shoulders or maybe his direct gaze, an unlikely bearing for a slave bred from countless generations of slaves. Of course, the Israelites were different: never intermarrying without the spouse converting; speaking their own language; and resistant to other gods and lifestyles. Thut dismissed his thoughts and halted the slaves' progress toward the dais.

For moments Thut looked at them. Determined to rid himself of this nuisance so he could fish in the Nile's swelling waters and fantasize about Hatshepsut's downfall, he spoke directly to Ramoses. *"Haii!* You are back. I trust the brick quotas are being met even without your assistance."* Gazing at the older man, Thut called for a scribe to verify the figures. The Israelites were keeping up. "Have you come with another ultimatum from your desert-dwelling god, then?" To Thut's surprise, Aharon spoke. His voice carried easily throughout the chamber.

"We have come—"

Thut cut him off. "Perform a miraculous sign, if indeed you do come at the behest of a god." Ramoses and Aharon exchanged a brief, matter-of-fact glance, then Ramoses stepped forward and threw down his shepherding staff.

Thut felt an icy hand grip his throat as the wooden staff slowly began to writhe. Its end raised up, and Thut stared into the dark, mesmerizing eyes of a hooded cobra. It was the most enormous serpent Thut had ever seen, standing at least three cubits high, swaying slightly, half its length coiled on the floor.

The others in the courtroom stepped back, their cries and yelps of fear swallowed as the snake perused the company with cold, predatory eyes.

The prince was transfixed, oblivious of the sounds of retreating nobles, of his guards drawing their swords. Ameni, head of Pharaoh's division in Avaris, stepped to his side. Thut tore his gaze away and motioned everyone back. Ramoses and Aharon stood calmly. Clearing his throat, Thut glanced away and spoke to his magi. "This simple trick can be repelled by your greater magic, my lords?"

Unhesitatingly Balhazzar, his Sumerian magus, stepped forward. "A child could do this magic, Your Majesty." After saying magic words over his staff, he threw it down. It too began to writhe and turned into an asp, slithering across the floor. The cobra waited until it came within easy range; in a flash of scales and fangs . . . the asp was gone.

Thut glanced quickly at Balhazzar. His face had paled under his towering red turban. "More simple magic?" Thut hissed. Another magus, Kefti Shebenet, threw down his staff, and before it had even completely changed, the Israelite's snake ate it. Halfheartedly the other four magi threw down their rods and staffs. Each was eaten in turn.

Thut looked back at the Israelite's snake. Apparently the magic was no longer simple. The serpent was now enormous, as if it had gained length from each of the snakes it had consumed. It stretched across the width of the room. Thut was glad the courtiers had left. No need to see and repeat this incident in Waset! He inhaled sharply as he saw Ramoses lean toward the snake and grab it by its tail.

Then all Ramoses was holding was a sturdy staff. Thut felt perspiration coat his body. It had all been a horrible vision.

Except that Ramoses' staff had previously been nothing more than a three-cubit-tall wooden stick, with knobs and small twists in it. Now it was straight and brightly colored, with a bronze tip that looked alarmingly like a hooded cobra, towering a cubit above Ramoses' head. Thut stood and left the chamber. The audience was over.

WASET

THEY BOARDED THE SHIP IN THE EARLY MORNING, the sun god Amun-Ra staining the sky with sherbet orange. Chloe heard the early morning chanting of the priests as probing fingers of light highlighted the white temple, casting its shadow across the water. She stood alone with her trunks.

Basha would not be going with her. Hatshepsut, living forever! had sent a note saying that Basha would meet her in Avaris; she had other duties to attend before she left Waset. Two guards stood beside Chloe, and although their swords were sheathed, she was certain that if she changed her mind, they would be drawn. She was being banished.

Her linen cloak barely kept out the morning chill, and she forced her teeth not to chatter as she stood observing Waset. The riverbank was already a hive of activity, with sailors and slaves loading the morning's shipping. She heard many languages, some of which she recognized as Babylonian, Kallistaen, Retenuian, and what she could swear was Greek. The narrow streets of the *rekkit* were filling slowly with women on their way to market, slaves hurrying to and fro for their masters, and children on their way to temple school. Almost like any other city, in any other time, in any other culture, Chloe thought. Despite the fact they worship statues and are half-naked most of the time, they really *are* like us.

Chloe had seen neither kilt nor collar of Cheftu this morning. She accepted the guard's assistance boarding the vessel. It was large: several tent cabins were assembled on deck, in addition to the block of rooms built in the center. Far above, fluttering in the morning breeze, was the standard of Pharaoh Hatshepsut, living forever!, a cartouche of her throne name stitched in blue on a white background.

Apparently Cheftu was not joining them, Chloe realized as they pulled away from the dock. As they lifted anchor, untying the heavy flax ropes that held the sails, she wondered if he were deliberately avoiding her, his banishment prize. The sailors ignored her, and she settled onto a stool, taking in the brilliant green palms, tamarisk, and sycamore that lined the shore and led up to noblemen's houses. She wondered which was Lord Cheftu's.

Then the wide paved road that ran along the Nile through Waset was gone and the shoreline became more agrarian. Fields stretched out in the distance, and whole families induced oxen or donkeys to turn the wheel of the shadoof and lift more water from the Nile. Chloe felt the warming sun on her back and crossed to the port side of the ship, where desert and deserted monuments filled her vision.

By lunch she had recognized no one on board. A servant gave her some roasted fowl and more of the teeth-jarring bread the ancient Egyptians ate. She was certain that a few more months of this bread would wear out her teeth. She ate her meal, throwing the bread and bones into the water, shivering when it churned with long, greenish brown shapes. Crocodiles.

The captain, Seti, approached her as the sun reached its zenith, urging her to seek shade. She let herself be led to a covered couch in one of the tent cabins set up on deck, where the heat and the constancy of the blue sky, green water, and red gold sand helped her nod off. Not to mention that she hadn't felt nauseated once. She jerked awake when they came to a stop. The sails had been lowered and Chloe could tell from looking at the sky that she had slept away most of the short winter day. She walked on deck.

They were at the water steps of an enormous estate, just to the north of Gebtu, the "other" said. Palms and fig trees shaded a terraced pathway that led up to a white house. Chloe saw figures coming down, carrying a traveling litter.

"My lady," the captain said, "Lord Cheftu requests you stay in his home tonight." He led her to the steps, an iron grip on her arm, indicating she had no choice. Two slaves gestured for her to climb into the litter. She alighted in a beautiful, cool garden, shielded from the setting sun by high limestone walls, pierced with patterns for breezes.

She was ushered into a high-ceilinged room with a blue painted couch and walls depicting underwater scenes of fish and a blue sky full of birds. It was exquisite. Oh, Camille, she thought, if only you could see through my eyes! She walked into the adjoining bathing room with clerestory windows and a small balcony. The fragrance of crushed flowers wafted up to her, and she saw the bath was drawn, flowers floating in the clear water.

Nebjet, Cheftu's old nurse and now his housekeeper, and the body servant Irini helped her out of her garments and into the deep pool. Nebjet and Irini dried and oiled her, then they opened a variety of trunks and chests for her perusal. Chloe ignored the question of why Cheftu had a whole woman's wardrobe in his house, just as she ignored the beautiful body servant. *His* body servant. Just because he hadn't mentioned anyone didn't mean there wasn't anyone in his life. Why would he tell her, a woman he obviously hated?

"Does my lady care to wear a color tonight?" Chloe nodded her head vigorously. Although most Egyptians wore only natural white, she was beginning to want some color. Blue, she knew, was for mourning. Yellow was the color of Amun's priesthood. Red was the color for soldiers. She didn't know any other symbolic colors.

Irini pulled out a finely woven pale green cloth, and Chloe clapped her hands in approval. At first it seemed to be only a huge square, but the girl brought the bottom two ends together like a wrap skirt and then crossed the two top corners, pleating as she went, and crossed the pleated fabric over Chloe's breasts, ending with a knot secured beneath her right breast. This created two perfectly creased sleeves that reached from her clavicle to her forearms. Again Chloe wished for underwear, though the color made the linen a little more difficult to see through. It didn't feel very secure, but then she wouldn't be doing much, she thought. Just eating—her one form of exercise! Irini brought out a selection of sashes, and Chloe picked a green one with embroidered silver ankhs.

She touched the embossed silver ankh around her neck. In the past several weeks she had read it repeatedly . . . RaEmhetep. The "et" of her name denoted her femininity. Her memory of that day in 1994, on the banks of the Nile, was becoming more and more faded. She had difficulty remembering what that guy even looked like. Her necklace was now longer, a fact she couldn't explain. While hers had been on a medium-weight chain to withstand her reservist weekends and her active lifestyle, this was on a fine chain with alternating lapis and malachite beads. Strange.

Irini combed Chloe's hair into a sheet of dully shining onyx and braided a band of tiny silver bells into it. She covered Chloe's eyelids in heavy green paint and rimmed them with the requisite black kohl. Chloe rejected all of the collars, settling for a cloisonné falcon pendant and light silver ankh earrings. She stepped into the sandals that had been specially crafted to fit her feet and waited.

She wished she had a real mirror so she could see what she looked like dressed up like an ancient Cinderella.

"Is my lady ready to dine?" a manservant asked formally. Chloe followed him up dimly lit stairs and out through a chamber to the roof. The sun had just set. Vibrant pink and gold still stained the sky.

"RaEm, you look lovely tonight," Cheftu said. She turned to him, seated beside a low table, his glowing eyes still visible in the fading light. She smiled in greeting and held her breath as he stood, solid and masculine, to escort her to the table. She felt the heat from his hand like a shock when he took her elbow and led her to one of the cushioned stools.

Chloe shook herself. On the one hand, this was almost make-believe; on the other, it was terribly and frighteningly real.

"Please take some wine," he said, offering her a glass. "It is from my family's vineyards by Lake Teftefet in the Fayyum." Chloe took a sip, and although sweet for her twentieth-century taste, it was still heady and delicious. She followed Cheftu's example, snacking on garbanzo-bean paste and vegetables as they admired the twilight.

Darkness fell quickly, and Ehuru lit the oil lamps, casting dancing shadows across the planes and angles of Cheftu's face. She tried to imagine him in a tuxedo, or Levi's and a T-shirt, and the images were most appealing.

It wasn't that Lord Cheftu looked like a Byzantine saint or a young Greek god. He was only an inch or two taller than she was, but he moved with the controlled energy of an athlete. His graceful strength, golden eyes, and cool distance reminded her of lions she had seen on safari with her parents. Hunting with her camera, she had watched the great cats observe the world around them before they lit onto prey, teeth and claws flashing. Of course, they were also the laziest animals she had ever seen. That didn't seem to apply to Cheftu.

His features were even, if a bit too blunt for her taste. His thick black brows, elongated by kohl, arched over his almond-shaped eyes and met at the bridge of his large, straight nose. His lips were full but always pressed tightly together, or occasionally stretched into a remote smile that revealed strong, white teeth—something, she was learning, that was unusual in Egypt. His eyes were ringed with black kohl, and Chloe had a feeling there was little they missed. He was an enigma, both scholar and spiritualist with the body of a statue. Bernini's *David*, with a fierce scowl as he throws the stones at Goliath, his perfection frozen in motion.

Although alien and disinterested, Cheftu touched a chord in her without even trying. He possessed a genuine masculinity that came from his actions, from his being. He didn't work out, he used his body legitimately: in riding, hunting, and archery. He didn't need a $2,000 Italian suit and a red Porsche to give him presence—it was tangible. He was rational and compassionate with everyone but her. Definitely not with her.

He was so real. Yet, she thought, looking at the amulet bound onto his upper arm, protecting him from demonic attack, never had there been a man more a part of his time. Cheftu was every inch Joe Ancient Egyptian.

He broke off his dissertation on grapes and vine dressing to stare at her. "My conversation bores you?" Chloe shook her head in embarrassment. Cheftu grinned, enjoying her plight, his teeth white in the torchlight. "Please suggest another topic. Would you care to discuss your upcoming nuptials? Perhaps your lovers? Why you are marrying Nesbek? Where Phaemon, your missing lover, is?"

Chloe stared at him, caught between anger at unjustified accusation and frustration at not being able to scream back. She bit the inside of her cheek. He stared at her with disdain until dinner arrived.

Nebjet placed broiled fish stuffed with almonds and dried figs before them with side dishes of pickled onions and leeks. The food was delicious, and Chloe ignored Cheftu while she ate. When she glanced up, she saw him staring in disgust at her appetite. Traveling through time had definitely increased it, and of course he'd been finished for a while.

Slipping behind his court facade, he was every inch the gracious host. Nevertheless, his mind was obviously elsewhere. Most of what he said was rehearsed, typical chatter with no intention of truly sharing. Chloe swallowed more wine as loneliness engulfed her.

Dessert was pastry filled with nuts, honey, and goat cheese. Chloe was dying for coffee and a cigarette but knew it was a completely futile wish. More desperate was her desire to talk—to somebody, anybody, about what had happened to her. The need to converse was so intense, she felt her eyes well up with tears. She slammed another glass of wine.

When they finished dessert Cheftu asked her if she would like to stroll around the grounds and garden, since they would be leaving early in the morning and she hadn't had a chance to see his estate. He guided her with one hand, a large torch in the other. His touch was impersonal, but it was human contact, and Chloe bit back the tears that threatened. Alcohol is a depressant, she reminded herself. Don't be so pathetically desperate for company. He's just doing his job. His pharaoh bloody living forever, assigned job.

She was amazed at the size of the estate. They walked from the house, which by even modern standards seemed large and comfortable, to the water's edge. It was all gardens. The flower garden was heavy with the fragrance of lotus, honeysuckle, and herbs. The vegetable garden was laid out with almost European precision, the many lettuces and types of onions in neatly marked rows. The vineyards, Cheftu explained, ran the length of the estate and were filled with a variety of grapes. He was experimenting with different mixes of grapes in wine. An ancient vintner. The moon was a sliver, the stars a shimmering canopy above them, as he took her to his medicinal garden. A small mud-brick hut stood in the center; Cheftu explained it was a storehouse and a laboratory.

The tension from dinner had faded, though Chloe was dying to ask him what his comments had meant. They walked in torchlit shadow for a few moments, Chloe reveling in the exercise and companionship, Cheftu silent.

"Lady RaEm," he finally asked, "since we are going to be together for several months, please, could you explain?" Chloe waited for another clue as she kept pace with his long, unskirted stride. He stopped walking and turned to face her. His voice was steady but throbbed with an intensity he couldn't hide. His eyes were blackened out by the night. "Would you have me beg?" he asked abruptly.

Chloe stared at him, confused. What happened to the cheery tour guide of a few moments ago? She refused to shrink from his dark gaze, and they stared at each other silently. Cheftu's voice was now brittle. "I have papyrus with me; I would like to know. I think you owe me, our families and our guests, that."

Chloe shrugged halfheartedly, swearing at RaEm for her incomplete memory. Cheftu's eyes glittered in the torchlight as his lips compressed into a straight line. She shrugged again, her face set in the international lines of not knowing what he was talking about. Apparently she convinced him.

"As you like, Lady RaEmhetepet—" He spat out her name. "I had hoped that in these many Inundations since we had seen each other last, we could at least be amicable, that once we dealt with past questions, we could have a reasonable physician-patient relationship, but I see that you have not changed, despite your new veneer. I will not question you again. I just fail to understand—" He broke off and turned away, stalking through the lovely gardens they had just shared. Chloe had to pick up her skirts and rush just to glimpse him. When they reached the patio, Cheftu bowed coldly and left her with a young slave.

Chloe followed her through to her rooms and sank onto the couch, her head spinning and the familiar nausea coming over her. She was helped into a robe and went in search of her chamber pot. Damn Cheftu for adding more stress, she thought, emptying her stomach. Afterward she tumbled onto her couch.

She was awakened by a gentle hand on her shoulder. Nebjet helped her dress, and Chloe accepted a package of rolls and fruit. When they reached the jetty, Cheftu was waiting in a common kilt and reed sandals, a cloak thrown across his broad shoulders. He acknowledged her with a nod and continued to oversee the loading of the ship. He wore a quiver of arrows, and a bow was tucked into his flax cloth sash. She climbed aboard and within moments of lying down was asleep.

The rowers manipulated the rough turns of the Nile the following day, the passengers watching in stark silence as the boat negotiated the twists and turns, banked by the captain and controlled by the men at the oars.

The next day they passed Abdo, the quay filled with people loading and unloading boats. In the shaded interior of her room, she watched the *rekkit* salute the royal standard of the boat. The crowd fell to their faces, with shouts of "Hail, Hatshepsu, Makepre!"

Then they were surrounded by the verdant solitude of the banks. All the land was used, but Chloe knew from the "other" that most of it belonged to Hatshepsut, living forever! or the priesthood of Amun. Night fell quickly, drawing a sheet of silvery stars across the sky. They tied up along the bank, for no Egyptian sailed at night. Chloe pulled back the cloth ceiling, staring into the heart of the universe until, slowly, her eyes closed.

CHAPTER 5

The days passed quickly. Cheftu avoided her, and she spent her time watching the Nile drift slowly by. Occasionally she saw groups of children clustered by the bank, waving and shouting to the boat, responding to the proud royal standard. Egypt loved her pharaoh. Chloe had taken some of the papyrus she'd had cut for conversing with people, and she started sketching. The inks the Egyptians used were cumbersome, so one night she had crept across the sleeping bodies before the fire and took some charcoal. Sharpening it into a decent point took hours.

She spent the nights by torchlight drawing on her notepad the children's faceless bodies, the boats and trees and flowers. As Ra's light tinged the world pink and gold she would hide the pad and fall into a brief but rejuvenating sleep.

Days later Chloe strolled around the ship, observing the workers and the slaves, feeling strangely out of place and yet quite familiar. They were on a straighter stretch of river now, the view from the prow nothing but water, water, water. Chloe's mind had begun to blur with the fields of emmer, flax, spelt, and wheat.

Little huts stood on the embankments above the river, and the "other" told her it was where the *rekkit* and the Apiru lived in corvée, keeping the irrigation channels clear and the walls strong. The huts were easy to build, a necessity because during the Inundation everyone moved to higher ground. As the Nile overflowed its banks and flooded the entire plain, only stone structures remained untouched: the houses of the gods. When the rivers receded, the lower priests were responsible for cleaning and repairing the temples.

Chloe was amazed that the Egyptians simply accepted the annual flood. In fact, they looked forward to it. Once a year their lands would be flooded out. Once a year they would start from scratch. When the waters settled, they returned to the same place and rebuilt their mud-brick homes, everyone working together. The only places exempt from the rising waters were in the desert, like the City of the Dead, opposite Waset.

The City of the Dead, where the tomb goldsmiths, sculptors, and artisans lived, was far enough away and high enough up that some of the inhabitants had lived in the same houses for generations. To the Egyptian mind that permanence was amazing. Only temples and tombs lasted forever. All else was a pattern of destruction and creation, life and death. Inundation and summer. This consistent repetition bestowed power and meaning, for only the known cycle was considered worthwhile and of Ma'at.

After two Egyptian weeks on the water, Chloe had no idea where they were. They had not passed a large city in days. The blue sky hung above them, dwarfing the tiny craft on the massive river pushing toward the Great Green. Sometimes at *atmu* Cheftu joined her. He didn't speak much, but then again, to have a conversation with someone who was basically mute was difficult. The notepad was helpful, but a tedious chore for making meaningless, strained conversation.

She spent a lot of time watching him. On board he had not bothered with all the gold and jewels she had seen him wear in Waset, though he still wore elaborate eye makeup and a headdress. Chloe wondered idly if he had male pattern baldness. As far as she could tell, he lazed around. Maybe he was like a lion in more ways than one.

He kept trying new spells and potions to make her voice work. The last one had been truly horrible. She suspected it was some kind of animal urine mixed with a green herb paste, kind of like a rancid pesto. She gritted her teeth remembering Cheftu's insistence that she take it. Being unable to verbalize intensified her frustration. Cheftu said whatever he wanted and walked away, not waiting for her scribbled retort.

The sun was setting when she heard him behind her. "Lady RaEm."

Chloe turned. His kilt and headcloth glowed in the fading light. She inclined her head in acknowledgment.

"We will arrive in Noph by tomorrow evening. I apologize for not keeping you better company this past decan, but perhaps you will allow me to remedy that tonight?"

Her quickly indrawn breath made him laugh, but without humor.

"Nay, my lady. I was thinking of a game of *senet*. There is a board in my room, and we can play here, under the sky of Nuit." He stood waiting. "My lady used to quite enjoy the game," he said, sounding slightly puzzled. "Has that changed in the intervening years?"

Chloe, fear of discovery welling up inside her, vehemently shook her head no. Cheftu sent a slave after the board, and they drew up stools at a low table by the bow. The crew were on the starboard side, eating and gambling, their normal evening's entertainment. Cheftu poured her a cup of beer and set up the board. Fortunately for Chloe, she had RaEm's memories of the game.

She won the first two rounds. The first was close, but Cheftu couldn't roll the exact number to get off the board, and Chloe came from behind and beat him. Cheftu took a sip of wine, laughing quietly as they set up for another game.

He met Chloe's inquisitive glance. "I was remembering when I first learned how to play. It was my sixteenth summer, and some of us had escaped the palace tutor. Thut and Hat were still stuck in class, and one of the older half-brothers, Ramoses, was back from the field. He'd been on some campaign in Kush for Thutmosis.

"Anyway, we crept into the harem, courtesy of one of the royal cousins, Seti, and played a game of *senet* for . . . assst . . . not favors, but rather information. It was a titillating experience," he said with a laugh. "The girls were a little younger than we were, but most had spent their whole lives preparing to bed Thutmosis the First. By the time we crept out, we were drunk with wine and half-insane with sensual knowledge. But we knew it would be death to be caught there, so we crept out of the palace garden and *most* of us went home." He fell silent.

Cheftu sent her a quick glance and then devoted himself to the board. Chloe sensed his withdrawal but didn't know why. She reached out and laid a hand on his forearm, imploring him to continue his story.

He jerked away.

Chloe sat, fuming and embarrassed, before he spoke. His voice was cold. "It is convenient you have no memory, is it not? At this point in life I imagine there are a lot of things and people you would rather forget. Unfortunately, I have to live with my memories." He turned away, his profile etched in the torchlight. He spoke contemptuously.

"Everything and everyone are just pawns for you. Just another way for you to climb to the apex of power that you so deeply desire. Was it all a plot, RaEm?" He turned to her. "From the beginning, just a way to take my body and my soul to add to your collection? I confess I find the company distasteful."

Chloe seethed . . . whether at Cheftu or RaEm, she couldn't decide. Whoever said that men were silent? Didn't discuss their feelings? What she wouldn't give for a little male repressiveness now!

Cheftu chuckled. "I believe Hatshepsut, living forever! should put you in the army, RaEm. You have more manipulative strategies than General Nehesi. The inconvenience of honor certainly does not hamper your methods." His glittering gaze met hers, and Chloe felt his bitterness to her bones. "Will Nesbek meet with your schemes? Or does he even know?" Abruptly he turned his back to her, saying stiltedly, "Will your ladyship please retire? I find I am weary of your company."

Chloe, with anger and tears mixed, stood up stiffly, gathered her cloak around her, and walked rapidly back to her makeshift room. She glared at the canopied couch as she wrapped herself in a robe. What could he possibly be talking about? What had RaEm done to this proud man that he could neither forgive nor forget?

At some point she had rejected him, that much Chloe knew. Why, though? She paced the tiny room until the crew's sounds died away. Feeling cooped up and stuffy, she put on her sandals and crept out of her room. They had docked, so she crept down the gangplank and onto the sandy soil. She headed in the direction of an abandoned temple to her right. Remembering the last time she had entered a run-down temple, she paused and leaned against the wall, wishing desperately for a cigarette.

And a voice. Someone to hear her cries of frustration, anger, and loneliness. This was so different from being alone. In every city, on any flight, there was always someone she knew was like her. Maybe not the same nationality or religion, but with the same concerns and fears and joys. Oh, God, why was she here? No one knew *her*. No one saw beyond what they expected to see. RaEmhetepet, the hotshot, sleazy priestess.

The stars were huge in the night sky. As she walked, tears began to fall. Finally her sight was so blinded that she sank into the rushes, drew her robe close around her, and sobbed. Cried for the loss of family and friends. Cried for the hopelessness of her situation. Cried out for some guidance, some help, some direction.

She flinched when she felt a hand on her shoulder, but it seemed gentle. The bare chest it turned her to was wide, hard, and very comforting. A man's hand caressed her head, his fingers smoothing her hair as her tears poured silently, racking her body with emotion. He held her gently, and as her tears subsided, Chloe became more aware of the smooth warm skin beneath her cheek, the resonating heartbeat beside her mouth.

She turned her lips to it and felt the arms around her tense. Dazed by the adrenaline rush through her body, she kissed his chest experimentally.

The man drew in a deep breath. Goose bumps rose on her skin. Recklessly Chloe began to kiss, assuaging the loneliness inside. Slowly, her mouth round and warm on her comforter's silken skin, her arms tight around his muscled back, she poured fire and passion through her mouth. He groaned. She felt the pulse quicken in his neck and followed the buried stream across his shoulder and down his arm to the crook of his elbow. Chloe licked delicately.

"Sweet Isis," he said in a ragged voice.

Chloe froze, the raging fire in her veins turning to ice. What the hell was she doing, necking with some stranger—make that *ancient* stranger—in the bulrushes just because he had an impressive set of pecs? Damn! She wasn't that desperate! The stranger sensed her mood, and she felt strong fingers try to lift her chin.

She pulled away. Then he kissed her, not abrasively, not commandingly, but the brush of a feather, and Chloe felt blood rush to her brain. Eyes shut tightly, she squirmed away, and the arms released her. Keeping her back to him, she raced back to the ship. She threw herself onto the couch to catch her breath and try to cool off before attempting to sleep. Emotionally exhausted, but physically frustrated, she tossed and turned on the Egyptian sleeping couch, finally throwing the headrest to the floor, and fell into sensual dreams of strong arms, ragged breathing . . . and a pair of golden eyes?

...

When she woke around noon they were approaching a metropolis on the west bank. Boats were tied for *henti* down the river, and the fields were the greenest she'd seen so far. As she watched she heard Cheftu's discreet cough behind her. She turned around. He was in court regalia: heavy gold earrings, a gold-and-white headcloth and kilt, and a huge, jeweled collar.

"We arrive at Noph," he said, his topaz gaze on her face. "We will go to the temple there and see if the Thrower cannot heal that which he created. Please ready yourself. We will disembark after eating." He inclined his head and strolled away, golden, glittering, and remote. Chloe immediately consulted the "other" about what to take.

Noph was the home of the god Ptah, who with Khonsu had created man on a potter's wheel, hence the name "Thrower." It was also one of the holiest sites in Egypt and the former capital. RaEm's memory could not supply any details about what would be expected of her, so Chloe took her notepad, the notebook of her sketches, and a kitchen knife. Why, she didn't know. She just felt safer knowing it was there.

The boat drew up to the dock, or at least as close to the dock as they could get. Just like cruise ships from Chloe's time, the boats were tied parallel and those passengers farthest out had to traipse over and through those boats closer in. One of the slaves from the ship took Chloe's basket, and she followed Cheftu until they stood on the dock.

It was the first time that she had been among the *rekkit*. She knew it was something the real RaEm would hate, but she was intrigued. All the bits and pieces of information she had heard from Cammy over the years made sense now. She finally understood her sister's fascination with these people who treasured life so completely that they wanted it to continue in the exact same fashion for all eternity.

Last night's catharsis had definitely helped her attitude, she thought.

Cheftu's hand on her back burned through the linen of her gown as he guided her toward the litters awaiting them. Although she would have preferred to stand beside him in the chariot, led by the two prancing browns, she understood that would not be appropriate. However, her curtain was partially open.

They passed through the ornamental city gates. The stone lintel was high above them, but the surrounding wall was very low. Noph had never been invaded, and the gate was not so much a defense as it was a frame for the magnificent temple in the center of town.

They passed through a marketplace. Hawkers were selling everything from Canaanite oranges to small dirt figures of Ptah planted with grain and now growing. They were supposed to forecast one's harvest. Chia gods, Chloe thought to herself with a chuckle.

Every few moments a food vendor would pass, the aroma of his wares wafting to her on the warm air. Fowl was sold, both fresh and roasted; honey-baked rolls with nuts wrapped in their centers; the salted fish that was forbidden to Chloe and most of the priesthood; fruits and sesame candy. It was almost like any Middle Eastern *souq*, with a glaring exception: no coffee sellers and no radios.

They turned right before the temple, going down a large avenue lined on both sides with huge whitewashed mansions. Each was surrounded with a fence and gate, but a few gates were open, sharing with the outside world a glimpse of flowering gardens and refreshing pools. They jogged along, the heat and motion making Chloe remember her stomach in a most unpleasant way. Just before she lost her lunch, they stopped.

Was this another of Cheftu's houses? Chloe searched her "other" memory, but the details of Cheftu's life and family were not there. Apparently an emotional memory, Chloe thought.

Her third-floor room was decorated simply; a ceiling border and wainscoting of blue lotus were painted on the whitewashed walls. In the corners of the ceiling were *ba*-birds. Chloe stepped closer. According to Egyptian thought, the *ba*-bird was a part of the soul that could leave the tomb after the person was dead. It was represented as a bird's head and the deceased's face. She smiled softly when the "other" told her she was looking at Cheftu's mother and father in their *ba*-bird forms.

With a sigh she sat down. A pillow graced the plain and ungilded couch, covered in fresh bleached linens. Chloe grimaced at the headrest. She hated the damn things and was tired of wadding up clothes to pad them. Then she touched the pillow and it collapsed beneath her fingers. Goose down. Praise Isis!

There was a simple dressing table and stool, and a game board was set up in one corner. Fresh lotus scented the room, and the sun gave light through the slatted clerestory windows. Chloe saw treetops and heard the melodic calling of birds. Once again, Cheftu's home was a peaceful haven.

A slave entered and led Chloe up to the roof. Noph was to her right and the river before her, boats tied to the dock and all along the shoreline. She saw people toiling in the fields to her left—fields that stretched for miles. The slave erected a cloth screen around the tub, and Chloe immersed herself in the warm water, leaning back as the sun caressed her skin and the woman washed her hair.

When her fingers began wrinkling, Chloe got out of the tub and wrapped herself in one of the linen towels provided. She walked back down the stairs, her eyes taking a few minutes to adjust to the dim room. Another woman, older this time, was there, sharpening a blade. She crossed her ample breast and asked Chloe to seat herself. Chloe watched in shock as the woman brought out silver shears and began to cut RaEm's ebony tresses. Chloe would have bolted, but the merest thought sent a wave of paralyzing terror through the "other." To refuse would be admitting she was a *khaibit* or *kheft*; kind of like a Salem witch refusing communion and thus sealing her fate. Chloe sat motionless as the woman shaved her head bald with a silver razor.

She rubbed a heady perfume into Chloe's skin—frankincense, Chloe thought as she was wrapped in a simple white gown. Fortunately there was a headcloth, so that she looked less like an egg. The woman outlined Chloe's eyes with red kohl. Not a good look; her green irises faded to gray by contrast.

The "other" told her that red was symbolic of flesh, and since she was going to the temple for a cure of the flesh, this was another depiction of her need. For a moment the thought of Cammy seared through her; what she wouldn't give for just ten minutes with the "other"! I've *got* to remember this stuff to tell her when I return! Chloe held on to that comforting thought as the alien processes took place around her.

They arrived at the Temple-of-the-Ka-of-Ptah at dusk. It was still late winter, and a chill breeze blew through the light cloak Chloe had been given. The temple appeared to be empty; yet Chloe heard echoes of voices beyond them. Built along the same plan as Karnak, it grew smaller and darker the farther into it they walked. Cheftu was several steps behind her as they passed through a towering cluster of columns, engraved with hieroglyphs so archaic that Chloe could scarcely read them. They came to a cross-passageway. Now it was almost totally dark. She looked over her shoulder and saw the white of Cheftu's kilt and headcloth. He motioned with his head to the left, and they continued walking.

Every now and then the yowl of a cat or the glint of a jewel in the wall painting made her stop. Cheftu stood motionless behind her, close enough that she could feel his heat.

They walked into a huge room with three pools. The sense of space was incredible. She couldn't see the walls on the other side. The pools were also large, even for someone who had grown used to the kitchen-size pools in Karnak. Torches (thank the gods!) were mounted around the perimeter, and Chloe walked to the second one, the only one filled with water.

"Nay . . ." Cheftu's voice echoed through the chamber. She turned, and he beckoned her to the third one. Three's a charm, she thought blithely. The pool appeared to be covered with a smooth platform of some sort.

Cheftu clapped his hands and two figures stepped to his side. Chloe took a step back before she realized they were wearing masks. For a moment she was looking into the feral stare of Anubis and the vengeful glare of Sekhmet.

However, they were only people; even in the dancing light she could see their perfectly formed human bodies. They advanced on her, chanting, and Chloe realized they were going to strip her. Cheftu's gaze was on her; she couldn't see it, but she could definitely feel it. Sekhmet held her shoulders while Anubis' black hands untied her robe. Her blood zipped through her veins, sweat beading her upper lip. The "other" ordered her to follow commands in such a fierce tone that Chloe didn't budge. But her heart raced as she debated how to defend herself should it become necessary. They stepped back, leaving her as naked as her first day alive—minus the hospital bracelet. She reached for her necklace. They had taken it, too.

Cheftu stood with his back to her as he lit a huge bowl of incense. He keened a prayer, but Chloe didn't have time to listen. The "gods" had fastened themselves to her arms and were walking her to the edge of the pool. Without even a countdown, they pushed her onto the platform. She stifled her scream as what she thought was solid footing dissolved slowly around her, leaving her thigh deep and sinking.

Cammy never mentioned drowning in noxious substances. What was it? Why did she continue to sink? She was now up to her waist. Despite her audience, Chloe struggled, trying to pull out her right leg which only succeeded in forcing her left leg deeper. She looked up in panic. The two "gods" stood beside each other, mute as columns, and Cheftu was hidden by the smoke of frankincense.

She was on her own. I've survived officer's candidacy school, she thought, I can do this, too. Easy to think, but as the thick substance caressed her belly and began to engulf her breasts, it was hard to formulate a plan. Was she some type of sacrifice? The "other" was totally incommunicado. Cheftu continued his prayers, and Anubis and Sekhmet produced sistrum and flute and began to play, the rhythms uneven but moving.

What the hell am I supposed to do!

The mud—at least that's what she thought it was—seeped around her shoulders, cradling her body in a lover's embrace as she stopped sinking and began floating. It was warm and soft, the texture of the London Ritz's whipping cream. When it became obvious this was all there was to it, Chloe began to relax. If I were at Elizabeth Arden's, she thought, this would cost a cool fortune. Her head felt very light as she leaned back and looked up at the ceiling. It was painted with stars and a depiction of Nuit, the goddess of night, swallowing the sun god Ra and birthing him every morning. Across one of the walls was a drawing of stick figures, each a representation of a god of the hour. She was surprised to see her own name—but then again, it did mean the astrological time of eleven o'clock.

As her vision grazed the hieroglyphs and drawings, she saw something that made her want to move to the edge of the pool. She couldn't move directly across—it was like walking in slow motion—but when she relaxed completely, her legs floated up and she could drift on the first level of the mud, pulling forward with her hands. In the far corner was her name again and then a doorway that opened up to the hieroglyph "Otherworld." Adrenaline pounded through her veins as Chloe squinted up to see the drawing above the doorway. She laid her head back in disappointment: only another bunch of stars.

Underneath it was what looked like a formula of some sort. It was a procession of alterations to her name: *RaEmhetepet, ReEmHetp-Ra, mes-hru-mesat Hru Naur RaEm Phamenoth, Aab-tPtah* . . . She translated. "Eleven o'clock in the evening, twenty-three after sun, natal day twenty-three times three, in the course of Ptah in the east . . ." But it was unfinished. Forgetting where she was, Chloe reached the edge of the pool, planted her muddy hands on the inlaid rim, and tried to lift herself. The mud sucked at her body and she gritted her teeth, using every ounce of strength left in her unexercised physique. Once past her hips, like a cork released from a bottle, she popped out.

She padded toward the corner, the mud on her body dripping a path, as she tried to see the other glyphs that time had erased. Cheftu's shout alerted her, and she turned. Anubis and Sekhmet were advancing with a linen towel stretched between them, their chanting loud and somewhat menacing. They wrapped her completely in it, not touching her once. Chloe was escorted over to Cheftu, who now knelt before the incense and appeared to be in a trance. Several of the torches had blown out, and a mist of frankincense floated toward the ceiling. It was dark, weird, and alien.

Chloe felt her heart thumping in her throat.

She turned around, trying to read the rest of the sentence, something about "prayer . . . what? . . . in the twenty-third doorway at twenty-three of RaEmhetepet." Chloe read it again quickly, committing the characters to memory—she'd have to figure it out later. Anubis grabbed her head and forced her to face Cheftu and now Sekhmet. Cheftu's stare was blank. The lioness goddess licked her lips, revealing a silver mouthpiece of extended incisors. Chloe backed up, but the solid body of Anubis held her still. Sekhmet held out her hand, and Chloe noticed it was beautiful, with long red painted nails, but when the woman turned it palm up to receive Chloe's hand, Chloe flinched. Sekhmet had the hieroglyphs of vengeance, fury, and justice painted on her wrist.

Cheftu leaned forward to whisper in her ear, "Give them your arm, RaEm. They are only making you an amulet. It will not hurt for long." He sounded tired and a little irritated. Chloe stuck out her arm and felt Cheftu seize her wrist, a linen glove on his hand so he wouldn't get muddy or wouldn't have to touch her, Chloe didn't know which. Sekhmet lowered her head and bit Chloe's wrist, tearing the flesh horizontally. Chloe was instantly dizzy as she watched her blood well, then rush out, the pressure of Anubis' hands on her shoulders and upper arms helping to quickly fill a shallow clay pot.

Cheftu wrapped her wrist with linen, and Chloe closed her eyes, trying to regain her equilibrium. It didn't hurt. Yet. The bizarre threesome led her to the altar, where Cheftu mixed her blood with mud from the pool. He sealed the mixture inside a scarab mold and laid it on the edge of the incense table. The "gods" had vanished. Chloe put a hand to her forehead. Still dizzy.

"My lady," Cheftu said, indicating a partitioned area, "go wash and re-dress. We have one more ritual." Chloe stumbled behind the partition and found her gown laid neatly across a basket. There was nothing on which to sit so she leaned against the wall for a moment. All the frankincense was giving her a headache. She didn't see any water but discovered as she toweled off that the greasy frankincense ointment made the mud come off easily.

She dressed in her robe and necklace again, missing underwear for the first time in several days. Actually, at this moment she missed everything about her world. Even *The Simpsons.*

The last part was easy. She drank some murky water while a priest dressed in red with mud stripes on his face tied the blood-mud scarab around her bandaged wrist. Then they left, stepping into the cool night. Chloe breathed deeply of the fresh air, scented with the smell of growing things, and accepted Cheftu's hand into the litter. Her wrist was beginning to throb, in time to the headache between her eyes. Why did they shave my head? Chloe thought morosely as she nodded off to sleep.

Hands helped her inside the house and up the stairs. Others laid her in the fresh sheets, rewrapped her bandage, and left her alone.

• • •

Chloe's first thought in the morning was that it would take forever to grow her hair out. Awakened and dressed before first light, she appreciated the slave rubbing a salve onto her arm and placing a cloth headdress on her head. With some makeup she would feel almost human again.

They left Noph, pulling away from the sleeping city as the golden-tinted fingers of Ra caressed Egypt with life and light.

When she was finally alone, Chloe wrote down the words for the formula. What did it mean? Her fingers drifted from time to time to the scarab on her wrist. It had been baked almost black, but the lines that showed the shape of the beetle had been painted green, the wings red and the rest left black. A silken cord, attached at the head and tail, kept it tied flatly against her wrist. She still smelled like frankincense, and her hair had grown like shaving stubble, overnight. Never again, she vowed, would they chop off her hair.

Period.

She walked on deck after lunch, the sun warming her back through her simple linen shift. She wore a headcloth, held in place by a circlet representing her office, and had ringed her eyes with kohl against the sun. The river grew more crowded the closer they drew to the Great Green. Cheftu was seated on the port side before a table and appeared to be drawing. The young bearded slave they had picked up in Noph sat beside him, shuffling through a stack of scrolls as if he were looking for something. Two humps appeared on the western horizon, and Chloe walked to the port side.

Cheftu looked up at her in surprise. "My lady! Can you speak?" She shook her head no and then opened her mouth for a demonstration. Cheftu's glance dropped momentarily to the amulet on her wrist, and he said, "I see. Maybe tomorrow."

She agreed and pointed to the growing shapes behind him. He looked. "The Pyramids. Surely you have seen them?"

Chloe tried to hide her excitement. The Pyramids! Finally something she recognized from her world! She shook her head no. Two trips to Cairo and she'd seen them only from a distance. Someday she wanted to climb them.

Cheftu watched her, frowning slightly: "I thought Makab took you after your parents flew to Osiris?"

She shook her head vehemently. Maybe he had taken RaEm, but it was nowhere in the "other's" memory. Cheftu smiled, a real smile, his golden eyes light and his teeth white against his dark face. "I take it from your barely restrained enthusiasm that you would like to visit them?"

She nodded emphatically, smiling for the first time in days.

He chuckled. "Always full of surprises, my lady. We have no litter, so we'll have to walk. I think the avenue from the river is still fairly easy going. Shall we see Ra die tonight from the apex?"

Her smile said it all.

"Then you must rest this afternoon, my lady."

Chloe smiled again and practically skipped back to her room. If only there were some way to take her notebook! She looked through her collection of custom-made sandals and picked the sturdiest ones, checked that she had a kilt, shirt, and cloak, and lay down, waiting until twilight.

She awoke periodically during the afternoon, her excitement making it difficult to sleep. Finally she saw long shadows and rose to dress. Cheftu met her at the stern, his young Apiru slave and two other *rekkit* beside him. His amber glance assessed her, and he smiled. "Are you ready, my lady?" She smiled and nodded as Cheftu looked at her a moment longer. "Then let's be off."

Seti had anchored them at an old dock, and they walked easily down it and onto the land. Chloe could see the remnants of an avenue that had been wide and sphinx lined but was already worn from more than a thousand years of use. The Pyramids grew before them, their tops puncturing the night sky. Their limestone casings were chipped. Cheftu explained they'd once been tipped in gold before the Hyksos had raided them.

It felt good to move again, Chloe thought. Her muscles were already sore and she thrived on the ache. She was living life, not just drawing it! Chloe matched her stride to Cheftu's, the slaves trailing behind. The sphinx was almost completely buried, only its eyes, still painted, and forehead visible above the sand. Cheftu was strangely quiet until they stood before the Great Pyramid, its name even in this antiquated time.

As detailed and exquisite as Karnak was, this Pyramid was a counterpoise of grandeur and majesty. Chloe craned her neck to see the top. The rocks she'd always imagined as stair steps were actually taller than she was. Chloe stood in silence, staring up with wonder. It was a few minutes before she noticed Cheftu was no longer looking at the masterpiece of ancient engineering, but staring at her.

"Amazing, is it not," he said, gesturing to the building. "Legend says it took twenty years to build, though I know not how. Would you like to climb it?" Chloe indicated the enormous height of the rocks, and Cheftu chuckled. "Not from here. The limestone is unscalable. It was one of Cheops' protective measures. On the other side are steps. Some ancient Nophite pharaoh used to come up here to think, so he had steps cut into the rock. However, it is still quite a climb." She gestured for him to lead the way, and they began to walk around the base. Chloe was amazed at the total absence of life around them. There wasn't a village, a field, or even an ancient tourist booth. They were alone.

The slaves followed at a distance, carrying torches and a large basket that Chloe hoped held dinner. After a fifteen-minute walk, they reached the other side. The moon had risen and the stars were out, casting their light on the moonlike surface of the shifting sands.

Cheftu found the steps and guided her to them. "Go before us, and be careful. These steps are hundreds of years old and slippery. I will be here to catch you if you trip, so do not worry." Who is going to catch you? Chloe thought, but she began to climb. Though the steps were normal size, years and countless feet had worn them down so that each step dipped in the middle. About a third of the way up her lungs began to burn, Cheftu noticed and called a break.

Each climber settled against the larger stones, looking across the endless desert, the miles of undulating silver sand. When Chloe regained her breath she started off again, Cheftu close behind. Her feet began to blister in the sandals, and she thought wistfully of a decent pair of boots, but when she looked up into the limitless, starry night, she forgot about her feet, the time-travel conundrum—everything except this majesty.

Chloe was sweating when she finally placed her trembling foot on the top.

The top of the world!

The wind was fierce, whipping at her headcloth and chilling the moisture on her face. When the Hyksos had taken the gold-covered top, it had flattened the Pyramid, leaving a plateau the size of her Dallas flat. She walked to the eastern side, overlooking the Nile. It stretched as far as the eye could see, a filament of black-and-silver light, weaving Upper and Lower Egypt into one of the greatest civilizations the world would ever know.

There were no lights, except the pinpricks she could see on their small craft far below. It was so barren. They were alone under this enormous expanse of silver-spangled sky. Cheftu's voice came to her on the wind, offering food and warmth.

The slaves had formed a shelter and heated wine. Chloe sat down inside it, next to Cheftu, enjoying the lack of wind, and stared up at the sky. She didn't recognize many of the constellations and couldn't ask Cheftu what they were. He handed her a cup of warmed wine and the predecessor to a pita-bread sandwich. She bit into it hungrily, crunching the goat cheese and cucumbers as she relaxed against the ancient stone.

They were blocked from the slaves' view by the shelter, and the intimacy of their position poured through her veins. Chloe was preternaturally aware of Cheftu's deep breathing, the way his long fingers moved as he spoke, as he gestured toward the sky and drew pictures in the air to illustrate his stories. Silvery light touched his body, gilding its hard smoothness, and the spicy warmth of his skin enticed her. Chloe gulped. Moonlight madness, that's all she was feeling. Besides, she had no hair! What kind of man would be interested in a bald woman?

However, in these moments she glimpsed what might have been between them . . . between Cheftu and RaEm. No telling what kind of *kheft* he'd think her if she told the truth. If she could tell him the truth.

He pointed, resting his cloth-covered head next to hers. "That is the star of RaShera," he said, pointing to Venus. "There is the constellation of the thigh of Apis." Chloe looked long and hard but couldn't make out how they had perceived a bull's thigh in the night sky. Of course, it wasn't any more difficult to imagine than Cassiopeia in her chair, but Chloe always had a hard time with that one, too.

"It astonishes me how, no matter where we may travel away from the red and black lands of Kemt, there are always our gods in the sky," Cheftu said, his velvety voice raw from the wind. "When we were returning from Punt, sometimes the trip would seem so long and the people so foreign, it was a comfort to look in the sky and know Ma'at was maintained."

She looked at him in surprise. Cheftu had gone on that fabled journey to Punt? The trip that Hatshepsut had considered the ultimate feat of her reign? She longed to ask him more.

"You did not know I had traveled, RaEm?"

She shook her head no.

He smiled bitterly. "I should not be surprised, should I," he said to himself. "*Assst*, well. In Assyria they have ziggurats. They are like the first Pyramids we ever built. They sacrifice animals to their gods and draw their attention by cutting themselves. They have very bloodthirsty gods. Then in the Far East, the people are very small and dark. They stick needles in you to relieve pain." He chuckled. "It works, but I cannot see any Egyptian standing for such treatment.

"In the islands of the Great Green, young men and women vault over bull horns as a worship to their gods. The women wear many-layered dresses, but leave their breasts uncovered. Stories say there used to be a great empire, its power stretching across the sea. However, they got greedy and their gods have almost destroyed them twice by raining fire." He sighed. "No matter where one goes, though, the sky is the same, Ra is born and dies every day and night. The stars dance on Nuit's skin in every country." He sat in silence, his eyes as dark as the night above them. "There is HatHor," he said, pointing. "It is almost her season."

Chloe felt his gaze on her.

"I hope you are able to serve her again, RaEm." His voice was personal, intimate and low, the former sarcasm and bitterness missing. She turned her head, meeting his warm glance, his gold eyes lit with reflections of the stars above. Hesitantly he touched her jaw, his thumb caressing her lower lip. Chloe didn't breathe as she moved toward him. Cheftu met her, his lips soft and gentle, a questioning heat that burned through her body. She felt the impact of his kiss in every cell, heat rushing from her extremities inward. His thumb stroked her chin as he angled his face over hers. Chloe began to melt, but he pulled back abruptly, looking away.

"There is Ptah, far in the east," he said conversationally. Chloe didn't give a hoot about Ptah at this point but looked up anyway, trying to calm her pounding heart. "He has left the house of HatHor and is now heading toward Isis and Nephthys." Her mind jarred. What had he said that was so familiar? She put a hand to her head, bending forward and away. "Ptah in the east"? What was that from?

Cheftu sat up next to her, his warm arm around her shoulders. "Are you well, RaEm?" She shrugged, barely hearing his question. He touched her chin and turned her face to him. Ptah and HatHor left her mind as blood surged through her body. Cheftu sat immobile, staring intently at her lips.

She licked her lips, inhaling his wine-scented breath, so close that she could see the texture of his skin. The moment stretched into eternity as he bent his head and kissed her, his fingers caressing her chin and jawline, his touch tentative but fiery. He traced the seam of her lips, and she tasted the rough texture of his tongue as he teased her, swallowing her excited gasp when he gripped her neck and pulled her closer. His kiss was lazy and warm, and she held his hand to her neck, feeling the blood race beneath his satiny bronze skin.

When he drew back, his eyes were dark, unreadable. He swallowed hard, and she tried to collect herself. They were both breathing heavily in the cool night air. What had happened? Why was he suddenly so cold? He released her as if he'd been bitten, and she quickly let go of his wrist. They stared at each other for a moment.

Cheftu looked stunned, then angry, then he was Lord Cheftu again—flawlessly polite and remote. In a fluid motion he drew to his feet, his voice rough. "When my lady is ready to return, I shall be waiting." She watched his star-spattered figure walk to the southern side of the Pyramid, the wind blowing his cloak flat to his body.

She sat, letting her pulse return to normal and her anger to full boil.

What a jerk! One thing was certain: she now knew who the stranger in the marshes had been; the recognition of his touch had warmed every molecule in her body. He'd kissed her again with a hopeful restraint, as if he were afraid to really touch her, then hunger had overtaken restraint. She had been a most willing participant, too. Damn. Sighing, Chloe leaned back, staring into the blackness. Why did she care, anyway? He was an alien to her, a member of a lost race. Soon she would be returning home. So why did those thoughts give no comfort? Why did she want to see, feel, and know more of Cheftu? To break beyond the facades of nobleman and healer? He hates RaEm, she reminded herself. RaEm is who you are. She rubbed her necklace across her chin as she shivered in the night air.

Cheftu glared into the wind. What had come over him? He knew RaEm was available for bedding. In fact, her easy willingness cooled his ardor. At least it had before. By the gods, he'd never touched RaEm like that or been touched by her so intensely, so bone-shakingly close. A pity he didn't want just her body. . . .

In the many years since they had last seen each other, he had missed her childlike surprise and freshness; but it was gone, it had been gone for many years. Still, there was an unfulfilled sensuality and femininity in her touch. A purity. The gods must be laughing at that! Her perfect kiss had been a falsehood—further proof of what an amazing deceiver she was, this priestess of the goddess of love and mirth. She and all she touched were lies, alluring reflections that faded with the introduction of truth.

Then by the gods, why could he still taste her?

•••

Chloe awoke in the afternoon, feeling as though she'd been hit by a train. The walk back from the Pyramid had been grueling. Her feet had bled from a dozen blisters. The sand rubbing into the wounds had been like salt. Cheftu had walked ahead of her the whole way, never looking back to help her, leaving that chore to his slaves. When they finally reached the boat she had kicked off her sandals and clothes, crawled into bed, and covered her head, letting sleep take her away.

However, with the brilliant day around her, the turquoise sky, blue river, and all-encompassing foliage, she found her mood improved. The river began to split into the many branches that formed the delta of Goshen, and Chloe settled into a chair by the stern, watching the multitude of birds and fish. Surreptitiously she sketched their markings, more details with which to complete her drawings that night.

They had to arrive soon; she was almost out of papyrus.

• • •

Two days later she *was* out of papyrus. She spent her nights filling in details and shading. She actually slept some, too. Reproducing the Pyramid eluded her, and Chloe doubted anything other than a wide-angle lens on a Hasselblad would do it justice. In addition, her nausea returned. She lay in bed for two days, taking only soup and bread.

Her personal physician ignored her.

CHAPTER 6

GOSHEN

Thutmosis III was awakened, as he was every morning, by priests chanting a welcome to Amun-Ra. He pushed off the linen covers and sat up, running a hand over his shaved head. Arbah, his slave, entered and knelt.

"Make haste!" Thut commanded. "I am late to sacrifice this morning, and I have special guests coming in from Hatshepsut, living forever! this evening. Not to mention those strange omens of disaster in the Great Green. Whatever happens there could affect Egypt!" As he spoke, Arbah ran his bath, steamed the towels for Thut's face, and instructed that the prince's white-fringed kilt be pressed.

Before Ra moved much farther in the sky, Thut rode down to the temple to sacrifice another offering for a good growing season. He leapt down from his chariot and joined the saffron-clad priests who chanted as they walked down the water steps: *"Praise to thee, Father-Mother Nile, that rushes up from the underworld and gives breath to the dwellers in the red and black lands of Kemt. Hidden of movement, a darkness in light. Which waterest the plains and valleys which Ra hath created to nourish all life. That givest drink to the dry places which have no dew from thy brow. Beloved of Geb, controller of Tepu Tchatchaiu, that maketh every workshop of Ptah to flourish. He who maketh barley and createth spelt . . ."* A commotion to his right caused Thut to pause.

"What is the problem that we cannot worship first?" he shouted to Commander Ameni, who detained two men. Thut clenched his fists when he recognized the two troublemakers. Striding toward them angrily, he said, "Have you come with your petty requests and idle threats again, Apiru?"

"We come to ask Your Majesty to grant us leave to go into the desert."

"Why?"

"As we have said before, we go to worship and sacrifice to our God."

The prince walked away, demonstrating that he thought them and their god no threat and of no consequence. He walked down the water steps, where Ramoses stood before him. The Apiru raised his bronze-tipped staff in the air and brought it down with a crash on the river Nile. Thut stood back, arms crossed, watching the performance. Strangely, there was no ripple. The waters were still.

"He who is, God of the Israelites, Elohim, has again sent me to you," Ramoses said. "He said for you to let his people go, to worship him in the desert. But," Ramoses noted with a grim smile, "you have not listened to him. So he says, 'That you will know that I am Lord of all, the water will be changed to blood. The fish will die and the water will reek. You will be unable to drink or use this water." He fixed Thut with a glowering stare.

"Anything your uncivilized 'el' can do," Thut scoffed, "the great magi of Egypt can also do. Turn the river, the source of all life in Egypt, to blood? The gods will not allow it!" His face paled as he saw the river behind Ramoses churn, as if just being struck.

Suddenly fish started rising onto the surface of the river, belly up, catching in the reeds along the shoreline. His courtiers gasped and whispered among themselves. He turned to his priests and phalanx of magi.

"You incompetent fools," he hissed. "Will you wait for the Nile to clog, or will you act now? Stop this, instantly!" Sweat broke out across his wide forehead, and suddenly the weight of his headdress seemed overwhelming. He clapped his hands and faced Ramoses.

"I will continue my morning prayers if you have taken the time you wished, Apiru. I will not let you, or your people, go into the desert. Ever! Now begone from my sight!" As he spoke, he extended his arms to be rinsed for prayers. The priest hoisted the jar of water and poured from his shoulder.

Gasps turned to shrieks as the clear water fell on Thut's hands and turned to fresh blood, thick, slippery, and still warm. Thut looked with horror at his hands.

The blood of Egypt.

Looking at the floor, he saw that all the water, once it touched him, had turned to blood. Seeing Ramoses had left, Thutmosis rounded on his magi, his countenance all the more frightening with spatters of blood on his white kilt and gold collar, droplets already darkening on his face.

"By the gods! Do something! Should the Glory of Egypt—" He caught himself. "Should the *consort* of the Glory of Egypt be captured in the spell of a foreigner!" He drew in a deep breath and said through gritted teeth, "Clean up this sacrilege!" Fish were already rotting in the warm sun, and Thut knew that by high sun no one would be able to work by the river.

His Egyptian magus Menekrenes came forward. "I know the spell, gracious Majesty." Thut gestured. Menekrenes turned toward the pots still full of water and, eyes half-closed, began to chant. The slaves brought forth another jug of water. The magus, still chanting, reached down and with a swift movement grabbed a handful of water.

It turned to blood in his very grasp. With an angry shout, Thut turned back up the pathway to the palace. A frightened priest ran to his side. "Prince! You must finish the prayers! More than ever they need to be completed." Menekrenes stood immobile, staring at the rapidly drying blood on his hands. The other magi deserted him.

Thut walked to the edge of the water and looked across the red and churning river, the stench engulfing him. Raising his blood-spattered arms, he intoned to the cowering priesthood and the dying fish, "Lord of finned life . . ." Thut heard himself and leaped forward in the liturgy. *"If the Nile is weak, all the world suffers, prostrate."* Thut hoped that wasn't to be prophecy. *"Sacrifices are few and the* rekkit *are made low. When he-she rises, joy bubbles from the lips of men, rejoicing in living. Creator, sustainer, he-she who brings richness to the earth rejoices. Lord of verdant life, drowning evil, nourishing good. Creating life for livestock, offerings for all* neter. *Replenishing and restoring life— feeding the poor. Causing trees to flourish to the uttermost desires so that men may not lack in them."* Thut finished the prescribed prayer but, without precedent, added his own words. *"He who would defeat the god of slaves and make Egypt rich with land, food, and trees. He who rejects the curse of the foreigner and rewards the faithful worshiper. O, Father-Mother Nile, we beseech thee!"* Thut ignored the gasps his addition brought and backed away from the Nile, his nostrils pinched.

Dismissing his retinue, he began to walk to his apartments. Surely this insufferable Apiru, Israelite, or whatever had not cursed his private baths and pools. The priests had dispersed, and only three brave courtiers followed at a distance, most of them spies for Hat.

The group came to the first level of a series of lotus ponds, and Thut stopped abruptly. "These are still clean and clear." He walked up to a pond, gestured for a lord to remove Thut's sandals, and he stepped in the water. No sooner had both feet entered than red stains began snaking their way from Thut into the clear water. He jerked out his feet with an oath, his toes covered with warm, gooey blood.

"Give me your kilt, Nakht," he growled to his least favorite of Hat's spies. The unlucky nobleman flushed but unbelted the finely woven linen and handed it to Thut, his proud head high despite his nakedness. Thut wiped his feet dry and clean and threw the linen at Nakht. Coldly Thut said, "My Majesty will retire to my apartments." He gestured toward the pool. "I do not wish to see this muck at all."

His retainer asked, "Should the Great House be warned of this?"

Thut caught his eye. "Do you think this has truly affected the whole Nile? Such a thing is impossible! I do not know how the Israelite did this trick, but I think perhaps my error was in underestimating his magical capabilities. I am sure it was only for our benefit. It will soon pass. The Great One," Thut said with growing solicitude, "has greater tasks to occupy her valuable time and resources than a squabble with the local slaves. Let us not bother her."

So saying, he turned and followed the private path to his apartments. He intended to spend the rest of this bloodbath feasting, fighting, and fornicating. Part of him hoped this little trick did inconvenience the royal wench under the Double Crown.

Lips in a grim smile, he summoned his body servant. "I will have nothing but wine to drink, and I will be bathing in milk. See to it."

THE SUN WAS HOT on the wooden deck as Chloe stared idly across the blue green water. An earthy perfume of unwashed men, stagnant water, and fertilized soil rose around her. Cheftu had smiled stiltedly at her this morning, and Chloe promised herself she would be pleasant but distant. It didn't help when his scrutiny dropped to her lips and she felt blood pound in her ears. He'd gone into his room to pack his medicines and scrolls, for soon they would arrive in Avaris. She would have to dress herself for that. God alone knew how she would pleat and fold her gown without a slave. Ahh, Velcro.

A scream rent the air.

"Blood!"

Chloe leapt to her feet, but she felt Cheftu's restraining grip on her shoulders. He held her back from the slave, who was screaming and swearing. Gallons of blood covered the deck, the stench in the harsh sunlight revolting. Covering his face with a cloth, Cheftu firmly pushed Chloe onto her stool and walked forward. He looked around, a peculiar expression on his face, his skin gray beneath his tan.

He's looking for a body, Chloe thought. Though it would have to be a horse to carry all that blood. She gazed out across the Nile, the blue sky, green bushes, and red water . . . She stood up slowly.

The Nile was red. A thick, viscous red, and as she watched, dead fish rose to the surface. She opened her mouth to scream, but no sound came out.

The ruckus behind her on deck was gaining in volume as Cheftu tried to make sense from the slave's ramblings. She turned to him, but he was focused on the slave.

Only a bolt of lightning would get his attention, she thought. Chloe looked away, but as she did so, she saw something as familiar to her as a telephone and far more accessible. A bow and a quiver of arrows. She looked again at Cheftu, but he was still ineffectively engrossed.

Chloe bent down for the bow and pulled an arrow from the quiver. As she did, she saw the edge of a papyrus page. Pulling away the cloth that lined the inside of the quiver, she saw a stack of scrolls wrapped around inside. Why was Cheftu carrying pages inside his *quiver?* She looked for another moment; she saw the top page was black with writing. Probably spells, she thought.

A cry returned her to the present, and she nocked the arrow, pulled the bowstring, and released it. It sighed faintly as it flew over Cheftu . . . and into the Nile. Cheftu watched its path, and a shocked silence hung over the ship for a moment as the whole crew looked out onto the bloody red water. Then he barked, his voice hoarse with horror.

"Sweet Isis, mother of the gods!"

The sailors' terrified cries joined his, and Chloe turned to look out across the . . . whatever it was. She turned back sharply.

No water. If something was wrong with the Nile, there would be no drinking water. Although people could last a long time without food, water was a necessity, especially under the burning rays of Ra.

She marched over to Cheftu, who stood looking into the Nile, his face blank, his golden eyes wide. She waved a hand in front of him and he turned to her, his gaze foggy with disbelief. Pulling out some papyrus and summoning RaEm's memory, she wrote the simple hieroglyph that meant life or death to them all. Water. When she looked at him again, his vision had cleared and the set of his mouth was resolute.

"ARE THERE JUGS OF WATER on board?" he asked Seti.

"Aye, my lord," the captain responded as his hands twisted the hem of his kilt. "What curse has befallen on Egypt, my lord? Are you not a great *hemu neter?* Can you not purify these waters?"

Cheftu looked at him grimly. "If this *is* the working of the gods, do you think I, a mere man, can change their desire? If this is the working of natural causes, perhaps they can be discovered and rectified," he said. There was no need to mention that if not, Egypt faced certain disaster.

Slaves brought out the water jugs, and Cheftu was pleased to see there was enough water to get through the next few days, if it were rationed. RaEm was already there, silently listing people and determining how much water for each. Cheftu gazed at her for a moment, caught in a welter of emotion: distrust, admiration, disbelief . . . and desire. He felt his body tighten and redirected his thoughts. The woman he thought he saw was just an illusion. For whatever purpose, it suited RaEm to be helpful now. Do not be deceived, he admonished himself.

"We must stop and gather more water from the marshes." He dismissed the group and followed Seti to the tiller, looking for a safe place to disembark for the few hours needed. As they steered into a tiny niche, Cheftu glanced over his shoulder.

As if she felt him watching, RaEm paused in her tallying and raised her head. Cheftu looked into her brilliant green eyes, indeed the color of Canaanite stone, but clear. She winked at him and he looked away, smiling.

• • •

They arrived at the torchlit water steps of the palace at Avaris. Night had fallen, and Chloe was amazed at how dark it was. At least now the stained waters were no longer visible.

Cheftu motioned for her trunks to be taken, and they stepped onto the dock, the heavy scent of night-blooming flowers masking the rot of dead fish.

The chief herald announced the approach of Thutmosis III. As he was not yet pharaoh, the courtesy title "living forever!"—required every time a pharaoh, living or dead, was mentioned—had not been added. That should make him easier to refer to, Chloe thought. He also did not require obeisance. She and Cheftu remained standing, waiting. A short, squat man with distinctly military bearing walked toward them. He wore the red crown of Lower Egypt and was clad in gold: gold-fringed kilt, gold collar, and multitudes of bracelets and rings. Even the kohl around his eyes was gold, reflecting a dozen torchlights. He stopped a few feet away so he would not have to look up at them.

Cheftu inclined his head. "Greetings, Horus-in-the-Nest. Life! Health! Prosperity! Your royal aunt-mother, Pharaoh Hatshepsut, living forever!, sends her hope that glorious Amun-Ra watches over you." Thut's beady brown eyes looked like pebbles in muddy water, Chloe thought.

Through a clenched-teeth smile Thut asked coldly, "How is she? She who wears the double crown?" Without waiting for a response he turned to RaEm and extended his hand. "This is the lovely priestess, then?" As he touched her, a searing pain pounded through Chloe.

Clutching at her throat, she gave an agonized scream and tore at her chest with gilded nails. Her throat was on fire! She couldn't breathe! She clawed away at the fire, but Cheftu grabbed her wrists before scratching brought relief.

He looked into her wide and rolling eyes, fear and pain dilating her pupils until they were black pools. She continued to scream, a piercing, heartrending wail.

"What in the name of Osiris is wrong?" Thut yelled. Then, just as suddenly as her outburst began, she collapsed, unconscious.

Cheftu caught her falling body.

"Is the lady mad?" Thut asked.

"I know no more than you, Prince," Cheftu said in a monotone as he lifted her body into his arms. "Please lead me to the lady's apartments and have a bath prepared."

Thut summoned a slave to meet Cheftu's needs. "But, Your Majesty," the slave protested fearfully, "how is she to bathe with no water?"

"It is your head to find some," Thut growled.

ONLY THE REMOTE FLICKER OF A TORCH WAS VISIBLE when Chloe woke. She saw a dark-haired girl lying on a mat beside her couch, with a jug close by her hand. A raspy voice came through the darkness, startling the girl.

"The lady needs liquid," Cheftu said, and Chloe saw the white of his kilt, a ghost moving toward her. He took the cup and added something to it, then sat next to Chloe. Gently he lifted her shoulders and held the drink to her lips. It was cool, so cool, and she gulped it thirstily.

He chuckled in the darkness. "By Isis, priestess, there is more."

Chloe wiped her mouth with her hand and instantly felt lethargy reclaim her body. He'd drugged her, but at this point she didn't care. The pain was gone . . . anything was worth that. Cheftu eased her down, his fingers fluttering, across her face, a strong and gentle caress. She nuzzled into his broad hand with a sigh and fell asleep.

Chloe awoke with a strong drumming in her ears, but when she moved her head it became less insistent. She placed her hand on the surface and opened her eyes in surprise when she felt warm, hard flesh. Cheftu was beside her, one arm flung over his face, the other hanging off the couch. She was pillowed against his smooth chest, her bare leg crossed over one of his. Feelings of embarrassment warred with contentment.

He must be exhausted, she thought, and quietly crept to the chamber pot. She looked over her shoulder and watched him for a moment: the strong, determined lines of his face relaxed, his sculpted body at rest. Most of it, anyway.

The water was lukewarm, but she stepped in and began to wash. Silence enveloped the palace, and she heard early morning birds calling outside. Cheftu muttered in the adjoining room, and Chloe froze. What had happened yesterday? What should she do? What did this mean? Silently she sat thinking, then she heard the door close quietly. He'd gone. Rinsing off, she went back into the room where Basha was setting out the Perfuming of the Mouth.

She crossed her breast. "Welcome to Avaris, my lady. Is there anything you need this morning? Your stomach? It is well? I see my lady has already bathed."

Chloe noted Basha's condescending, insolent tone, a tone RaEm would never tolerate. Fear of discovery made Chloe do what she thought RaEm would. She walked across to the trunk and picked it up, dumping all the garments on the floor. With a kick worthy of RaEm, she scattered the garments and noticed the hauteur vanish from Basha's face.

"Of course, my lady," she said hurriedly. "Your ladyship's linens will be attended." Basha grabbed the clothes while Chloe stood, foot tapping. She moved with speedy grace, and after the door closed Chloe smiled and laughed silently. That should prove that RaEm was just as obnoxious and arrogant as she had ever been.

Ergo, she was the same person.

· · ·

Morning sun drenched the sky in mists of lavender, orange, and pink, a pastel reflection of *atmu*. Chloe circled her eyes with kohl and stepped into the warming dawn. The sun rose higher and higher as she finished her meal and paced through the slightly overgrown garden. Thut probably did not care much about fripperies like neat flower beds.

Seeing no one else about, she knelt and began weeding, memories of Mimi's many rose gardens clouding her mind. A budding fig tree was almost obscured by an encroaching vine, and Chloe sat cross-legged on the ground, clearing some growing space for the tree. She was astonished at the feeling of accomplishment when, a long, sticky while later, she had weeded the area around the tree and several of the empty beds completely. Smiling, she felt comfortable and restful for the first time since waking up in HatHor's chamber.

"Why does the lovely lotus RaEmhetepet stay in the midday sun? Will she not wilt, she who is truly of the night?" The deep bass voice was heavy with sarcasm. Chloe twisted around to see Thutmosis in a dusty kilt and blue-and-white leather helmet, leaning against a date palm behind her. She could smell the sweat and dust of his body. She began to kneel, but he reached out and clasped her shoulder.

"Please, my lady, do not trouble yourself with court manners. You will find those of us banished to this wet land are not so . . ." He paused and then, with a glint in his eyes, said, "ceremonial in our greetings. Although if you would care to offer me a drink, I would be honored to take it with you." His release of her arm was a caress, and she wondered why he was here, alone. Didn't princes have bodyguards and entourages?

She got up and poured him a cup of wine. Although he was obviously thirsty, he sipped carefully as he watched her from under bushy black brows. His gaze wandered, taking in her short, scraggly hair, her round perspiring breasts, her hands crossed protectively over her gently rounded tummy, and her long legs outlined through the thin linen. Chloe, determined not to be flustered by his intent appraisal, swallowed shallowly and met his gaze. He grinned, showing jutting, yellowed teeth.

"I am afraid I have forgotten how to play the foolish romantic games of the Wasetian court. I am more a man of action. You are not beautiful," he mused. "You lack the softness of a woman. Your eyes belong to a *khaibit*, but your allure is legendary. Will you dine with me tonight?"

Chloe, smarting from his unflattering comparison to a bloodsucking ghost, smiled grimly at him.

"The lady is under strict command to rest and heal," a velvet voice said from behind her. Walking smoothly up to Thut, Cheftu gestured to Chloe. "Hatshepsut, living forever! was most insistent. Though she did not believe this would be the best place for the lady, I persuaded her that, as a prince among princes, you would encourage the lady to heal so that she can return to the Silver Room of HatHor. She is the sole defensive priestess of the twenty-third hour."

Chloe stared at Cheftu's bold-faced lie; Hatshepsut had *wanted* to send her here. However, when Thut muttered his compliance and walked away, she was impressed at Cheftu's rescue. He inclined his head politely to the prince, and Chloe studied this ancient lord. He was remarkably alive this morning. Flushing, she remembered where she woke up, and the scent and feel of his skin against hers was suddenly all too real.

Quickly she walked over to some overgrown grapevines. She knelt and began to weed. Cheftu crouched beside her, his nearness unnerving. His braceleted arm almost touched her. Did he feel anything? Nervous sweat trailed down Chloe's back.

"A word with you, my lady," he said quietly. "Since your memory has failed you, I would remind you that there is great mistrust here. For your safety it would be well if you could get a guard." She glanced at him. She could protect herself; the last thing she needed was someone watching her all the time. She really would go mad.

"Has that which you feared made itself apparent?"

Chloe looked at him, an eyebrow raised in query.

"Holy Osiris!" he swore. "Must I speak to you as a wanton?" He looked away, and Chloe noticed the white lines around his lips. Again, he wasn't as in control as he seemed. "Are you with child?" he blurted out.

Chloe sprang up, outraged. She opened her mouth to read him the riot act, when doubts assailed her. She didn't know what it felt like to be pregnant, and though she thought she had a few of the symptoms, she could not be certain. She certainly hadn't missed any periods. Chloe licked her lips and shrugged halfheartedly. What did she know?

Cheftu looked away, but not before she saw the disgust in his glance. A long moment passed before he said, "Very well, then." As he stepped toward her, she stepped back. "I will not harm you, but with Osiris as my witness, you must trust me." His eyes were hooded, his face solemn. He seemed sincere enough, but he was a diplomat, a courtier. That was his job. Should she put her life in his hands? A man who had accused her of being a tramp the first time he'd spoken to her? Not bloody likely.

She watched him silently. Sure, she thought. Tell you I'm from the future and watch you burn me or beat me or wall me up or whatever Egyptians do to traitors and madmen! Cheftu walked away, shaking his head as he left, his striped headcloth brilliant in the sunshine.

Chloe spent the rest of the day quietly. She puttered in the garden, weeding and completely ruining her linen robe, until Basha suggested she take a rest. Exhausted from her strange arrival the night before, she slept until after nightfall.

When Cheftu sent after her for dinner, she sent a note saying she would eat in her room. When Thut sent a slave to retrieve her for dinner, she again declined. After a long bath (in old bathwater) she strolled with Basha down to the river's edge. By starlight the water looked thick and heavy, like oil. The acrid smell burned her nostrils, reminding her of something else, another time she had smelled this same odor. Blood, a lot of blood. Doesn't matter, she thought dismissively.

Chloe longed to ask questions about how the water, or lack thereof, was affecting the country, but she didn't want to take the time to write it out when probably only Cheftu or Thut would be able to reply. She trudged back to her room and fell into a dreamless sleep.

Two days passed in silence. She gardened, drew, and ate. She slept a lot. Her hair was growing; in a couple of days it would probably even lie flat.

Basha announced the next day that the Apiru had asked Thut when he wanted the curse lifted from the Nile, and Thut had said tomorrow. "Though why he did not say today, my lady, I fear I do not know," she commented. Chloe agreed. A bath *would* feel good. Although it was not summertime hot yet, all the foliage and water in Avaris made the place feel muggier and warmer than it actually was. Kind of like Houston.

Chloe walked into the wilting garden and wondered how she would entertain herself for the next several weeks or months. When would her voice return? When could she go home? How?

The stench of the Nile was horrendous. Hundreds of fish lay dead and rotting on the shore. She saw the slaves were cleaning up. Despite the overseers with long whips and short tempers, their lack of enthusiasm was notable.

Chloe returned to the palace and was stopped by a shout.

"My lady, my lady!" Chloe turned to see Cheftu's Apiru. "Health! Life! Prosperity! My Lord Cheftu inquires if my lady is up to dining with him tonight? He also said this was yours and begs your forgiveness in not delivering it earlier."

Chloe accepted the small scroll and cracked open the seal. It was written in messy hieratic. "You anger me, RaEmhetepet. Your childishness is wearing thin. I expect to be received differently when next we meet." It was unsigned, but she turned it over. The seal was from Nesbek's house. What was this about? Glancing around, she rerolled the papyrus and tucked it in her sash. She was tired of not understanding what was going on in her adopted lifestyle, and the "other" was ominously quiet.

Suddenly she felt she was not alone.

"Surely if the lady is well enough to stroll in the heat of the day, she can break bread with me tonight?" Chloe could tell from his tone that he was not asking permission . . . he was commanding her. Thutmosis looked at her. "My lady?"

Chloe did not want to eat with this man whose gaze wandered over her as if she were on the menu, yet she knew no alternative. The story of her life recently. She nodded assent and turned away. He may be the prince, but this is my garden, she thought grumpily.

She clapped imperiously for Basha. After impatiently scrawling a note, she sent the girl for Cheftu. Maybe he could get her out of this mess. Or bring his own date.

The thought of Cheftu with another woman made her even crankier.

• • •

She was seated in her cool room when Cheftu entered. She handed him her brief note describing Thut's request.

"My lady has received a royal invitation," he said. "Do you have second thoughts about accepting?"

Chloe stared at him, frustrated with her inability to communicate. Could she be overreacting to Thut's stares and invitation? Cheftu watched her through narrowed eyes. Slowly she shook her head. Somehow she would be fine.

"Does my lady feel, um, unsafe with Horus-in-the-Nest?" he asked gravely.

She shrugged, uncertain and embarrassed. Cheftu considered for a moment, his long-lashed gaze never leaving her face. "I shall send a guard with you." He paused; for a moment an expression of very human confusion crossed his face, then he spoke, cold as ever. "I confess I do not understand your concerns, RaEm. Thutmosis has been your goal for years, so why the facade of fear? This is the opportunity you have lusted after; or are you playing the reluctant maiden for my benefit? I assure you, it is unnecessary." Chloe averted her face. His words and manner were offensive. RaEm may have been free and easy, but she, Chloe, had a different standard.

Kissing strangers in the bulrushes and enemies on pyramids notwithstanding.

Cheftu grabbed her and pulled her close to his side, wrenching her arm cruelly. His eyes were no longer opaque, and with blazing revulsion they raked her face, yet his touch warmed her. Once more gaining his precious control, he thrust her away and walked rapidly from the room.

"Get over it!" she wanted to scream. His sniping, his barbed comments . . . in the other facets of his life he seemed to be reasonable and rational, but not with RaEm. Basha jolted into the room. "My lady," she said, anguished, her gaze open, "how are we to prepare you in such a short time?" Chloe entered the bath and saw fresh water. Apparently

Thut's Apiru had quite a lot of power. She allowed Basha to undress her and climbed gratefully into the inlaid pool, bracing herself for hours of pampering and toilette.

• • •

The moon had already risen when she was ushered into Thut's private apartments. Torches flickered across the beaten-gold walls, portraying the triumphs of Hatshepsut.

Thut stood in the corner, his wrestler's body draped in gold-fringed linen. A red leather collar spanned his wide shoulders, matching the gold-and-red *henhet* crown, the cobra and vulture standing out in solid gold. He stepped toward her, his hands extended.

Although Chloe stood almost a foot taller, the power of his body was overwhelming. She began to wonder if her hooded guard, tall and muscular though he was, would be any help if Thut decided he wanted more than just companionship.

"Come forward, Lady of Silver. I see you have dressed according to your name." Chloe grasped his warm, meaty paw as he scanned her. A filmy veil of silver cloth encased her body, her only jewelry a filigree silver collar and a white flower in her hair. Though her eyes were ringed with black, she had worn no other makeup or fragrance, despite Basha's obvious attempts to make her as alluring as possible.

Since her own hair made her resemble someone in the latter stages of mange, Basha had covered it with a white-and-silver headcloth. A wig was out. The "other" said that wearing a wig to a private dinner was parallel to offering a date a selection of condoms when he came to pick her up. Not a signal Chloe was interested in sending.

She looked around the room, avoiding Thut's murky gaze. A curtained room stood off to the side, a low rumbling coming from it. She looked at the prince; what was the noise?

He dropped his gaze and called for wine, seeming suddenly nervous. The noise stopped and something heavy fell. A human groan. Was someone hurt? Immediately she was standing in the doorway, the curtain over her shoulder.

It was a studio. A potter's studio.

Chloe blinked and turned to Thut. He drew himself up, refusing to look at her. "It is my hobby," he said stiffly.

She walked in. He was a craftsman? The room's simple whitewashed walls had been used as drawing boards. Imperfect ideas were sketched out and polished in the same hand. A high shelf was lined with bowls, statuettes, and molds. Two large pots were spattered with liquid plaster, and at one table were works in progress.

Picking up a double-handed jug, Chloe turned to Thutmosis. He took it from her grasp, explaining the handles were still wet. Chloe looked at her hands, slightly smudged with paint from the detailed artwork of ram's horns she had held. Beside a bar was a high stool, an unfinished sculpture before it. Bast?

She looked at his paints and a literal, physical yearning gripped her. With a shaking finger she touched his palette. It was rectangular, carved of ivory, the wells for color inscribed with etched hieroglyphs. Ocher, lapis, cadmium, white, malachite, gold, and black. She rubbed the paint between her fingers, gauging the consistency. A little more liquid and it would be perfect for papyrus. Oh! Paint! To be able to create in color!

Thut coughed and Chloe realized she'd wandered through his personal chambers with the disregard of a three-year-old. She felt herself blush and turned, expecting a reprimand. Thut fixed his gaze to the left of her nose. "The projects in the kiln are complete, if you would like . . . ?"

Chloe smiled, the first genuine smile in what seemed like days. They walked to the back, where the air grew hotter and heavier. Through waves of heat she saw large jars, the same double-handled design, and flat plates with painted centers. She leaned down over one to get a better look.

"My lady . . ."

Chloe turned on her heel and walked swiftly through the studio, absently noting the throwing wheel. It felt as if her whole body were red with embarrassment. Pornographic pottery! The picture she'd bent down to see was difficult to comprehend . . . because of the . . . gymnastics the couple were involved in. She slammed a glass of wine.

Out of the corner of her eye she saw the guard. He stood erect, his tanned skin sheened with sweat in the torchlight, his face hidden by a leather mask. She saw that his biceps were pale . . . almost as if he wore armbands, something only nobles wore.

Thut touched her back and she spun, stepping away.

"Does it surprise you that a prince would do something besides rule and conquer?" His nostrils were flared, and Chloe realized he was offended. She shook her head.

"In your understanding of men, Lady of Silver, do we all seek nothing except destruction? To maim? To kill? Do you think conflict is all we live for? Do you think the beauty of life, a child's smile, a beautiful wall painting, a poem of longing . . . that these things are beyond us?"

She backed up.

"A man can be both a conqueror and appreciate the creating arts." He reached for his belt, unlatching it so that the gold-and-leather strip dropped to the ground with a soft thud. "Although I would hate for you to doubt my word." He lunged for her and Chloe ran, dodging the columns and skittering on the mats. He grabbed her wrist, his hand a vise, and twisted it behind her, kissing her with the fury of an outraged ego.

His tongue pressed against her teeth as she turned and twisted. She had height, but he was strong—and angry. He squeezed her breast painfully, and Chloe kneed him. Growling with anger, he threw her away, blinking rapidly. "How dare you refuse my royal attentions!" he said through gritted teeth.

"How dare you defile a priestess of HatHor!" she retorted. "Your manhood is not in question, Horus, your manners are!"

Chloe couldn't tell who was more surprised to hear her speak.

Thut stared with dropped jaw, and the guard stumbled after taking a step toward her. Was she speaking this strange language in her own voice? She pressed a hand to her throat. Thut took a step back, and she ran out of the golden chamber, her guard trailing. Elated, she turned to him. "Where is Lord Cheftu? I must speak with him tonight!"

He shook his head vigorously and in a somewhat choked voice said, "I will tell him my lady's good fortune after I see you safely to your apartments."

Chloe shrugged. He left her at her door and she entered the chamber, whistling. Basha came running out of her adjoining room.

"My lady?"

"Basha, I can speak! I can speak! My voice has been returned to me!" Chloe clapped her hands in delight, grabbed Basha, and began waltzing around the room, stepping all over the girl in the process. "I can talk, I can sing, I can chatter, I can yap—" She looked up and saw Cheftu staring at her from the doorway. He looked stunned, and his body was glazed in perspiration. Chloe stopped and thrust Basha away from her.

"My voice has returned, Lord Cheftu."

She saw his pulse jump as he smiled a wide, courtly smile. "You must be so pleased, Lady RaEm. His Majesty's kisses must carry the healing powers of Thoth himself."

Chloe's face froze. "So the guard was also a spy?"

"Horus-in-the-Nest has presented you with this gift, my lady," Cheftu said. "The slave was instructed to pass on His Majesty's gratitude and pleasure." He stabbed her with a wrapped parcel, a narrow box tied hastily with ribbon.

"I did not—"

Grabbing her arm, he said loudly, "Let us go to the garden, my lady." When they stood beside the fountain in the center of the lotus garden, Cheftu turned to her. "You endanger the lives of us all, RaEm! Your careless behavior is even now in the ears of priests from here to Waset! The Great House will not be pleased. Now your unborn child can be said to be either the incarnation of Amun or the son of Horus-in-the-Nest! Your ability to speak after 'seeing' Thut will read like treason to the Great House. These are uncertain times. You will be in danger. You had best pray Thut is generous with you!"

Chloe pulled her arm out of his grasp. She recognized now what the pain had been when they'd first arrived. It had felt like a zillion fire ants camping out in her throat and chest—the same burning itching that had presaged gaining feeling back in other parts of her body after she'd arrived in ancient Egypt. So she had had the ability to speak for several days but had never tried. *Haii-aiii!* However, her anger toward herself was quite different from her anger toward this uppity man who was always unhappy with her, no matter what.

She said sarcastically, "I ask your great mercy for my voice having returned at an unfortunate time. I have done nothing wrong. Now I may return to the Great House in complete safety, able to explain my actions and assume my responsibilities. Why do you care, anyway? I'm just another notch on your Thoth-headed stick! Your position is secure. I am healed and I am safe!"

Cheftu's face was shaded in the moonlight, but his hard grip around her waist and his long-fingered hand pressing on her tight belly communicated clearly. "Safe, my lady? When even now proof of your broken vows grows within you? When your betrothed, Nesbek, your former lover Pakab, or the soldier Phaemon is the father and could betray you at any moment? Or is it another of your other debauched Egyptian nobles?" He shook her slightly. "Are you mad?"

Chloe's thoughts raced. For the briefest second a man's face flashed before her; his mouth was open, and his eyes were round with disbelief. Before the image faded, she saw blood gush from his mouth. A pair of hands, woman's hands, were covered in his blood. She damned RaEm to a personal hell for not cataloging her memories. Who was that? Why had she seen him?

Cheftu had terrifyingly good points about a father. She placed her hands on his. "If there is a child, it shall not suffer due to my short-comings."

"Then you'd best proclaim it to be the offspring of Amun-Ra, priestess. Say it is a man-child to marry the princess Neferurra and help her rule over Egypt. Then, though Pharaoh herself will hate you, you will have the nominal protection of Hapuseneb. Or rid yourself of it. Herbs grow here along the Nile—"

She cut him off. "Nay. This is a life. I will find a way to protect it." It's not even my own, she thought dazedly. If it *is* at all.

"Meanwhile you also need protection from—" Cheftu's grip lost its intensity but gained in familiarity.

"From Thut," she interrupted. "He would have bedded me tonight had I not shocked him so."

"Maybe from Thut, but also from me," he murmured as he lowered his lips to hers. His kiss was as different from the bestial grunting of Thut as the sun from mud. Chloe's head swam as she leaned into him, feeling the hard heat of his body as she wrapped her arms around his neck, pressing him closer, inhaling his intoxicating scent. She opened her mouth and felt electricity flow between them at contact. When he pulled away his breath was rasping, his eyes gleaming in the dark like a wild animal's.

"What is this enchantment, RaEm?" He lifted a shaking hand and drew it down the side of her face, tracing her lips with the slightest touch. "Why do I desire you and despise you in the same breath? You are no mystery to me, yet I long to know more. Have you cast a spell on me?" He dropped his hand at Chloe's silence and bowed abruptly. "I bid you good evening, my lady," he said, and vanished into the darkness of the garden.

Chloe stood there, trying to catch her breath, to forget the feel of his demanding body, blocking out every other thought on this incredible night.

She still held the gift from Thutmosis. Slowly she unwrapped it.

It fit in her hand. The colors were still wet from Horus' use, the delicate brushes now tucked in the carved pocket beneath the cartouche-embossed lid. His artist's palette.

CHAPTER 7

The morning sun was already creeping across the painted floor when Chloe jerked awake. Soon Basha would be in with the Perfuming of the Mouth. Thank the gods it was only fruit and milk, because even the memory of scrambled eggs, bacon, and coffee sent her out of bed in search of her chamber pot.

A few minutes later, face cool with perspiration, she leaned against the whitewashed wall. She'd ignored the signs long enough. All the wishing in the world would not change what was now a fact.

Apparently she was pregnant, and if this being sick and feeling tired all of the time was pregnancy, then pregnancy *sucked*. Chloe doubted she had slept this much in her entire life. Who was the father? As her mother had always said, "It takes two to tango."

A product of mostly conservative societies, Chloe viewed the sexual conduct of her own country with a mixture of revulsion and surprise. She was still a virgin, a tough decision at times, but one she did not regret.

Her decision dealt partly with opportunity. Most of the guys she went to school with had also been military brats, unwilling to commit to any relationship in a world where one could be yanked away with a phone call. The fear of pregnancy was very real. Unmarried motherhood was never an option; in the Middle East a girl would be killed by her male relatives for disgracing the family name. Likewise she wouldn't want to shame her parents. They expected the most from their daughters.

Most important, however, was Chloe's knowledge that she could not stand to share so intimately with someone and then lose him. Perhaps because of her lifestyle, sexual intimacy had never seemed worth the risk: to not only get naked, but to bare her heart and then be dumped. That part seemed inevitable, to judge from her friends and even by Cammy's short-lived marriage. To wake up alone and abandoned would kill Chloe inside, and she knew that. So she dated, had fun, and made friends of the men who wanted to take her to bed. Maybe it was cowardly. However, it was the only solution she saw.

Joseph had been her one serious boyfriend. He was an Italian American Jew she'd met on a study tour of Italy. He was Orthodox, studying the jeweler's art on the Ponte Vecchio before taking his place in the family business. Their relationship had been less sexual and more romantic. Picnics (of nonkosher foods), walks through the narrow streets, quiet dinners. Even poetry. The tension was there, but he was already engaged, so they both exercised self-control.

They'd known their relationship could go nowhere, but Chloe had been entranced. All her life she had heard negative things about Israel and the Jews, since Saudi Arabia and most of the other Arab countries in which she'd grown up were not among Israel's fans. Then there he was, larger than life, with a thirst for beauty and self-expression that rivaled her own. He'd been beautiful—Michelangelo's David in a black suit with a wide smile and gentle spirit.

So, either because of strength, weakness, or cowardice, she was a virgin.

However, RaEmhetepet was not. She had obviously violated the sacredness of her season of serving. She must have been pregnant before Chloe stepped into her skin. So some guy knew the whole story and was waiting for her to . . . to what? Chloe shook her head, the reasoning always returning to the same point. Banishment was the penalty for RaEm's transgressions and her lover's. Was that what was keeping him silent? Maybe there were too many possibilities to be certain? Again the face—the blood—the woman's hands—flashed through her mind.

She flinched at the sound of sandals in the corridor. Damn, am I nervous, she thought, hoping it wasn't the enraged prince regent. He'd sent her the palette; perhaps he'd forgiven her? Basha came in, balancing a large tray with fruit, beer, and pastry. At the sight, Chloe's stomach rebelled and she turned away.

Later, while lying on a table and being massaged with a lemon-scented oil, she felt a tiny movement deep within, as minuscule as the fluttering of a transparent hand and as significant as the opening of an otherworldly door. She dismissed the slave and sat up, staring at her naked brown belly in amazement.

It moved again. There was life inside her! Chloe covered her stomach protectively, a surge of unknown, fierce emotions coursing through her. "I will take care of you, my little stranger," she whispered in English. "Somehow it will all be okay." She caressed the hardness under her oiled skin; it felt like a tiny ball, lodged between and above her hipbones. "I will protect you," she muttered in awe.

Later Chloe was seated before her dressing table when her visitor was announced. Basha prostrated herself on the floor, and Chloe watched in amazement as a petite woman with the bearing of a goddess stepped into the room. She was trailed by five other women, all dressed alike in white cloaks and silver collars.

Chloe stood, accepting the delicate hand extended to her, racking her brain for information. "Life, health, and prosperity," she said before she clapped her hands and bade Basha get chairs and refreshments. She noted the look of surprise on several of the faces when it became apparent she could speak. Basha returned, instructing the Apiru slaves to position the tables and chairs, setting out wine and fruit.

The leader—Chloe still couldn't remember a name—hadn't stopped staring at Chloe, observing every nuance of her appearance. It made Chloe intensely nervous, considering her recent discovery.

"My sister is recovered. I am pleased, as is our mother HatHor," the woman said in a low, melodious voice. "You shall return to serve the mother tonight, RaEmhetepet."

Chloe smiled, trying to keep outwardly calm. How did she serve the "mother"? If it was tonight, how could she prepare? She drank deeply, stalling for time, her mind racing. One of the other maidens leaned forward and helped the leader—*what was her name?*—out of her cloak, and Chloe choked.

Dangling from her throat, on a delicate silver chain, was Chloe's silver ankh. Actually, not Chloe's, but one almost exactly like it.

The woman leaned forward, calling for water, and Chloe could see the inscription on her necklace. "Little sun," a nickname for five o'clock in the evening. Chloe calmed herself and glanced around. Each woman was wearing the same necklace, but Chloe could not see all the names.

Holy Osiris, she thought. Then the knowledge came rushing in. She was one of the priestesses who prayed through the night, guiding the weakened Ra through his darkened course by praising and singing, invoking the aid of the goddess of love on his behalf. A defensive priestess.

From the time the moon was full until it was horned, she would spend those nights from eleven o'clock until midnight, dancing and singing before the silver statue of the goddess.

Some other nights they would all be summoned to make predictions and would drink the "goddess's milk" and look into the future. Tonight was such a night, and the others could not do it without her. Such was RaEmhetepet's destiny because of her birth date and her ancestry.

This knowledge filled her mind in seconds; suddenly she knew everyone in the room, most of whom she had trained. ReShera, five P.M.; Ruha-et, six o'clock; Herit-tchatcha-ah, seven o'clock; AnkhemNesrt, eight; RaAfu, nine; Gerchet, ten; and Chloe, as RaEmhetepet, was eleven. Petite ReShera was the next most powerful priestess and also a member of the sacred Sisterhood who policed the temples. She was also the missing Phaemon's twin sister, though Chloe remembered nothing of him.

Chloe's gaze flickered to the blue band ReShera wore around her waist. A mourning band. "I am sorry for your loss," she said, indicating the belt. ReShera's eyes flamed with intense passion for just a moment, and the other priestesses held their collective breath. Basha dropped a goblet on the stone floor.

ReShera looked down. "The gods will deal with me and Phaemon, I am certain," she murmured. Her gaze met Chloe's. "About tonight..."

"I look forward to speaking with the goddess," Chloe said. "Although I am unfamiliar with her temple here."

The priestess smiled and said, "It is a secret temple. I will send a litter for you before Ra departs the horizon, sister. Tonight is very important. This desert god of the Apiru is disturbing Ma'at and we must divine what the mother would have us do. Perhaps there is impurity among the priesthood and this is our punishment. We must prepare." She rose to her feet, and the attendant maidens rose with her. "Until the *atmu*," she said, and they left. Basha once more prostrating herself.

•••

Cheftu joined her for lunch, withdrawn but amusing. They played several games of *senet*, one of which Chloe actually won. As they were tidying up the pieces, Chloe asked, "If you were to be something else besides a healer, what would you be?" His face twisted in surprise, then he put on his court mask.

"Why do you ask?"

"Does it matter?" She shrugged. "I guess from seeing Thutmosis and his love of pottery. One doesn't think of pharaohs caring about small things like that."

Cheftu looked at her, his gaze open for a moment. "I would be a scribe."

"Sitting in the marketplace, writing letters for the ignorant?"

"Nay." He looked away, a sad smile on his lips. "I would be a scribe of the times. Tracking the reigns, the traditions, the wars, of Egypt." His tone turned sardonic. "You, RaEm? Would you be the wife of a dozen men?"

Chloe stiffened. What a jerk! She'd tried for peace and look how he'd behaved!

"My lady, I apol—"

She cut him off. "Good afternoon, Cheftu. I must prepare for my duties of office tonight." Her shoulders were stiff as she walked away . . . she had only two hours.

When the litter arrived, she was dressed. After two hot baths and an icy one, Basha had started sharpening a blade to shave Chloe's head. No way. Whether or not she was in RaEm's body, with RaEm's genes, Chloe wasn't going to run the risk of cutting her hair again. It had just started to be manageable, and she knew it would take forever to grow out. It wouldn't do to go back to her own time looking like a radiation victim. She'd have enough to explain as it was. And she *was* going back.

Basha was shocked, but she was also obedient and put away the shears and razor. She pulled out the pleated white tunic Chloe was to wear and a long, fringed shawl. After slipping the tunic over her head, Basha tied the shawl, thoroughly covering Chloe's hips and thighs.

Now why can't I dress this way all the time? Chloe thought. It certainly was not underwear, but it covered just the same. The shawl was beautiful, its blue and white stripes shot with silver threads and tiny embroidered horns and ankhs.

Basha brought out the jewelry trunk, and Chloe, consulting her "other" memory, selected a silver circlet with horns, a disk, and a filigreed feather, and a malachite-and-silver bracelet. Basha then tied a headcloth of woven silver on Chloe's head, the folds falling over her shoulders and down her back. She put the circlet on top and bowed.

"My lady is ready?"

Chloe wondered at the lack of makeup, but when Basha draped her in a hooded cloak, she got the feeling it wouldn't matter. She heard the jingle of tiny bells in the hallway, and when the door opened she saw a similarly shrouded person waiting.

She noticed the other woman was not wearing sandals, and turning to Basha, saw she was once more prostrated. Who is this that Basha should behave this way? Chloe thought, then forgot her question as she was helped into the waiting litter and its curtains were drawn.

Once inside, a powerfully sweet odor assailed her, and Chloe had to breathe through her mouth to keep from gagging. They were carried up and down streets, until the light coming through the curtains had almost faded.

When they stopped, Chloe was the first to climb out, almost falling out when she realized she was stepping on another person. They were at the doors of a small temple, its ruined columns covered in ivies and vines—quite a bit different from the encroaching desert in every other temple location.

She walked through the hypostyle hall, for the temple was built according to the plan of Karnak. The paint had long ago faded from the hallway walls, and the jewels had been removed from the depictions of HatHor and her various myths.

The opposite wall told the story of HatHor going to Nubia, where she had assumed the shape of a wildcat and wrought absolute destruction until the god Thoth, in the guise of a baboon, cajoled her back to Egypt.

Chloe could read every word and had the smallest vision of a schoolroom where she had written out the story many, many times as punishment for . . . for what? Oh, joy, she thought. Another unanswered question.

They walked to the back of the temple, threading their way through a dense forest of HatHor-headed columns. They stepped into the goddess's chamber, and Chloe looked around. The walls had once been covered with silver, the "other" said, but most of it had been removed, leaving only a glint of the sacred metal here and there.

The barque where the silver statue should reside was empty, but there was a low table with the ritual offerings of grain and beer standing before the clearest depiction of HatHor. Goddess of music, dancing, laughter, drunkenness, and love, she also foretold the future of children, in the form of seven exquisitely beautiful women. Each of the maidens here was a physical counterpart to each of the seven HatHors. Egypt was the child whose future they would predict.

Oh, Camille, Chloe thought, you would not *believe* this!

They sat down at scattered tables, each place designated by a goblet and plate. Chloe saw her name, RaEmhetepet, etched on the silver and chose a nearby chair. Each of the maidens sat down, ending with ReShera next to her. In a motion they all pulled off their hoods and dropped their cloaks around them.

The six HatHors sat looking at her, and Chloe had to agree they were the most gorgeous women she had seen in Egypt, including Hatshepsut. No one was wearing makeup, which served to accentuate their beautifully sculpted features. Some were tall and willowy, others, like ReShera, petite and delicate. All were wearing the silver cloths and circlets. She alone wore the horns and disk and Feather of Truth. They were like an ancient sorority, Chloe thought, amused.

It seemed to be up to her to get started. As she glanced around, a child brought a silver dagger and laid it before her. Chloe raced through her mind, searching for some of RaEm's clues, but could locate nothing except some chants for an Apis fertility ritual.

She looked to ReShera, bewildered. "Sister?" she prompted.

With a gentle smile ReShera placed a hand on her wrist. "The mother understands, RaEm. I will take responsibility. May I have the sacred dagger?"

Relieved, Chloe handed it to her and watched as she walked to a far alcove. Slaves led forth a white cow hidden there. It must be drugged, Chloe thought, because it just stood there, watching the dagger with almost human eyes.

She looked around. The maidens were weeping. Silent tears streaked their perfect faces as they watched ReShera approach the cow, torchlight flickering off the silver threads in her shawl and headcloth.

She stood before the cow and slowly raised the dagger in the air. Throwing back her head, she began her prayer in a high, keening wail that echoed through the empty temple, freeing the spirits to worship.

"O Mother HatHor, Divine Sister of Amun-Ra, Lover of all Beauty, Defender of the Sacred Eye, please come to thy own. In desperation for thy goodwill we seek the flesh of this animal. Nurture thy own through its blood and milk. Guide thy own for the continuation of Ma'at, the holy balance of the universe. Gird thy own like lionesses to seek that which has weakened the holy order of priesthood. Mother, grant us thy power, thy ruthlessness, they all-seeing vision."

She plunged the knife into the cow, its anguished moo mingling with the wails of ReShera and the maidens. Blood spurted from the wound in the cow's side, and slaves ran forward with silver pitchers to catch the flow. As soon as the pitchers were full, ReShera removed her shawl and stanched the wound. The cow was led away and ReShera brought the pitchers to the table.

Chloe began to sweat: things were looking pretty strange. A slave poured the steaming blood into their goblets, and Chloe resisted the urge to cover hers with her hand; she didn't dare. Gerchet clapped her hands and the servants came forward with what looked like a stew but smelled like curdled milk. They scooped a portion for each maiden; Chloe wanted to gag. It was some kind of meat stew, cooked in milk.

ReShera raised her hands to heaven. *"O Lovely HatHor. Bless thy own as we consume our holy meal. Prepare thy own for the Field of Reeds in the milk of thy provision, just as this kid was prepared for eternity in the milk of its mother. Bless us, Mother Goddess."*

The priestess dropped her hands and lifted her glass. "Tonight we need special assistance from the mother. We must set aside our daily concerns and live only for her knowledge." She turned to Chloe, her hand outstretched. "The vial, my sister."

Chloe stared at her. Vial? Closing her eyes, she remembered a tiny, detachable part that slipped onto her circlet. Slowly she reached up and found the silver disk. She couldn't get it out. "Allow me, sister priestess," ReShera said, and, standing, pulled out the two-inch round disk.

Tapping it smartly with a long fingernail, she popped it open and then put a pinch in her goblet of warm blood. Holy shit! Chloe thought. What am I in for? Camille never mentioned drinking blood or doing drugs! ReShera handed the vial to her, and Chloe had no choice except to add a pinch to her own "beverage." Herit-tchatcha-ah dug into her meal, tearing the flesh from the bones and soaking it in the milk before she ate it. Chloe followed suit, trying not to think about what she was eating. It couldn't be worse than chocolate-covered locusts, she thought. She *hoped.*

Finally the meat and milk were gone, and ReShera raised her goblet. The maidens, including Chloe, followed suit and drained them. Chloe swallowed harshly, her face twisted in a grimace behind her goblet.

Each woman set down her cup, not wiping away her macabre mustache. Chloe felt the blood begin to dry on her face, but table manners didn't appear to be much of a priority.

The slaves cleared away the dishes, then the table, and just around the time Chloe was about to fall onto the floor, they brought cushions. She felt strangely light as she stared up at the dark ceiling. RaAfu began to wail, then each of the women joined in. Unfortunately, to Chloe's twentieth-century ears they were not all in the same key, but another part of Chloe opened her mouth. When in Egypt . . .

AnkhemNesrt began a prayer. Everyone chimed along, not at the same time and definitely not in the same pitch. Chloe sang, too, neither comprehending nor recalling the words that came from her mouth. Something about seeing into the future and protecting Egypt . . . but Chloe wasn't certain.

Her mind filled with hazy memories. She was watching herself with an Arab, their bodies laced together like ribbons, straining, seeking pleasure. Camille was in the doorway, shocked almost beyond recognition. The Arab man looked familiar as he covered himself. Chloe reclined naked and unashamed in the bed, her large brown eyes hostile and angry.

Ruha-et's piercing yowl brought Chloe out of her reverie. Gerchet's wails had become screams, and when Chloe struggled to sit up, she saw ReShera weaving around the room, eyes wide and pupils dilated, promising to be HatHor's hand of vengeance, to cleanse the priesthood so that Egypt could defeat the slaves' desert god.

Then, like a top that had lost momentum, ReShera spiraled around backward and fell flat, her voice cut off midscreech. Leaning on an elbow she barely remembered having, Chloe watched the twisting, tortuous dance of three of the maidens. Chloe thought it was seven, eight, and ten o'clock, but what with everyone wearing the same clothes and . . . it was bloody hard to tell.

She started to giggle at all of them, staggering around like some ancient version of the Seven Stooges, stepping on each other, crashing into walls, tripping over nothing. Her giggles grew louder as she got to her feet and careened after them. It was like bumper cars, only not as jarring, since she couldn't feel anything.

The torchlight joined in the dance, the orange flickers fading to white and then turning into . . . Gene Kelly! What was he doing in ancient Egypt? He looked so young!

She opened her mouth to ask, but before he could answer he morphed into a huge Dr. Seuss Starbelly Sneech. When she reached out to touch his belly, someone grabbed her arm and pulled. They let go, but Starbelly was gone, just a large flaming brazier before her.

She looked around the chamber. The maidens had collapsed on the floor, like heaps of crumpled laundry. Chloe yawned. It did look comfortable, so, with all the grace of a felled sequoia, she joined them.

• • •

Chloe awoke in her own room. It was still dark, which was good, since even the reflection of the moon on her linen sheets made her wince. The pounding in her head gave the term "hung over" a profoundly nasty meaning. She eased out of bed, moving very slowly to keep the room from spinning out of control.

What did I drink last night? The memory of her copper-scented cocktail sent her lurching toward the bath chamber. Unfortunately there was a wall. The impact knocked Chloe to her knees as Basha screamed out, "My lady, my lady!"

The slave girl came running toward her, sounding like a dinosaur out of Jurassic Park. *"Are you well, my lady?"* she screamed. Chloe clutched her head, leaning against the wall.

Quietly and succinctly Chloe whispered, "My head is exploding. I am about to die. If you make one more sound, I will have you skinned alive."

Basha gasped in fear. Evidently the slave girl had no sense of humor. Chloe was led to her chamber pot and left in silence.

• • •

The morning sun grazed Chloe's face, and she pulled up the blanket and turned over. Amazingly, she felt okay, at least compared with last night. Memories of the nasty liquid Basha had forced down her came rushing back, but at least her stomach stayed where it was.

As for last night, talk about hallucinating! She laughed aloud when she remembered the Starbelly. I always loved Dr. Seuss, she thought, chuckling. But those other memories? Couldn't be me, and certainly not with Cammy watch—

Hold a bloody minute, Chloe's mind raced. What if what I saw was not a memory, not a dream, but a look at the future? We *were* asking to see the future. But why would I have brown eyes? The answer hit with such impact, she fell back onto the couch. RaEmhetepet had had brown eyes; now she had green. What if RaEm kept her own eyes and stepped into my skin . . . in the twentieth century! What could she be doing to my life?

Could that drug have opened my mind enough to see 3,500 years into the future? I don't believe in these ancients' gods, but that was potent stuff I drank. Could it have done that? What else could it be? What is she doing to my life? The pain on Camille's face had made her almost unrecognizable. Who was that guy? Why would he sleep with RaEm? He doesn't think it is RaEm. He thinks it's me! Damn!

Basha was not around, and Chloe ran to the chest, looking for the circlet she had worn last night. It was nowhere to be found. Frantically she tore through the other chests, spilling kilts, sheaths, collars, and sandals into a gaudy multicolored mess on the polished floor. It was not here.

Chloe was startled by a knock on the door. Seeing no Basha, she crossed the chamber and opened it. Cheftu stood there, impressive and approachable in a simple kilt, headcloth, and faience collar. His golden eyes widened briefly, and Chloe thought she even saw the corner of his mouth lift for the briefest second.

Then he was Cheftu. Confusing, frustrating, arrogant, watchdog supreme. Cheftu, who'd thrown her olive branch in the fire. "My lord?" Chloe inquired in her haughtiest "RaEm" tone.

He inclined his head. "Life, health, and prosperity! The prince has invited us to join him fowl hunting in the marshes today." He looked away. "I was unaware you would be, uh, indisposed, this morning."

Chloe looked down. She was wearing a brief sleeping shift, and she could feel her hair in short clumps on her head. The desire to wipe away Lord Cheftu's obvious opinion that she did nothing except scream and faint overrode all else.

"I am quite well, my lord, and would greatly enjoy such a journey. If you will but wait a few minutes, I will change and be with you." She stepped back to admit him to the room and saw with satisfaction the surprise, quickly hidden, on his face. She walked ahead of him, clapping her hands for a slave.

"See that my lord is served the Perfuming," she instructed, "and begin my bath." With what she thought was a singularly gracious smile, Chloe left Cheftu seated on the delicate reed chair as she raced into her sleeping room ready to strangle an already scared Basha.

In record time for an Egyptian noblewoman, Chloe stepped into the sitting room. Cheftu rose to his feet, again surprised. "My lady . . . ?"

Chloe walked to the chair opposite him and bade him sit. "I too need to break my fast. Please join me." In silence they ate crusty rolls and juicy fruit, though Chloe turned away with a grimace the fresh milk Cheftu offered.

He kept sneaking sideways looks at her. Chloe tried not to smirk. RaEm had rarely risen before the midday meal, she knew. She always took at least two hours to dress. Did I beat *that* record, she thought, munching triumphantly.

Cheftu was surprised. Be honest, he told himself, you are shocked. The prince had requested RaEm's presence, and Cheftu had told him it was a hopeless cause, but he would ask nonetheless. Provided she was still speaking to him after yesterday. By the Feather, her question was so uncharacteristic!

He arrived here, and RaEm herself had opened the door, looking for all the world as though she had just left her lover's couch, and informed him she would go. Then she'd walked in, only a few minutes later, as radiant as the sun, a short kilt swinging above her sleek, shapely legs and a linen shirt displaying a sense of modesty he had seen in RaEm once. A modesty he found decidedly alluring.

She finished her meal and stared out at the garden, her legs crossed and one sandaled foot swaying. Her short hair was unadorned, and except for kohl around her eyes, she was not made up. She was more appealing than Cheftu had imagined.

"A bead for your thoughts," he said quietly.

A bittersweet smile crossed her lips. "My family."

"Have you heard from Makab?"

"Makab?" She looked startled. "Uh, nay. He is not much for corre-spondence," she said quickly.

Too quickly, Cheftu thought and frowned. The Makab he knew wrote almost constantly. He watched her eat some dates, her long fin-gers gracefully picking out the pits—something wasn't adding up. Her questions, her mannerisms, her movements, her attitude. *Haii*, holy Isis, her kisses!

The effect she had on him was devastating. He felt like a green boy, shaky and uncertain. He cared, he actually cared what she thought. By the gods! Was he mad? He knew what type of woman she was. She was bored and banished, and of course she would become what he wanted; she could not stand to be alone. Once back in her own environment, she would again grow her scales and fangs. Remember that, fool, he chided himself. She wouldn't be a good deceiver if you weren't deceived.

● ● ●

The outing was in honor of the seven HatHor priestesses. They very rarely traveled beyond Waset or their home nomes. It also was a cele-bration of having water again. Though dangerously bereft of life, the Nile was once more a muddy blue green. Not only had the blood killed the fish, but the crocodiles and a lot of the waterfowl had starved. Egypt was hunting the remainder. Great conservation technique, Chloe thought wryly.

Thut had prepared three boats and assembled a group of courtiers and soldiers to fill out the numbers. Each of the golden barges was flying Thut's cartouche, embroidered on the red of the military. Chairs and tables sat clustered in groups on the deck and near a sheltered rest area, curtained from the sun's heat. Another skiff was outfitted for dinner, and the smells of baking bread and brewing beer carried on the breeze.

The seven o'clock priestess was impressed with Cheftu. Chloe saw that immediately and was surprised by a jolt of—*surely not jealousy.* A lean young noble walked over to Chloe, and Cheftu excused himself. After retrieving a flagon of wine, he folded his long body at seven's feet and proceeded to flirt outrageously with her.

Chloe focused on the man standing before her. He was in his mid-twenties, but the firm lines of his face had blurred with rapacious living. He took the throwing stick from her hand and gently swatted her with it. "RaEm, my dearest protégée. I miss you since you have taken to playing with Nesbek. Is that exclusive now? Or is your form of punishing me to let others taste your talents?" His voice was like a whiny child's, but his gaze spooked Chloe. Another one of RaEm's old lovers. Pakab. Again he hit her with the stick, this time not so gently. "Has Bastet got your tongue?"

The next time he raised the stick, Chloe caught it on the way down. Pakab looked surprised, then a sneaky smile spread across his face, emphasizing his full, sensuous lips. His eyes glittered for just a moment. "Just so, priestess. It is best to play it straight in *his*," he emphasized, "presence." Pakab leaned forward and whispered into her ear, "It is so good to have you back in Goshen. Please forgive me, for I cannot wait for us to play again." He tongued her inner ear and Chloe flinched, but Pakab was already walking away, his arm around one of the older "ladies" of the court.

Chloe felt ReShera's gaze on her, and her blood chilled at the woman's look of reproach and horror. Chloe tried to smile, but ReShera turned away. The beautiful day suddenly palled. Cheftu occasionally looked her way, like a nursemaid, but was utterly focused on the elegant features and expressive hands of seven. Chloe didn't even bother recalling her name in Egyptian.

Thutmosis was his usual bellicose self, his throwing stick in the air more than in his hand, the naked serving girls swarming around him like bees to lotus. He looked over at Chloe periodically but made no move to approach her.

Chloe finally understood the phrase "alone in a crowded room."

RaEm had little talent with the throwing stick—that information was available readily enough—and Chloe didn't have the heart to try. All the faking, the constant charade, even the lack of underwear, was fully exhausting. The knowledge that RaEm could be wearing her skin and ruining her life . . . and now with the child . . . Chloe refused to pursue the thought. At some point she would have to escape or hide. As HatHor's priestess she was not allowed to have a child outside of the marriage laws. Of course, she was also supposed to be a virgin, but the law had been amended so that she had to be "pure" only during the time she served in the temple.

Chloe looked at the other maidens, these beautiful, seemingly pristine women from the best families. Did any of them have her secret? She doubted there was an ancient Egyptian maternity home where she could be a Jane Doe. She gripped the side of the boat, watching as one of the many trained cats leapt into the marshes and retrieved a bird felled by Thut's stick.

Clearing her mind, Chloe watched the succession of birds that dropped out of the sky—less as the day passed and the participants imbibed. Cheftu was having a grand old time, his head in the lap of seven and ten caressing his feet. Chloe felt invisible. Okay, jealous. And lonely . . . bone-jarringly, wrenchingly, lonely. When could she go home? Anything to see Cammy's rotten color sense, to hear Mom rant on about this acquisition and that technique and oh! your father's amazing whatever . . . anything Father did was amazing to Mom. To see Father fill his pipe . . .

The blue green of the Nile blurred.

Chloe felt a warm hand on her shoulder.

Thutmosis stood behind her. "I hope you will dine with me this evening, Lady of Silver. It . . . we have gotten off to a bad start. I would like a chance to remedy any false impressions you may have." Chloe was touched by what was obviously a taxing and humbling speech, delivered with all the charm of which Thut was capable.

"I would be most honored, Prince," she lied. They stood in uncomfortable silence for a while before the noise of a group of women retiring to change gave Chloe the chance for which she had been searching. Mingling with the delicate flowers of Egyptian society, Chloe went to the other skiff, where linen curtains were set up so the women could dress. She noted that the curtains only accentuated what went on behind them and saw that the men on Thut's boat seemed less inclined to hunt and more inclined to gawk. Probably the whole point.

The seven HatHors gathered together, and Chloe noticed that outside of necessary information exchange, they did not actually speak to each other. In fact, the group seemed quite strained, the tension thick enough to strike with a throwing stick.

By the time Chloe was dressed her mind was hopelessly muddled. She reached for her necklace, holding on to it fiercely. It was the one thing still recognizable in her life. Yet it was different. She looked down at it. The vision of the brown-eyed Chloe leapt before her. A brown-eyed Chloe with a silver chain ankh that also said RaEmhetepet. She dropped the ankh on its malachite-and-lapis-beaded chain against her breast. It looked like hers, but it was RaEm's. Her necklace, like her whole life, was gone. Replaced by an imperfect reflection of the reality.

She joined the others on the party barge. The deck was arranged like a theater in the round, ladies seated together on one side, nobles on the other. In the center was a circular space for Thut's many entertainers. Lotus garlands were draped the length of the vessel, and all guests were handed a blue lily for their costumes. Like most of the women, Chloe wore hers in her wig, fastened so that the cup of the flower fell just across her forehead, bathing her in its fragrance.

Baskets of fruit and flowers adorned small tables. Beautifully painted false columns rose above the company's heads, giving the illusion of a portico floating on the Nile. Chloe noticed bags of water tied in the air, suspended between the columns, and the "other" told her it was to ward off mosquitoes.

Metal dishes reflected pools of light, the wind flitting shadows across the retinue and the still water. Far above them the stars hung, their reflections in the Nile doubly draping the night in brilliance.

Slaves wearing wigs and strategically placed strings of beads wandered about, offering cones of scented wax for people's heads. In the course of the evening the cones would melt, dripping their fragrance into wigs and onto clothing, placating that most important of Egyptian senses, smell. Chloe thought it was disgusting—long greasy fingers that caressed her neck and slid farther down onto her sweaty skin—but since she was wearing a formal wig this evening, she paid little attention to the mess.

Everything smelled: the waxy perfume, the bushels of flowers draping everything that was still, the sweat of the scurrying Apiru and aroused guests, the wine and beer, and above all, the stink of the Nile marsh. Chloe felt nauseated again.

Each guest had a glass goblet. Young boys, bodies shaved, their youthlocks braided with ribbons, passed through the company, filling them with date wine or beer. After about three sips of a very potent wine, Chloe felt her heavy wig gaining weight and her stomach wrenching in protest. Though she was dying of thirst, there was little else to choose from, so she contented herself with watering her drink.

A hush fell over the crowd.

Thut was announced, and Chloe crossed her breast in respect, as did the entire company. As Thut took his seat, a slave scurried over to Chloe, inviting her to join Horus-in-the-Nest. She noted with surprise that the slave was not Egyptian, but of another, lighter-skinned race. He was just painted to look Egyptian. The entertainment was beginning. Chloe felt her body involuntarily begin to sway to the beat of the sistrum and the wail of the double flute.

She smiled warily at Thut as he leaned forward and tucked a lotus into her gown, between her breasts. Then dancers came in, whirling in flashes of scent and skin, torches glinting off their jeweled belts and collars. They were not Egyptian; Chloe was astonished to see a redhead, her long hair braided into thousands of tiny strands, leading the group. They whirled like dervishes, jumping over each other and leaping into the air. The "other" recognized them as Kefti. The dance grew slow. As the spinning became a seductive sway, Chloe noticed that conversation had all but halted and quite a few perfume cones were beginning to melt. Next to her she heard Thut's heavy breathing as he watched every movement the redhead made.

Chloe didn't see Cheftu anywhere.

She tried not to care, engrossing herself in the intricacies of the dance and the sonorous plucking of the several harps. Once more the dancers increased their pace, and the group, including Chloe, clapped along.

Finally the girls collapsed into graceful bows at Thut's feet, their breathing rough from the exertion of the dance. The assembly cheered them lightly, more so when the redhead was motioned forward and Thut handed her a ring from his own finger.

She was a tiny thing, Chloe thought, barely five feet, most of it covered in flame-colored braids. The girl looked up at Horus for a brief moment, and Chloe saw that her eyes were brown and heavily lashed—and that she hated Horus with every bone in her delicate body. The dancer dropped her glance quickly and bowed again, but not before two of Thut's nobles exchanged glances and put their hands on their daggers. Several of the girls were pulled onto nobles' laps as they passed through the party. The redhead was untouched; the claim Horus made on her was unbreachable.

Next came the wrestlers, an Egyptian favorite. They circled each other in the small space, their wide bodies clothed only in fishermen's pierced leather loincloths. Their backs were tattooed, not in Egyptian motifs, but in a delicate, curving tracery that created flowers, gardens, birds, and fish from ink and skin. They jumped at each other, encouraged by the wine-induced crowd, grappling like lovers. The party grew more boisterous, clanging their glasses on the tables. Chloe noticed that the heavily segregated group had become much more mixed. Even a priestess or two was seated next to a bejeweled noble.

Everything came to a halt when the cupbearer Rekhmire presented the stuffed and roasted birds to Thutmosis. The wrestlers drew apart, bowed to Thut, and left. One by one the dishes were laid on the low table beside Thut. When no more plates could fit Thut bellowed, "Serve my faithful ones, Rekhmire!" The cupbearer bowed before the cheers of the intoxicated crowd and began passing around the crispy birds.

"I have had yours especially prepared," Thut said to Chloe as the cupbearer presented it. She swallowed hard. The "other" flooded her brain with information. For Thut to kill and have her served the bird was an accepted courtship ritual. They would eat it together, perhaps even feed each other the choicest bits. This was not the gesture of a sleazeball. He was taking the first step toward marriage.

Chloe glanced around the room. Thut's wife, Isis, was not here; presumably she was watching his son, Turankh, who was the heir to the throne and Thut's pride and joy. "My lady? Does it please you?" She met Thut's muddy gaze, then dropped her glance to the crispy fowl. It looked yummy, if you liked blackened food. The smell of baked honey and figs rose from it, and she lifted a hand.

Thut placed a hand on hers. "Wait for the taster, Lady of Silver." He motioned to one of the slaves standing by, who crossed his chest and accepted the piece of Chloe's roasted duck. The taster chewed and swallowed as the company looked on, this spectacle much more exciting than the slowly swaying musicians. He bowed again and departed, but Thut held Chloe's hand firmly in his own. Smiling in the depths of his dark brown eyes, he passed her his cup. "Wait for a few more moments, lady," he said, watching her drink.

Another slave was directed to go through the same for Thut, and he had just torn a piece of the meat from the bone when a shout went up from the other side of the room. Rekhmire immediately ran forward. The slave who had eaten from Chloe's hand was collapsed on the deck, his hand to his stomach as he heaved dryly, his whole body shaking.

Thut bellowed for a physician. The group watched the slave, yet no one moved to help him. Chloe saw the tears of pain race down his face as his body tried desperately to rid itself of the food. Sweat coated her body, icy trails running down her back despite the heat of the evening. *That had been her food.* The world receded until all she heard was Thut blustering about who had been responsible for the food preparation. How could he get sick so quickly? Was he allergic? Was he poisoned? the "other" asked.

The slave sank into unconsciousness, his shadowed form shrinking into the darkness. The party was silent as Cheftu ran onto the deck and knelt over the body of the slave. Chloe walked forward shakily.

The man lay facedown. Chloe crimped her nose against the odor of the contents of his stomach spattered with blood and mucus along the wooden deck. Thut stood, his lip curled in disgust. "I would know who tried to kill me!"

"My prince," Cheftu said, "he is unable to hear your questions."

"Rouse him, then!" Thut spat.

Cheftu licked his lips, obviously irritated. "My prince, the man is ill. No one tried to kill you. He is just sick as one of the hazards of preparing food in the heat of Ra."

Thut's brow lowered. "Then take him back to Avaris and have him watched. I want to know the moment he awakens . . . and how this food affects him." He clapped his hands and turned to his guests. "Lord Cheftu will see to this slave. Let us continue our feast!" Obediently they walked back to their chairs. The graceful musicians began to play, and the slaves unobtrusively started to clean.

Chloe saw Cheftu boarding one of the smaller skiffs, directing the slaves to carry their companion. Cheftu's kilt glowed in the flickering torchlight, and Chloe realized with a shock that he was not wearing any of the jewelry and makeup an Egyptian would. Or a headcloth. His hair, which she had never seen before, was thick and black with just a glint of blue in the torchlight. He had looked so familiar . . . and so touchable.

She quickly scanned the deck of the other ship, which was preparing to sail, when she saw the larger blob of white—a sheath—blend with the white of Cheftu's kilt.

Chloe jerked her gaze away. Seven was gone; Chloe knew with a sinking feeling that the priestess was the reason Cheftu had been unadorned and absent. Pasting a fake smile on her face, Chloe suddenly reversed her earlier decision and took the large blue glass cup the slave girl offered her. Thut was engrossed in conversation with his nobles, so Chloe downed her drink, determined to forget every aspect of the evening. Soon.

• • •

Once again, she awoke hung over and uncertain as to how she had gotten to bed. I've got to stop doing this, she thought as she hid her head under the linen bedclothes to avoid the bright rays of Ra.

Basha crept into her chamber, offering a tray of milk and fruit in a whisper. Chloe took a sip of the milk, then ran for the chamber pot, one hand clutching her head, the other her stomach. Someone pounded on the door, and her stomach curled into a tighter knot. Go away, she thought, tears streaming down her face. Basha was gone quite a while, and when she came in, she avoided Chloe's gaze. With gentle hands she guided Chloe to the massage table and began rubbing a soothing mint lotion into her heated skin. She massaged Chloe's temples as Chloe thought about the past few nights. Was this RaEm's lifestyle? Party all night and sleep most of the day? She had to modify her behavior if— no, make that *since*—she was pregnant. Chloe closed her eyes as Basha's motions became drugging.

"It is the beginning of the month, my lady," Basha said. Her voice was wobbly. "Shall I call a seer for you?"

Chloe searched through her memory, and the information she found was scary. Like most upper-class Egyptians, RaEm had her horoscope cast almost every day, and the way the sacred sticks fell determined her daily actions and decisions. However, Chloe also saw that since she had been "out of favor" with the gods, not having her horoscope read for the past several months was perfectly acceptable. Assuming RaEm's haughtiest tone, Chloe responded, "Of course, you foolish girl. As if you need ask such a thing! Do it immediately!"

Basha ran from the room, leaving a sticky mess in the center of Chloe's back. "I didn't mean *immediately* immediately," Chloe said to the empty room.

BASHA RAN FROM LADY RAEMHETEPET'S APARTMENTS, fleeing the lady's wrath. She was so hard to understand. Most of the time she was nice— demanding, since she was unwell so often, but appreciative. Quite unlike her normal behavior. Then there would be these outbursts, and she would be the same hated mistress who had beaten Basha and threatened her until she came under the protection of the Sisterhood.

The girl stopped running and took refuge from Ra's heat under a tree. It was so sticky in Avaris, not at all like the clean, dry heat of Waset. No one was around, and Basha carefully removed the papyrus roll that had been addressed to Lady RaEm. No less than the Great House guard had delivered it. The herald was most insistent to hand it to the lady in person, and Basha had resorted to lies—RaEm was ill and contagious—to buy herself time. She needed to go to the hidden temple and give this to her mistress. She smiled to herself, imagining how pleased the great lady would be with her. She arched her back against the tree; how would she be rewarded?

"Basha?"

She jerked to attention, crumpling the papyrus in her hand, hiding it behind her back. Lord Cheftu! "My lord." She knew her voice was cracking. He smiled and inquired after Lady RaEm, his pale eyes noting briefly the hand behind her back. He made her nervous, this big, reserved man. Her mistress said he was not to be trusted; he had failed the Great House.

"What have you?" he asked with a smile. Basha realized belatedly that she had not been paying attention to the conversation.

"My lord?"

"A sweet from the tray of the lady?" He smiled ingratiatingly and took a step closer to her. "I will not betray you. Will you share a bite?"

The edge of his collar touched her bare breast, and she recoiled. His flesh stank, heavy and alien. "Have no fear, little one, I will not harm you." He lied easily, she thought. His gaze was fixed on hers, his lips moving, telling lies. ReShera said lies were all men knew. In the blink of an eye his hand snaked out and grabbed her wrist, pulling her into his arms so he could see the papyrus.

The words he muttered she did not recognize. They were not Egyptian. He thrust her away from him, pale beneath his dark skin. Basha didn't wait for his permission but fled. She didn't know where the temple was, but she would find a contact. If this missive caused an *erpa-ha* to pale, her lover needed the information.

CHAPTER 8

Chloe was sitting in the peaceful garden, watching the wind stir the blue lotus and fuchsia bougainvillea, when Basha ran to her and fell at her feet like a melodramatic heroine.

"What is it?" she asked, sitting up straight.

"My lady, they killed her! She confessed and they killed her!"

"Killed whom? What are you talking about?" But Basha was weeping, talking about guilt and innocence, how it was all her fault. Chloe pulled the girl up and slapped her sharply across the face, the only instant remedy for hysteria that she knew.

Basha was immediately silent, her eyes sparking with a hate she didn't try to disguise.

Recoiling from the slave, Chloe sat back in her chair. "What happened?" she asked, trying to smile yet chilled by the expression in the girl's eyes.

"The dancer confessed to trying to murder Horus-in-the-Nest by poisoning your duck," Basha stated, her gaze now on the ground. Her tone was curt, but Chloe didn't have the nerve or the heart to reprimand her.

"The dancer?"

"The Kefti dancer."

Of course! Chloe thought. The girl's obvious hatred for Thut, noted not only by her. "She confessed?"

"After two days of questioning," Basha answered dully. "At first she denied it, but they persuaded her that she was guilty. She said she'd poisoned yours because she knew it was impossible to get to his."

"How——?"

"Drawn and quartered by His Majesty's favorite four steeds." Basha's voice was hollow, and she had begun to shake. Shock, delayed shock. Why?

"Basha," Chloe said, but the girl was beyond hearing her. She got up and knelt beside her. "Basha?" She lifted a hand and winced as the girl cowered, shielding her face. "I only slapped you because you were scared," she explained softly. "Basha?"

The slave was frozen, staring at the ground, her shoulders hunched as if warding off a blow. The terribly brief class Chloe had taken in psychology told her the girl was probably a victim of some sort, but Chloe couldn't guess more. She pulled Basha up, careful to move slowly, and led her into her sparsely decorated room. Automatically Basha curled into a fetal position, and Chloe pulled a light blanket over her. Cheftu would know what to do.

She heard steps in the main room and stepped out. Nesbek stood there, glowering at her. "Up to your old tricks with the slaves? Why waste your talents, my lady?"

Entering the room slowly, she looked at this repulsive stranger whom she, RaEmhetepet, was supposed to marry in less than three months' time. She could not fathom her instant and all-encompassing loathing for him. However, it rose like a fever from every pore in her body. She'd avoid him at almost any cost.

He bowed slightly over her hand, and Chloe's skin crawled when he turned it palm up and licked. Two palace servants watched every move, and Chloe fought the urge to yank back her hand and flip him like a stranded roach. That would not be politically correct—he had something on her, and she had to know what. However, she couldn't keep her lip from curling in revulsion. He saw her expression, and his eyes darkened with an unnamed passion.

"My touch causes your petals to wither, Lotus? It used to make you bloom." Chloe withdrew her hand and wiped it covertly on her sheath. She dismissed the servants and walked into the garden, struggling for some diplomatic way to tell him she would rather mate with the crocodile-headed god Sobek. She gazed at the ground, the picture, she hoped, of innocence.

"Nay. It is not you, my lord. I find all such contact displeasing." Too late she realized her mistake and felt blood rush to her face.

"Who else have you allowed to touch you, sacred priestess?" His words were polite, but he threw venom with each word. He advanced and seized both her wrists in a surprisingly crushing grip. "I know your little secrets, RaEm," he snarled. "I would also know your reasoning behind this coyness." He dropped her hands and stepped back. "Is the prince in your sights now? He would not stomach the real you. The lovers I am so generous to share you with would be cold and alone." Nesbek smiled, his gold teeth flashing. "He would be appalled if he knew your fondness for bruised slaves. Do not be a fool, RaEm! He would demand your death and leave you unburied and unmourned."

The ancient Egyptian part of Chloe blanched at the thought. To be forgotten in this world and the next. Her bodiless *ka* flying endlessly through time and space with no rest . . . ever. Nesbek let RaEm have lovers? What a strange relationship. And bruised slave flesh? That might explain Basha's cowering. Chloe managed a shaky smile. "I have the protection of the throne. I have nothing to fear."

Nesbek laughed, an annoying sound like the snuffle of a pig. "I am having a small entertainment tonight, and you are the guest of honor." His glance flickered beyond her as he leaned toward her. "Even your precious prince will attend, but still know it is for you." Nesbek's face was close, but he turned away from her lips, thank the gods! "I miss you, Lotus."

He pressed his face into her neck. "Why are you so cold to me? I think you will warm again when you see the young prizes I have found for you."

Chloe grimaced but couldn't pull away from the vise around her wrists. She yelped in shock as he sank his teeth into her bare shoulder.

"*Haii*, RaEm, to hear your cries again . . . *Aiii*, aye, you will like your presents. Apiru." Eyes smarting with the sting and her stomach churning with disgust, Chloe wondered if he'd had all his rabies shots. His grip had loosened and she pulled away.

"I think you shall entertain us tonight well, priestess," he said as his reptilian tongue darted out to the bright red smeared on his lips. "Being back where you belong should restore your fire. You will dance for us . . . and share your other skills. I will send for you at the twenty-fourth decan." He smiled again and then said in a voice as cold as stone, "You will not like the penalty if you disappoint me." He blew a kiss at her and slunk away. Chloe sank onto the stool, head in her hands, her face mottled with rage and fear.

What was their relationship? Was he blackmailing RaEm? Did they have an understanding? At times he seemed as though he were playing at being harsh, that it was expected. Her chilly reception had been noticed; didn't he realize she wasn't RaEm?

She looked at the already darkening flesh of her wrists and the bite on her shoulder. What had she stepped into? This was not part of anything Cammy had ever mentioned about Egypt. What could she do? There was help, no friend, no one to turn to, even for comfort.

She thought of Cheftu, of the obvious hatred he had for her, as well as the physical desire. Or Count Makab, who although her only relative obviously disliked RaEm as much as Cheftu. Or Basha, who obliquely hated her.

No one. She was on her own.

How did one refuse the attentions of a soon-to-be-king and his lecherous courtiers? She had only hours to formulate a plan. Maybe she could run away . . . but where? With a baby on the way, what could she do? Have it in secret and then give it to some family and try to blend in with the common Egyptian folk?

She was dead in the water. Crocodile bait. RaEm didn't have the faintest idea how to do anything except order people around and perform HatHor priestess rituals. Chloe could learn, but she didn't even speak the same dialect as the *rekkit*.

There had to be some alternative. She slumped with her head in her hands. A discreet cough jerked her head up. Cheftu. For a second the sensations of seeing him in a clinch with her sister-priestess enveloped her. He seemed unaffected, as cool and removed as ever.

"My lady. Life, health, and prosperity to you. How do you fare this afternoon?"

"I am well," she lied.

Cheftu studied her in silence for a moment, his long golden eyes moving from the bite on her shoulder to the mottled color in her cheeks. His jaw tightened as he spoke. "As it is the beginning of the month, I wondered if you wanted your horoscope read?"

Chloe shrugged. Not unless it contained the phone number for the flight out of here.

He bowed slightly and turned away.

"My Lord Cheftu?" Chloe said anxiously.

He half turned back. "My lady?" For a moment he looked almost approachable. Then the haughty mask slipped over his features, and with a slight inclination of his head, he left.

By THE TIME CHEFTU REACHED HIS APARTMENTS he had ceased to be angry. RaEm was RaEm. This new vulnerable look was only a trick from her basket of manipulative skills.

A soldier was waiting for him. After the appropriate greetings he read the note from Thutmosis: an invitation to join the army on a brief camp in the desert. His refusal was not accepted, and Cheftu began to wonder if this was Horus' way of keeping the competition for RaEm at bay.

The shared fowl had shocked everyone. With Hatshepsut, living forever! withdrawing her favor from RaEm, she needed a powerful protector. Unfortunately, a court magus was not appealing enough.

The guard was waiting for him to gather his clothing and then escort him to Thutmosis' side. Who would watch over RaEm? Since when did she need anyone to? he asked himself derisively as Ehuru packed his bag. How did the slave girl fit into it all? Obviously she was Hat's spy—but why would she steal a document from Hat if she already knew?

Questions were still pounding Cheftu's brain, multiplying in the sunlight as he stepped into the chariot and followed Thutmosis and his contingency of soldiers into the desert.

By NIGHTFALL CHLOE WAS POSITIVELY ANTSY. She paced her apartments, picking up objects, then setting them down. Cheftu had not returned, and soon she would have to either run away or brazen out the evening as best she could.

Neither was an appealing option. Surely it couldn't be all *that* bad, she reasoned. Just a party. Maybe she'd have to fob off Nesbek, but she'd had practice evading amorous drunks. Still, she doubted he would be as easily manipulated as a frat rat. If the prince tried anything—

She jumped at Basha's approach, anxiety and fear making her fierce. "Curse you, *kheft!*" she yelled. "Sneaking up like Sobek to destroy me!"

Basha stiffened as if Chloe had slapped her again. "I only follow Ma'at's desires," she said, her eyes downcast and hand trembling.

Chloe was sick of Basha's cryptic statements and nervous disposition. She grabbed the hesitantly offered drink. "Begone!"

Tossing it back like a shot, she grimaced at the gritty texture. Just like Egyptian bread, she thought sulkily. Angry and wanting to lash out, she threw the alabaster cup against the wall. Feeling better, she called for assistance to dress. She would simply have to outwit them—somehow.

EXHAUSTION HAD WHIPPED CHEFTU'S BODY, yet his mind would not cease questioning. The papyrus he'd seen for only a second in Basha's hand had been from the Great House. In the scroll, Hatshepsut, living forever! had informed RaEm that her behavior was unacceptable and she stood on precarious ground. RaEm must have been shocked, though it had not stopped her from accepting the violent love token from Nesbek.

Cheftu turned on his stony bed, ignoring the star-hung night and the sonorous snores of the hundreds of men around him. The time had come for him to make his decision. Why couldn't he? To go against the wishes of Pharaoh was something no true Egyptian would contemplate. To Cheftu, the poison placed in his hand by Hatshepsut, living forever! for RaEmhetepet was nothing short of murder.

He did not want to believe RaEm had betrayed the truths of the Sisterhood she purported to believe, yet the hard swelling of her body was the last confirmation necessary. If she survived the miscarriage and the incident remained unknown, RaEm's position might survive noticeably unscathed. He had thought that was Hat's wish.

Or she could die. He feared that was Senmut's wish. Was it now Hat's also?

Cheftu had been startled by the protective instinct RaEm demonstrated when they spoke of the unborn child. Even the most vicious creature Khonsu created had some admirable traits, he reminded himself. Since learning about his former betrothed's lifestyle, Cheftu had come to regard her as among the most predatory. Despite that, the memory of her soft mouth beneath his sparked lightning through his veins.

The woman was poison. He knew that. She infected his blood and would ruin him if he allowed her. Still, he could not kill her or the unsuspecting babe she carried. Instead he would give her something to imitate the drug yet not unsettle the unborn.

What about the hapless slave who had died in the night, after vomiting blood? His all-too-human cries still rang in Cheftu's ears. Had that been an attempt at assassinating the crown prince? Aye, the dancer had confessed, but what mortal after two days' torture would deny anything? More important, she'd named no accomplices. It did not add up.

He knew that Hatshepsut would never, even in the direst circumstances, allow Horus-in-the-Nest to be hurt. She respected the blood of her father that ran in Thut's veins. No doubt he would already be on the throne if he had been her son. But he wasn't, and she could not let the power pass from her hands right now. However, she would never commission or approve his death.

Cheftu mentally reviewed her trusted ones. Would Hatshepsut's faithful bodyguard, Nehesi, do this without her permission? Nay. He would never go against his commander in chief's request. Hapuseneb? Nay, because Thut III was the offspring of the god, and the high priest of Amun-Ra would never risk the god's eternal wrath or the disruption of Ma'at.

That brought the question to Senmut, Hatshepsut's beloved vizier. He had risen from a common peasant to be second in the land. Cheftu smiled into the night. Senmut had thirty titles alone, one of those an *erpa-ha*, a hereditary prince of Egypt. Did he hope to kill Horus and then take Hatshepsut to the temple and declare himself Senmut I, living forever?

Nay, Senmut would not go against the wishes of Pharaoh. If that was his intention, he would have done it years ago. Years before the miracle.

Cheftu remembered that day. He had been among the many from the palace school who had sneaked into the courtyard of the temple, aching to see Amun-Ra in all his golden glory. It was one of the many feasts in the Egyptian year, when the god traveled in his golden barque from Karnak, upriver to Luxor Temple, for a visit.

Hatshepsut had already begun her singular reign but had not openly thwarted Thut III. She had merely sent him to the temple to be instructed as a priest, appropriate for a boy who would rise to godhood. Cheftu, already inducted into many of the temple's mysteries, had been surprised when the barque on which Amun-Ra sat stopped before one of the many *sem*-priests on the temple steps. This one, however, was wearing the blue-and-white ribbons of royalty in his youthlock.

As a stupefied Egypt looked on, the god had inclined his head, his words lost in the roar of the people's applause. Young Thut III had fallen to his knees, and the surrounding priests had dropped onto their faces. Hatshepsut, living forever! and Hapuseneb had finally come out of the temple, and they had seen the last moments. Thut had stood up, raising his already meaty fists in the air, and yelled, "Amun-Ra declares me pharaoh!"

The populace fell to the ground in awe, shouts of "Thutmosis Makepre, living forever!" drowned in the dirt. Cheftu had dared to raise his head and look at the reigning sovereign. Hatshepsut was shaven headed for the occasion. In the shaft of scorching sun, she was the incarnation of Amun-Ra: full of awesome power.

Her skin was painted gold, and like the gold tissue of her kilt, it appeared to glitter with the power of the sun itself. She had raised both of her hands, projecting her low and lovely voice. "My father Amun-Ra has spoken. He has declared himself pleased with Horus-in-the-Nest. Thutmosis will succeed me when I fly to Horus and Osiris." Her voice had risen with emotion as she spoke. The population, awed by the sight of the ripe and sensuous man-woman, their living god and the defender of Egypt, had shouted, "Hail, *Heru uatt* Hatshepsu Ma'atkepre, living forever!" until the cries echoed back and forth from the shrouded temple to the cliffs across the Nile, gaining in strength and fervor.

Cheftu too had cheered, overwhelmed at the mystery and power of this golden creature, caught up in the paganism of the moment and the contagious enthusiasm of the crowd. Thut had slipped out with the other *sem*-priests, and Cheftu knew Hapuseneb would ferret out who was responsible. They would be in the House of the Dead by nightfall—if they were even given the courtesy of an embalming and not thrown directly to Sobek.

He sighed as the vision of the bright, golden day in Waset faded into darkness. Where were they all now? The boy had grown into a formidable man, truly the conqueror of Egypt—if his aunt would let him. Still Hat hung on, trying to interest her gentle daughter, Neferurra, in the succession. The whole court, however, recognized that Neferurra wanted nothing but to stand by her cousin's side, clinging to his arm as consort.

Every minute of his thirty-one years pressed down on Cheftu. All the living those years had encompassed suddenly amassed in aches and pains. His soul cried out in lonely exhaustion. Why could he not be a simple physician? Or take over the family lands and ferment the finest wines in Egypt? Would he ever have a good and gentle woman to hold in his arms as they watched Ra fade on the horizon, exchanging glances over the rims of their cups? Children? A legacy of his blood to carry forth? He realized he was tired of the court's intrigue and the constant burning both ends of the torch while trying to hold on to the middle. He sighed wearily. At least his stomach was calm.

He missed Alemelek, the trust, the lack of fear. Their complete understanding.

There was no reason to rush back to the palace. Doubtless RaEm was locked in Nesbek's arms. He forced his mind away from the vision of her lovely brown limbs tangled with that scorpion. Would he never be free of her web? Just when he had come to terms with having loved a fantasy in his youth, he had met her again. Although she was not the same woman. Or was she?

Bleary-eyed, he forced himself to be still. In the distance he heard a muttered exchange as the guards changed duty. Then he slept.

CHLOE DREW A DEEP, SETTLING BREATH and stepped down from the litter. Nesbek's delta house was a large white block in a thicket of biological fecundity, and she could already hear coarse male laughter on the heavily perfumed air. She walked up the path and into the courtyard.

She saw nothing except bodies everywhere. Intermingled. Men with women with women with men with men. Holy shit! *It was a genuine, no-holds-barred orgy!* Bile rose in her throat as blood rushed to her face. What had she gotten into? Anxiety rose in her like fever, and sweat broke out on her back and upper lip.

Nesbek was sprawled on a low couch, one fawning male licking his toes, an overdone woman fondling him openly. Nesbek himself had his hands on a slave girl barely in her teens. He pushed them away when he saw Chloe, shouting for silence. His gold teeth glittered in the torchlight.

The writhing, undulating mass of humanity ceased momentarily in its headlong search for gratification.

"The Lady RaEmhetepet, my betrothed," he shouted. "She shall share with us her amazing talents!" He turned a darkened glare her way, growling, "I trust you have exorcised that cold spirit? Do not shame me, RaEm. Hurt me." Then he smiled.

Chloe gulped. For a split second she could hear those same words—"Hurt me"—in another voice, and she saw bloodied hands and a man's face. It flashed through her mind in a millisecond, but Nesbek's salacious grin obscured the vision.

Show time.

She tried to look away from the collection of body parts, most in someone else's possession. There was no place to focus, which was proving difficult anyway. She remembered what her speech teacher from high school said and imagined everyone in long underwear. She hadn't seen most of these people before, but the "other" recognized them. Hell, the real RaEm could name everyone in the room, although the prince was missing.

Chloe heard a thin, reedy note rise and knew even before the prodding of the "other" that it was her cue. Clenching her teeth, she dropped the cloak. The room grew expectantly silent. Chloe felt lusty glances race across her form. Her breasts were covered only to their silver-painted tips by a silver-and-turquoise collar. The beads around her hips were even more humiliating. Even though it was culturally permitted, she felt *nekkid*—sick and sleazy. Dear God, she thought, don't let Mimi watch this! She raised her arms and cautiously let in RaEm's mind.

An overwhelming surge of power flooded her being, and she realized with a start that dancing was the one thing RaEm truly gloried in doing. Her passion was so great that a little of the feeling had overflowed into her rational memory. Afraid she would end up a part of the orgy if she let RaEm have her way, Chloe took RaEm's guidance in small and tidy lumps. Consequently Chloe was less sensual and skilled than RaEm. Fortunately, so many of the guests were tripping on an ancient amphetamine that Chloe doubted they recognized her as a fraud.

As the tempo increased she spun, ducked, twirled, and gyrated. The room spun, ducked, and most definitely gyrated with her. In fact, it began to do some things she did not have the agility to follow. She ceased her whirling and landed in a semigraceful heap on the floor. The applause was weak. When she looked up, she saw the "audience" had directed its attention to the doors.

She was still panting from her dance when she saw what, or rather who, had gained the party's attention. Two Apiru slaves, bound and naked, were led toward her. Chloe closed her eyes briefly. She was having trouble seeing, and she had to concentrate on getting to her feet without further dislodging her already askew beadwear. Her head throbbed and there was a painful tightness in her chest. Her leg muscles were spasming. She leaned against a column, trying to regain some equilibrium. Then Nesbek met her at the raised stage and handed her a whip. He kissed her on the mouth, squeezing her breast, though Chloe felt it only distantly. "Do what you do so well. We have waited a long time for this," he whispered before slapping her bottom with a beaded flail.

She stared, speechless, at the heavy leather thongs that flared into a multitude of ends. Chloe, afraid that she was now seeing double, tried to count the straps. When she reached ten for the second time, she gave up. Where the bloody hell was this place? What was she supposed to do?

Nesbek, drunk and supported between two naked and oiled young men, turned from the bound slaves to his guests. "Now, my honored lovers, let that which we have long awaited, begin. Inflame us, RaEm," he said, backing away.

Chloe looked at the slaves, trying to sharpen their fuzzy images. A young man, probably fifteen or sixteen years old, and a girl about the same age, were tied to posts, spread-eagle. Neither of them spoke a word. They stood with bowed heads, backs to the crowd, accepting their fate. These kids should be worried about the prom, Chloe thought, though she knew in this time they were beyond marriageable age.

An arc of pain shot through her. Her mind went blank. Pain reached up from her back into her chest, and she flinched, causing the end of the whip to twitch. The Apiru girl recoiled in response, her fear bringing a pleased muttering from the crowd. Their anticipation surrounded Chloe like a putrid smog, a heightening of sexual tensions in the incense-scented room. Small animal sounds reached her ears; the "other" explained what they were. Chloe swallowed bile again.

A second cramp gripped her. Chloe stood still, grinding her teeth as her body became a playground of sharp and dull prods, pokes, and stabs. The Apiru girl was crying, and the boy whispered to her in their own language. A pep talk by the tone of it, Chloe thought muzzily. She gasped, fell to her knees, and dropped the whip as another spasm seized her. Behind her eyelids she saw flashes of red and black, the patterns dizzying in their continuous changing. She opened her eyes in a moment of lucidity.

The guests were grumbling, and Nesbek stared at her, his face ashen. "Do not shame me!" he mouthed with a look of such loathing that she felt it even through the ever-intensifying agony in her body. Cupping her belly, Chloe sank to the floor. Through strobelike flashes of iridescent red, splotches of chartreuse, and lines of black, she saw Nesbek standing over her, his arms widespread, holding back the crowd. Amid

cries of "Leave her, she's ill!" and a tussle of bodies, she felt herself lifted. After a brief blackout *she* was tied between the posts, Nesbek's shouts of "Nay!" vibrating through her body. She couldn't see, couldn't hear, but the fury of the disappointed party was palpable.

The cramps drove her down, hunching over her knees, trying to control her anguish. She bit into her lip and tasted blood. Part of her mind realized the muffled shrieks she heard were her own. The sensations in her body were so intense, she didn't even feel the first kick or punch.

For what seemed like eternity she hung between new and growing tortures in her womb and those elsewhere on her body. Vainly she tried to speak, but the bestial murmuring of the advancing crowd drowned out her mutterings. Finally a painless and peaceful sensory night fell across her. Chloe felt nothing else.

CHEFTU TURNED ON HIS COUCH. Ra streamed brightly through the garden door; it must be past the noon meal, he thought. Still weary, he remembered the hard stone pillow from the night before and lay indulgently in the clean linens. The clear blue sky and the swaying palm fronds refreshed him; he was content. Thutmosis had been skeptical about his "prediction" that had brought him back to Avaris, a simple trick Cheftu rigged. Being a seer had its uses. The portents had been dark, Cheftu had only deepened the contrast. His lie had gained him readmittance to the palace and four more days without Thut or any others, save the palace guards.

A scrabbling at the garden door drew his attention. Drawing the sheet across his naked body and rubbing a hand vigorously across his face, he walked out.

His Israelite Meneptah, a gift from Alemelek, stood before him. Cheftu reached forward and clapped him on the shoulder. "It is good to see you, most worthy student."

Meneptah crossed his chest in a gesture of respect. *"Hemu neter.* Health, life, and prosperity."

Cheftu looked at him. "Why did you not notify Ehuru of your presence? It is late, but would you share the Perfuming with me?"

Meneptah's brown gaze dropped. "Nay, *Hemu neter.* I come to you because I believe there has been an . . ." He stopped. "Please, master, come with me."

Knowing the Meneptah would never venture this boldly to see him unless there was some great urgency, he returned to his room, dressed, and followed the Israelite's fast pace through the winding paths until they converged on a road. Ra was hot on their uncovered heads, and Cheftu felt the gold screws in his earrings begin to burn from the sun. "Meneptah, if I had known we were walking to Noph, I would have brought my chariot," he half jested.

"It is not much farther, *Hemu neter.*" They walked in heavy silence for a while longer, then Meneptah left the road and followed a scratched-out path through the heavy green underbrush. Cheftu pulled a whisk from his belt and swatted at the swarms of determined mosquitoes. They stepped into a clearing, and Cheftu saw mud-bricked town houses huddled together. An Apiru village.

Meneptah hurried to the second house and sent the door flying against the wall.

Cheftu followed him through a dark warren of rooms. Meneptah knelt beside a pallet on the floor and pulled back the window curtain. Cheftu felt as if Set's hand had seized his throat and was siphoning all the air from it. The sun's piercing light revealed a battered figure lying on the mat, mud covered, bruised, and wrapped loosely in a linen sheet. *RaEmhetepet.*

"Where did you find her?" Cheftu growled to Meneptah. "How long has it been?"

• • •

A makeshift litter swung between Meneptah and one of his cousins as they walked back to the palace. Cheftu reached out a steadying hand. RaEm's skin was boiling, a true sign of the *ka* fighting against an intruder. Cheftu's wrath built and burned as he reflected on Meneptah's tale. Thank the gods one of the Israelites had found her this morning.

Where could she have been that her evening ended in an irrigation ditch by an Apiru village? Who had left a priestess for dead? Obviously not the prince regent. Phaemon was vanished, Pakab was in Waset, so it must have been Nesbek. Her other dissolute lords were ensconced in Upper Egypt.

The group turned onto the road, and Cheftu wondered if she should be taken to her own apartments. He decided she would be safer in his; why had Basha not come to him? She knew he was responsible for the priestess. Nay, he and Meneptah would take turns guarding her until Cheftu had some answers. This did not add up.

He looked at the swaying litter beside him. Her brown skin was unnaturally flushed, and there was a deepening bruise around one eye . . . it would be a while before she could open it fully. There was a gouge in the flesh close to her jawline. Any closer and it could have taken off her earlobe. Cheftu felt his gorge rise at the thought of what instrument did this. He knew RaEm had a reputation for less than accepted appetites; was abusing and being abused one of them?

He remembered tagging along with his older brother to one of the seedier brothels. Though he had been losing his dinner from cheap wine, some older boys spoke of a woman in black who would whip you for an extra thrill and an extra fee.

A brief grin flashed across his face when he thought about the boy he had been. Naive. Egypt was all he had wanted, all he had lived for, all he had absorbed. Ironic now that Egypt was all he had.

They had almost reached the heavily guarded palace gates, and Cheftu shook his head, dispelling the memories. They had no room in his life. He was Cheftu *sa'a* Khamese, physician to Pharaoh and inheritor of his family nome.

She *needed* him. For the first time ever.

The most pressing problem was how to get her inside without anyone seeing and reporting. A familiar shout made him motion the Apiru behind some low bushes, and he approached the gate.

The commander smiled in recognition. Then Cheftu saw it fade when he noticed the bloodied *shenti* and the lack of makeup and collar on one of the *erpa-ha* of Egypt. Ameni jumped down from his chariot, waving away the remaining guards. "Life, health, and prosperity, *Hemu neter.*"

"I would have your oath of secrecy, soldier."

Ameni crossed his chest. "It is yours, *Hemu neter.*"

"The priestess staying here was wounded and left for dead. We must tend to her and assure no one sees her weakness. Hatshepsut, living forever! herself will want to know how this has happened and who dared to kill the most powerful moon-priestess of HatHor."

The soldier's face was rigid, but Cheftu saw a little of the color fade. He bowed quickly. "I will serve your lordship for the good of Egypt."

Cheftu smiled quickly. "It is good to know, my friend. I need to get her inside unnoticed."

He bowed. "It is done, my lord."

"The gates are open, go quickly," Cheftu said to the Apiru. He instructed Meneptah to hurry ahead and have Ehuru prepare a room for the lady. Also to find a trustworthy slave from among Meneptah's people.

They carried her in and lowered her body onto the sleeping couch in an adjoining room. Cheftu assembled his instruments to begin his examination. Observation was key; her hair was matted and sticky from a combination of mud in the ditch and the fat from a perfume cone. . . . He looked more closely at the gouge on her neck. It was scabbed over and crusted with mud. Apparently she got it *before* she was left to die. He pulled the remains of the sheet down farther. The savage bite on her shoulder was festering. Cheftu's lips curved in distaste.

He yanked off the linen altogether.

Cheftu felt the blood leave his face as his stomach churned. RaEm had been cruelly beaten. Her belly was purple and red from the abuse, her legs and crotch black and blue. He could trace the marks of the multitailed whip that had wound around her body. That was the gouge in her neck. There was another opposite, on her waist, and a third on her upper thigh.

By the gods! Cheftu choked back the revulsion he felt, looking at her fine limbs, swollen and discolored, caked with streams of her own dried blood.

Meneptah brought a pitcher of recently purified water, and Cheftu gently washed blood from her wounds. He applied an herb paste to the cuts, in case there was infection, and covered her with sheets to prevent a chill.

RaEm was deeply unconscious, yet occasionally she jerked, as if on the end of a child's toy. Cheftu removed the mud scabs from the gouges and was applying a final poultice to the one on her neck when the scent of fresh blood reached his nostrils. Shouting for Meneptah to get more cloths, Cheftu wrenched the linen off RaEm.

She lay in a pool of her own blood, her color fading even as her life hemorrhaged away.

Acid burned his belly. Rapidly he checked for other signs, cursing himself. RaEm had taken, or been given, a poison that was serving as an abortifacient. He had seen it before. The poor male slave who had died earlier in the week—he had had no child to give and so had choked on his own bloody vomitus as he'd bled internally.

Had Pharaoh ascertained that he, Cheftu, would not give the poison to her? Had she found another accomplice? His mind flickered back to the final meeting before they had left Waset. "A confidential medical mission" was what Pharaoh had said as Senmut had handed Cheftu the packet of poisonous herbs. The way Ra-Em was found in the temple had raised even more questions, adding fuel to the flame of Hatshepsut's paranoia. The blood on RaEm's hands had belonged to someone else, but whom?

Now *this* blood. Was it self-inflicted? Had RaEm taken the easiest path, as she was inclined to do, or had the poisoned duck the other night been intended for her and not the prince?

A corner of his mind registered the chanting priests, their voices rising and falling in the corridor. They had been summoned. Even they knew the woman was dying. Or were they expecting it? Where were the HatHor priestesses?

Blood poured from her, and soon her unborn child would. If only he truly were a magus, really did have powers outside himself . . . if that were true, he would save her and spend a lifetime accepting her gratitude. Cheftu slapped himself mentally. Whatever changes had taken place in RaEm, she would more likely spend a lifetime flaunting her health before him with other men than thank him.

It seemed to Cheftu that when he looked into her now green eyes, there was another person looking out at him. Someone whose beauty resided not only in costume and jewelry, but in character and goodness. She was genuinely bewildered when he spoke of the past. And her touch! What had caused the change in her reaction to him? And his to her? It went beyond a physical desire—though that was a constant battle—to a recognition, basic and elementary. By the gods, he didn't know what it was.

Cheftu gritted his teeth, and yanked himself back to the present. A beating *and* poison. Someone was determined to kill RaEm. Was it Pharaoh's will? To go against the will of Pharaoh was death and inconceivable to an Egyptian mind. He smiled grimly. Praise Ptah, that did not affect him.

Meneptah raced in, another of Cheftu's medicine kits on his shoulder, fresh linen cloths in his hands. Cheftu grabbed the linen and began to staunch the flow of blood. He washed it away with warm water, his eyes stinging as he thought of the child who would never be; for the child that, by the Feather, he had once wished to be his. A quick examination showed it would be a matter of decans.

He took her hand and knelt beside the couch.

"RaEm, can you hear me?" Her pupils wandered behind tightly closed lids. He caressed her slender fingers in his own strong grip. "RaEm, it is forbidden for anyone to touch you. A pure priestess must be treated only by her sisters. However, they are not here." *You are not pure,* he added mentally. "You must let me know what you are feeling. You are losing the child, RaEm. Did you take something? Did someone give you something? I must know what poison holds you, RaEm. You must tell me what happened."

She moaned softly and was scaldingly hot. Calling for colder water, he bathed her through the hours, trying to ease her temperature. Fever killed suddenly with miscarriages.

"Have you had anything to drink? RaEm, where have you been?" His words were a litany, repeated endlessly as he dissolved mandrake root in a weak wine and soaked linen cloth in it. Patiently he dribbled the mixture down her throat. The herbs would ease her pain as she woke. If she awoke.

During the night Cheftu alternated between bathing her and making her drink. Through the smoke of incense he could see her swollen eye and the white patches of linen covering her wounds. The chanting in the corridor rose and fell, a monotonous hum that threatened to lull him to sleep.

Meneptah sent for his cousin D'vorah, and the two of them helped RaEm onto the birthing bricks as her body convulsed with premature contractions. She could not sit upright, so the Israelites each held an arm, placing her calves to either side of the stone, where Cheftu knelt, waiting for the unborn. Sometime during the interminable night, amid her halfhearted groans and cries, a small package of flesh was forced from her womb. Cheftu gave Meneptah orders to find a small sarcophagus and turned away, his lips pressed into a tight line. Then he cleansed her body, ridding it of the infection. Soon, may it please Amun, her fever would lessen.

Who had been the father? RaEm's relationship with Phaemon was well-known; ReShera had introduced them. Would a guard of the Ten Thousand and brother of a priestess have touched RaEm when she was in her serving season? Where was Phaemon? How could he make her endure this pregnancy alone?

When Ra finally greeted the world, RaEm had broken into a sweat and Cheftu felt the worst danger was past. He ordered the clerestory windows uncovered to dilute the suffocating incense wafting in from the priests in the corridor.

RaEm slept through the day, waking at times to scream and beg in a broken, indiscernible voice, until Cheftu held her hands and soothed her with quiet words.

At the end of the second day Meneptah came to his side, startling him out of one of the many Bast-naps he had taken.

"My lord, bestir yourself and go bathe."

"I cannot, I dare not leave her. When she wakens she will be frightened. She will not recognize the room," Cheftu croaked. Meneptah allowed himself a brief grin as he glanced toward Ehuru in the darkened corridor.

"When she awakens and sees you she will believe herself to be in the company of a *khaibit*," he said, and brought a bronze mirror from behind his back. Cheftu was inclined to agree with him. Bleary, bloodshot eyes stared at him from a glob of running kohl. The dark shadow of several days' beard masked his face. His chest and kilt were spattered with bloodstains, and his fingers were dark green from crushed herbs. He groaned. Even his hair hurt.

"You are quite correct," he said slowly as he glanced at RaEm. She was sleeping peacefully now.

"My cousin D'vorah will sit with her," Meneptah said.

Cheftu stumbled across the receiving room into his own chamber. "I shall return shortly," he muttered as Ehuru called for a bath. Then he fell onto his couch, already snoring.

CHLOE OPENED HER EYES to a room flooded with light. For a moment disorienting images swam in her mind's eye. Then she opened her eyes completely. Correction, one eye. The other was swollen shut. She looked around, thankful for her twenty-twenty vision.

Where was she? This wasn't her Amber Street town house, that was for sure. She glanced at the woman sitting opposite her, and the reality of her trip through time whizzed through her head like MTV on speed. She felt her pulse double time as she realized she was RaEmhetepet, priestess of HatHor. Now a disgraced—and from the messages her nerve endings were communicating to her brain—seriously bruised priestess. With something disgusting spread on her stomach and breasts. Slowly she focused on her surroundings.

Her hand was being held by a beautiful young woman with hazel eyes and wavy hair. Behind her stood a swarthy young man, his beard and one-shouldered garment making him familiar. Cheftu's protégé, Meneptah. A slow smile that started at his mouth and reached his eyes greeted her.

"My lady! How do you feel?"

Chloe felt throbbing from a dozen wounds but shrugged. Her voice was rough. "I am better. What is this mess on my stomach?"

"I am glad you are better," Cheftu said from the doorway. She turned her gaze to him, and the young woman dropped Chloe's hand and crossed her chest in respect. "It is a remedy for your sickness," Cheftu continued. "A mixture of swallow's liver, beer bread, and healing herbs." Even as Chloe smelled the concoction he was describing, she was dazzled by his alien splendor.

The magus's robe hung from his broad shoulders to the floor, a frame for his bronze physique and pressed white kilt. As usual, his wig was perfect, his eyes ringed, and the wealth of jewelry on his body a little overwhelming. Chloe was unaccountably cranky that he should be so presentable when she lay there practically in pieces.

"My lord, you deign to visit a disgraced priestess?" she snapped. She was decidedly irate that he had not warned her of Nesbek's inclinations yet knew rationally that there was no reason to warn her. RaEmhetepet was just as corrupt. This knowledge did not encourage leniency, however. She glared at him through one eye.

He colored at her words, and Meneptah broke in, dismayed.

"Nay, my lady! Lord Cheftu has attended you these past several nights. He himself washed the blood . . ." His brown skin reddened in embarrassment, and Chloe stared incredulously at Cheftu. Squinting, she saw lines of strain around his mouth and violet shadows under his eyes. He stood stiffly, staring through her, indignation in every line of his taut, muscled body. Chloe was ashamed and momentarily mute.

"My lord," she tried.

"I did it for your family, woman," he said coldly, and stalked out. She was horrified at her behavior.

"Is my lady hungry? Does she thirst?" the young woman asked, changing the subject as she glanced, panicked, at Meneptah.

"Aye, call my slaves," she said, hiding behind RaEm's personality.

Meneptah looked uncomfortable. "My Lord Cheftu has instructed his personal slaves to attend you," he said apologetically.

"Why?" she snarled.

"His Lordship doubts your slaves have your best interest at heart. You were poisoned, and Basha has fled. This is D'vorah," he said, indicating the woman. "She will wait on you." With a slight bow he left, D'vorah following him to the kitchens.

Chloe winced at the aches and pains full consciousness brought to her attention. She tried to recall the events of the previous evening. Like an S&M video, the scene played through her head, and Chloe quickly turned it off, repulsed. What kind of twisted reflection of RaEm had she enacted?

•••

When Cheftu returned he found RaEm cradling her once more flat stomach. She pressed her trembling hands to it and looked up at him, her gaze bright, the confrontation of a few minutes before forgotten.

"The child did not live." She said it as a statement, as if fearing his response.

Cheftu reluctantly nodded affirmation, avoiding her stare. "We . . . we could not tell what it was."

She looked bewildered.

"Whether male child or a female," he mumbled.

"Aye." She closed her eyes, swallowing loudly. "How far—I mean, how old was it?" Her voice was barely a whisper, and Cheftu had to lean closer to hear her.

He turned away. "I would guess one hundred twenty-four to one hundred thirty-four days. About halfway through your time." He licked his lips and glanced down. "Who is the father, RaEm? He has a right to know."

She tried to sit up, inadvertently groaning at the pain. "Just yesterday, or was it yesterday, I realized I'd have a baby." Her words were rushed, spoken in a half whisper, fragile and cracking. "Basha must have given me poison, but I was too caught up in other things to pay any attention. I was scared and on edge and I didn't even know why. A premonition. Maybe I *should* have read a horoscope."

Cheftu watched the emotions chase across her face. The last was an achingly sad smile. She ran a tongue over her dry lips and swallowed, her hands clenching the linen sheets around her. He saw her bite her trembling bottom lip and fought the instinct to draw her to him, to comfort her.

Slowly she sank back onto the pillows, one hand caressing her necklace, and then she covered her face with her hands. RaEm made no sound, but her brown, bandaged shoulders started to shake. Certain she was mourning her child, he turned to leave, trying to honor the unborn's memory with silence. He gestured the waiting Apiru slaves away.

"Cheftu," she said brokenly, "please . . ." and reached out a trembling hand.

Cautiously Cheftu walked to her side and sat on the edge of the couch. He put a gentle hand on her shoulder. She threw herself into his arms and curled her legs up, half on his lap, burrowing against his chest.

Cheftu was dumbstruck. Who *was* this? To cry? In the presence of others? To care about something other than herself *enough* to cry? This was a different RaEm. Gently he caressed her sticky black hair, rocking her like a child, his words and voice drowned out by her racking sobs. The paste on her chest adhered them together.

Through her hiccuping tears he managed to interpret. "I promised to protect it," she cried. "How could I fail this? Only yesterday it was real! How could I do this?"

Cheftu winced at the agony in her voice. "Sweet Moonbeam, pain is a part of love," he whispered. "The god will protect you. Do not fear. You will have another child. *Assst.* This is but your first." He knew if she wanted two children to reach adulthood, this would be only the first in a series of ten or more pregnancies. Life was hard on the weak and defenseless.

He held her, a disgraced and disfigured priestess, and wondered, if she could pick something to change in her life, what she would pick. He wished it would be he. They could have created this child together, and then her grief would be lessened, for he would carry it. Her hair was matted, but he stroked it, wondering at her paradox. Strong yet vulnerable. Had he ever really known RaEm? Could he get to know her now?

Or was it too late?

●●●

Later, Cheftu picked at the roasted fowl on his plate, his mind still reeling from the warmth and compassion he'd glimpsed in RaEm. Ehuru entered, but Cheftu waved him away, craving privacy with his thoughts. Ehuru didn't leave. "My lord," he said in a quavering voice.

"Aye?" Cheftu demanded, irritated.

"It is gone, my lord," Ehuru blurted out. Cheftu saw the old man's face was tightly drawn, his gaze downcast.

Cheftu spoke slowly, softly. "What is gone?"

"The quiver, my lord."

His belly cramped, burning. The papyri. The notebooks. The knowledge. "Since when?"

"I know not, my lord. I have not seen it since you went to Pi-Ramessa."

"Is anything else missing?"

"Nay! Nay, my lord. Your jewels, your gold, your magic, it is all here."

"Except the quiver?"

"Why would someone take your quiver, my lord?"

Cheftu clenched his hands, willing himself calm. Why indeed? Except to ruin him.

BASHA SHIVERED IN THE MORNING AIR. "It is done, my lady," she murmured to the seated figure. "I also know that Lord Nesbek had an entertainment where RaEm once again indulged in lascivious behavior."

The woman laughed. "Nesbek is an example of the weakness and crudity of men. His only excitement comes from hurting or being hurt." Basha placed a quiver and a stack of rolled papyri on the small, inlaid table.

"Like RaEm? She likes to inflict harm, too."

"Nay, precious, RaEm is different. She fights inner demons, but not only those empowered by pain. She fears being alone and will pay any price for company. She should seek the goddess, the priestesses given her, but she seeks men with no understanding of the strength of Sekhmet. Fools who think they rule the world."

Basha took a stool by her mistress's feet, feeling the beringed fingers work through her hair, as comforting as when she was a child. "If she is engaged to Nesbek, why did RaEm sleep with Phae—?" Too late Basha realized she had infuriated her mistress. However, the priestess would not beat her but instead would ignore her, making Basha the least significant grain of sand in Egypt. "Mistress, I am so sorry!" She turned, pleading with Phaemon's beautiful twin.

"She will pay," the silver-clad woman said softly. "He is gone, destroyed by her evil, and she will pay." Her lover scared Basha when she spoke this way. Her lips would curl and her gaze would focus inward as she whispered secret words, hissing with venom. Her mistress could sit for hours like this, and it terrified Basha. Better RaEm's fury, even if it meant broken bones and scars.

Basha got up to leave, stepping quietly from the room as if her mistress were praying.

"You must remain here, in secret; you cannot return. I will protect you." Basha spun, looking at her. The color had returned to her face and she was fine. "Once your task is finished, this will be yours," the priestess said, handing Basha a small parcel.

Basha opened the box. "It is beautiful!" The golden scarab twinkled in the faint light as it twisted on a finely wrought chain. "Will you put it on me?" she asked, holding it out to her love.

A faint grimace of distaste crossed the woman's lovely features. "Nay. I cannot. You cannot wear it until . . ." Admonishing Basha like a child, she had her return the necklace to the box. "I will even inscribe a special prayer on it for you," the priestess said as she set it down. "Are you thankful?"

Basha clung to the beautiful woman, stuttering her gratitude. "I love you more than life itself, my lady!"

The woman smiled, her focus once more inward, and Basha felt a tremble of fear before losing herself in the passion of her kiss.

CHAPTER 9

Cheftu slipped into the audience chamber behind the foreign magi. He had checked on RaEm this morning; consequently he was late. The long, narrow room was already full of soldiers and courtiers, the antechamber crowded with petitioners. It was rumored some tribe from within the Apiru was threatening Egypt with terrors if they were not allowed to leave and worship their god in the desert. Cheftu knew that Hatshepsut wanted details.

He was just in time.

These Apiru were not impressive looking . . . they had the same dark eyes, skin, and hair as the rest of Egypt's populace. Only their unsanitary beards, body hair, and one-shouldered garments set them apart. They walked the length of the room, halted by a soldier's sword from getting too close to the prince.

One of the men bowed, his white-streaked beard reaching almost to his waist. He spoke in a melodious voice. "Horus-in-the-Nest, this is what the Lord of Creation says: Let my people go, so that they may worship me. If you refuse to let them go, I will plague your whole country with frogs. . . ."

Cheftu was caught up in the court's following. Across the painted and colonnaded courtyard, down the wide water steps leading to the Nile, they walked, Thut's entourage moments behind. The two Apiru halted beside a small stream, one of the many irrigation rills that led to Horus' private gardens.

Ramoses spoke to Aharon. When he handed him his beautiful, unusual walking stick, a buzz of nervous conversation rose from the crowd. Looking around, Cheftu saw Thutmosis surrounded by guards, watching. Aharon stretched the staff over the stream, then turned away. The Israelites walked quickly through the crowd, which parted easily before them.

All eyes remained fixed on the water. Silence reigned. Moments passed as Cheftu tried to still his pounding heart. Could the Israelite do as he said?

Suddenly the silence was pierced by a loud "Rrrrrrbitt!" as a huge spotted frog sprang from behind Thutmosis; surprised, Thut drew his dagger, impaling the frog before it was a cubit away. Suddenly the air was dense with the calling of frogs.

Cheftu looked back. Ramoses and Aharon stood by one of the ornamental pools, watching a brown green tide come up from the Nile. There were hundreds of frogs, all sizes and colors, leaping over each other and on top of everything.

The Egyptians, no strangers to frogs, nevertheless reacted with astonishment at this sudden invasion. Confusion reigned as soldiers tried to guard Thut, women shrieked, and everyone else steadily backed away from the living reflection of Inundation.

Thut turned on the two Apiru, forgetting his princely dignity in anger. "We shall see who is greater!" he bellowed. "Anything your puny desert god can produce, so too can the noble gods of Egypt!" The physician in Cheftu noted Thut's purple visage and the pulse pounding in his temple. He should be careful.

Balhazzar, the chief magus, had already walked back to a decorative pool and was producing frogs from its depths. Surprisingly, the frogs would not jump on or over the Apiru. They jumped in a wide space around them. All the other magi had started conjuring up frogs.

Cheftu almost laughed at the ridiculousness of the situation. Now the Egyptians were polluting their own pools! Before, only the Nile was responsible. His laughter stuck in his throat when he saw Thut staring with total revulsion at his magi.

"You impotent women!" he raged. "You have taken this trickery and multiplied it into a plague!" He grabbed a sword and advanced upon two unfortunate slant-eyed magi. One of them he ran through with the sword. The other vanished into saffron-colored smoke.

Cheftu slid back through the jostling crowd, looking for the Apiru. They were gone.

Wise choice.

Belting his kilt between his legs, Cheftu set out for his apartments in a leisurely lope through the gardens, his stride broken only by leaping frogs.

CHLOE'S EYES OPENED TO TOTAL DARKNESS. She felt pressure in her head and chest. The room was so stuffy! The very air was palpitating. Slowly she sat up, trying to control her slight nausea. She still had not adjusted to the total darkness. She shuffled to the garden door and leaned against it, listening. The peaceful crooning of the cicadas was gone. Some other noise had drowned it out, a sound she could not place.

She looked up, her mind clearing a little. The clerestory windows that made the room comfortable were blocked off. *Strange.* After she'd opened the garden door, she rubbed her eyes, trying to reconcile what she saw with what she thought she saw.

Before she could, a cold, clammy *something* brushed her naked leg, then another something. Chloe squealed and ran for the couch, squashing something yielding and damp under her foot.

Her cries brought Meneptah, who flooded the room with light. Chloe's eyes adjusted, and she saw the floor was alive with amphibians. They created a path for Meneptah.

"My lady," he said, "take my arm and I will lead you out."

Chloe stood on the couch, kicking off the frogs who dared jump up. Disgusting! Meneptah offered his hand, and she stepped down gingerly. They walked slowly toward the door, and Chloe noticed the frogs did not come close to Meneptah but crowded in on her. There must be a hundred of them!

She saw the open garden door and more frogs hopping into the room. Chloe and Meneptah joined Ehuru in the frog-cluttered passageway, progressing slowly to Cheftu's frog-free apartments. She tried not to step on them in her bare feet, but they were everywhere. The gushy feeling of crushed amphibian flesh made her shriek every time. Chloe blamed her reaction on the shock of the situation. At least that was what she rationalized to herself. In reality it was the frogs' size, coupled with their defiant stares daring her to step on them, that she found so disconcerting. She wasn't up to a staring match with anyone, particularly a frog. She ground her teeth and stepped carefully, clinging to Meneptah.

They reached Cheftu's door and Meneptah stood before it, barring it with his body. The frogs did not jump past him. Chloe ducked under his arm and slipped into the room.

Not a frog in sight. Meneptah closed the door behind them.

She looked around Cheftu's apartments. "Where is Lord Cheftu?"

"He is in the audience chamber with the Apiru and the prince," Ehuru said. "Thutmosis is asking the Apiru to intercede with their god and take away the frogs. My lord," he said, "claims that this god will take them away at the prince's request."

Chloe nodded.

"Now, my lady," he said, "please rest in the adjoining room and I will wake you when he returns."

Chloe yawned and followed him into the next room. After days of no activity, the gauntlet of a froggy hall had been wearing. She was so tired that even the headrest felt good.

CHEFTU ENTERED THE SMALL TORCHLIT CHAMBER. The walls were painted with the traditional scenes of Pharaoh smiting his enemies, with Thut's substitution of his dead father as pharaoh instead of Hatshepsut, living forever! A small but notable defiance, Cheftu thought. He bowed slightly to the other nobles milling around the room. After accepting a cup of date wine from one of the beaded servants, her eyes downcast as she moved among the men, he joined the others waiting for Thutmosis. The seven days of frogs had been awful. Thankfully no one had died from any poisons they might carry. It had just been inconvenient.

Never in his life had so many frogs left the Nile, though it was not uncommon for them to reproduce and overrun small areas from time to time. It happened infrequently and thus held no true significance. These frogs had been bigger and more aggressive than any he could remember: a deliberate snub to HenHeqet, the Egyptian goddess of conception and procreation, who was often depicted as a frog.

They stood as Thut entered the room, his titles intoned by a young soldier who also served as chamberlain. Cheftu found it interesting that Thut was dressed in his nightclothes—yet another way to scorn the Apiru—even if he did have to beg their mercy.

"Prince Thutmosis," said Balhazzar, "what shall happen?"

Thut seated himself and motioned for wine. "I have the Apiru's word that, as of tomorrow, there will be frogs only in the Nile."

The magi's faces broke into grins. One of Thut's confidants said, "They were not pleased that you would not let them leave to worship their god. How do you intend to avoid further curses?"

Thut drank deeply of his cup and then wiped his lips with the back of his hand. "I shall refuse to see them."

Affirmative murmuring greeted his comment.

"The times when this god has confounded us, he did it in the form of Ramoses and Aharon. So I shall simply refuse to see them." It was quiet. "The real problem," Thut said, "will be the dying frogs. We must organize means to dispose of them."

He motioned for a scribe and a map of the area. The rest of the night they created shifts and wrote directives to all the lords in the neighboring nomes, with strong suggestions of how to get rid of the millions of dead frogs on the morrow.

WASET

HATSHEPSUT TURNED IN SENMUT'S ARMS. Ra's rays were journeying across the golden floor, and she could hear Hapuseneb and his priests chanting at the door as they had every morning since she had crowned herself pharaoh.

> *"Awake in peace, thou Cleansed One, in peace!*
> *Awake in peace, thou Reborn Horus, in peace!*
> *Awake in peace, thou Eastern Soul, in peace!*
> *Awake in peace, Harakhti, in peace!*
> *Thou sleepest in the barque of the evening,*
> *Thou awakest in the barque of the morning,*
> *For thou art he who soareth over the gods.*
> *There is no other god who soareth over thee!"*

Senmut's dark eyes opened.

"The god's greetings to you, precious brother," she said softly. His lips twisted into a slow smile as he brought her face to his, slowly exploring her lips. Hat kissed back for a moment, distracted. She sat up abruptly. "Brother! What do you hear?"

He concentrated for a moment and said, "Nothing, save the passion flowing through my veins. Come to the couch."

She sprang away and walked to the garden door. Cautiously she opened it. Silence. "The frogs are silent!" After calling for servant girls, she rapped on the door and notified the soldiers standing guard that she and Senmut would go for a chariot ride this morning.

He was gone when she returned.

•••

Senmut joined Hatshepsut at the stables, where her horses stamped with impatience. He took in her abbreviated kilt and the red leather collar that just brushed the tips of her gold-painted breasts. She wore matching sandals, gloves, and a close-fitted crown with Egypt's cobra and vulture embossed in gold. He leapt nimbly into the gold chariot beside her, and they were away, Hatshepsut at the reins.

They raced away from Waset, up the Nile. It was glorious to feel Ra on their backs, to have the freedom of this moment. Hatshepsut turned wide of Waset and headed into the desert, the tiny chariot kicking up sand and careening wildly in the uncertain medium. Senmut leaned forward and kissed the straining muscle in her left arm, then settled back for a long, hot ride. The desert terrain flashed past, pale gold sand in undulating mounds, canopied by the turquoise blue of the endless sky. Hours later she let the horses slow as they came to the enormous rock face.

She turned to him, a smile on her wide lips. "Show me the progress, architect!" He stepped down and walked to the far side of the face, kicking back a pile of rocks until Hat could see the dark opening beyond. She followed as Senmut crawled down the ladder carved into the wall, and they were in darkness. Only the rhythmic chanting of workers in some other room indicated this was anything other than a cave. Hat's lips met his in a sweet and passionate kiss as they clung together in the dark.

In their tomb.

Senmut took the reins on their return, and Hat leaned against the side. "What is it, love?" he asked. Her eyes were filled with tears.

"I was thinking of the painting."

He had done it, a vision of their joined afterlife, as a gift to her. Afterward she had made love to him in the darkened dust, slowly and patiently, still as treasured as their first time together, when he had come to her, after the death of her husband and half-brother, Thutmosis II.

The stench met them before they saw the water. The frogs. It was as if Amun-Ra's hand had touched them in one moment and they had all died—all the different kinds, at different stages of growth. Already their bodies were alive with other life, spewing forth the maggots and flies that could quickly become a deadly epidemic. Senmut swatted away the clustering flies from his eyes with the leather flail of his office.

The *rekkit* had swept together the carcasses and left them to further rot in the sun. The smell was overpowering. Senmut looked to Hat, offering her his sop cloth.

She looked at him coldly. "The rest of Egypt must suffer; why should I bury my nose in a perfumed cloth? Drive slowly."

They passed through many small villages on the bank of the Nile, each with piles of rotting frogs. By the time they reached the palace gates, they were accustomed to it.

GOSHEN

THE FEAST WAS MANDATORY. Thut, in an attempt to raise a nervous morale, had planned a fantastic celebration. RaEm was still abed, recovering, but Cheftu's official presence was required. His glance flitted from one small table of nobles to another. He was certain one of them had placed Basha to kill RaEm, not to mention abort the child. Cheftu drank from his cup. Who was the father? Where could he be? Had he fled? Cursed cowardly swine, Cheftu thought. Impregnating her and leaving her alone to face the consequences.

He saw a servant enter and present Thut with a beautiful glass vial. The room was full, perfumed cones melting, their sweet scent mingling with the hundreds of bouquets of fresh flowers. Amidst the laughter and feasting, Thut opened the jar, apparently a gift, and poured it out.

Dust.

Cheftu could still see the grains falling through the air when they came to life and dispersed from the table. Nobles and slaves alike began to swat and slap, trying to kill the tiny bugs.

Thut looked over to the magi. "Do something!" he bellowed. Balhazzar, by far the most advanced magus, looked around the room. The food and wine were ignored as people fought the determined insects.

"Prince Thutmosis," Balhazzar said quietly, "I can do nothing. This is indeed the finger of a god."

Thutmosis stood, bringing the whole party to their feet, then threw his golden cup at Balhazzar. "Get out!" he yelled. "Begone from Egypt by dawn tomorrow or your life is forfeit!"

Balhazzar bowed deeply and left the room. Thut sat heavily on his stool. "We celebrate, friends!" It was a command. Cheftu watched as the nobles sat down and began to eat and drink . . . and swat and scratch.

THE GNATS MERGED INTO A PLAGUE OF FLIES as the week progressed. The heat was intense, but Chloe was improving. She thought she might actually survive. The fever after her miscarriage had drained her strength, but her bruises were faded and her wounds were scabbed over and healing. The "other" was livid about Basha's duplicity, and Chloe still had no answers as to who the father was. She now was healthy enough to resume her priestess duties. Cheftu kept his distance; the caring, gentle healer she had glimpsed had reverted to a coolly methodical physician who checked her body with emotionless scrutiny. But D'vorah was always there, gentle and pale, with a sweet smile, making up for his callousness.

Chloe walked through the palace at Thut's request, noting that these flies were not *just* huge Egyptian flies that crowded the eyes, but *biting* flies. She was wrapped in several swathes of linen, leaving visible only her eyes, surrounded by heavy kohl, and her feet, covered by lace-up sandals. The flies bit through the cloth, again and again, until Chloe wanted to scream from frustration. Bumps rose and swelled beneath her linen.

She was admitted to a room inhabited by similarly clothed people. For a moment she grinned. They looked like a bunch of walking mummies. She recognized a few faces from her dancing debut. No Cheftu. Thut turned to her. He had not and did not know anything, it appeared. Nesbek had just used Thut's name as a prod she couldn't resist. May Sobek bite him on the backside! She should have known a man with the desire and sensitivity to paint pottery would shun the rank vulgarity of Nesbek's hobbies.

Thut addressed them. "You are among the most powerful workers of the gods in Lower Egypt. You are some of the most landed nobles in Lower Egypt. I have called you because an evil deity seeks to destroy Egypt. The things that have happened here, my couriers report, have happened everywhere. Pharaoh's court in Upper Egypt is in turmoil, and the Great House spends whole days interceding for the people in Karnak. I need your wisdom. Egypt needs your wisdom."

A magus spoke. "You must let these Israelites go to worship. There is no other solution. They are, after all, only a part of the Apiru. They have never assimilated, and perhaps when they return they will be more willing to be Egyptians, to accept our ways."

A few murmurs greeted this suggestion. Thut paced the front of the room, looking for all the world like a caged beast.

"Egypt will be ruined if they do not go!" a nobleman cried.

He was interrupted by a wealthy landowner. "What will we do without the Apiru, or the Israelites, or whoever this pitiful band is? We will have to return to ancient times, where we can build only during the Inundation and only with our own *rekkit*. It will once again take decades for temples to be repaired, for tombs to be built." His outburst was applauded.

Menkh, Proclaimer of the Truths at On, spoke; his high-pitched voice was calm, but his words were disturbing. "This must be a god we are dealing with, and he is ridiculing our gods. First he strikes at Hapi, the god of the Nile. The lifeblood of Egypt becomes blood that robs life. Fish, one of our most important resources, are killed by the thousands. That in itself is enough to start a famine. We are bartering with a proud god." He reseated himself in silence. A few people squirmed in their seats, uncomfortable with the thought of an angry, powerful, unknown god.

A Zarub businessman, Khabar, patting his enormous belly as he stood, endorsed killing all the troublemakers and then not worrying at all.

A smattering of applause greeted his words, but Thut frowned. "I will not have the death of a prophet or priest, however insignificant, on my hands. I will not murder for convenience. How do we know that this god, if he exists and has power here, will not send a more powerful plague as punishment?"

The group sat in silence, dividing into those who would keep the slaves and kill the leaders to avoid more plagues and those who would let them go in exchange for peace.

A familiar voice broke the silence. Chloe turned to see Lord Cheftu, lounging against the far wall. "Majesty," he said, "if indeed these plagues are allowed to continue, they will wreak destruction. Thus far the Nile turning to blood poisoned and killed the fish. The lethal content in the water forced the frogs onto dry land. They have died and been left to rot, their carcasses germinating these flies." He walked forward, his face dark against the many layers of his linen wrapping. "These flies will poison our livestock, killing a main source of meat and labor. If Egypt does not die, she will surely take generations to heal." He turned to face the group. "Each of these curses has been worse than the last. How long will we wait before this land is utterly destroyed?"

Dead silence greeted him. Djer, a priest from Aiyut, spoke, a crafty expression on his long, weathered face. "Majesty, perhaps we can come to an agreement with these Israelites. Let us open our temples to them, throughout Egypt, for three days."

Thut grunted.

"For three days they can offer sacrifices, dance, worship as they will," Djer continued. "This way their request is met, yet we can keep our workforce. If need be, we can even gift them with stone utensils or some such."

Thut chewed the corner of his lip. "I approve." He looked over the group. "Egypt thanks you for your efforts. You are dismissed, except those within the priesthood."

Chloe hid from Nesbek's speculative gaze by sliding onto a stool behind a large potted citrus. Cheftu was already gone. She sighed. He was as elusive as a fly swatter in this cursed land. As she pulled the linen closer around her face she felt the bites on her forehead and nose beginning to swell and itch.

The prince faced them. "The Israelites are waiting for me in the adjoining room. Be prepared to send couriers to your temples in preparation for usage of their sacred rooms." He left, escorted by two soldiers at each side.

The second underpriest of Amun from Noph was spluttering with rancor as he sat next to Chloe. "My lady!" he erupted. "Will the Sisterhood allow such a sacrilege? It is unthinkable that some lowborn foreigner should be allowed in the presence of Amun! Ma'at will be ruined! This is unheard of! It is no wonder that Pharaoh does not allow her nephew the throne," he whispered. "He has no decency, no respect. This is appalling."

Chloe ran a weary hand over her face, gaining two additional bites on her hand for her trouble. "It is surprising," she said.

"Will you allow this to transpire in HatHor's sacred complex?"

She shrugged. "If we do not, there will be no one left to worship. The people will perish, either from poison, disease, or starvation. We must decide which is the worst of the two evils. We are between a hungry Sobek and Set himself."

He shook his head in reluctant agreement. "We—"

He was cut off by Thut stalking back in. "The flies will leave," Thut said. "But they refused to worship in our temples. They claimed the people would stone them, a valid point." He sighed heavily. "I have given them permission to go into the desert, but only a certain distance."

One of the priests spoke up. "So Horus-in-the-Nest has been cowed by slaves?"

Chloe looked to the speaker in shock. Was he stupid? How did he dare to speak that way? Thut's face had reddened, but his expression was contrite.

The priest continued, "I am an old man and have seen many Inundations, so I can speak my mind freely. What if these other tribes within the Apiru seek to manipulate for their freedom this same way? Egypt could be left almost desolate! My Majesty Hatshepsut, living forever! will be displeased that you have negotiated with slaves."

Thut's lips drew into a fine line. "My esteemed aunt desires peace above everything. She would rather have fewer slaves than have a curse laid upon the land every ten days. I am the one in power here. I have decided." He turned on his heel, exiting.

The old priest followed him, his thin, failing body wrapped in cubits of linen, the leopard skin of his office draped over the whole ensemble. The group began to break up, priests dispersing to Lower Egypt's various temples.

Chloe slipped out beside a side column and noted with surprise that Ra was almost gone. The air was thick with buzzing, and she half ran to her apartments, the flies stinging through her linen wrappings. She was cursing with itchy frustration as she rounded the bend leading to her rooms. The guards who customarily watched every gateway were gone, and she got a few more bites as she glanced down and noticed her sandal was untied. I'll be inside in a matter of minutes, she thought hurriedly.

And promptly tripped. The tightly wrapped garments prevented her from catching herself in time, so she fell on her face. Chloe rolled over immediately, trying to avoid the fly-covered ground, trying to keep the nasty bugs out of her eyes. Swearing volubly, she got to her feet, testing ankles and arms to see that nothing was damaged. Then, frowning with gritted teeth, she turned around.

Nesbek stood before her, his rotund body wrapped in the rich red of which he was so fond. Chloe snarled, too angry to be afraid.

"My lady."

She did not shout, but her scathing words cut. "I am not your lady. Get away from me, you son of a *kheft!* I do not know what secrets you hold over my head, but I am finished with you! Your presence is a stench in my nostrils! Your lifestyle repulses me almost as much as your appearance." She smiled, enjoying the release after months of playing the simpering, ineffectual priestess. "Should you ever touch me or attempt to contact me again, I will see you impaled!"

His face purpled with emotion, and he raised a hand to strike her, "Aye, RaEm! You have returned to me!" Suddenly she didn't give a damn who saw her or what they thought of her actions. She threw off her robe.

Chloe deflected his wrist and circled him, ignoring the flies and the falling darkness. Her hands went up in a defensive posture as he leapt at her. She sidestepped neatly, and Nesbek fell hard on the fly-covered ground. He stood up, frowning slightly. "I like your new game, RaEm. Is the loser the victor in this one also?"

"What?" His words made no sense.

He turned back to her, and she saw with a vague degree of alarm that he now held a jewel-hilted dagger in his hand. "Big stakes, Lotus."

She narrowed her focus. He rushed at her, dagger arm raised. She dodged the knife and stepped aside, grabbing his arm as she flipped him over her shoulder. He landed flat, the wind knocked from his lungs, his knife out of reach. She retrieved it while Nesbek lay panting for air.

"I will keep this," she said. "If you ever come near me again, I will sink it into your . . ." Chloe trailed off but stared pointedly at Nesbek's kilt. "As for whatever you think you know about me, you will forget it. The RaEm you would have married is dead."

His eyes bulged. "RaEm? What do you—"

"Our engagement is finished. Agree to this or I will go to the prince regent himself and share how you entertain. He is a sophisticated man, but decent, I think. I am certain he would be appalled at your tastes. I know Pharaoh would separate your head and shoulders for it." She knelt beside him, holding the knife to his face, which was a sickly grayish yellow, his eyes dark reflective pools in the failing light. With a poisonous smile she said, "Do we understand each other?"

NESBEK GRUNTED AGREEMENT, afraid to move his head in case she decided to enact Hatshepsut's punishment for him right now. What had happened? Where was his adventurous, risqué fiancée? RaEm stood, tucked the dagger into the sash around her waist, picked up her cloak, and walked to her garden gate.

He lay on the ground, getting his breath back, confusion and anger surging through his veins. He felt a shadow and looked up to Lord Cheftu. The *hemu neter*'s face was shadowed, but his sibilant whisper was as easy to understand as the sword Cheftu held poised over Nesbek's privates.

Nesbek braced himself and felt the prickling of cold sweat break out across his body. He had been surprised by RaEm's behavior and more than a little aroused. Perhaps it was another game? . . . They'd played with knives, flails, whips, and slaves, yet he couldn't imagine how this fit in. She sounded adamant. Was she teasing him? Priming him? Perhaps she didn't mean it.

Cheftu, however, was an excellent sportsman and had been RaEm's betrothed. Now he was her personal physician and, from what Nesbek could see, was still attached to her.

"I believe our Lady RaEmhetepet has had enough of your attentions, my lord," Cheftu said quietly. "While I think the punishments she has suggested for your future are appropriate, I would *relish* delivering them myself."

He crouched beside Nesbek, whose eyes were screwed shut in apprehension. Cheftu's cool hauteur was replaced with marrow-freezing venom. "If you so much as look in the lady's direction while you still draw breath, I will personally send you on a barque through the underworld."

Nesbek recoiled from Cheftu. He wanted to reply but very much feared that would be Cheftu's excuse.

As if he could read Nesbek's mind, Cheftu spoke. "By the gods! I hope to see you creeping along this garden wall tonight, so I can leave your body for the flies."

Nesbek's stomach roiled.

"Do you know what flies can do to a dead body? I doubt Osiris himself would welcome your stinking, infested flesh. How could you let your own betrothed be dumped by the road like refuse? What river scum are you?" Cheftu placed the knife at Nesbek's throat. "What have you to say for yourself?"

Nesbek swallowed, wincing as he felt the sharp blade slice his skin. He was getting hard.

"Speak, you river rat!"

"It was not my fault! The crowd, they were angry, disappointed. Too much to drink."

"And?" Cheftu moved the knife to new skin. Nesbek felt icy sweat under his kilt, and his genuine fear of this powerful lord suddenly killed all passion.

"I got her away before the whipping began. I took her to your Israelite's village." He winced as he felt more sticky blood trickle behind his ear. "I knew you would find her."

Cheftu was motionless. "So you left her in the hopes of saving your own yellow-skinned neck? What if she had died?"

"I . . . I had someone watching to make sure she was found. I could not let it get out she had been with me. My sister would cut off—"

The golden lord chuckled, low and nasty. "Your bloodsucking allowance? Or that impotence that hangs between your legs?" Cheftu stood up, sniffing Nesbek's blood on the knife. "You stink of coward down to the drivel that runs through your veins. Get away from here and never approach RaEm again. If you do, I wonder how your sister will respond to the letter I will write?"

Nesbek sat up. "Please, my lord, RaEm is the only one who understands that I need to hurt . . . it's the only way—"

Cheftu kicked him lightly in the chest, holding him to the fly-covered ground with one sandaled foot. "The only release you get is from hurting others. I have heard this about you. RaEm is no longer interested. Find yourself another victim."

He stepped on Nesbek, and for a second his full weight was on Nesbek's chest, a compression that felt too close to death. "You will return to me here before we see Ra crest the horizon. You will have all your miserable belongings and a reason for your departure that I can tell the prince. Or it will be the last sunrise you ever behold."

Nesbek scrambled away, fearful and angry but relieved to still be alive.

Cheftu brushed flies away from his face and eyes and turned toward RaEm's apartments. He saw light glowing from within and wished he would be welcome, if for nothing more than a cup of wine and a game of *senet*. He would stay and watch for Nesbek all night. He didn't think Nesbek would hurt RaEm. He seemed to care for her in a weak, self-centered way that made Cheftu's stomach burn. However, in the event that he was wrong . . .

Drawing his linen cloak closer about him and waving away more flies, Cheftu sat on the ground, preparing for a long night. The moon rose, full and fat, its light lending a daytime brightness to the garden. Cheftu seated himself under one of the many sycamores and watched the climbing white flowers open and flood the air with their hauntingly sweet scent. A night bird began singing, its notes climbing up and down the scale. After a while the flies didn't bother him.

Cheftu cleared his mind carefully, relaxing the different muscles in his body, conquering the distress that had him taut as a bow, wishing the fire in his stomach would subside. He was fighting sleep when he saw RaEm's light extinguished. The flies were fewer.

Aching, he got to his feet when he saw RaEm's garden door open and a white-clad figure slip out. It was RaEm, her drifting walk now filled with purpose. She headed straight for the river, and he followed close behind. Periodically she stopped and listened, then continued on her way. Upon reaching the deserted bank, she sat on a mud-brick wall. From inside her cloak she brought out three sticks tied to form a triangle, with a stick behind it, on which the whole thing rested. She laid a piece of papyrus across it and began to mix ink.

She's drawing again, he thought. He had become familiar with her nocturnal habit while they were on the Nile. He'd thought it strange, but then again, she'd been so sick during the day that it was her only form of entertainment. He'd certainly been an ass. Yet here, in the middle of a plague, in the middle of the night, after holding a knife to the throat of the murderer of her baby, she was drawing again. He watched as her few quick strokes re-created the present scene, almost as if this moment had been frozen in time. Obviously this was more than a casual hobby. Would she ever make sense to him?

He was confused by the contradictions that constituted RaEmhetepet, and his confusion increased exponentially as he watched her. He would have thought her heartless had he not been the one to cradle her when she'd realized her child was gone. Had he not heard the anguish in her voice, he would have classed her as a heartless snake tonight. However, since he did know those things, the effort, energy, and resilience she was exhibiting left him in awe.

Moonlight caressed her short black hair, gave her large green eyes a catlike glow, and kissed her full lips. He felt a tightening in his body, a blinding rush. He was used to his physical reaction to RaEm, but he also felt his heart tighten as he thought about the tenacity of this woman. Had he ever really known her? She had been a child, really, that night he'd crept out of Pharaoh's harem and met her in the garden. She had been beautiful and fragile, but so fearful of everything. Now the memory of her kiss on the Pyramid obliterated those faded moments and added to the already uncomfortable pressure beneath his kilt.

What had happened to that young girl? What had caused the corruption? It was too easy to blame Nesbek or Pakab. There had to be an internal reason that made her seek the forbidden. How could he know what it was? He hadn't seen her for years, until they were formally introduced at Hat's festival and RaEm had invited him to her estate in Goshen. Would he ever know? He leaned against one of the many trees lining the bank and, keeping RaEm in full view, nodded off.

CHLOE LOOKED AT THE DRAWING. It was difficult without a finer tip, but she had captured the moon's path across the Nile, rising above the clusters of trees. Sighing contentedly, she packed up her ink brushes and folded up her makeshift easel. Holding her still-drying work in one hand and her full linen pouch in the other, she began to walk back to the palace. The eastern horizon was already fading to gray.

The sight of a hand lying in the grass was almost her undoing. The early dawn highlighted it, etching the square-cut fingers in ivory, firing the tiger's-eye scarab ring with a demonic glow. Chloe stifled a scream and dropped her things. Cautiously she walked around the back of the tree.

Cheftu.

Blood drained from her face and she fell on her knees, covering his face with kisses, her throat half-choked with sobs before she realized he was warm and breathing.

And now awake. Very awake.

His strong arms encircled her, pulling her onto him, to his hungry lips and night-blackened eyes. She felt blood pounding in her temples and nervously licked her bottom lip, staring at Cheftu. It was the wrong thing to do. His gaze flickered to her lips. She hung there in the air above him, caught like a hare in a snare, frozen.

He reached up with a finger and traced her lips oh so slowly. Taking her lips' moisture onto his slightly trembling finger, he licked it slowly, his heavy-lidded gaze searing hers. Chloe gasped. His bare chest and legs scorched her, and she moved toward him, crazed thoughts careening through her mind. Damn, she thought dazedly. For the first time the fact that he had been dead and buried for thousands of years before she was even conceived didn't matter a jot. What mattered was the heat coursing through her, the heaviness in her breasts, the pulsing in her body.

She lowered her face as Cheftu glanced up. Abruptly he sat up, his head colliding with hers. Painfully.

"RaEm," he said hurriedly, confusedly, "it is almost first light. I must be on my way . . . I . . . have an appointment."

Chloe, hand still rubbing her jarred jaw, noticed that he refused to meet her gaze and leapt to his feet with more speed than grace.

"Where are your materials?" he asked as he brushed dead flies from his kilt and cloak. Amazingly, there seemed to be no flies in the air.

Chloe picked up her bag and carefully rolled up her drying papyrus, reluctant to have Cheftu learn more than he already had. She said nothing, ignoring the protests of her still-intrigued body and swearing at the comments from her bewildered brain. They started off at a brisk walk, avoiding all contact. A brush of arms and the air charged between them. Cheftu motioned for her to precede him, and they walked single file. Soon they were back at the garden gate. Cheftu opened it for her and she walked by, her head raised proudly, trying not to feel his rejection of her attempted kiss—or his lack of interest.

"RaEm," he said, his voice hoarse, "although other business takes precedence at this time, I hope we can continue our"—he stumbled for a moment—"*conversation* at a later point. This evening, perhaps?"

Chloe, thoroughly stung by his explanation, kept her face averted. Conversation was the pseudonym he was using for their moonstruck behavior? She answered crisply, "I think not, my lord. What I was about to *say* has no bearing or significance." Take that, she thought. "It would have been regretted instantly."

His granite grip on her arm forced her to look at him. "If you must again disembowel me before my death," he growled, "have the decency to speak to my face, RaEm."

Chloe stared at his chest, feeling his anger. His long-fingered hands burned through the linen on her arms, and suddenly the tension, the timing, the excuses, did not matter. She didn't care about what he said or did . . . she wanted him. She wanted that tracing finger to touch her in magical ways and those sensual and well-cut lips to curl back in ultimate pleasure. Not to mention his body . . . well . . .

Cheftu felt the change in her body. What had been resistant stone became molten metal, and RaEm surged into his hands. She raised blazing green eyes to him, and Cheftu's breath lodged in his throat. Purposefully and slowly she licked her full lower lip, and his stomach twisted as blood rushed away from his brain. He stood immobile. The invitation in her look was engraved with gold, but still he stood, hesitant to move forward yet wary of stepping back and seeing the door between them close.

Involuntarily his hands clenched her arms tighter, and she moved closer within their embrace. He watched helplessly as she leaned forward and pressed her lips to the pounding pulse in his throat. He heard a sharp intake of breath when she licked the spot, then opened her mouth wider to suck on it.

Dazedly he realized the gasping breaths he heard were his. Of their own accord his hands roamed up and down her back, cupping her and pressing her to him. She was like lightning, leaving every inch of his flesh alive and smoking.

Shafts of morning sun were ignored as they sank to the ground, hands frantically caressing, lips frenetically exploring. Cheftu was still more observer than participator when a loud exclamation interrupted them.

He crouched in front of RaEm, grasping both of her wrists in one of his hands, ready to protect her. Commander Ameni stood before them, his blue eyes quickly taking in RaEm's rosy-tipped breast and Cheftu's jutting kilt. Ameni looked embarrassed under his tan and fixed his eyes slightly to the side of Cheftu. He ignored RaEm completely.

Cheftu looked around himself in disgust, seeing through the eyes of the soldiers. Every surface was covered with dead flies. They were both dirty, RaEm's gown was ripped almost to the waist, and the bags of her equipment were strewn across the fly-covered grass.

He colored as he thought about the lack of restraint demonstrated, compared with the ideal for which all Egyptian men strove. To be in control, respectful, courteous, and above all, never overcome by emotions and passions. He was appalled at himself. This was what he was going to do with the woman he loved? To take her like a rutting animal in the public park of a palace? Automatically he backed away from his thoughts, inquiring of the guards what they wanted.

He accepted the cartouche-embellished note and waved away the soldiers with as much arrogance as he could afford. He watched them walk out of sight and turned to RaEm. The heat of passion was gone. She had covered herself and was looking at the flies with the same disgust he had.

He got to his feet, arranging his kilt as best he could, and handed RaEm the missive. He plucked his crumpled cloak from the ground and brushed off the dead flies. Frowning, she gazed at the page and then dropped it as if it were a serpent.

Cheftu picked it up. It was a letter from Hatshepsut, living forever! to Thutmosis: Cheftu's stomach burned as he read it.

"My dearest and most noble nephew. Life! Health! Prosperity! How generous is your offer for the priestess RaEmhetepet's hand. My Majesty is sure the most congenial Lord Nesbek will not hesitate to give RaEm to you, as it is My Majesty's wish. Please be married forthwith. My Majesty awaits the news of her increasing. May Isis and Nephthys bless your union."

Cheftu read the scrawled note in the margin. "My Lady RaEm. The happy occasion is tonight. Join me at *atmu*." It was signed with the cartouche of Thutmosis III. RaEm stood beside him, her face as pale as her cloak.

His own face as stiff as a funeral mask, Cheftu handed her the note and bowed. He could not, *would* not think. "It seems congratulations are in order, my lady."

RaEm said nothing, absently fingering the slit in her dress that revealed the whole length of her brown leg, allowing her a stride that matched his. "Does this mean I will be the royal consort when he becomes pharaoh?" she asked as they walked to her apartments.

Disdain rose in Cheftu's throat, a burning bile. *It was the same old RaEm.* How could he have thought differently! Aye, she was kinder in some ways and had picked up some new habits in the years since they had seen each other, but she was undoubtedly the same conniving, manipulative, grasping, social-climbing *kheft*-maiden of his dreams and nightmares.

Desire drained as he turned to face her. "My lady, you know as well as I do that unless Thut sees fit to elevate you to royal consort, you will only join his harem and the few wives he already has. Someday Thutmosis will marry his cousin Neferurra to legitimize his ascent to the throne. She will be divine consort."

Surely that couldn't be surprise in her eyes from his words? Then again, she could be so single-minded in her greed as to forget Ma'at and the whole balance of creation, too! He sighed. "If . . ." he paused, remembering her miscarriage. Would she be able to have children now? Only the gods knew. "If," he repeated, "you begin increasing soon, and give birth to a boy, then perhaps you will become a royal wife and be the mother of the next pharaoh after Prince Turankh."

They reached the door of her apartments. Cheftu was not surprised that all her belongings were gone, except for one small trunk. RaEm was horrified. She stalked through the room. "How dare he take my things before I have even agreed to this marriage! That swine! That insufferable male pig!"

"Lower your voice, my lady. Epithets are not the way to endear yourself to your husband. Surely he was just acting to make things easier for you today."

Even as he spoke, Cheftu knew he was lying. Thut had taken her belongings to show her the inevitability of the situation. She had no choices. Pharaoh had decreed, and everyone from the lowest slave maiden to Cheftu himself belonged to her and would do her bidding. His gaze flickered to RaEm, who sat in front of the bronze mirror, staring fixedly at her reflection.

He closed the door and went to her side. "My lady, it has been a shock—"

RaEm interrupted, her voice listless. "Why do you call me 'my lady'? This night you have called me RaEm . . . or was that only because I threw myself at you?" She hesitated, and Cheftu opened his mouth to speak but closed it when she continued. "What a horrid fate, to be married to a long-dead stranger who cares nothing for me beyond the black hair and golden skin he sees."

Cheftu stared at her, saw her clenched fists on the table, her legs crossed and woven together as she leaned forward on her forearms. She seemed to have forgotten he was here. But only for a moment.

She turned to him, panic in her green eyes. "I must get away! I cannot marry this man! I cannot be a part of this history!" She leapt up and grabbed his hands in hers, pleading with him. "I beg of you, please help me escape this! I must get away before tonight!" Her impassioned cries surprised him.

"My Lady RaEm, you do not know what you ask." He wriggled his fingers out of her grasp. "You are overwrought. You had no rest last night, and you are still recovering from your, uh, ordeal." He looked away, hating to see the openness in her gaze fade. "I shall send Meneptah with a draft for you. It will ease your concerns for tonight." He pulled away and backed to the door. "You should bathe and prepare yourself, my lady. Where is D'vorah?"

RaEm turned back to the mirror, hiding her face in her hands, her voice muffled. "Perhaps you are right, my lord. I shall take the draft and rest. Please go."

Cheftu felt uneasy about her acquiescence, but maybe that was just his suspicious nature. With a slight bow, he left her and closed the door. He tied his kilt between his legs and raced for his apartments, hoping Nesbek was still there, his bags packed.

●●●

Chloe waited until the sound of Cheftu's rapidly departing footsteps had faded. Then she went to the trunk left her by Thut. Life was spinning out of control, and though she had resolved to make this century work for her for now, marriage to a prince, though he wasn't as bad as she had originally thought, had not been in the bargain. There had to be some solution. Despite her best efforts, she could think of no feasible alternatives. She sat silently, staring, until the knock on the door.

Two servants entered, an unwieldy object balanced between them. Chloe dismissed them and began to unwrap the linen. The box was two cubits square. She pried off the top and the sides fell away, revealing a Thutmosid creation.

It was graceful and very, very large. Chloe looked at the detailed painting and felt blood pound into her cheeks. "He said he would get me and he has," she whispered. Was this a sample of what he expected on their wedding night?

The art was two-dimensional, but it only made the pictures that much more graphic. Couples gamboled around the vase, and Chloe looked over her shoulder, almost expecting to see Mimi and her mother. She threw the linen over it, shaking and flushed. The *Kama Sutra* in plastercraft.

Another knock.

Meneptah entered, eyes downcast, a vial in his hand. "His High Lord Cheftu said to mix half of this with wine and you should be rested by afternoon, my lady." He backed toward the door, intent on exiting. "One more thing, my lady," he said. "D'vorah went to her village and will return shortly to attend you."

"Please thank her, and tell her there is no need. I am to be wed tonight."

Meneptah looked stunned. "My . . . my . . . lord has not mentioned such a thing," he stuttered.

"*Haii!* Well, it seems Thutmosis only today received a reply from the Great House."

Meneptah frowned. "Thutmosis?"

"Aye. He had Hatshepsut, living forever! void my engagement to Lord Nesbek."

His gaze dropped to the floor, his voice calm again. "I wish you happy, my lady. What a great honor."

She walked to him and lifted his chin with one long finger. "There is no honor in marrying someone I neither know nor love. I had no say in this matter." She turned away, whispering, "Holy Osiris!"

"Pharaoh's power is absolute, my lady."

Chloe's voice was taut and strained. "Go from me now, Israelite. Pray to God for me, for I need his aid."

He left, and Chloe wondered at her words. She believed in God enough to think of him with capital letters but had never believed he intervened in people's lives on a personal level. That was up to the individual. In this case, herself.

The garden beckoned her. It was a lovely Egyptian day, one she would remember for a long time to come, it seemed. Mentally she shrugged away the acceptance of the situation that seemed to be threatening her on every side. She'd somehow get out of this.

She knelt beside the trunk and looked through the clothing and jewelry left there. There remained enough to be suitably dressed for her wedding tonight. She questioned the "other," for there was a ritual dress in which a priestess married. Maybe if the clothes were not here, she could barter for a few more days? It would give her more time to make escape plans. To her dismay, she found the pectoral of her office and the matching horn-and-disk headdress. She could marry legally.

It was just noon. Chloe paced her room, wondering how to pass the day. What she wouldn't give for a book, anything to take her away from these next few hours.

The Egyptian half of her mind knew what a boon was being bestowed upon her. Once Thutmosis got her pregnant, her life would be hers to order as she saw fit—demanding separate living quarters or spending her days sketching in relative luxury. She could even hire a slave to take care of the child when it came. If she could get pregnant. She clenched her hands into fists. To have to know Thutmosis intimately . . . Oh, God, please, *couldn't* it be someone else!

The sibilant whisper of RaEm's mind urged her to take this easiest path, told her it would not be as bad as she anticipated. The prince would treat her differently once she was his.

Her twentieth-century mind bristled at the thought of belonging to any man with no say in the matter, despite his rank.

She had never wanted to marry, but then she doubted she had ever been in love. All her life people had told her that one day she would meet Mr. Right and then she would want a permanent relationship. Or would it be His High Lord Right? Chloe kicked *that* thought in the groin. Cheftu had made it abundantly clear she should marry Thutmosis.

She crossed the room and picked up the vial, warm from the sun.

I'm not supposed to be here. My interference in this time could change all of history, she thought. Although Chloe didn't think *she*, individually, was that important, every show or book she could remember about time travel emphasized that history should not be changed. If each person was like a stone thrown into a pool . . . the ripples could rock a boat, if far enough away. What kind of ripple could my presence cause? I can't go through with this—no matter what the cost. Any chance to get away, I've got to take it.

CHAPTER 10

B y sundown Chloe was dressed. Another serving girl had come; Chloe hadn't even bothered asking her name. She stared at her Egyptian reflection, ready to wed Horus-in-the-Nest, soon to be the Mighty Bull of Ma'at. The slave had left, leaving Chloe a few minutes to herself before the chariot arrived to bear her away.

They were to be married at a small temple on the bank of the Nile. There would be no honeymoon except for tonight. Thutmosis didn't want to leave the Israelite situation. She would be moved to the harem except for the nights.

She drank from the vial Meneptah had brought, instantly feeling it course through her veins. Cheftu had suggested only half, yet she'd taken the whole thing. She hoped it wouldn't be fatal. It was now a lot easier to step away and observe herself; she felt almost ethereal. Closing her eyes, she breathed in the scent of flowers from outside the door. The silver-and-white image in the mirror opened her eyes anew. Chloe smiled, and the priestess RaEmhetepet smiled back.

There was a knock on the door, and Chloe turned to it. When Cheftu entered she felt the familiar jolt of attraction shoot through her. He was dressed in white and blue, the long cloak of his office falling from his shoulders to his leather-shod feet. His stare blazed from beneath lapis-painted lids, and the lapis stones hanging from his ears reflected the torchlight.

He stood close to her, so close she could feel his warm breath on her face. Languidly RaEm raised her eyes to his and saw his withdrawn expression. "His high and mighty Lord Cheftu," she drawled. "Did not your mother tell you that frowning all the time will give you lines on your face?" She saw the angled muscle in his jaw clench as he held his tongue.

RaEm reached up a hennaed hand and stroked his smooth cheek. "Do you know that I can count on one hand the times I have seen you smile? I can count with a closed fist the times you have smiled at me. I want to see you smile, mighty lord." She resolved in her drug-fuzzed mind to change his dour expression. With a wicked lift of her silver-painted eyebrows, RaEm grabbed Cheftu between the legs. His expression *did* change— from surprise, to shock, to anger, and, as she continued to hold him through his kilt, feeling him lengthen and harden, to resentful desire.

She threw back her head and laughed, and Cheftu's face darkened with fury. "I am not your toy, RaEm," he said through gritted teeth. With a hard hand he grabbed her wrist, putting pressure on the bones until she was forced to release her prize. Still holding her wrist, he looked into her eyes.

"So, even now you would take another man? Go to your husband with my seed still sticky on your thighs?" His smile was humorless. "I would be careful, priestess; I might have been young, and Nesbek jaded, but you are going to marry a man who will, eventually, be pharaoh. He will kill you if you are unfaithful. *That* would be justice."

He stood silent, his chest rising and falling as he tried to regain a measure of self-control. "I have come to escort you to the temple, as it is unseemly for Thutmosis to do so. I do not know why he does not just bed you, as most of Egypt has." His gaze was dark with disgust. "It is sad to see a man with such potential overcome with lust for such a slattern. However, he is only a man. I, for certain, am no Feather of Truth concerning you!"

His voice filled with a bitterness that raked across the priestess. The sharp pang of loss stunned Chloe beyond the effects of the drug. Within herself, she cringed. What was perfectly natural for RaEm was unthinkable to her. Unfortunately she had done it, had succumbed to the impulse to get his attention. Bloody hell, she'd gotten it.

The Egyptian mind within her was stunned. Lord Cheftu had spoken blasphemy! Each pharaoh was the god incarnate, so much more than a man. Cheftu's words could get him killed.

Chloe felt a deep stain of humiliation cover her face and chest, most of which was exposed. She recoiled from the revulsion in Cheftu's face;

she could feel his flesh shrink from hers. She was an abomination in his sight; he would be pleased to be rid of her.

With a painful realization Chloe admitted she would miss him. Each day without seeing him was dark, and each time she did see him, a little more of the intimidating mask he wore would slip, revealing a man she greatly admired . . . and liked.

She turned on her heel; she had to try. "I am so sorry, Cheftu! I know not what pain I have caused you. I wish—oh, how I wish things could be different! *Haii-aii!* For the love of Isis, help me!" Humiliated and shocked at her outburst, Chloe walked away, back stiff, praying the floor would open beneath her.

Cheftu stared at RaEm's nearly bare back. Her skin glowed like warm amber in the torchlight. The simple white sheath molded to her rounded hips and fastened around her newly trim waist with a silver cloth. She wore a formal braided wig, the tip of each braid banded in silver. The silver horns of her office rose a cubit in the air, making her whole appearance seem even longer and leaner than reality.

He closed his eyes and inhaled. She no longer wore a heavy fragrance; now it was light and fresh, reminding him of green gardens filled with laughter and joy . . . a garden they had known only once. He ground his teeth. By the gods, this was not helping. Underneath his blue-and-white headcloth he could feel a headache beginning. Acid bubbled in his stomach like *rekkit* soup. This night from hell was not even under way; a headache was not a good omen. Once again he directed his thoughts to the silver statue across the room.

Nothing made sense. RaEm was driving him to madness! He could never predict her behavior. On the one hand she was brazen, crude, and available to any male, not attributes to recommend her to Cheftu. On the other . . . ? RaEm turned to face him, expressionless, and Cheftu looked, really looked at her for the first time.

It had been years since he had seen RaEm after . . . well, after. Many Inundations of travel and experience. He had grown and matured during that time, was no longer the disjointed, gangling youth he'd been. Surely in that time RaEm would have changed, too? How much change could be from maturation? He would almost swear on the sacred bull of Apis that her face had changed—not just filled out, but that the bone structure was actually different. A pity ancient Egyptians didn't keep portraits, Cheftu thought. Hapuseneb had said she looked different, but Cheftu had ignored his words, at the time more engrossed in Alemelek's revelations and death.

The light touched her features, her long, straight nose, her slanting cheekbones, the tiny cleft in her chin. Cheftu blinked, trying to look through a haze of time and prejudice. Her lips were fuller, her forehead not so broad, her features not so flat. He felt as though he were straining forward, trying to see an image through a veil.

RaEm seemed to come back to herself, and Cheftu jerked when he realized the standard-bearers were beating on the door. RaEm walked to him, and Cheftu realized that she was taller than before. She had always been taller than most women—indeed, even than some men. She used to come up to Cheftu's chin, yet now they could see almost eye to eye. *Much taller.* How much of this was the difference between an inexperienced, innocent child barely into puberty and the jaded older woman before him?

Excitement mounted within him, and he dared to wonder. Was it possible? Could his fondest hope that he was not unique, not alone, be true? Quickly he reviewed his recent association with her. More and more seemed to be clear. It would explain so much: from the eye color change to her obvious confusion regarding their past association, the time he thought she was dancing with Basha when she got her voice back, the physical ease she had now that had never been there before, not to mention her newfound talents. How could he be certain? It was the only logical—or illogical, depending on one's perspective—explanation.

She was *not* RaEmhetepet.

You are only wishing for the moon, he told himself. You've never really gotten over her, and now you would delude yourself into thinking the most impossible thoughts. It's not utterly impossible, another part of his mind said. He tried to remember where she had been found when she'd become his patient. Was it in HatHor's Silver Chamber? Was it possible? What had Hapuseneb said?

They walked through the hallways, mounting the prince's new three-person chariot. Cheftu stole a glance at her, standing beside him. Now that he looked at her, he wondered how he had ever believed she was RaEm. I thought she was RaEm because that was who I expected her to be. Just like everyone else. We see only what we expect, and she has kept up the charade, doing whatever necessary to make us believe it.

Were her hungry kisses part of the charade?

Cursing himself for a blind fool, he wondered how to get her away. They must talk. Anything beyond talk was too remote to wish for. She could not marry Thutmosis, that was certain.

Cheftu's mind raced as the horses brought them ever closer to the little temple where this woman would be sealed into the annals of ancient history. She was holding the side of the chariot with a death grip, the silver of her rings cutting into her fingers. He wondered how to break through the facade, how to let her know they were the same.

Suddenly, with a scream from the horses, they were thrown to the side as the chariot halted, spilling them onto the sandy, stone-pocked street. Instinctively Cheftu reached for *her* and tried to shield her from the ground as they fell. As she landed, hard, on top of him, he acknowledged that this woman also weighed more than RaEm had. As they stood up, he looked behind him, madness churning in his mind. The standard-bearer's chariot was coming up fast.

Their driver came forward, a puzzled expression on his florid features. "My lord, I cannot explain it, but the horse seems to be dying." His voice was full of confusion, but Cheftu rejoiced.

The other chariot pulled up and he walked over, his arm around the unresisting priestess. The darkness was almost complete; there would be no moon, just stars. He explained the need to get the "Lady of Silver" to the temple before the service. It was imperative that she prepare herself before she left the service of HatHor and joined the Sisterhood of Sekhmet, as all these particular priestesses did.

Thanking Amun-Ra that this chariot could hold only two people, he ousted the driver and the standard-bearer, claiming he would deliver RaEm to the prince.

Praying whatever had befallen the other horses would leave his pair alone, he whipped them through the dark streets, heading not toward the waterfront, with its torchlit temple and waiting prince, but back to a hidden Apiru village in a copse of trees.

•••

Cheftu closed the door behind him, turning slowly to face Chloe, seated woozily on the couch. "We can stay with the Apiru, they will hide us. When they leave, we can go with them."

Chloe hung her head in relief. "Thank the gods!"

Cheftu licked his lips nervously. "However, there are a few conditions." He refused to meet her bleary gaze. "You cannot tell anyone about the goddess HatHor. Their desert god is jealous and is their sole deity. This is a special concern because many of the Israelites have embraced HatHor, which may bring trouble. Even while their unknown god smites

Egyptians, Apiru flock to HatHor's temples and buy her amulets and statues."

Chloe shrugged. It would be a relief not to pretend allegiance to a lifeless silver statue.

Cheftu sat on the folding stool across from her and reached for her hands. He seemed to have forgotten their heated words earlier this evening and was making every effort to help her. Warily he looked into her face. "Second, and most important, we must be wed."

Chloe jerked her hands free and sprang from the couch. "Married! Why is that?" Inwardly she raged that she could not avoid matrimonial bonds in this lifetime. At least Cheftu was an improvement over her other two offers, even though he thought she was a whore. I acted like one, she said to herself, remembering with a shiver the throbbing handful she had held.

Cheftu lifted his hands in an almost European movement of resignation. "It is their culture. A man and a woman cannot stay together unless they are married. More important, it will protect their own people."

"From what?"

He smirked. "From intermarrying with idolaters. If we are together, then the chances of us leading someone else astray are slimmer. They are suspicious—a powerful priestess and an *erpa-ha* joining their band? They will, however, do it out of gratitude for Meneptah's training."

"So what does this involve?" Chloe asked, not certain she wanted to stay with people who didn't trust her. Not that anyone in the palace did. She sighed.

"They have a . . ." Cheftu searched for the words. "A ritual. After that we stay together in a room for eight days. Then we can join them and they will hide us as best they can."

Chloe stared at the flaking whitewashed wall. Glancing over to Cheftu, she saw him looking at her, his face a slate of indifference.

"We have no choices, do we?"

He rose and came to stand beside her. Looking at her, he said softly, "Nay. No choices." Staring into his golden eyes, she saw resignation, fear, and a little hope.

She turned away. "When?"

"Immediately."

"Make the arrangements."

He inclined his head and left. Chloe stared out the wide window that opened onto a walled courtyard. She looked down at her garments.

Apparently this *would* be her wedding dress, despite the change in grooms.

The door opened and the room filled with Apiru women, who wore one shoulder uncovered yet veiled their hair. D'vorah, her hazel eyes glowing, embraced her, then directed the others. Chloe rinsed in the hip-bath, then put her linen sheath back on. D'vorah rimmed Chloe's eyes in black kohl and applied ocher paste for lip color, then replaced her silver jewelry, including the headdress and pectoral that made this wedding official.

It also signed Cheftu's death warrant. Just exactly what would be the penalty for marrying the prince's intended? Beheading? Being flayed alive? Hot pincers? Chloe shivered. What could she do? They had to stay together so they could leave with the Israelites, and they surely couldn't return to the palace. Yesterday had amply demonstrated, however, that being alone with his gorgeous, irresistible body for eight days would result in sex. Period. She didn't even *want* to say no. Where was the fear? Would he leave her? Would she experience intimacy with a stranger and then be dumped?

Putting her head in her hands, she cast around for a single, pleasant, reassuring thought.

She remembered Cammy's wedding, all in white with orange blossoms; granted, the marriage hadn't lasted long, but the service had been beautiful. Her eyes filled with tears. Cammy should be here, reminding her she needed something old, something new, something borrowed, and something blue. Chloe sniffled.

Let's look at the glass half-full, she thought. The groom could qualify as the old, her coloring as the borrowed, the silver sash with blue embroidered ankhs . . . but nothing new. She wiped away her tears, trying not to smear the heavy kohl.

Someone knocked on the door. She rose to open it.

"My lady is ready?" inquired a wide-eyed woman who had introduced herself as Elishava. She explained that D'vorah was not allowed to assist from this point, as she was still a maiden.

Chloe shrugged. It was bad enough Cheftu thought the worst of her, but could she live with his death on her conscience?

Grasping Chloe's arm, Elishava led her down narrow steps into the courtyard filled with people. The Apiru had managed to find a few lotus blossoms and arrange them in a jar in the center of the area, under a small canopy of striped cloth.

Elishava laid a restraining hand on Chloe's arm as she fumbled in the sleeve of her cloak and brought out a bracelet. Chloe accepted it with trembling fingers. It was exquisite.

The wristband was composed of three rows of malachite, lapis, turquoise, and glass beads, threaded between three silver spacers. The clasp was a malachite scarab with the inscribed verse "Love thy wife sincerely. Fill her belly and clothe her back. Oil is the remedy for her body. Make glad her heart all thy life. She is a profitable field for her lord."

Something new.

Chloe placed a hand to her forehead. She was so warm. How could Cheftu be so hateful and yet so gentle? Obviously this was a gift from him; no Apiru would have a piece of jewelry crafted this painstakingly. For whom was it originally intended? She opened the clasp and slipped on the bracelet, watching the colors deepen in the torchlight.

She stood waiting to be summoned. It must be almost dawn. Although Cheftu had known the way, it had taken several hours to find this place. Perhaps Thut would encounter similar difficulties. Perhaps they would live. Chloe yawned behind her hand as her eyes burned, and her head weighed an easy ton.

Apiru men and women milled around the courtyard. Suffering and hard work had aged them before their years. Nevertheless they were alive and content now, drinking beer and gathering together to observe the big happenings in their small village.

Her breath stuck in her throat when she saw Cheftu. He stepped from a house across the way, flanked by Meneptah and another, older, Israelite. Cheftu was magnificent.

His white linen kilt accentuated the bronzed muscle and sinew of his legs and upper body, tied around the hard flatness of his belly. A rush of heat flowed through Chloe. The stones on his collar and arms and in his ears caught the light and held it. His face was set, emotionless, but she thought she saw his pulse jump when he saw her.

Of course it did, she thought, he's looking at his executioner! Chloe was led out to him, her hand placed in his. She looked into his eyes, and he winked at her. She was startled. Did ancient Egyptians wink?

"You are lovely," he whispered, and tucked her hand under his arm, smiling when he saw the bracelet there.

Was this the same man as earlier? The one who'd called her a slattern and said he felt sorry for her bridegroom? The one who'd said justice would be her death?

The ancient leader stood before them and spoke hurriedly.

"According to the words of Moshe and the tribe of Israel, thou art consecrated, one to the other, from this time forth."

Cheftu took her hands in his and looked into her eyes, searching. "By all that is holy," he repeated after the leader, "I take thee, RaEmhetepet, to be my wife, both now and forever, in heaven and on earth." He stopped and swallowed. "I do pledge thee my undying devotion."

The scribe handed them a document, and Chloe glanced at it, her brain in an uproar, and carefully signed her name in hieratic. Cheftu followed suit, and they were surrounded by the singing Apiru, led by a grinning Meneptah.

Grasping her around the waist, Cheftu kissed her forehead, and they were guided back to the house. Amid blessings of many children and a good night they were pushed into the same room as before and handed a hastily prepared tray, and the door was bolted behind them. Chloe thought the entire process took less than an hour—yet she was *married.*

They were captured on the third floor, with no escape except to jump from the window. That they had nowhere *to* escape was the problem. Because she had rejected Thutmosis, they had to run from his anger. Now Cheftu would pay the price. At least, she hoped, she wasn't messing with history.

"Come, lady," he said. "Let us drink some wine and talk. It has been many Inundations, and we have eight days to relive every moment." He poured two cups and they began to sip. *He* seemed jittery.

So she was supposed to consummate a relationship with a stranger who had been dead 3,500 years before she was born? So much for true love and romance! Shakily she downed the rest of her glass.

Cheftu refilled it. "Please, do not fear me," he said, his voice low. "I know this is not what you wanted. I am sorry I could offer you no alternative." She looked into his eyes, darkened in the half-light. He moved slowly toward her. "Moonlight, I will not hurt you. I have cared for you, protected you, and although this is unexpected, we can make it work. I am sorry for the things I have said; let us forget them." He was watching her very carefully, his golden gaze intent. "Let us start again, as two new people."

Chloe tried to speak, but her voice sounded strange in her ears, and her tongue felt as though it were wrapped in cotton. "I am also sorry for you," she managed to say. "You are forced to marry a woman who once betrayed you . . ." Her words were stilled by his finger on her lips.

"This is past. We live today. Today we are together, and I hope stronger for it. You will be safe. That is my first concern." The tenderness in his gaze robbed her of breath. He reached for their cups. They both threw back their drinks as if they were tequila shots and not hon-eyed wine.

Chloe closed her eyes as the warmth traveled through her chilled body, mixing with the drugs she had taken earlier. When she opened them again she saw Cheftu had walked to the window and stood facing out, his sculpted body in black relief. She walked over to him and kissed his shoulder. He was warm, solid, and slightly salty. She kissed again, opening her mouth to taste more of his satiny skin.

Pleased with the sensations coursing through her, she trailed kisses down his arm, nipping at the cut muscles, licking his skin. Cheftu stood immobile, jaw clenched. "If you could do anything tonight, Cheftu, what would it be?" she asked, running her fingers down his tensed arms.

He exhaled. "RaEm." He swallowed. "RaEm, I would put you to sle—Ah, nay. I would see that you get—" He winced, his hand moving to his stomach. She saw fine moisture bead on his cheekbones. Rising on her tiptoes, she kissed his face, the tinge of salt tingling her lips. Cheftu's eyes were closed and his jaw was clenched. "I am sorry I hurt you before," she whispered. Clumsily she touched his chest, his bronze skin warm beneath her fingertips. "You know what I would want tonight?"

"What?" he barked.

"I want you to open your eyes so I can see your thoughts."

He opened his eyes. Their amber depths were warm but guarded. He probed her with his gaze. Gratefully resigned to being with him, she reached up and touched his lips with her own. Although they were pressed tightly together, they were warm and yielding. Cautiously she took the tip of her tongue and traced their outline. He exhaled loudly but didn't move toward her.

His reaction was her strongest encouragement, and she ran her hands over his smooth chest, the ropes of muscle and tendon throbbing at her touch. Chloe leaned her forehead against him. "I have always thought you beautiful, my lord," she said. "We've treated each other harshly—"

He pressed a finger to her lips. "That is in the past, RaEm."

"Promise?"

He hesitated. *"Assst . . ."*

"Will you seal it with a kiss?" She was being bold, throwing herself at his ancient feet. Chloe felt blood rush to her face. He'd married her to save her skin. He didn't really want her. All the guys who'd tried to take her to bed and the *one* she wanted . . . She turned away, humiliated.

His grasp on her wrist was bruising. His mouth was on hers, hard and searching—angry, frustrated, and restrained. Chloe snaked her arms around his trim waist, pulsing with his energy. Cheftu pulled back, his voice harsh.

"RaEm, you are half out of your mind with a sleeping potion! You do not know what you are doing. You do not know what you are doing to *me!*" His gaze glittered in the dim light. "Please, take no offense. Just go lie on the couch and get some rest. We can, uh, talk about this again when you awaken."

Chloe traced the whorls of his ear. "Do you want me to stop, Cheftu?" she whispered. "Am I so offensive you would rather spend your wedding night cold and alone?" His hands clenched the cloth of her sheath.

"RaEm, I am trying to be honorable," he ground out. "I want to . . ." His voice died as she kissed down the column of his throat.

"You want to what?" She followed the line of his thigh with her hand, the fine linen soft on her palm, warm with his heat. Chloe felt every muscle of restraint the length of Cheftu's body. His breath was coming quickly. He spoke, his voice ragged, the words fast and angry.

"This is your final choice, Moonlight. If you touch me again, I am going to make us husband and wife." He caught her chin in his hand and forced her to look into his eyes. "I will *not* be divorced. Either call a slave to undress us and I will lie to anyone about the validity of this marriage, or let me undress you and we will be together in flesh and spirit. No secrets and no boundaries."

Chloe stepped back, trembling.

This was real: this man, this time, this marriage. The lines around Cheftu's mouth were white with strain, and his eyes were dark and shadowed. His stance was wary, his hands flexing by his sides. A fine sheen of sweat covered his torso, and the golden collar around his neck and broad shoulders rose rapidly with his breath. Why RaEm herself had ever rejected him, Chloe could not imagine. Cheftu was as genuine and three-dimensional and alive as it got. She swallowed, her voice breathy with nerves.

"Do you want me?" She slowly raised her eyes to his. Heat zipped through her body, heavy, rushing, liquid heat. There were no doubts in that look.

Chloe reached behind her head and unlatched the heavy silver collar that hung past her barely covered breasts. She untied her sash, releasing the rest of the linen dress, which slipped down her rib cage to her hips.

Was he even breathing? She removed the silver circlet on her head, its two filigreed horns seeming to move with the tension in the air, and her shining black hair fell free. She stepped close to Cheftu, so he could feel the heat of her body in the cool room.

"May I undress you, husband?"

He groaned as he pulled Chloe close, kissing her whole face, eyes, lips, hair, and neck. Chloe gasped as his lips traced down her body, his hands trembling as they caressed her. He was silent but thorough, filling her mind with a white haze of sensation. He stepped back, his eyes wide and dark on her, as if weighing choices. With impatient hands he wrangled out of his kilt and sandals. Finally he had shed everything except collar and headcloth, which Chloe yanked off before she stepped away.

Cheftu looked like a statue.

He was shaped from living bronze and feathered with soft black hair. She felt a tremor of fear as she looked at him and thought about the textbook technicalities, then all thoughts vanished as he pulled her onto the marriage couch. He would not leave her; this she knew.

Then there were no thoughts, only the feeling of Cheftu's hands running up and down her body. He kissed her, his tongue rough, then soft, intimating what would follow. Blood pounded in her temples, tingled in her fingertips, and rushed, centering itself in her body. They teased and touched and tormented until Chloe was panting.

She watched his mobile face, his amber eyes glancing up to melt her bones to honey. Cheftu's hand crept from her waistline, lower. He murmured against her mouth with the pleasure of discovery. Chloe's back arched; her skin felt singed below the surface. She was climbing a mountain of pleasure, each caress goading her along the path. She pulled him onto her, twisting beneath him, lost in a realm of experience.

"Are you ready?" he asked hoarsely.

She murmured unintelligibly, and Cheftu bent to kiss her as he entered. He froze when he felt the tearing in her body. She shrieked into his mouth, suddenly tense and rigid.

"By the gods," he gasped, "this is not possible! This cannot be true!" he said, his voice harsh. He caressed her face and tried his damnedest not to move. Tears trickled from the corners of her eyes, and her little pants were not from pleasure. She was hurting and scared. He had done this. Sweat ran down his back as he wondered what to do; how could he have known? Then her tension drained as her eyes closed. Her lush lips curled into a smile.

"This is nice," she murmured, and when she moved, her quick-drawn breath communicated to his barely held control. Urging his response, she caressed the taut muscles in his shoulders and arms.

Cheftu braced himself like stone, trying to ignore the tight embrace of her body as he debated rapidly what to do. This was the answer he needed. This was more than he'd dared to hope. Everything was changed. She wasn't RaEm . . . but who was she? No one's wife, that was certain. Her voice was rough with desire, the caress of her hands inflaming. What could he do? In a moment the answer would be moot. With surprising strength she wrapped her legs around his waist, pulling him deeper. Cheftu groaned and yielded.

Cheftu suddenly held her close, his eyes shut as he stroked her body inside and out. Once again he started her up the mountain, leading her until Chloe was immersed in a freezing pleasure that blacked out everything except his face. She felt his body tighten and release, then he laid her down as she drifted in the last gleanings of pleasure.

A few minutes later he brought her a linen cloth, dipped in warm water. With a gentle smile he pressed it between her legs. "This should stop some of the trembling." He climbed onto the petal-strewn couch beside her.

Gathered to his chest, Chloe dropped off to sleep.

・・・

Chloe awoke as Cheftu entered the room, carrying a tray. Morning sun streaked the floor. He kicked the door shut behind him, and Chloe blushed. It seemed such an intimate thing, sealing them in alone, together. Remembering that he was an ancient stranger, she felt awkward suddenly.

"How are you this morning?" he asked, sitting beside her.

The memory made her blush . . . and smile. "My mouth feels like I have eaten papyrus stalks."

He grinned. "The tonic. You took it all?"

"Aye."

"I thought you might." He handed her a goblet of beer and then kissed her after she had drunk. After a lengthy interval he pulled away.

"Moonbeam, we must talk." His voice was breathy, but his look was serious. He withdrew to the stool across from her and watched her through saffron eyes that were deadly intense, despite the tremor in his hands.

He poured them milk. "This was your first time to be with a man."

It was a statement, not a question. "However, you miscarried a child at one hundred twenty-four days."

Chloe bit into a hard roll and tried to chew slowly.

"What magic is this where a woman is pregnant, yet untouched?"

Bloody hell . . . she'd forgotten about that. Not the pregnancy, but that she was the one who had allegedly gotten pregnant and had also lost her virginity last night. She swallowed, thinking furiously. The truth? Yeah, right. Although Cheftu seemed open to ideas beyond the range of his senses, how *could* he believe the truth? That concept of change was too far removed from the ancient Egyptian mind.

"Holy conception?" she offered with a weak smile. He looked stricken, though with Hatshepsut's entire reign built on the very concept of a god impregnating a human, she couldn't imagine why.

"I would think a god, *especially*, would batter down the maiden door," he said sarcastically. "You are my wife. You made that choice yourself, even after I gave you the only alternative I could. We have seven more days here . . . until the end of the week. We apparently have a lot to learn about each other. I will not have a marriage with secrets or boundaries. Neither will I betray you. I have pledged myself, and will be true."

Miserable, Chloe swallowed. She had heard of women in the desert who were like a virgin every time. What would be her excuse when after seven days she was not? Quite frankly, she didn't want to wait seven days. Cheftu was looking at her quizzically, his gaze full of . . . what?

"Cheftu . . . please believe me . . . but, I cannot tell you now."

"Someday you will?" He stared at her a moment and then got up and stretched, once more relaxed. "You, *assst*, the time I came to heal you, you had been in the temple, correct?"

"Aye."

"What happened to you there?" He turned to face her. "Did the god Amun visit you and fill you with his child?"

"Nay. I don't know what happened."

He knelt down, his face level with Chloe's. "You are certain you don't know what happened that night? Where the blood came from? It was all over you. Your clothes were in rags, yet the priests in the adjoining room said you had been there since *atmu*. Where is the soldier you were meeting there? What happened to Phaemon? What is your secret?"

Chloe gulped. *He knew.* Somehow he knew and was giving her a chance to explain herself. Even she couldn't explain the blood. The man's tortured face flashed before her again. The soldier? Phaemon?

She could kill RaEm.

Cheftu stood and walked away with a sigh. Chloe watched him pace the room, his stride swinging the fringed edge of his kilt around his muscular thighs. She visually traced the curve of pectoral down to the ripples of his stomach. After a few minutes of seeing his bronzed body flex and release, she felt distinctly heated. "My lord?" She pulled back the sheet.

The physical sensations were drugging . . . but he was emotionally distant as he returned to her. Chloe kissed him harder as she felt tears prick her eyes. Her husband, yet they were married strangers in a world of mere sensation. He wouldn't even look at her. Cheftu rolled onto his back, pulling her above him.

"RaEm?" His voice was hoarse, his tone expectant.

Chloe swung her hair before her face, surrendering to her nerves and hormones. He still wanted RaEm. It was worse than her worst fears. She'd lost her heart, and he didn't even know her real name.

⸫

Chloe woke first and snuggled closer to Cheftu. She looked at his broad forehead, arched black brows, and almond-shaped eyes. With a butterfly's touch she traced his jawline, his long, straight nose, the wide lips that were capable even now of sending shivers to her most intimate interior. She curled up, her head on his chest. The despair of last night had faded. There really was something to that concept of being more relaxed after sex. Not making love, she reminded herself, just having sex.

"You look like the cat with the cream."

"More like the cat full of cream," she replied. He chuckled and kissed her forehead gently. Turning onto his stomach, he faced her.

"Look at me, my beautiful cat." His voice was soft, his look pleading. "Explain the garden to me, please. Why did you say those things? Why did you want to hurt me so?"

"I thought the past was past, my lord," she hedged. How could he think she was RaEm? Because he wanted her to be. He loved RaEm.

"It is past, RaEm," he said. "It matters not, not really, but I am curious."

Chloe fingered the linen sheet in front of her and took a stab. She'd been living a lie, why not another one? "We were so young. We knew nothing of life and needed more time to be sure."

Cheftu looked down, the sun picking up blue highlights in his hair. "We didn't speak in the garden, RaEm. Do you not remember? This was our only conversation." He leaned forward and placed his lips on hers, light as air and soft, melting her own. She gasped and opened her mouth, and Cheftu explored, slowly and provocatively, its interior. When Chloe was reduced to fluid, he pulled away. "Do you remember now?"

"If we didn't speak, why did you accuse me of saying unkind things?" she said.

Cheftu pulled away. "That too is out of your memory, Moonlight?"

Chloe shrugged, looking away. "There is a lot I do not remember before the accident."

"It is hard to remember when you are not the same person, *haii?*" His expression was earnest, his gaze open and tender. "Who are you? From where do you come? Please, please tell me."

"Why do you want to know more? . . . I am the priestess of—"

"Nay," he said. "I know you are not."

"Why do you want to know? You want me to be RaEm. My story would be madness. You wouldn't believe a thing," Chloe said, half turning away.

He pulled her back to face him. "Oh, my beautiful sister, I will believe you . . . anything! I have bartered my life to protect you. I deserve your trust. Give me truth!"

"What is truth?"

Cheftu looked at her intently, brushing the fallen hair away from her face, caressing her bottom lip with his thumb. Chloe fought to still her breath in his embrace. "Truth is that I knew RaEm." He took a deep breath. "Intimately. I became a man with her." Chloe tried to pull away, but Cheftu caught her close to him, her face pressed against his chest.

His voice resonated through his body. "You look similar—indeed, to most, almost womb-sisters. However, your bodies are not the same. Your mouths are not the same," he said, pulling her back to look into his face. "RaEmhetepet only took from men. She never gave." He smiled. "You give, even when you are hurting.

"You are so beautiful, both inside and out. RaEm had only physical beauty, though it took me almost to the marriage altar to find out." His fingers traced her features, and Chloe looked at him, her eyes filled with tears. He caught a tear on his finger before it dropped and stroked the saline across her lips, his breathing becoming harsher. His gaze was intent yet calculating. He took another deep breath. "Also, because your eyes are different. They are so clean and fresh, like your soul. But they are also observant and appreciative . . . as green as the fields of *ma belle France*."

PART III

CHAPTER II

After months of hearing an alien language that she could both understand and speak, the French out of Cheftu's finely chiseled Egyptian mouth was like an icy blast.

Chloe jerked away from him. *"What did you say?"* she cried in English.

He lunged at her, his eyes pools of amber fire, his grasp iron on her wrists. He babbled incoherently for a few moments until he finally said, in hardly discernible English, "My darling, you have also traveled? From where do you come?"

Chloe looked into his face; his excitement was palpable and unrestrained. Was it too much sex, not much sleep, and very little nourishment? Or just the resounding shock of hearing French from her ancient Egyptian husband? Maybe simply because she could think of no other response? Whatever the reason, Chloe said, "Holy shit," with a definite American accent and fainted.

$$\overline{\bullet \bullet \bullet}$$

"RaEm, RaEm," a rough masculine voice said. *"Plaire à Dieu,* why do you not wake up?"

Her eyes snapped open. Cheftu knelt over her, fanning her face and calling to her in a mixture of ancient Egyptian names and French invocations. Regrouping her thoughts, Chloe reached up to touch his face. He swiftly kissed her fingertips.

Speaking slowly in English, she said, "Do you understand me?"

His face lost some of its deep color. *"Oui, ma chérie."*

"Do you speak English?"

"Yes. I speak more than twenty languages—most of them dead."

Her hand froze, because the bulk of questions she had to ask him would not organize themselves inside her fogged brain. She sat up, and he stared at her with fully widened eyes, all his masks of nobleman, priest, healer, and magus gone.

"What is your name?" he asked slowly, stumbling over the syllables. "You are English?"

"Chloe, and I'm an American. Mostly."

"From where?"

"The United States," she answered.

His brow furrowed in confusion.

She tried French. *"Des États-Unis."*

He waved away her response. "It is a bagatelle. What year?"

"Nineteen hundred ninety-f . . ." She never finished; his face turned gray.

"The twentieth century?"

"Oui."

He dropped her hands and turned away, burying his face in his hands. *"Haii, mon Dieu . . ."* He shook his head back and forth.

Chloe sat in silence. "Cheftu, what is, was, your Christian name?"

From the muffling of his hands she heard, "François." He faced the wall and dropped his hands. "I left my time of 1806." He turned to face her. "Do you know the name Napoleon?"

"Of course. He was defeated by the British at Waterloo in 1815."

He glanced at her, not comprehending. She reached out to touch him, quiet the confusion in his eyes.

"So the time in the temple, when you didn't remember, that was when you came through?" he asked.

"Yes. I don't know *what* I came through, though. When I got here I thought for a while that I was ill, or dreaming . . . but then . . . I realized I had somehow traversed a time-space continuum and ended up here." Her English words, spoken rapidly, fell into a confused pile at his feet.

He stared at her as though she had two heads. In a cracked voice he asked, "The hieroglyphs, they have been interpreted? They can be read?"

Chloe frowned at him. "Of course."

"Who broke the formula?"

"Some guy named . . ." She bit her lip in concentration, trying to recall that name she'd heard so many times from Cammy, the name in so many of those books.

"Haii?" Cheftu's face was lined with expectancy.

Chloe snapped her fingers. "Champinion . . . no, wait, that's mushroom in Spanish. Umm . . ."

Cheftu stood up and walked to the window, his movements jerky. "Champollion?" he asked, his voice a monotone.

"Yep. That's it."

"Il l'a decouverte sans moi," he said in an anguished undertone. He faced the black night, his arms braced on the window frame.

Chloe was frozen, her mind spinning. Who had discovered what without him? But more important—he was like her! He knew what it was like to be removed, without warning, from everything! Since he was still here, he obviously hadn't found a way back. She stared at his bronzed back, trying to let the astonishment sink in. Eighteen oh six . . . He was more than 150 years older than she but the same in this day and age.

It was comforting that the man she loved was not of a race and mentality completely foreign to her. He was European . . . though she didn't know how long he had been here or anything else. She looked at him and knew that regardless of his age, his nationality, or his name, she loved Cheftu. Not for where he was from, but because of who he was, the risks he took, the level of care he showed. The way he made her feel.

She walked to where he stood motionless. Chloe took his arm and guided him to the couch. "Sit, my beloved brother," she said, seeing his blank, staring eyes. What was wrong with him? Was he in some sort of shock? Speaking softly in Egyptian, she pushed him down, wondering what to do if he really were ill. He stared blankly at the ceiling.

"Cheftu, Cheftu, wake up, greet the night, the RaEmhetep," she said. No response. She checked his pulse: it was racing, and his breath was coming in little animal pants. What could have been so horrifying? Napoleon losing the war? Someone else finding the key to the hieroglyphs? What did it matter, here and now?

She took some wine from beside the couch and sprinkled it on his face. He didn't even blink. She splashed water on his face. Zip.

Biting her lip in remorse, she slapped him across the cheek. He did not respond, didn't even flinch. She sat on the stool, thinking and getting scared. What had made him freak out? Finally she shouted in French, "François, François, you must wake up, Champollion is doing it without you!"

He roared alert, cursing and swearing as he stared blindly. Chloe reached to gentle him, and he jerked her to his body, growling with fury, lost in an unseen world. Shaking with emotion, he backed her into the wall, kissing her until her lips were raw, filling her with his demonic energy. His hands molded her to him; his nakedness and strength were overwhelming.

Chloe waited for him to take a breath and then ran. He caught her before she took two steps and brought her back against his chest. Her wriggling attempts to run inflamed him further, and she felt his heat and hardness against her back.

He was speaking in ragged French, decrying someone for betraying him, for not believing in him, for not waiting for him. He seemed to think she was the tool of whoever had deceived him and whispered about the pleasure he would take in extracting his revenge. Chloe resisted him as he pressed against her, his hands never leaving her body, his lips and tongue reducing her brain to a pile of red-hot ashes.

Then he began stroking her, and Chloe felt herself merging into him. His touch had gentled, and his caressing hands were pushing her over the edge. They fell onto the couch, his cheek rough against her shoulder. She was trembling, hot and ragingly hungry for him. Then he pulled away.

Once more he stared, unseeing.

She ran her fingernails down his bare chest. He hadn't mentioned another woman. All other questions could wait until afterward. "Do not dare leave me this way," she hissed.

With a snarl he pushed her onto her hands and knees, his arm around her waist. She felt his touch as he filled her, groaning with excitement, kissing her neck and shoulders. The experience was consuming, as if he had suddenly become an octopus, and her every need was being met simultaneously. He held himself close to her, moving slowly, seductively. Her ears burned with his words, emphasized by his hands and lips.

Chloe was exhausted and energized, more alive and more real than she had ever felt. The intimate smells of sweat and sex mingled around her until she was drunk on sensation. The world consisted only of the heat and sweet vibrations building like a fever inside her. Then he pulled up, fixed his hands on her waist, and thrust so deeply that she was sure he'd touched her womb. She fell into a hundred, thousand pieces, sobbing Cheftu's name, and he collapsed over her, wiping away sweaty hair and salty tears.

• • •

When Chloe woke up she felt like an earthquake victim the morning after. The boundaries, the walls and floor, had shifted. Nothing was what she thought it was. She was glad to be alone, to ponder the changes. Cheftu was French. François. A shudder rushed through her . . . pleasure and fear. What would happen now? Wincing with an assortment of strained muscles and already developing bruises, she limped to the chamber pot.

He was not there.

She hobbled to the window, taking care not to be seen naked. Just the normal courtyard scene, people rushing to and fro . . . no graceful, strong, misplaced Frenchman. Surely he wouldn't have left her? No, she might not know five things about him, but she knew he was honorable and that he wanted her. He would return. Was he sad that she wasn't RaEm? Chloe wandered back to the couch and fell onto it, luxuriating in the cool linen against her skin.

The quiet opening of the door woke her. Cheftu came in, solemn as a funeral. He knelt and took her hand. Without looking at her, he spoke in his heavily accented English. "My behavior last night was unforgivable. To use you as a whipping post for my anger is horrible. I don't even know who you are, yet I treated you like a whore." He raised his amber gaze to hers. "Worse than a whore." He swallowed. "All I have done since I have met you is berate you for the past, a past you do not even know."

Chloe sat stunned. He was far removed from the remote but beautiful man she had come to know. He focused on some point beyond her. "This is not the way I would have behaved normally." He licked his lips, which were swollen. "Last night was a series of shocks." She was silent. "Although that is no excuse for my behavior." He looked up into her face, his breath catching as she trailed her fingers through his hair.

"What shocks?" she asked, then flushed as he arched an eyebrow. "Besides the obvious."

He bit his lips. "There is nothing that matters anymore about my former life. It is gone. My vocation, my dreams, my family—" His voice cracked. "Deceased, for hundreds of years." He looked up at her. "Now is the only thing that matters. Keeping you safe, riding out this political storm." He rose to his feet, his eyes blazing as he faced her.

"The most shocking thing last night was—I realized I love you." He continued without missing a beat, "You were a maiden and I took you like an animal." He groaned, rubbing his face with his hand. "I cannot believe I actually did that. I have never before lost control."

Chloe pulled his hand away, staring into his golden eyes. "*What* did you say?"

"I love you. Those vows I made came from my heart."

"For me, or RaEmhetepet?"

"You. From the twentieth century. Who asks 'what if' questions and paints in the night." He paled as he spoke. "I still cannot believe this," he muttered.

"For how long?"

"What?"

"How long have you loved me?"

Cheftu chuckled. "It began when I saw your enchanting derriere."

"Enchanting?"

"Mmmmm, *oui*."

"And then?"

"Your grace in handling Hatshepsut, living forever!"

"I fell apart later. Dealing with history has never been my forte." Sorry, Mom, she apologized mentally.

He twined a finger in her hair. "I desired your body when you almost shot me." She frowned in confusion. "With the arrow," he explained.

"I have excellent aim," she said. "Right over the prow and into the water."

"Mmm," he said. "Although I was lost forever when you asked me 'why.'"

"Why?"

He slid his hands down her arms, then gripped her low around the waist and pulled her to him. "Why this, why that. What would I do if . . . those many questions seduced me, word by word. I saw your soul. A person who questions and creates. I knew I loved you then . . . and only you, *chérie*."

"You hid your feelings well," Chloe murmured, breathless.

"I had hoped my actions would speak for themselves. I tried to care for you, protect you, give you the time you needed to become accustomed to me again." He smiled grimly. "I had to keep from entrancing the assorted lords and soldiers you collect like flies!" He kissed her tenderly, barely brushing her lips with his. Speaking against her mouth, he said, "When I followed you off the boat that night, you were weeping so, I thought my heart would break. Then, when I touched you, you melted into me, needing me, wanting me." He kissed her again, hungry. "I had already lost myself with RaEm once. I could not understand why I did not recognize your flesh. Indeed, you warmed me more than fire."

Chloe held him close and felt the steady thrumming of his pulse underneath her hands. "I liked it, Cheftu," she whispered. "I liked everything then, and," she gasped with remembered pleasure, "everything last night."

He pulled back her head to look into her eyes. "Everything?" Passion flared in his look as her hands lifted the edge of his kilt.

"I think lovemaking is probably like ice cream, *glace*," she mused. "Lots of different flavors for a lot of different occasions."

Cheftu pulled her back with him, toward the couch. "Flavors? *Haii?*" He smiled. "Like mint and orange and honey?"

She smiled, unbelting his kilt. "Let me tell you about an institution in my country . . . it is called Baskin-Robbins. . . ."

• • •

Chloe turned in his arms, much later. *"Haii* . . . coffee with cream is a nice flavor."

Cheftu laughed, his chest shaking her. "Thirty-one flavors is an intimidating number, *chérie*. Do not tell me I create them on my own?"

"No . . . I will be some assistance. However, my sweet tooth has been satisfied. . . ." She waited a beat. "For a while."

"Praise Isis!"

She punched him on the arm gently. "Talk to me. I miss hearing English, or French, or whatever you want to use."

"Bien. What shall I tell you?"

She sat up, suddenly energized. "Everything! Your story, how you came through, what it was like for you. Your family, your job, how it felt to go from being French to Egyptian."

Cheftu was quiet for a long time as the room became darker. "I was sixteen. My brother was a member of Napoleon's army of scientists and surveyors. I tagged along to help. Nothing was too lowly a task: carrying, digging. I was learning all I could about Egypt, though I was already a linguist in my own right." He chuckled. "I even turned down a university position to travel with them. I was in passionate love with ancient Egypt, her mysteries, her secrets. I wanted to know her completely." He shifted his hand to Chloe's breast, holding her in the darkness, her heartbeat against his hand.

"I made a habit of creeping out after dark when we were close to great monuments. I would walk through them, picture them as I thought they had been. One night I wandered into Karnak. I stepped into HatHor's chamber and found myself in a maelstrom of senses. There was someone else there, another boy my age. I grabbed him, though it was too"—he searched for the word—"too clouded to see anything. When I woke up it was in the clothes of a *w'rer*-priest in the Silver Chamber of HatHor.

"For days I could not see, and the physicians said I mumbled unintelligibly. When Cheftu the boy awoke, it was to another family, another world. A world in which I was perceived as a man. The head of the household. Because of my 'experience' they said I was chosen of the great god and so I was indentured to serve the *neter*-priests, and I learned their secrets."

She sat in silence. She would *not* ask.

"For two years I did not leave the House of Life. Humors, herbs, spells, and surgery were my life. Then I was free to leave, to work as a healer." He sighed. "I was a foolish youth." He twined his fingers through Chloe's hair. "My family are aristocrats. Nobles of Egypt. It was time to seek a wife. Actually, it was quite past time. I had kissed RaEm once in a garden, though I did not know who she was at the time. Later, I met her at a feast of Pharaoh's." He glanced down. "They, or rather you, have always been close. One of Hat's few female friends.

"RaEm thought me attractive, and since she was unmarried and not serving in the temple that season, she invited me to visit her country house in the delta. She had been a priestess since childhood, so she had grown up much faster with no supervision, no stringent rules. Though younger, she was very skilled. I was hot-blooded and ruled by my, well . . . Before I knew what I had done, I had bedded her." He stopped for a moment, and Chloe felt the tension in his body. "Or, rather, she had bedded me."

He sat quietly for a few minutes, staring into the night beyond the window. "I rushed home, ashamed, scared, wanting to offer for her. I felt it was my duty. To the Frenchman in me there was no other choice, but I knew marriage to be very serious. Unlike my own country, adultery is not accepted here. So I went to my father, who approached her father, and the contract was written.

"Since we were both from the aristocracy, it was decided there would be a wedding feast. Her family came, her friends, my family and friends. Even Pharaoh sent a gift. However, RaEmhetepet never came." He spoke matter-of-factly, with no trace of his former anger and rejection.

Chloe searched her second memory for a clue, a word, a token to explain RaEm's actions to the man beside her. "And?"

Cheftu pressed his lips together in a tight line. "Of course, it only grew more embarrassing as the night passed on. I heard later that she had been on a hunting party with the viscount of the Anubis nome. She never explained, or apologized. It had simply slipped her mind."

"What about her parents?"

"They were humiliated, of course. Such disrespect for elders was unthinkable. But she was truly little better than a stranger to them. She'd been taken to the temple before her second birthday. I knew her better than her parents did."

"Did you love her?" Chloe hated herself immediately for asking.

"I thought I did. If love meant accepting responsibility and fulfilling duty. *Le vérité est* she was imminently desirable. Wealthy, beautiful, wild. She enhanced my pride." He chuckled. "Until I was left alone at the feast. I learned about the deception of pride then. It is an ongoing lesson."

He kissed her shoulder, watching his hands move on her skin. "I will love you, Chloe—'young and verdant'—such a fitting name," he murmured. "I look at you, and wonder how I ever thought she was beautiful. When we made love, Chloe, it was more than just a joining of flesh, it was *making* love, and in those moments I know I have never felt passion or excitement or true unity before."

Chloe's eyes welled with tears as Cheftu bent to kiss her lips. His mouth caressed her with a tenderness that shook her to her soul. When he pulled away his eyes were glassy.

"Now to have someone who truly understands me . . . where I come from. For so long I have been unable to speak, to truly share my thoughts and feelings. Oh, *ma chère.*"

∴

"Which flavor was that?" he asked, his voice slurred.

"I think we will make that strawberry," Chloe whispered against his cooling skin.

"J'aime la saveur fraise!"

"If you had to do it again, would you, Cheftu?"

He chuckled. "Which part, *chérie? The fraise* or the—"

"All of it. At any major turning point."

"Aii, would I leave everything to take up a new life in this time?" His body had stiffened, and she opened her eyes.

"What is wrong?"

He shrugged, as French a gesture as if he'd been wearing a beret. How come she had not seen it before? She hadn't been looking for it. Hadn't expected it. He was quiet for so long, she had drifted to sleep.

"I cannot say." He heard her questioning grunt and spoke. "To stay here, to go there. To be a linguist or a physician . . . Egypt or France . . . I must believe that *le bon Dieu* knew what was happening and placed me here. To consider more would be to court madness and depression."

A furtive scrabbling at the door jerked them off the couch, twisting on linen and patting down hair.

"My lord?"

"Meneptah?" Cheftu had the door open almost before Chloe was dressed. She drew her linen sheet closer. The Israelite was covered in powder and stank of smoke. Cheftu lit the torch. "Sit, tell us what brings you here."

"Life, health, and prosperity, my lord," Meneptah said hurriedly. "To begin, Thutmosis wants your skin, Lord Cheftu. He was outraged and humiliated that you stole away his bride. All the court cowers. If your gods had not been looking out for you, chances are he would have already found you and removed your head, regardless of the favored status you have in Waset."

Cheftu grimaced, "I doubt that status is valid any longer, my friend. What kept him from looking?"

"Elohim struck with another plague."

Cheftu and Chloe exchanged startled looks. "The murrain of cattle," Cheftu said wonderingly under his breath.

Meneptah looked startled but agreed. "Our leader, Moshe—you call him Ramoses—warned the prince to move all cattle indoors. Prince Thutmosis did not listen, and thus almost all the cattle he owned are dead. This is reported true in most of the delta. Except for ours."

"How long did this plague last, or is it still going on?" Cheftu asked.

"The prince sent immediately for Moshe and asked him to intercede with God for the safety of the Mizrayim."

Chloe looked at Cheftu in confusion. He answered her with a smile, "It is Hebrew for Egypt. Has anything else happened?"

Meneptah smiled broadly. "Oh, aye, my lord," he said. "The whole court, in both Waset and Avaris, have been struck with a pox. Even the magus Shebenet himself was unable to stay in the presence of Moshe. Everyone in Egypt, except us, has been affected."

Cheftu's interest sharpened. "A pox? What are the symptoms?"

"This dust," Meneptah said, gesturing to the ashes all over his cloak and hair. "It came from a dust that Moshe threw into the sky. It stands more than a cubit deep in some areas. When it falls on Egyptians it makes boils and open sores on them. They begin to fester and seep with blood, pus, and a grayish fluid. What is it, my lord? I must know how to medicate people."

Cheftu brushed some onto his hand and held it before the flame. A stripe of welts broke out on his palm. "Has your leader made any other predictions about the future?"

"A killing hail will fall soon. We have all been told to stay in our houses. Moshe told the prince that also, but we shall see if he listens. You must keep yourself safe, my lord. You must stay here."

"What has fallen on you is volcanic ash," Cheftu said. "Tell me, have there been loud noises from beneath your feet, or reports of great waves along the Great Green? Fire in the sky?"

Meneptah was pale beneath his tan. "Three fishing villages were swept out to sea at the mouth of the Nile. The priests of On proclaimed the fire a sign of Amun's wrath against Elohim . . . but this large noise, this I do not know, my lord."

"Meneptah, if this dust is cubits deep on the ground, then the predicted island in the Great Green must have erupted. The hail your Moshe predicts will be mixed with the ash, and twice as deadly. "

After directing Meneptah on how to mix a poultice and prepare the tribes for the coming hailstorm, they bade him a good night and fell into bed, not realizing it was morning.

•••

The clatter of horses and chariots jerked Chloe awake. Cheftu was already up, standing by the window, listening as the decree was announced in *rekkit.*

"The Regent, Thutmosis the Third, declares the threats of your prophet do you no good. No one shall leave Egypt with his wealth or his family. Those wishing to leave without flocks, wives, or children must report to the palace to be approved."

Chloe rushed to the window and watched the soldiers in their blue-and-white helmets march by. "That's awfully harsh treatment."

"Thut's pride is wounded. Your escape has shamed him, and he is taking it out on Egypt," Cheftu said grimly.

Chloe stepped behind him. "This is my fault?"

"Not exactly . . . you are his excuse to behave like a schoolboy."

"I feel so much better," she replied sarcastically.

"This is a disaster. He will break Egypt on these terms. I should go back to Thut, beg forgiveness for marrying you, and try to dissuade him from this path of destruction." Cheftu sounded less than enthusiastic.

Chloe whirled him around to face her. "That is not safe! It is not sane! To do so would bring death! Why would you do such a thing?"

Leaning against the wall, his gaze distant, Cheftu spoke. "Are you familiar with the history of the Jews?" He didn't wait for her reply. "These plagues are from the Bible."

Chloe sat down on the couch, blinking. "The Exodus?"

"*Oui.* I believe so. Though I thought another pharaoh was on the throne." He chuckled. "I even presented that paper on it. . . ." He trailed off. "No matter. If I am remembering correctly, the next plague should be . . ." He ticked off on his fingers. "We've had blood, frogs, gnats, flies"—he turned to her—"it must have been the murrain of cattle that killed our horses on the way to the temple." He crossed to her and held her close. "For that chance I thank God."

"The volcanic ash must be another plague," she said.

"*Oui,* it must be the plague of boils." He got to his feet. "I must go plead with Thutmosis. If things continue this way, Egypt will be destroyed." He bent to pick up his crumpled kilt.

Chloe got to her feet. "If you do dissuade him, are you not playing God? This Exodus is the bedrock of Judaism for all time!"

Cheftu watched her with a grim smile. "I do not think my efforts are enough to change God's plan. I also think to do my duty as one of Egypt's advisers, I should try. Thut will not kill me. I am one of the favorites of the Great House. Even he would be cautious when dealing with one of the hereditary princes of Egypt."

Chloe stared. He was already kneeling, fastening one of his sandals. "What about the Apiru? Aren't we escaping with them?" she demanded.

He paused, bowing his head to look at the floor. "The answers are not so easy anymore, Chloe," he said, his accentuation of her name sending a shiver down her spine. He turned to look at her, his eyes molten in the golden rays of morning. "We can talk later, but now I must act." He reached for his heavy belt.

Chloe snatched up her gown. "We go together or not at all."

His glance flickered over her. "If you were a Frenchwoman, you would be too weak from *amour* to consider roaming about the country-side during a plague."

She was almost outraged until she saw the side of his mouth twitch with amusement. "American women are hardier." He helped her adjust the straps of her dress and fasten her collar.

Gently he dropped a kiss on her neck. "I will miss these slow days with you, my lady. In all that may transpire, know that you are my heart. *Je vous aime.*"

She leaned back into his warm chest, her pulse jumping in her throat. Apparently French in his time was still very formal. Cheftu kissed the top of her head, then moved away, grabbing his cloak. "Cheftu, isn't this going to ruin our credibility with the Apiru? We're going to have to sneak out. We're breaking their traditions after begging asylum." She looked around, her gaze sharp for their belongings from years of staying in hotel rooms. "Are those your armbands?"

"They are a small payment for those who have risked their lives for us. Perhaps it will enable them to forgive our social gaffe. If they do not see us leave, they cannot be questioned about where we go. Thut will not be able to punish them."

Theoretically, Chloe thought.

The door opened directly onto an inner courtyard, making them visible at once. It wouldn't work. Cheftu crossed to the window and looked out into the deserted outer court. "This is the only way." He kissed her briefly. "I will send someone for you as soon as possible."

She looked out the window. It was a drop, but there were niches and crevices in the crumbling wall of the building for foot- and handholds. She gave a mighty yank on her sheath and pulled off half of the skirt so it ended just above her knees, then swung over the side.

She hoped she'd remember her brief rock-climbing seminar. Cheftu sputtered protests in the room above her, but Chloe was determined to go with him. She skimmed her feet and hands, moving from hold to hold until she was a few feet from the ground. She dropped and rolled, the shock of the hard landing absorbed in the roll. Cheftu dropped next to her, grabbed her hand, and shrank into the faint shadow of the building.

"Should I know anything more?" he hissed. "Besides *glace* and your arachnid tendencies?"

They dodged through the village, running from shadow to shadow. The soft whinny of a horse got Cheftu's attention, and they were soon standing in a lean-to with a pretty bay mare and no chariot.

"Can you ride?" he asked in French.

"Not very well," she said in Egyptian. "These horses have not been broken for that. Won't it be dangerous?"

"No more so than anything else we have done," he said wryly.

Cheftu reached around the horse's neck and hoisted himself up. With a loud whinny she pranced in the stall but apparently decided his weight was no worse than a chariot. Chloe looked up at Cheftu, daunted by the size of the horse. As she looked around for a mounting block, the "other" told her Egyptians didn't *ride* horses. They would think Cheftu truly a magician when he showed up like this. He reached down for her, and with a heave that almost unseated him, Chloe was seated, precariously, behind him, thinking fondly of underwear as she arranged the remains of her dress.

The horse didn't like two passengers and began to buck, trying to rid herself of the weight. Cheftu laced his hands through her mane and held on with his knees. Chloe wrapped herself tightly around him as they jounced around. The mare kicked away the lean-to walls and ran into the square, Cheftu and Chloe clinging to her back. Amid the confused cries Cheftu pulled the side of her head, forcing her toward Avaris. Determined to free herself, she bolted.

By the time the horse slowed, Chloe was exhausted. Cheftu was still hunched across the horse's back, guiding her by pulling at her mane. She hated it, yet Chloe knew there was no other way to goad her—she wasn't trained for this. They stepped out of the overgrown greenery and were on a small road when Chloe noticed it was dusk.

At least at first glance it seemed like dusk, but the sun was still high in the sky. Cheftu yelled something over his shoulder that was lost on the rising wind. When he slapped the rump of the horse and she took off again, Chloe barely had time to grab his waist. The wind began to howl, furiously whipping the foliage and swirling dust. The horse reared when lightning flashed across the sky. Chloe scrambled to stay seated, Cheftu her anchor.

The world was a cacophony of sound as the sky grew darker by the minute. Soon they would be unable to see anything. With a giant boom the skies opened and it began to hail. She crouched farther over Cheftu's back, cringing from the onslaught. Amid the steaming rain was small, pea-size hail. Miraculously, every piece missed them.

When they turned onto a wider road leading into Avaris, Chloe gasped. Fires burned everywhere as hail continued to fall. Each piece was larger; sizzling rocks the size of oranges battered trees. Chloe saw the brutalized bodies of wild dogs in the desolate streets. Cheftu yanked the horse toward the palace. They pulled up to the gates, and he slid off the horse to seek admittance. He pushed the heavy cedar . . . and it swung in. There was no one on duty. Chloe jumped down, and the horse reared and bolted, running beneath the leaden sky.

Chloe and Cheftu ran toward the covered walkway. Once underneath, she looked out at the strange world. The hail was larger: Chloe had no doubt that being hit now would be fatal. She also noticed that when the hail landed, a small flash of fire would ignite the ground, resulting in grass fires that burned despite the damp. She shivered and Cheftu drew her close.

They walked unchallenged through the empty hallways and porticos of the prince's palace. When they reached the audience chamber, voices could be heard from inside. Cheftu halted her and they stood, eavesdropping unabashedly.

"I must do this!" thundered a voice, recognizable as Thutmosis'. "In Avaris alone more than a hundred have died! We must summon him! There is no other choice!" The words of the other man were lost, but the thinly veiled derision in his tone was not. Thut cut him off. "Enough! I have spoken!"

They waited for a moment, but no one came through the towering doors and no other sounds were audible. Squaring his shoulders, Cheftu walked up and pushed open the doors.

Thut spun around, noting their presence with a lifted eyebrow. *"Haii-aii!* The fugitives return." He continued pacing. This is a pleasant shock, Chloe thought, having expected death or prison.

Cheftu crossed his chest in respect. "Another plague, Prince?" he asked calmly.

Thut looked at him from beneath lowered brows. "Aye, magus. Have you any advice for the Egypt you have betrayed?" His voice was cold, his movements marked.

"Aye, Prince. The God with whom you fight is going to win."

Thut stopped pacing and faced Cheftu. "Are you a convert to speak so firmly? Or have you and my aunt-mother conceived this plot to undermine my claim?"

"I am neither, Prince. However, I have seen"—Cheftu struggled for a moment—"the future. If you persist in this hardheartedness, you will not be in it."

Thut approached him, wary. "Are you saying that Horus-in-the-Nest should beg the pardon of a minute god who has neither temple nor treasury nor priests?"

Cheftu looked him directly in the eye. "He is an all-powerful God who has the width and breadth of time and space as his temple, his treasury all imagined wealth. His priesthood one day will cover the earth."

Chloe listened to the conviction in Cheftu's voice. Thut must have also heard it. He turned away, his shoulders hunched. "I have already sent for Ramoses." He walked up to his stool on the dais. "It seems that Pharaoh Hatshepsut, living forever! is also journeying this way." He gestured toward the stools to the left of him. "Please, sit and join me as I plead with a shepherd-slave for the life of Egypt. After I deal with him, I will deal with you. You were wise to let my temper cool." He cast a bitter glance at Chloe.

Cheftu looked back at Chloe, and she followed him to the gilded stools on the floor at Thut's foot. They sat in silence. Chloe looked around the room with its plain stone floors and etched alabaster columns. Behind Thut was a huge mural with the pharaoh smiting his enemies, the same picture that would grace every pharaoh's tomb, along with the list used since the dynasties began, enumerating who would be killed. The list never changed, regardless of who was on the throne. To the people of Egypt whether or not Pharaoh would win was not a question—it was a foregone conclusion.

The more powerful the pharaoh, the more powerful the common man. That was why Thut tried so hard to fight against this "desert god." He truly believed that with his actions went the reputation of Egypt, Chloe realized.

The doors opened and two men, clad in long cloaks and beards, walked in, covering the length of the room in seconds. They inclined their heads toward Thut, waiting for him to speak. Thut waited for innumerable moments. "The golden god's greetings to you, Ramoses and Aharon."

The taller man stepped forward. "Call me no longer Ramoses, as my Egyptian mother did, for I acknowledge no Amun-Ra. Rather call me Moshe."

Chloe almost choked in excitement. Moshe? This was Moses! De Mille wasn't too far wrong about how he looked, though his charisma made even Charlton Heston fade in comparison.

Thut's face darkened with anger, but he held it in stiff control. Ignoring Moshe's request, he said, "Ramoses, take away this plague." He spoke with an imperiousness that would have done Hatshepsut proud.

Moshe spoke, not with arrogance, but with mind-numbing confidence. "I am not God. He hears only prayers. He commands me, I do not command him. Will you let us go? Or will your pride continue to destroy this land you have been given?"

Thut sighed deeply, the weight of the past months starting to tell on his fleshy features. "Please," he said, the entreaty sounding odd on his lips. "Pray to your god for me to take away this torment. I . . ." He paused, the seconds turning into minutes as he sought for the words he had never before said, a concept he had never before understood. "This time, I have transgressed." He stopped, surprise on his features. "This Elohim of yours is in the right. I and my people are in the wrong. Intercede with your god for us and go, for we have had enough. You need not stay in Egypt any longer." He fell silent, his mud-colored eyes almost black in the near darkness of the echoing audience chamber.

Moshe spoke, and Chloe could see Cheftu's lips moving along with Moshe's words. Did he know his Bible stories that well? "When I have gone out of the city, I will spread my hands in supplication to Elohim.

The thunder will stop and the hail will no longer destroy, so that you will know all the earth is Elohim's, even Egypt. But I know you are still not a believer in our God and you still do not respect his power."

Thut had no further comment, and without any acknowledgment of Thut's status the Apiru left the room, the click of the embossed door jolting them all.

Thut turned to Cheftu. "So, magus, have you seen enough of Horus pleading? Will you tell my pharaoh that I am not fit because I am moved by the destruction of my land? Or should I end your life before you chance to betray me again?"

Cheftu fell gracefully on his face in obeisance. "You have averted the greatest disaster Egypt will ever know and have ensured for yourself an afterlife of peace, Pharaoh," he said.

Thut looked shocked; Chloe was stunned. Cheftu was swearing fealty to the pretender to the throne? He could be killed for treason! She looked into the shadows that encompassed most of the room. Any spy could be there, memorizing his words to take back to Pharaoh.

Thut walked to where Cheftu lay on the ground, then raised a foot and placed it on Cheftu's neck. "Your oath is taken, High Lord Cheftu sa'a Lord Khamese, vizier of the Oryx nome. Shall you serve me and serve Egypt for your breath and life?"

"Aye, My Majesty," Cheftu said into the floor.

"Then rise, magus." Cheftu got to his feet and accepted a ring Thut took from his right hand. "Why do you do this, Cheftu? You who have been Hat's friend and counselor for my lifetime?"

Cheftu took the ring and placed it on his left-hand little finger. "Because you must keep to your word. Now I am a trusted counselor, so you will listen to my words. You must honor your vow to this God, Pharaoh."

Thut snorted. "For everyone's safety, do not call me 'Pharaoh.' For Osiris' sake, do not harp on this like a papyrus hawker. I said they can leave, and they can, under my stipulations." He smiled wickedly. "I am not such a fool as to let them leave forever, Cheftu," he said, clapping his new lord on the back. Cheftu's expression became grim again.

"You cannot defy this God and win, Majesty."

Thut glowered at him. "I am Horus-in-the-Nest. My word is Ma'at."

"Will you hold to your word, My Majesty?"

"As it suits me, my lord."

Cheftu looked away, disgusted. "May my wife and I have shelter here?" He was challenging Thut with the relationship. Chloe moved to stand by his side.

Thut growled, his eyes agate. "Aye, but if you ever flout my will again, the jackals will feast on your flesh, magus. Take this used priestess from my sight, and stay far from my chambers and my gardens. I will send for you when your presence is required."

Cheftu and Chloe then bowed stiffly, hurried across the stone pavement, their bare feet making no sound. Once outside they saw the sky was brightening, and true to Moshe's God's word, the hail had stopped.

The destruction was unbelievable. Outbuildings were crushed to the ground. People who had been caught outside were flattened under hailstones as large as basketballs. The gardens were in shambles, vines ripped away from buildings, the odor of crushed lotus rising up through the flame-scented air.

They walked the length of the palace without seeing another soul. Entering Cheftu's suite, they found Ehuru on his mat, the rotten stench of his open sores making Chloe gag. Cheftu knelt at the side of his faithful servant, commanding Chloe to bring water, cloths, and his herbs. Covering her face, Chloe stepped into the chamber where Cheftu slept. She picked up the woven papyrus basket that contained vials and jars, grabbed some fresh linens from Cheftu's couch, and walked into the bathing chamber for water.

She laid everything down by Cheftu and stood, calling for servants. None came. She stepped into the narrow servants' hall that ran through the entire building, where the same smell of rotting flesh reached her. Lighting a torch, she saw the place was littered with ill Egyptians, their burst boils draining onto the mud-block floors. She ran back to Cheftu, repulsed and angry that God could do such a thing.

Cheftu had bandaged Ehuru and was mixing an ointment. The manservant had not woken, but he was breathing easier. Chloe grabbed Cheftu's arm and more linens. "There are more, Cheftu. A whole hallful need your help," she said, dragging him into the servants' hallway. With a muttered oath he knelt by the first victim.

Hours later Chloe stumbled into the bathing chamber. The water was colder than she would have liked, but added to the scented sand bar, it was refreshing and cleansing. Cheftu came in after her, spattered with a variety of noxious fluids and staggering from exhaustion. He sank under the water, and Chloe paddled to him, massaging the kinked muscles in his neck. She washed his torso until his burnished skin glowed in the torchlight. Cheftu leaned against the side of the pool and drew Chloe to him. Burying his face in her neck, he held her.

She leaned into his body, feeling every inch of water-softened skin from the tops of his feet up his strong thighs to his flat abdomen and the curved muscles of his arms. She felt his steady heartbeat and ran her fingers through his dark, wet hair.

"I love you," she said quietly beside his ear.

His arms tightened around her in acknowledgment. "That gives me air to breathe, Chloe," he murmured. His arms relaxed and his breathing became slow and even. Chloe pulled away, realizing he'd fallen asleep. She stepped out of the pool and tapped Cheftu on the shoulder, jerking him awake long enough to follow her into the bedroom. She handed him a robe and grabbed a blanket before they fell onto the couch.

• • •

Shouts from the next room roused Cheftu. He looked at Chloe, snuggled into the sheets like a cat, one hand curled beneath her face. He tucked linens in around her and went to the sitting room, closing the lightweight door behind him.

Ehuru was on his pallet, stirring. Two soldiers stood inside the room. A faint odor of illness still emanated from them, and neither was standing with the precision of the military. They crossed their chests, and one spoke:

"Horus-in-the-Nest requests your presence in the audience chamber, my lord. We will wait for you to wash and dress."

Cheftu waved to the chairs and table. "Then please seat yourselves before you fall. I would call for refreshments, but the servants are all unwell." The soldiers sat down, and Cheftu went into his bathing room, rinsed, and donned his robe. Without disturbing Chloe, he dressed for court, but in the blue of mourning for those who had died. After strapping on a leather belt and collar, he left the room, unable to shave himself or apply the necessary makeup. It felt strange to greet the world this way, a breach of proper etiquette, but this was a national emergency.

If Thut did not keep to his word, it would be a national disaster.

While following the guards through columned walkways unattended and unswept, Cheftu realized the palace was in shambles. They entered the audience chamber through one of the side passages. He was startled to see so many people present, but they were all sick. Open wounds from the previous plague were healing but still unsightly. No one was shaved, and very few had indulged in the elaborate toilette required for court.

Thut was dressed for battle, from his blue-and-white leather helmet to his leather shinguards. He sat on his stool, reading a missive. Cheftu bowed to him and began to move away, but Thut called to him. "It seems my aunt-mother has heard of my actions," he said, voice accusatory. "News travels too quickly." He glared at Cheftu for a few moments and then waved him away. "Even now the Israelites await my pleasure."

Cheftu seated himself with the nobles, listening to tales of lost and wounded acquaintances, of how the plagues had affected everyone from Hapuseneb to Nesbek, down to the papyrus gleaners who lived in the marshes. Some men were angry and wanted retribution. Others wanted to kill the "questing Apiru sons of Set." Still others wanted the slaves to leave, with their flocks and families, and never, ever return to the red and black lands of Kemt.

The chamberlain, leaning against his staff at the end of the room, banged it on the floor and in a feeble voice declared the entrance of Moshe and Aharon.

The doors opened and they walked in, looking taller, stronger, and far more fit than every Egyptian in the room combined, Cheftu thought. They approached Thut, sketching bows in the air.

"You have requested this audience, slave?" Thut said. Apparently his pleading from the day before was not to be repeated.

Moshe did not seem surprised but spoke in ringing tones the words François had learned in one of the many lessons of Père André's catechism.

"You break your promise, Prince, therefore this is what Elohim, God of the Israelites, says: 'How long will you refuse to humble yourself before me? Let my people go that they may worship me. If you refuse to let them go, I will bring locusts into your country tomorrow. They will cover the face of the ground so that it cannot be seen. They will devour what little you have left after the hail, including every tree that is growing in your fields. They will fill your houses and those of all your officials and all the Egyptians. It will be something never seen since the time of Menes-Aha, the unifier of Egypt, until this co-regency of Pharaoh Hatshepsut and Thutmosis the Third."

The court was transfixed, staring after Moshe and Aharon as they left, the door slamming shut with finality. Almost as if a spell were broken, the group began to buzz.

Thut stomped one sandaled foot on the floor. "Silence! You sound like a gaggle of geese in the marshes!" He held up his hand. "This has arrived from Pharaoh Hatshepsut, living forever!" The group fell silent. "She is even now on her way down the Nile to assist us. She commands"—his voice echoed through the chamber—"that the Israelites be brought to heel." His muddy gaze found Cheftu. "She is displeased with the way I have handled this situation. She wants the slaves to stay. She says that 'Amun-Ra is more powerful and will vanquish or assimilate this barbarian desert deity.' Those are her exact words."

The nobles began clamoring, and Cheftu rose to his feet, as one of the few who could stand unassisted. "Prince," he pleaded, "the hail was destructive. It erased our annual crops of flax and barley. The wheat and spelt were protected, still unbudded. This God has given us a way to survive. Let them go!"

Thut's face reflected his inner struggle: to do what was best for Egypt and suffer the ridicule of Hatshepsut or to choose Hat's favor and the hordes of locusts? Cheftu sat down. There was no question who would win. "Curse Thut, and curse his stubborn pride," Cheftu muttered through gritted teeth.

Sennedjm, a wealthy lord and merchant in far-off Mediba, stood. He was young and healthy with a reputation for being an honorable and just man. The group quieted. "Thutmosis, my friend," he said, "we have fought at each other's side, we have traded stories of our wives, and our children have played together." He turned to the other men. "My son Senenbed, though only eight summers old, longs to be a general in Thut's army when Pharaoh ascends to Osiris." The men in the group grinned, each of them thinking of the family that awaited their return. The young lord looked back to his friend the prince and raised his hands in supplication.

"Thutmosis, how long will you let this man catch us in his snare like a hunter? We have no protection, and his god has a very sharp sword, ready to divide our bones and marrow. Let the people go, so they may worship their god. Do you not yet realize that Egypt is ruined?" Sennedjm looked beseechingly at Thut, and the surrounding courtiers applauded him, both for his eloquence and for his nerve.

He sat in silence, and finally Thut motioned to the solitary slave in the chamber. "Bring the brothers," he said. The atmosphere in the room changed as a peace with their actions floated among the nobles. Once again the Apiru entered, their reed sandals slapping on the stone floor.

Thut stopped them with his hand when they were midway down the hall. "Go and worship your 'elohim,'" he bellowed. "Tell me who will be going."

Cheftu pinched the bridge of his nose and rubbed his eyes tiredly. This disaster was not going to be averted. He didn't need to hear Moshe's answer and Thut's ever more enraged rejoinders to realize an even greater plague was coming.

He watched through a veil of depression as the two soldiers who could stand drew their swords and chased the Apiru from the room. Damn your eyes, Thutmosis III, he swore. Cheftu slipped undismissed from the audience chamber and went back to his apartments.

Someone was feeling better, he noted. The halls were swept and the smell of fresh baking bread rose in the hot, sunlit air. He entered his chamber and found Ehuru, eyes bright, sitting up and instructing two young Israelites on how to get food from the kitchens and where to take the linens for washing. Meneptah was seated at the table with Chloe, and they were eating from a tray of bruised fruit. He crossed his breast with respect but also smiled widely at Cheftu.

Chloe, apparently alerted by his expression, hurried to his side. "What is it? What is the problem?"

Cheftu let himself be seated and took a sip of wine. Speaking in his heavily accented English, he said, "Do you know what is the Passover for the Jews?"

"Aye," Chloe said, paling as she glanced at a confused Meneptah.

"It appears it will happen. The prince has not backed away. He is determined to destroy Egypt."

Chloe began to peel an orange. "What is next?"

"Locusts, tomorrow." Cheftu accepted the portion she handed him and looked at Meneptah. "My friend," he said in Egyptian, "you must listen carefully. Your prophet Moshe has foretold that locust swarms will come tomorrow and destroy the land. You must prepare for the journey into the desert."

"The plagues have never affected us before," Meneptah protested.

"God did not say you would be the exception this time," Cheftu said. "You must protect yourselves. Marshal whomever you can and go to the fields and along the river. The garlic and onions are almost ripe, the trees are filled with fruit; pick everything. Before you go to your couches tonight, seal up all your food tightly. Leave out only bread and beer. Then, when the locusts leave, you will still have green nourishment. Go, my friend."

Meneptah rose to his feet. "Will you and the lady RaEm be traveling with us?" He looked from one to the other.

Cheftu answered evenly, "We have not decided, but we still have time to decide."

The Israelite walked to the garden door. Cheftu's call stopped him. "Do not come back to the palace unless and until I send for you. Egypt is angry, and you wear the clothing of your tribe. You are in danger."

THEY SPENT THE AFTERNOON DOING as Cheftu had recommended to the slaves: scrounging for onions, lettuces, fruit, and flavorful herbs along the riverbank. Ra was dying by fire that night, and the sky was shades of crimson and gold as Cheftu paddled their skiff around in the mosquito-laden evening.

When they returned to the palace, Cheftu ordered a dinner and bath for them, dismissing Ehuru to the servants' dining hall. He poured Chloe a goblet of wine and held it to her lips. She sipped the heady fermented dates, tingling at the look in Cheftu's eyes. "The next days are going to be from Set," he said. "Let us enjoy each other while we can."

"Your wish is my command," she said teasingly. A bandaged slave brought in a tray with bread and honey-roasted fowl, and Cheftu dismissed him with a smile. He drew Chloe close to him, resting her against his chest, cradled between his thighs.

Holding her in his arms, he tore pieces off the bird and fed her, watching her intently. She tried to serve him, but he gently placed her hands in her lap. "Allow me, beloved." They said nothing, and Chloe feasted on the sensations of their bodies touching, firing her anticipation.

She took another of the honey-dripping pieces from Cheftu's fingertips, but as she did, she licked off the honey, shivering when he inhaled sharply. He continued to feed her, but some of his dexterity was gone; his hands shook.

Chloe licked the honey off his fingers again, chuckling at Cheftu's muffled moan. He reached forward and covered his fingers with the sticky substance, then reached inside her linen robe, caressing its warmth onto her skin. She gasped, her head thrown back. "What flavor is this?" she asked, breathless. Both hands now covered with the sticky sauce, he caressed her, from her shoulder down her flat abdomen, coating her thighs, and then, softly, creeping together to meet over her throbbing center. She looked at him. "Please," she whispered.

"Patience, beloved." Gently he disentangled himself and went to the table for a drink of water. "We must make it last, Chloe. Hell comes tomorrow, and I do not know when we will be together again, fed and safe. We will need this memory between us, as sustenance." He set down the goblet. "It is still only the beginning of the terrors."

He turned. Chloe was breathing deeply, the tracks of honey glistening designs on her brown skin. Kneeling beside her, he raised her chin with a finger and tasted her lips. They were sticky with honey and hungry. He taunted her with long kisses, twisting his fingers in her black hair. "Lie back, beloved," he said, and pressed her away. She lay, without comment, her robe around her waist and her green eyes glowing.

He filled his mouth with the sweetness of warm honey, his hearing dimmed with desire. Her skin was soft and supple under the sticky coating, the muscles tightly knit together, undulating gently with his attentions. Her hands moved over him, pressing him to her body. Cheftu pushed himself up, but before he could move over her, she scooted away from him, close to the dinner tray. He swallowed hard as she untied her robe and laid both hands in the dish of honey.

She drew to her knees and pressed her hands on her body, slowly, slowly, moving them down, a look of sensual abandonment in her eyes. Her head fell back and her eyes closed, and he heard her tiny gasps as the warm honey trickled over her sensitized skin.

His breath quickened as she caressed her breasts and moved across her belly between her legs. Unconsciously his fingers moved as if he could feel her. She turned back to the honey dish and poured the remainder over her hands and moved toward him. He untied his kilt and let the fabric and the underapron fall away, his eyes focused, entranced, on her cupped and dripping hands.

They met thigh to thigh, belly to belly, and Cheftu kissed her deeply, tracing the warm streaks on her skin. When her lips began to move down his chest, he ground his teeth. She took one of her cupped hands and poured the remaining honey across his torso, creating a slow water-fall across the plain of his chest and abdomen. He groaned as her other honey-coated hand gripped his stones and stroked upward, drenching the hard length of him with honey.

Chloe followed the tracks of honey across his smooth chest, her teeth teasing his flat nipples. His hands gripped her derriere, pulling her to him. She withdrew with a sizzling smile and continued her kissing pilgrimage.

Cheftu sank onto his haunches, his body now glistening with sweat in addition to honey. Then Chloe's mouth was on him, and he fell back on his forearms, staring blindly at the ceiling as he felt her tongue caress him, nipping, swirling. He was shaking with control, letting his naked goddess of love work her magic behind a veil of black hair and honeyed skin.

Desperate to not unman himself, he began to count the types of grapes in his vineyard, in Egyptian, French, *and* English. His long fingers scrabbled hopelessly against the floor as wave after wave of sensuality assaulted him. "Aurelia, Lenoir, Blanc du Bois, Champanel, Chardonnay, Chenin Blanc . . ." Her excited moans were not helping. They battered his body and emotions. "Fredonia, Concord . . ."

Chloe leaned over him. "Do you want to torture us both, Cheftu?" she whispered. "Why do you not let go?" He felt the welcome weight of her body on his, and the stickiness further fired his already inflamed brain.

"I did not want to lose control while—"

She smiled at him, tempting in her candor. "I want you to. *Tout est doux en amour.*"

His eyes bulged as white-hot lightning shot through his veins. *Haii-aii!* Indeed, in love all was sweet! He spoke hoarsely, urging her to release his passions. Instead she lay on him, her movements, lips, and hands almost driving him to a frenzy. When he reached for her she lifted up.

"Patience, beloved," she whispered with a wicked smile. "You must have patience."

He, Lord Cheftu, whose patience and control was, if not legendary, then at least well-known and respected. When he saw only red behind his closed eyelids and his arms felt as if they were forged metal, he felt her weight leave his chest and the soft fall of her hair on his belly. She engulfed him, and Cheftu shook like a tree in a khamsim, the gradual growing within him increasing until he felt himself explode, his fingers tangled in Chloe's hair.

When at last his *ka* returned to him, he felt Chloe snuggled against his side, the honey on her body cool and tacky. She leaned over him for a kiss.

"So what flavor was that?" he asked.

"*Assst.* For you it was double-dip, chocolate-sprinkled, caramel walnut cookie dough splendor. *I* had vanilla." Cheftu lay still, feeling his heartbeat return to normal. "Are you asleep?"

"Naaaaay," he murmured.

He heard her smile. "Well, go to sleep. That is all you are good for now anyway."

They awoke, cold and shivering, in the darkened room.

"Come, beloved," Cheftu said, his voice rough, and clinging together, they stumbled into their room and curled up on the couch, shivering and messy. Then Chloe gently drew Cheftu onto her body, asking with her mouth and limbs. As Cheftu climaxed he saw tears streak down her cheeks. "Why do you cry, beloved?" he whispered. "I have not hurt you, have I?" He gathered her close, kissing her face and hair.

"Nay. It is just that when we are making love, your pleasure is mine. When you are vulnerable with me, it is a gift." She wiped her eyes. "I guess it is hard to believe we are together. That somehow in this mix of time and space we found each other. I guess there is a God."

"Aye. He brought us together. We will never part."

"Never."

***

Chloe sat up, wide awake. She was motionless, listening in the darkness for whatever had awakened her. Cheftu was still asleep, his legs tangled in with hers. It came again, a high mournful cry, and she relaxed when she realized it was the wind, whipping through the air cones on the corners and roof of the palace. They were there for ventilation, and the high winds sounded eerie as they whistled through the channels.

She lay back down, curving her body next to Cheftu's. His arm possessively pulled her close, holding her imprisoned against him, even in sleep. Chloe snuggled closer, feeling the hairs on his legs tickle her bare bottom and thighs. Sleepily Cheftu kissed her shoulder, and Chloe lay still, listening to the wind, perfectly content for the first time in her life.

Her feeling of contentedness was much diminished in the morning. She had dreamed of Camille, walking through the ancient Karnak Temple, searching for some clue to the whereabouts of her little sister. She had been crying and blaming herself, and Chloe had awakened feeling irritated that Cammy was taking the blame. If anyone is to be held accountable for my being in this predicament, she thought, it's me. If I ever return, I'll never go in someplace where I'm not allowed.

Even Cheftu's exploring morning hands and welcoming body set her teeth on edge. She jumped up from the couch, and Cheftu woke fully, sensing her different spirit from that of the passionate goddess of the night before.

She barked for slaves and went in for her bath. Cheftu lay, staring out the high windows. The sky was yellow—bright, but brittle. He drew on a kilt and walked into the garden. It was hard to tell what the time was; the sun was hidden. Far to the east he could see a shimmering saffron-colored cloud. Though he had never experienced a locust cloud, he was sure that it was approaching. He ran back inside, summoning slaves and making the final preparations that he could.

Cheftu stepped into the bath chamber and shouted, "Get bathed and dressed immediately, RaEm!"

When Chloe emerged, feeling slightly more at charity with the world, Cheftu was gone. The room had been changed. Already the lack of air was making it stuffy. The windows were sealed off with mud bricks, the air cones boarded up the same way. Smoke from torches on the walls made her eyes sting. Even the garden windows were closed, the delicate alabaster reinforced with mud bricks. "He certainly worked fast," Chloe said aloud.

Ehuru appeared in the doorway. "Come, my lady," he said. "Lord Cheftu awaits you in the garden."

Chloe followed him down the long hallway to the colonnaded porch, where those nobles staying in the palace had gathered. Most of them the "other" memory recognized, but not the man standing with Cheftu in deep conversation. Chloe was surprised to see he was holding a baby, wrapped tightly but already sporting the youthlock of a young Egyptian. Cheftu watched her warily, and Chloe winked, sorry for her snappishness earlier.

"Beloved," he said, addressing her, "this is Count Sennedjm of the Ibis nome." To the count he said, "My wife, the Lady RaEmhetepet of the goddess HatHor." Sennedjm smiled at her, his attention floating between the small talk they made and the three young boys scampering through the battered garden. The baby in his arms was sleeping soundly, and Chloe felt a catch in her throat as she looked at the chubby face with its arching black brows and pink pucker of a mouth.

The air was suddenly filled with static electricity, and Sennedjm broke off in the middle of a story to look to the east, where everyone else's scrutiny was fixed. Thut stood before them all, the papyrus scroll from Pharaoh still in his hands. The brittle yellow sky was obscured by a large metallic-looking cloud, so dense and so huge that it became like twilight. Chloe stood rock still, head craning back to see into it. Cheftu moved closer to her, his body tense, his expression somber. The wind picked up, blowing away the broken trees, causing kilts to fly into the air and wigs to fly off. And blowing the papyrus from Thut's hand.

The group hurried under the protection of the portico and continued to watch. The wind began to blow away bits of the cloud, and a loud buzzing replaced the roar of the storm. Thut alone stood in the garden, his golden collar and wig gone, his legs apart in a soldier's stance, holding out against the buffeting of the gale.

The cloud began to fall. *It was raining locusts!* Chloe screamed as they hit the ground, their bodies clinking with the impact. They were huge. Chloe had seen locusts before, had even eaten them on a dare. These, however, were enormous!

Locusts were part of the grasshopper family, she remembered, built with the same powerful legs and colored green, gold, and brown. Instead of the usual two-inch grasshopper, however, these suckers were three to five inches long and striped black and yellow. Already they were stripping the ground of its grass, in a low roar of chewing. Thousands had fallen and were marching, militarily, across the garden, devouring every living thing in sight.

It was like watching a color film fade to black and white.

Cheftu looked over to Chloe, his jaw set and his lips in a thin line. She saw pity and regret in his golden glare. People scattered back to their apartments, and even Thut retreated to the portico. More locusts fell every minute, marching over each other, charging to the greenery, climbing up walls to eat the remaining vines, covering the trees, tearing away the protective bark, and eating the fresh green leaves. Chloe felt sick.

Cheftu had moved to Thut's side. The prince was staring out at a brown, useless garden, and the locusts marched into another garden.

"My Majesty," Cheftu began, and Thut jerked toward him. He didn't even know we were here, Chloe thought. "Should you go inside, Prince?" Cheftu asked.

Thut's elongated brows drew together. "Nay. I will take my chariot and go to the fields. We must see the level of destruction in Egypt." Cheftu bowed and turned, as Chloe heard Thut say under his breath, "Since we are responsible for it."

Others had not prepared their quarters for the locusts, so Chloe and Cheftu spent most of the day going into different apartments, sealing off the windows and passages and then assigning slaves to kill the remaining locusts. They were especially hard to kill, their bodies seemingly encased in armor. Eventually they were destroyed, and the inhabitants were ordered not to unseal the spaces. The weather was not cooperating. It was unbearably hot and dry, and by nightfall everyone's nerves were on edge.

Word got round that Thut had spent the day in the locust rain, traveling through the delta to see the destruction. He sent couriers down the Nile to intercept Hatshepsut, living forever!—everywhere, it seemed, there were locusts. When Thut got back he had gone silently to his apartments and dismissed all his retainers.

CHAPTER 12

When the sun rose the next morning, Cheftu was gone. Chloe dragged out of bed and walked into the receiving room. He was kneeling by the garden door, patching the drying mud bricks in the doorway. A high squeal came from outside. She put her hands to her ears. "What is that?"

"The locusts. They shriek in the sunlight." He pointed to the table. "Put the wax in your ears."

After kneading the greasy tallow between her fingers, Chloe filled her ears; the annoying locust ringing ceased, but she was still able to feel the vibrations from millions of locusts. She put on her sandals and stepped into the corridor. It was filled with migrating locusts. Gritting her teeth, she stepped down, crunching some of the locusts to mush, while others walked across the tops of her feet. By the time she reached the kitchens, food was the last thing she was interested in, but she wanted to see exactly what they were going to eat. A few slaves moved about in the outer courtyard, the honeycomb-shaped ovens belching smoke and the aroma of fresh bread.

The cook was surprised to see a noblewoman but seemed to appreciate the effort since she was so shortstaffed. Everyone was deaf with wax, so they communicated by sign language. Chloe was a little disconcerted to see one of the slaves shoveling in locusts to be used as fuel. She took several loaves of bread in her covered basket and a pitcher of milk. By the time she got back to the apartments, the top of the milk was full of locusts.

I wouldn't mind them so much, she thought, if they just wouldn't fly at me and spit on me. Walking across the garden was like something from a Hitchcock film. All around was the sound and a million echoes of chewing, biting, tearing, and destroying. Her sheath was covered with bugs, and she had to hold back screams as they crawled up her legs beneath her skirt and inside her linen wrap.

When she reached the hallway, she shook off and stomped the locusts on her person, skimmed out the milk-covered locusts, shook locusts out of her hair and dress, and stepped inside. Most of the morning was gone, and so were Cheftu and Ehuru. Chloe lit one of the smoking torches and seated herself, putting her feet upon the stool opposite and wrapping her skirt tightly around her legs. She tore off a hunk of bread and ate it, then poured some of the warm milk in a glass but couldn't drink any more after spitting out a spare locust leg.

The locusts were working against the soft mud brick, and Chloe saw in the torchlight that it wouldn't hold much longer. Despairing, she went into the bedroom—crunch, stomp, crunch—and retrieved her lousy excuse of a notebook.

Closing her eyes, she tried to picture the nightmare outside. The recently budded trees were bare below their bark, the walls were naked, and locusts clogged the pools. She recalled the resigned terror on the faces of those few people she had seen.

•••

The light gutted in its holder, leaving Chloe in tomblike darkness. Swearing, she slipped on her sandals and stifled a scream as her foot touched one of the locusts, then moved slowly toward the torches. They were all used, their oil gone, leaving a dry, straw-textured club. She peered in the direction of the garden gate, trying to discern any light through the cracks, but she couldn't see any. Surely I didn't sketch away the whole day, she thought. However, it seemed more and more likely.

She shuffled toward the hallway door, gritting her teeth at the flutter and brush of wings and legs of the disturbed locusts. Upon reaching it, she yanked it open and stared into the dimly lit depths. She pulled a lump of wax from her ears. Blessed quiet! One torch glowed at the far end, and Chloe saw the starless night beyond. What I wouldn't give for a watch, she thought. Though I'd prefer a cigarette or even a decent pencil!

Turning away from her unproductive thinking, she looked up and down the corridor, but there was no sign of life anywhere, unless you counted the millions of bulging-eyed eating machines scattered the length and breadth of Egypt. She walked outside—crunch, grind, pop. Her gown was spattered with the spit of the locusts, the brown stains looking like blood in the feeble light. Shuddering, she drew her arms close and looked around.

The destruction was staggering. The topography was flat; every tree and bush that had stood was now level with the ground. Then Chloe heard the low buzzing roar of the creatures eating. She brushed them off her face and arms and looked back to the palace for signs of habitation. It was mostly dark, and Chloe wondered if the people had just gone to bed or gone to their town homes or country villas until this was over.

Mechanically picking the bugs off her body and clothing, she walked back to her rooms, taking the torch and the spare that was kept behind the holder. Once inside she threw away the milk, which had curdled in the stuffy heat, squashed more bugs, and settled down to more bread, some locust-skimmed water, and a night of drawing.

When she sat up and stretched at dawn, Cheftu had still not returned. Where the hell was he? She refilled her jug of water, locust free thanks to the expedient of covering it, and munched on the stale bread. Peeking outside, she saw the sun had risen and was already burning high and bright. She withdrew at the light and at the sight of the many locusts still gnawing away at what was left of the vegetation. She plugged her ears again. Exhausted, she stumbled over locusts to the couch, fanning the sheets to make sure they were clean, or at least locust free, and lay down, falling into a deep and dreamless sleep.

She jumped when she felt the touch on her elbow and turned over to see Cheftu's servant, Ehuru. "By the gods! What happened to you?" He was blackened with smoke, his eyes red and bleary, and he had vicious-looking burns on his hands and arms. His eyebrows had singed off, and Chloe saw for the first time that he was shaven headed, having lost his wig at some point.

He gave a sketchy reduction of his usual bow and said in a rasping voice, "We have been seeing to the Apiru all night, my lady. My Lord Cheftu was concerned you would worry and sent me to check on you."

Chloe got up and forced him to lie down. "Rest just for a moment," she said, overriding his protests.

"On my master's couch? It is unthinkable, my lady!"

"Ehuru, do it. It is my order."

"My lady, I—"

"Ehuru!"

"This is for you, my lady," he finally said, handing her a papyrus scroll before his eyes closed and his low snoring filled the room.

Stepping into the main room, she broke the Oryx nome seal and read the hieratic scrawl. "Beloved—there has been a fire, many are wounded. I am sorry to leave you but must assist all I can. I shall return to you, keep faith this will not last long." Then, instead of his name, he had signed in fluid, flowing script, "François." Chloe smiled as she traced the letters with her fingertip, the locusts forgotten momentarily as she remembered his lovemaking.

However, if her nineteenth-century–ancient Egyptian composite husband expected her to just keep the home fires burning until the men returned home, he was in for a shock. Fires were disasters. Misplaced and hungry people, disorganization, and chaos were her specialty. Cheftu would be dealing with the victims, but who would help the confused survivors?

Chloe smiled to herself. I'm the up-and-coming Red Cross—no, make that Red *Ankh*—brigade. Would Cheftu like this? No. Would Ehuru let her come back? No. Would that matter? Chloe twisted her—RaEm's—ankh necklace. No.

• • •

Actually, Ehuru wasn't nearly as difficult to badger as Chloe had expected. He didn't think the burned village was a place for "my lady," but his eyes filled with tears when he admitted that aye, the Apiru did need help.

They left in the afternoon, a horrifying, post-Apocalyptic walk. No greenery remained anywhere. Stubs that were once trees bristled obscenely from nude, dusty soil. Locusts covered the sides of buildings, eating vines and flowers, staining everything tobacco brown. The beautiful whitewashed buildings, clean and neat even among the *rekkit*, were discolored hovels.

The sky, a brassy, alien blue, seemed harsh above the moving, living black-and-yellow earth. Chloe wept, her lips compressed to avoid the odd, flying locust.

Doggedly they kept walking, stomping and crushing the bugs, staining their feet and ankles with locust innards, like a macabre vintners' dance. She was certain her legs were numb, for even those bugs that crawled up her dress she blithely brushed aside. Praise HatHor she had fashioned a tight, impenetrable diaper.

They arrived after *atmu*, and Chloe gasped when she saw the village. It was like an El Greco: eerie gray smoke against the night, tortured figures, and unholy, glowing flames in the distance.

Cheftu and Meneptah had set up a makeshift surgery in a tent to the side of the remaining house. Light glowed behind the smoke-stained flax curtain, and locusts moved on the outside, weighing down the fabric.

Lying on the locust-covered ground were bodies. "They are laid out in family groups," Ehuru said, his voice flat.

Chloe was grateful for the darkness, though the white glow of bare bone and the horrifying stillness were graphic enough testimony to the deaths. The stink of burned flesh hung like a mournful cloud over the smoldering remains, and Chloe's stomach was empty before they stepped into the square.

The survivors clustered here. Those too weak to live had been given painkillers and waited to die, to meet their jealous God. Those who were relatively unscathed sat in shock, staring. The slaves had no organization: water sat in jugs a hand's reach from those dying of thirst.

Everywhere, covering everything, were locusts. They buried the dead, they poisoned the wounded, and they crawled on the living.

It was the closest thing to hell that Chloe could imagine. She felt scared and sick and wished violently that she'd never come. "The well is filled with locusts," Ehuru said. "We cannot get to the water."

"My lady?" The harsh voice, tear filled and vaguely feminine, halted Chloe. She scanned through the darkness, the lumps of flesh moving and still.

"D'vorah?"

The Israelite girl stepped forward, and Chloe stifled a shriek. She had been badly burned; her hair, eyebrows, and eyelashes were gone, leaving crusted dark wounds, a gruesome relief on the girl's sooty face. Her hands were bandaged, yet she smiled, her lips cracked and bleeding. "Why have you come, my lady? This is no place for you!"

Chloe bit her lip to hide her revulsion. Medicine had never been appealing—she hadn't even been able to carve open her frog in junior high biology. Even cuts and bruises on her own body seemed foreign and horrible. It had taken three tries before she'd completed her first-aid training, and even then she'd been sick afterward. However, this was D'vorah, the young woman who had been with her through the miscarriage. The one who had held her hand when Chloe had spontaneously burst into tears. It wasn't just a sick, scabbed, wounded person. It was a friend.

Tears streaming down her cheeks, Chloe hugged her gingerly, feeling D'vorah's delicate bones beneath parchment-dry skin. The girl sobbed, racking sounds that led to globs of black phlegm bubbling through her lips. Chloe was pinned between pity and horror. "How is your family?"

"Gone, my lady. All gone."

They sank onto the locust-covered ground, the wails of mourning blending with the low drone of destruction. Chloe held the girl, listening. To save their master's fields from the locusts, for he was a good man, the Apiru had started fires, using smoke as a deterrent. The foreman was gone, but it was a typical choice to make in a locust storm.

It had worked well until the wind had suddenly shifted. Within moments the mud-brick village with its dried reed roofs had burst into flame.

"I was sleeping downstairs," D'vorah said. "With the children—Ari, who is five, and Lina, who is eight." She put a blistered hand to her mouth. "They never even awoke!" She coughed again, and Chloe winced at the dark blood mixed in with the black mucus.

"A popping sound woke me." She crossed her arms on her knees, watching the locusts climb up her burned hands. "I carried the children to the window, but I could not put them through! It was too high, and I was too weak."

D'vorah said that while she had stood there, trying to fit her smoke-dead siblings through the clerestory window, the roof had crashed in, raining molten brick and the scorched bodies of her parents and older siblings.

Meneptah had been outside and had battered the windowsill and dragged D'vorah through, but not before a jar had exploded, inflaming her hair and scorching her face.

Chloe rocked the burned girl in her arms, caressing her shoulders, picking the locusts off her burns.

— — —
• • •

"Lady RaEm?"

Chloe opened her eyes to see a black figure bent over her in the dawn. She and D'vorah were lying together, arms around each other. Chloe twisted her body, protecting the girl. "What do you want?" she snapped, half-asleep and scared.

The man stepped back hastily, crossing his chest. "It is Meneptah, my la—"

"Meneptah! I am so sorry! Please, I was asleep. Come, see D'vorah."

The Israelite bent over the sleeping girl. His hands were clean, the only part of him not black with soot. His touch was painstakingly gentle, reverent, and when Chloe looked at his face, the expression in his eyes, she doubted D'vorah would be without a family for long. She slipped away, seeing the destruction for the first time.

It had been a much larger village than the one in which they were married. Forty, maybe fifty two-story homes had clustered around dirt tracks all leading to the center well and the square.

Nothing but the shack at the end, where Cheftu's surgery was, still stood. Charred squares and rectangles were all that remained of street after street of homes. How many people had there been? How many had survived?

The sun was already hot on Chloe's neck, and she couldn't fathom the agony for those who were burned. Shelter, water, and food were what these people needed.

She needed Ehuru. She needed some slaves. Chloe bit her lip, wanting to see Cheftu but afraid to disturb him. His work was saving lives; she could wait.

— — —
• • •

Chloe recruited five Apiru women, grieving and in need of a task, and sent them to the palace in the care of Ehuru.

While they were gone, she and three teenage boys who were hurt, but not badly, proceeded to clean out the well, taking turns going inside to sift out buckets of locusts. Chloe was convinced that at least forty thousand locusts had fallen in the well. It was horrible, the dank, clammy darkness, the crawling bugs, grabbing handfuls of piled and drowned locust bodies, and throwing them in the buckets to be hauled up.

When the well was clean enough—in other words, only thirty percent locusts—Chloe instructed the returned women to weave a linen well covering from the palace sheets.

She and her three boys left, returning with stripped tree trunks. With mud, niter, and crushed locusts they mixed a cement to fix the trees in the ground solidly. Then they stretched layer after layer of linen sheeting across the four trunks. Carefully, on linen and branch stretchers, they moved the survivors into the shade.

When one of the women fainted from hunger, Chloe knew they had to eat. Ehuru had raided the palace kitchens, returning with fat, lazy fowl, honey, and flour. Though she didn't speak the language of the women, they communicated in the international and eternal way of all culinary mavericks. The flour and eggs became soup, a kind of cross between chicken dumpling and egg drop, Chloe thought, and finally they fried locusts and served them with honey, a bittersweet treat for the Apiru.

Chloe thought the locusts' taste was better disguised under chocolate, but there was a certain mean satisfaction in crunching the little monsters who had terrorized her for days, awake and asleep; a distinct vengeance to rip off their legs and wings before cooking them.

When the people came in from the fires in the fields, Egyptian and Apiru working side by side, Chloe saw that they had water to rinse with and drink, then soup and locusts. For three days she worked, never seeing Cheftu but instructing Ehuru to see that he took some soup. Another village on the edge of the estate had caught fire, and Cheftu was dealing with their casualties while Chloe organized their survivors. The locusts were soon the sole foodstuff, but the well was once again sweet.

They no longer fell from the sky, but they were still piled about three deep everywhere there had been grass. She crunched through them without thinking, her face set in a permanent expression of revulsion. The noise of their hammering jaws had become an audient wallpaper; she didn't hear it but knew it was there at all times.

She didn't know she'd collapsed until she woke up to face a black-stained, furious, proud *hemu neter* spouse. They had done all they could do; it was time to go home.

• • •

Thutmosis' palace was still deserted, except for the slaves and the ever-present locusts. Chloe and Cheftu absently trod them into the floor on the way to their apartments and inside. Cheftu was gray beneath the soot but refused to sleep until he was cleaned. Chloe thought he would probably drown if he tried alone, so she led him toward the bath chamber and helped him unfasten his kilt and sandals as she sat him on the stool and skimmed the water for locusts.

"It is not fresh or warm," she warned, and Cheftu croaked in a facsimile of laughter.

"Anything is cleaner than I am, and I have felt enough heat to last a lifetime." He sank into the water, not caring, and Chloe began washing off the soot and grime. He was crisscrossed with scratches, and the black hair on his arms had been singed, the roots standing up like bristles. His hair was oddly burned, patches here and there, leaving small areas of his scalp pink and peeling. Chloe washed his face, noting the beard growth and trying not to irritate the angry red marks that looked like claws or fingernails. His hands were blistered from the heat; Chloe wondered how he had taken care of others when his hands were so wounded. The fingernails were cracked and torn, the small black hairs that graced his fingers torched. His eyebrows were singed, but he suffered no major damage.

Then she saw his back. He must have stood with it directly to the fire, she thought. The blisters were raised and filling with fluid, and it looked as though a branch had fallen across his shoulder, touching his upper back and part of his upper buttocks. He had fallen asleep in the cool water but jerked awake when Chloe touched him.

"What happened, Cheftu? What was it like? Talk to me," she asked softly.

He groaned and whispered, his lungs also damaged. "People were screaming, running with their bodies on fire, seeking some relief. The houses went up in moments, the smoke killing those still asleep." He sighed heavily. "I arrived too late to do anything. Meneptah and his mother had been staying with family. It is a boon of the god that they were awake and in the square when they saw the wind change and the sparks fly." He ran a hand over his face. "As you saw, most of the people who survived have lost their hair, or eyebrows, and have blistering burns. Those who were badly burned have died, which is merciful. We could do nothing for them."

Cheftu looked at his hands, the torchlight warping their shape under the water. "I am concerned about my hands. They are my, our, life, our livelihood." He pulled one out from the water, looking at it closely. "The burns do not go farther than the first layer or so of skin. With some oil, they should be well soon."

"What about your back?"

"It does not matter. I have no medicines left." He shrugged, wincing. "Get me oil and a feather. Stroke the oil on and we will hope for the best." He finished rubbing off what black he could and staggered from the pool. She heard his snores before she was out of the water.

•••

A knock sounded on the door and Chloe, startled out of sleep, answered it, still tying her robe. It was a royal guard, and he handed her a scroll, inclined his head, and instructed Chloe to give it to Lord Cheftu, *erpa-ha.*

"He was wounded and is resting."

The instructions were to open it immediately, the guard said, so reluctantly she walked into the bedroom and knelt by Cheftu, kissing him gently on the forehead. "Beloved, you must wake up." She touched his shoulder and then jumped back as he rose to his feet, swearing when he felt the pain in his back. His hair stuck out in singed clumps, and he was wearing a formidable frown; when he saw Chloe he lay back down.

"Thought someone woke me," he mumbled, already half-asleep.

"I did. This is for you. From the prince." She extended her hand with the papyrus.

He read it in silence, one hand propping up his chin. "Ramoses was called in and heard the prince's request that the locusts leave. Thut says that Ramoses did not demand anything for removing the plague. He did not repeat his request for freedom. However, he seemed regretful." Cheftu rolled the papyrus and sank his face into the oil-drenched linens. The temperature in the room was rising rapidly, and Chloe felt her robe sticking to her body.

"How do you feel this morning?" she asked quietly. "I was not sure if I should cover your back or leave it uncovered."

Cheftu turned to her, one eye visible above the rise of the couch. "Did you use the oil?"

"Aye."

"Then all we can do is let the body begin to heal. I really should make an amulet; maybe an entreaty to Sekhmet to alleviate some of the pain," he mused.

"Would another bath help?"

"It would feel like heaven"—he swatted an inquisitive locust off the couch—"but would soften the skin so that when I put a bandage on, it will stick like mud brick to my back. You will have to tear it off every time to clean the wound."

"That is barbaric!" Chloe said. "Have you no other solutions?"

"There are no solutions! That is what I would recommend to any of my patients. I can do no better. There is no proven 'cure' for burns." Chloe poured more oil on his back, and Cheftu sighed as it cooled and relieved, momentarily. "I would do a lot for a bottle of good cognac right now," he said.

She smiled at the back of his head. "I do not have cognac, but the woman in the kitchen gave me a bottle of something to drink when she heard you were burned." She walked to the table in the receiving room and brought it back.

Cheftu sniffed at the neck. *"Rekkit* water of some kind."

"Can you tell what's in it?"

"A lot of alcohol," he said with a short laugh. He took a swig, and Chloe saw his mouth twist in distaste, but he continued to drink. More than half the bottle was gone by the time he handed it back.

She lay down next to him, their bodies inches apart. "Do you want to talk about it?"

"Nay. Many good people died, whether they were Apiru or not does not matter."

"Ehuru said you saved some people."

"Ehuru exaggerates. God saved them, I simply ran in and picked them up." His voice was muffled, speaking into the bed linens.

"When did you get your burns?" Chloe asked quietly.

"When we got there, the flames were moving from house to house by the moment. I ran for the last house. Inside there was a young boy, maybe five summers old, cowering in the corner. He was surrounded by fire, and I could hear his cries above the crackle of the flames. Baked locusts were all around. I ran forward, urging him to get on the table and jump to me. The flames were not licking very high yet. Finally he did, and when I had him in my arms I turned to run out the door, but it was filled with flames. So I ran to the clerestory window.

"I do not remember how we got out, but Ehuru said the beam struck me as I was crawling through the window. I must have fainted." He fell silent.

"The boy?"

"Little Caleb? He has some blackness in his lungs, but he is fine otherwise." They lay in silence together until she heard his breathing, deep and regular. Chloe inched off the bed, kicked the locusts out of her sandals, and left the room.

Cheftu lay asleep for the better part of three days. He woke to take some chicken stew and water. Ehuru came in the second day he was asleep, and they alternated over Cheftu's care. Chloe either continued her series of drawings and sketches or slept on her time off. One day she went to the village, where they were rebuilding, making mud-and-locust bricks. D'vorah was healing but busy with the remaining village children. Their master and the foreman had not returned yet.

The locusts were still everywhere, but they had stopped eating the day Moshe said they would. They just *were*. Then one morning Chloe woke before the sun, and when she went outside she had to rub her eyes to make sure she wasn't dreaming. The ground was moving! Like a black-and-gold carpet, the locusts were moving, marching across the ruined gardens and palace, methodically walking west.

Then, as if following the orchestration of a giant hand, they lifted wings and rose, up into the air, the mass of them, riding the westerly wind to the sea. Chloe ducked to avoid those taking flight close to her and watched in amazement as the star-strewn night was obliterated with the glittering mass. She stood for hours, watching as the cloud grew smaller and smaller. The only locusts left were the old and sick, still hobbling westward ho!

• • •

For almost a week things were normal, Chloe thought.

At least as normal as time-traveling back to an ancient culture, falling in love, getting married, and planning treason could be. Not to mention drinking blood and tripping out on prehistoric peyote. Aye, if that was your idea of normal, things were way cool.

The slaves had returned, the palace was clean, and everyone was preparing to receive Hatshepsut, living forever! A large feast was to be held in three days, and the hairdressers and ancient couturiers were being snatched up by the incoming nobility who had left their servants at home.

Cheftu was up and moving around, a loose linen shirt covering his back, and he was taking smaller amounts of the drink the cook had provided. Chloe had not gone back to the kitchens since the return to normalcy. Cheftu had treated a variety of people, from the ladies who were ill from so much river travel to the burned slaves whom Meneptah ministered to under the *hemu neter*'s supervision. Cheftu had not been home before the fifth watch in as many days. Doctor's jobs had not changed much in the intervening years, Chloe thought. They still spent all their waking hours in practice.

She walked alone through the gardens, ruined by the locusts yet vainly sending forth green shoots, which would be collected for Hat's feast. It was almost time for the noon meal, Chloe thought, walking toward the flat-roofed palace.

Suddenly, night fell like an anvil. Chloe quickly looked up. The sun was faintly visible through the enormous black cloud that now hung between heaven and earth. Then it became darker, and Chloe realized she couldn't even see her white gown in the darkness. She heard cries from the people in the palace, invoking Ra. Their shrieks became more panic filled as it grew darker. Chloe knew, however, that the gold god in Waset had no more to do with this sudden darkness than her sister, Camille.

It was the last plague before Passover.

She could almost see her old boyfriend Joseph's family's table in Florence, the extended family wearing their finest clothes, each silver place setting accompanied by delicate gold-etched blue Venetian glass goblets, in which each person had dipped a finger and recited the plagues in unison. "Blood, frogs, gnats, flies, cattle, boils, hail, locusts, darkness, death of the firstborn."

Each drop of ruby red wine represented one of the ways God had used the elements to bring Egypt to its knees and free the Jews. Chloe stared upward.

She could see absolutely nothing. Even her sense of direction seemed to be obscured, and she hardly knew the way back. Using the frightened cries as an auditory beacon, she began walking toward the palace. The whitewashed walls might as well be covered in pitch, she thought, for all the good they are doing me. She continued walking forward, hands out-stretched. She touched something solid and felt around the sides. A door. As she stepped inside, the cries that had been faint became rau-cous. Male and female voices echoed within the mud-brick walls, sounding like a terrified army.

"Why does someone not light a torch?" she asked aloud, trying to sense whether anyone was there. After feeling around, and tripping more than once, she came to the conclusion that she was in their apartments, or in ones so similar that it didn't really matter. She felt along the wall for a torch, then lit it. At least she thought she did. The sounds were all there, the sputter as the flame caught and grew. But no light. Nothing.

Mystified, Chloe recalled the last arrangement of the room. She found a stool by scraping her shins on it and sat down to think. How long did this plague last? She tried to remember that one Passover meal; what had they said about the plague of darkness? Damn! I sure wish I'd paid more attention to the story, she thought, instead of wondering what Joseph had been thinking about me. . . . Oh, well, if need be, she could just sit here for the duration. Nothing had lasted too long, though we could have done with half as many locusts and still called it a major plague. Still, God had been pretty merciful, she thought objectively.

Chloe smiled into the darkness, relieved that for once she knew what was going on. Her smile faded as she heard the genuine terror in the voices around her. Screams, cries, pleading with Ra not to abandon them.

Her heart began to hurt for these people—in their eyes, their god was dead. Hesitant, and afraid of the surfeit of information she might receive, she turned to the "other." She barely had time to close the mental door before she drowned in ancient thought. Sorting carefully, sitting in the dark, she looked at the world from RaEm's perspective.

All she saw was chaos.

Ma'at had been cast down. The eternal balance of the universe was off-kilter. There was no rhyme or reason, only pain, confusion, and betrayal. Even RaEm, for all her sadistic sexual practices and betrayal of her religion, was numb.

To RaEm, the darkest depths of Egyptian hell, the pathways through the underworld, were now here. Darkness, creatures seeking human destruction, uncertainty, and death hovered anywhere light could not flourish. This wasn't just an eclipse or whatever Chloe's twentieth-century mind rationalized. It was the end of the world. Unimaginable horror was being realized. The Egyptians were superstitious. Like most primitives, they perceived evil in darkness and good in light. This plague was evil personified—and the stark terror it invoked in the Egyptian soul was enough to drive one to madness.

RaEm's mind cried out to the goddess she had dishonored and the eternal sun god who was no longer visible. She raged and wept and cowered, begging and pleading for light. Chloe closed the mental door. She couldn't handle RaEm's shaking bewilderment. The fear and dread were too all-encompassing.

The darkness seemed like a living thing, heavy as a woolen blanket and as smothering. Chloe held up her hand and couldn't see it before her face. Her natural impatience was not going to let her rest for these days while Egypt cowered. Where was Cheftu? Slowly she got to her feet and shuffled toward the garden door. The fresher air greeted her, and she felt the flooring change beneath her sandals.

It was no longer the springy grass of weeks ago, but the earth still had more give than the stone pavement. She craned her head back, searching for light of some sort: sun, moon, stars, alien spaceships, she didn't care. They just weren't visible. Trying to visualize an aerial map of the palace, she began to walk cautiously toward the main audience chamber.

It was much quieter now—Chloe couldn't sense any people around her, and the grounds seemed ominously quiet. She tripped over the raised edge of a tiled path and stepped onto it. If her memory was accurate, this would lead to Thut's private audience chamber. She shuffled along, her arms outstretched for protection.

A piercing cry from the east made Chloe jump and swear. It came again, high and keening, sounding more like a warning than anything else. The sound of rapidly approaching footsteps encouraged her to step close to a wall, any wall, and she heard a runner pass her, breathing evenly, heading toward Thut's chambers.

How did he know where he was going? she wondered, and stepped away from the wall. Halfway down the long corridor—at least she assumed it was the long corridor—Chloe heard the resounding echo of doors being thrown against the outside walls and the clatter of armor and a multitude of sandals. A rumble of male voices bounced around her, so that she was retreating as the voices advanced, but without gauging their actual proximity.

Thut's voice came to her, obviously displeased. "This could not be worse timing! When I consulted my horoscope this morning and it said a red rooster would crow for me today, I should have sensed disaster! This deity of the Apiru is determined to bring Egypt to her knees. Will it not be a surprise for Ramoses when Hatshepsut, living forever! confronts him!"

Aii! Apparently Pharaoh had arrived.

Chloe flattened out against the wall as the group came toward her. She could see nothing, the darkness was so intense. Thut's voice had taken on its customary tone of command as his company turned into a passageway.

"Summon this Moshe and his brother to the main chamber. Find Ameni and my guards! This time they shall see Egypt in all its glory!" His voice was biting. "Glorious Hatshepsut, living forever's throne should be placed on the dais. See that it is so!" The rest of Thut's commands were lost under the tramping of the many pairs of sandals that echoed through the corridor. Where could Cheftu be? Chloe began to make her way to the audience chamber. The darkness should enable her to hide in a corner and hear all that was happening.

Stepping slowly away from the wall, she retraced her footsteps, hunting for the cross-passageway that would take her to the chamber.

LORD CHEFTU PACED BEFORE HIS PHARAOH, living forever!

"So what is the fear here, magus?" Hat asked, her voice pitched higher than usual, the only evidence of terror at this midnight at noon.

"My Majesty, for many weeks this God has visited these plagues on Egypt. Only by letting this people go will we escape with our lives."

Hat shifted in her seat. Cheftu couldn't see her, even in the torchlight, but the rustle of linen on gold and the tap of her tapered nails on the armrests let him know she was irritated and impatient. "Since you have been gone, my lord, I have been using another's services. He is not as efficient as you, but he does have an explanation for these plagues. He said it has almost nothing to do with this prophet. Now, I hear the Lady RaEm has both regained her voice and lost the bastard she was carrying. Is this true?"

"Aye, My Majesty," Cheftu said, wondering at her sources.

"Good. She is now wed to Thut, and that should keep him out of my way for a while."

"My Majesty——," Cheftu began.

"No more now, magus. Let us go to the audience chamber of Thut's lamentable little palace and see this prophet put in his proper place."

"But My Majesty——"

"Oh, do stop interrupting, Cheftu!" She clapped her hands. When the slow footsteps of a slave were audible, she said, "Prepare my cloth-of-gold kilt and skirt. They have wanted to negotiate with Egypt, and indeed they shall!"

Cheftu sighed softly. Whatever would be, would be. "Where is the noble Senmut?" he asked. Hatshepsut rarely traveled without him. It grew ominously quiet.

"He is working on a special project. First, he is finishing the details of his parents' tomb. Although he is of poor stock, he is an honorable man in the ways of Ma'at."

Cheftu bowed, though in the darkness the movement was pointless.

Hat continued, "There is no need for him to leave his work to deal with some insubordinate slaves."

"A special project?" Cheftu said. "Has not Senmut created the most beautiful of all monuments to My Majesty in her mortuary temple at Deir El-Bahri? How could even such a magnificent artist as Count Senmut surpass that?"

"He is not creating something beautiful, but he is creating something divine and eternal." Her tone was final. "My Majesty is the pharaoh of Egypt, living forever! I have brought peace and prosperity to this land. There is no need for My Majesty to answer to anyone."

"Aye, My Majesty. However, the peace you have brought is being challenged, both in Goshen and in the south. The Kushites are testing their strength once more. Surely you should take the army and crush this rebellion before it grows full-size? Cannot the gold be better used that way?"

Hat's tone was icy. "My Majesty is aware the country is seeking blood. My Majesty knows that men want to go to war and the sons whose lives I have saved in these years of peace are now chafing in their security. Still, My Majesty will not sacrifice Egyptian mothers' hopes and joys to meet the needs of a bored male populace! I am surprised at you, Cheftu! You have always been the voice of reason. The one time I dragged you to battle you refused to fight, but instead treated the fallen of both sides. Has being in the rage-filled presence of my nephew-son changed all of that? Or are you simply suggesting that My Majesty step down and let Horus-in-the-Nest take the double crown?"

Cheftu tried to still the fear in his throat. His guts twisted and gurgled. Did she know about the oath he swore to Thut? Or was this simple anger at being out of control of what was happening to her beloved country?

"My Majesty," he said cautiously, "I want what is best for Egypt. I have given my life to serve her. It concerns me that the people are discontent with the peace and prosperity you have provided in the god's wisdom. Would it not be better to take a small army and defeat the Kushites? Would that not meet the needs of the people better than building something more? Already you have restored so much of what Egypt lost in the time of the Hyksos; is that not enough?"

"It is not."

They sat in the darkness, Cheftu fearing the cold tone of Hat's voice. "Have you always shared your secrets with me, *Hemu neter?* My silent one?"

Cheftu frowned into the darkness. "I have, My Majesty."

"There is nothing you have kept hidden? No magic formulae, no hidden languages?"

Feeling trapped, Cheftu answered calmly, as his stomach boiled. "Nay, My Majesty. I have used my abilities for you alone."

"Do you swear this?"

"Aye." He hoped she did not notice his brief hesitation.

"By all that you hold sacred?"

"Aye," he said, confused and more than a little frightened. Hat would not normally act this way. What was wrong?

"By the *ka* of your friend Alemelek?"

Acid burst into his throat, and he swallowed and tried to control the cold sweat breaking out across his body. "I beg your pardon, Majesty?"

"Alemelek. You carry with you drawings he has done. Sketches and drawings unlike anything I have ever seen. All explained in a writing so foreign, it must be from the Shores of Night, for not even Set would do away with pictures of the gods."

So that was where his drawings had gone. The one of two things that Alemelek had asked of him, and he had failed. That which was intended for the future had been discovered now. What would the repercussions be?

"Who is your spy, My Majesty?"

"The same who saw that you would not help the Lady RaEmhetepet regain her position by ridding her of the baby, and had to do it herself."

Assst, Cheftu thought. The little serving girl Basha. She had disappeared the night RaEm had miscarried and the night his scrolls were stolen.

"It would seem you know all, Majesty."

"To the contrary, magician. When these things were discovered in your apartments here, it was decided to search your homes in Waset, Gebtu, and Noph. Do you know what we found there?"

Cheftu stood, numb. It was all over.

"More of that *kheft*-writing. Pages of it, bound together. Are they spells, magus? Or curses? From this world or another? Do you have a reasonable explanation why you would deliberately deceive your pharaoh?"

His mind raced as Cheftu stood in the darkness. She had found his notebooks, the many pages of notes he had written the first years he was here, hoping to use them in his research someday. The darkness was foreboding, and he wondered where his friend Hat was in this night-black room.

"I await your explanation, *Hemu neter*," she said, her voice frigid. He heard her move toward him. "For years I have held your counsel at my heart. For my lifetime I have trusted you." Her voice cracked. "It appears I have held a cobra to my breast." Her whisper was fierce: "Begone, magus. If this magic is so dark you cannot explain it to me, I want no part of you. Take your spells and your pictures and go back to the pit from which you came. I give you one week to leave Egypt, and if you ever return, I personally shall destroy your body and your evil."

Cheftu was shaken to the core. Leave Egypt? For where? For what?

"My decree stands for all time. No matter who is pharaoh, this decree shall be law. Just as my father banished the traitor prince who would side with the slaves against his own family, and ruled that his name never be spoken again, so I banish you!"

Hat threw the papyrus scrolls and his many notebooks at him. "Begone!"

Cheftu scrabbled to retrieve the years of documentation. She had left the room; he could hear her receding footsteps as she walked out on the deck. He gathered his things close and walked cautiously across the room, looking for a lighter black patch that would lead to the world beyond. Banished. From Egypt. He swallowed hard as he thought of his vineyards, his loyal servants . . . his wife.

Unimpeded by others, Cheftu walked across the deck. The voices he heard were weak, like the mewling of lost kittens. His sandaled foot found the downward slope of the ramp leading to land, and he inched his way down it carefully, the scrolls tucked into his belt, one arm holding the small notebooks, the other outstretched. He felt the give of sandy soil and heaved a sigh of relief.

For all that Hat knew, apparently his marriage to RaEm had slipped past. Would she also banish RaEm or leave her here to further tear apart his soul? Automatically Cheftu found himself on the way through the gardens to the palace. He remembered Ramoses. He, Cheftu, must be there when Hat had her confrontation, but he was reluctant to leave Chloe alone. He came to the gates, and his approach was noted by a scared sentry.

"Who goes there!" The soldier's voice trembled with fear.

Use it for all it's worth while you still have it, Cheftu thought. "His High Lord Cheftu! Open the gate, sentry!"

The soldier responded to the authority in Cheftu's voice. He went through the gates and hurried toward the audience chamber. He would stop here for a moment before going back to Chloe.

The presence of people was palpable. Their fear was like a rancid perfume in the air. They shouted out, "Who is it?" every time someone breathed. Fear of the dark and the evils it held was obviously a large part of the national consciousness, the scholar in him thought distractedly. He addressed the group at large. "When are the Israelite prophets expected?"

A swell of sound answered him, those calling for the Apiru's deaths, those pleading with the gods, and a few responding that the slaves had not yet been found. "Where is the prince?" he asked, and was met with a lot of uncertainty. There were rumors he was praying in his room or that he had gathered an army and they were going to kill the Israelites. Everyone seemed to know it was the Israelites who wanted to leave and that the majority of the Apiru were still going to be here, even if the Israelites departed. When they departed.

He headed back to their apartments. He must speak to Chloe.

CHLOE HAD JUST REACHED THE CORRIDOR to their apartments when she heard her name, her Egyptian name, hissed out. She spun around, trying to pinpoint the voice.

"Sister," the voice said, "the priestesses have been summoned. We must gain Ra's attention. He is ill and needs our help. ReShera would assume your position, but we dare not let her. She sees only with the vengeful glare of Sekhmet, not with the mercy of HatHor. Come with me, please, my lady."

Chloe strained to see through the blanket of darkness, but it was difficult. The "other" identified the voice as AnkhemNesrt, eight o'clock. Chloe doubted she'd ever heard her speak, but RaEm had.

"Will you come, priestess? I am scared. . . ." The soft voice trailed off, ending in a hiccup of swallowed tears.

Chloe pushed away from the wall, arms outstretched. "Of course, sister," she said, and felt the impact of a slender body in her arms.

The girl sobbed quietly. "Why has this happened, great lady? Why have the gods abandoned us? Ma'at is destroyed!"

Hysteria tinged the girl's voice. "It will be reestablished, AnkhemNesrt," Chloe said firmly. "However, we must listen to the demands of the Israelite's god. He alone can provide help through this time."

The girl was silent as they stumbled along the corridor. "How can he be more powerful than Amun-Ra?" she wondered aloud. "Never, never has the power of Ra been hidden! Not in all the dynasties of all the pharaohs. Not even in the time of the Hyksos! Who is this god?" Her voice was filled with wary respect.

"He is the beginning and the end. Who was and is and is to come." The words tripped off her tongue, and Chloe recognized they were words she'd heard in churches all her life. Then she realized she actually *believed* it. "Come, sister, we must hurry to the temple."

Easier said than done. The streets were empty but haunted, filled with the petrified cries of an invaded people. Their world was upside-down, and Chloe felt the spirit of fear stalking the streets. They hurried as quickly as possible through the blinding darkness, guided by AnkhemNesrt's sense of direction. Chloe feared total pandemonium would break out before long. The people were too scared. They almost were impaled by a young boy with a quick sword. It was definitely unsafe outside, disaster brewing.

Chloe's legs were beginning to ache when AnkhemNesrt came to an abrupt stop. "We have gone one street too far."

They turned around and at long last found the temple. They could hear the wails of the priestesses from inside, beseeching HatHor to aid Amun-Ra. They entered the main chamber, and AnkhemNesrt began to tug at Chloe's clothes.

"What are you doing?" Chloe whispered.

The girl stopped, shocked. "Undressing you, my lady. Of course, if you wish a more worthy priestess to—"

"Of course," Chloe interrupted, ready to slap herself. When would she learn to consult the "other" before opening her mouth! "We must dance unclothed for the goddess so that she will take off her clothes and thus cheer up Ra to come out of hiding." In Chloe's opinion it was one of the more ridiculous myths, but it was better than doing nothing, and the ancient Egyptian part of her was climbing mental walls in inactivity and horror.

In RaEm's world nothing happened that did not have a precedent of a thousand years. Repetition was worshiped, the steady, ongoing, never-altering prescription for life. Spontaneity was not valued by ancient Egyptians. Change was shunned. Individuality was not prized. Improvement was inconceivable.

To be a part of the cycle—birth, life, marriage, children, and death—or the cycle of the land—Inundation, Growth, Harvest, Rest: these were the sacred rhythms; anything that stepped away from them was to be feared and mistrusted, dismissed from memory as quickly as possible. For the first time Chloe understood that this aberration in Egyptian history would never be recorded.

These plagues, this crisis, would be forgotten; after all, it happened only once.

They walked on toward the others, the air heavy on Chloe's naked body. The priestesses were rubbing ashes on each other, mourning the loss of the fulcrum of their existence, Amun-Ra.

ReShera had been silent since Chloe entered; she handed the silver sistrum to Chloe with rather more force than necessary. Allowing RaEm slight control of her mind, Chloe began to move the sistrum and dance, the slow movements straining her muscles and the words of the other priestesses ringing in her ears.

"Oh! HatHor! Save us from eternal night!
Oh! Lady! Retrieve the sun for us!
Bring back the equilibrium of Ma'at!
Fill us with your glory!
Let not the darkness win!
But restore to us thy life!
Oh! Ra! Come back to us!
Oh! Amun! Leave us not!
Oh! Gods! Save us from the darkness!
Keep us in your eternal light!"

Chloe's voice was rough with tears as she heard the pleading of the women around her. What had begun as singing became wailing—lost, pitiful, hopeless. For hours they danced and sang, heaping ashes on their heads and tearing at their hair to invoke the goddess's pity, so she, in turn, would persuade Ra to shine again.

The night did not lift, did not lighten. Finally, all her limbs trembling, Chloe sank to the floor. Sweat ran in rivulets down her naked body, mixing with the ash and forming a thick paste. She ran a hand through her hair, pushing the short strands away from her face. Her mind was blank, numb with RaEm's rising terror and her own pity for those around her.

AnkhemNesrt sank to the ground beside her. "We will rest now, great lady. Perhaps it is night and the god will rise in the morning?" She laid a warm hand on Chloe's naked leg. "Do you wish to sleep in the White Chamber, lady?"

Chloe didn't want to move, even for a room at the Hilton. "Nay, sister. You may if you wish."

"The prince will come tonight, lady. Are you certain? It is your responsibility."

Something in AnkhemNesrt's voice made Chloe drag her weary mind to the "other." After a few seconds she said decisively, "Nay. You must serve the goddess, AnkhemNesrt. Unless you wish for someone else to go?"

AnkhemNesrt almost collapsed with relief. "Perhaps ReShera, lady?"

"Very well. Summon her and tell her, please," Chloe said as she drifted to sleep.

CHEFTU TRIED TO KEEP A REIN ON HIS PANIC. Just because Chloe was gone did not mean anything was wrong. He paced the room for the third time in as many minutes. Ehuru was there, silently fearful in the darkness. They had lit several torches; at least they thought they had. It made no difference.

The sound of running feet in the corridor stopped him. The high, panicked voice of a child announced that the prophets would be with Thut and Hat (though he was much more respectful) in six decans, and a runner would announce when the court would convene.

Ehuru stirred. "Should I prepare a bath, my lord?"

Cheftu chuckled despite himself. "Aye, Ehuru. I could use a wash if you can find the water."

Ehuru's laugh joined his own. "If that is what my lord needs, that is what he shall be provided." Cheftu heard the retainer's shuffling steps leave the room. He sat on a stool, drained. Hands clenched, he leaned forward. What could he do? Soon things would be beyond his control.

First he must provide for those who had served him so faithfully, Ehuru among them. Second he must find Chloe and explain all that had happened—warn her of probable danger. He must liquidate what he could of his holdings and get gold. They must make arrangements to leave. By ship? Could they go to Kallistae? No, it was gone in the eruption. Retenu? Hatti? Where was safe? What had survived this disaster? Where would the approaching famine be the least? He ran a hand over his blind, bloodshot eyes and the scruff on his face. They must pack.

His long fingers tapped at his side as he crossed the dark room again and again and again.

CHLOE WOKE WITH A START and a horrible crick in her neck. She was sitting against the wall, arms across her knees, providing a pillow of sorts for her head. She longed to stretch out but could feel the soft, warm body of AnkhemNesrt curled around her feet, like a kitten cuddling its mother. Then her leg cramped and Chloe stood up, painfully, clasping the wall in support. It was a few seconds before the charley horse subsided. AnkhemNesrt was sitting up, whimpering into the darkness.

The spells and prayers and chants had not worked. It was still darker than night, and Chloe fought the desire to scream at her blind ineffectiveness. Instead she drew AnkhemNesrt to her feet, her arm around the naked girl, guiding her to the main chamber. Another aerobic workout, Chloe thought. She had no idea how long they had been asleep, but she heard the others stirring.

She picked up the sistrum, fumbling for a few minutes as she found it, mixed in with her clothes. The jangling woke the others, and soon they were dancing in a circle, their prayers now unspoken pleading, heartrending, and hopeless.

The clatter of armor, swords, and sandals brought them to an abrupt stop. Footsteps drew nearer. A booming voice rang through the chamber, and Chloe recognized Ameni.

"Mighty Pharaoh, perfect in Ma'at, Child of the Sunrise, Daughter of HatHor, Hatshepsut Makepre Ra, living forever! commands all the Ladies of Silver to her audience chamber this morning." He waited a moment. "We are here to escort you."

Chloe could feel the women looking at her. Where was ReShera? "We shall join you, Commander," she said. "Allow us to complete our ablutions and dress."

"As you wish, Lady RaEmhetepet." Footsteps retreated to the hallway.

"Is it morning, RaEm?"

"Why does Pharaoh, living forever! want us, lady?"

"How are we to dress, lady?"

The questions converged on her, and Chloe used her best commander voice to still their fears, get most of the ash washed off, then everyone dressed with no mirrors, servants, or even the eyes of a stranger to aid them. Chloe called roll. ReShera was still missing. No one wanted to search the dark temple for her, and RaEm had no memory of the place. Very well, Chloe thought. She can just stay here. The women's hands linked as they walked out to meet their escort.

THE ROOM'S DARKNESS WAS HEAVY with the mingled presence of several hundred people. Cheftu couldn't see them, but he heard their frightened whispers, the rustle of linen, and, overall, the stench of fear-filled sweat. He stepped toward what had always been his position, apologizing to those people he walked on and into.

Neither Hatshepsut nor Thutmosis had yet entered the room, and he tried to keep his thoughts away from where Chloe could be and why she wasn't here. How did he know she wasn't? Would he be able to sense her presence in this great darkness? Had it been three days? Was light once more going to shine?

The chamberlain hit the floor with his heavy staff. His voice was full strength again, though Cheftu thought he heard a quaver of fear in it. "Hail, Horus-in-the-Nest," he called out. "Inheritor to the throne! Prince of Upper and Lower Egypt, Beloved of Thoth, Seeker of Ma'at, commander in chief of the armies of Pharaoh, living forever!" Cheftu heard the solitary steps proceed through the throng and ascend the steps and then a creak of wood as Thut sat down.

Again the chamberlain banged his staff. "Hail! Hail! Hail! Pharaoh Hatshepsut, living forever! King of the Red and Black lands! Defender of Ma'at! Beloved of the goddess! Daughter of the sun! . . ." The rest of the litany was lost in the rising noise of everyone falling on their faces. Even the chamberlain was quiet as the click of Hat's sandals traversed the length of the room. As soon as she mounted the dais and seated herself, Cheftu heard the synchronized pace of her private Kushite guards taking their positions around her throne.

"All may rise!" the chamberlain bellowed, and Cheftu joined the rest as they rose to their feet.

"Nobles of Egypt!" Pharaoh's voice throbbed through the room, heavily sensual and commanding. "Those who have given your blood to defend the integrity of our gods and our land! My Majesty gives you thanks. My Majesty gives you honor, and My Majesty commends your faithfulness!" What should have garnered a round of applause instead met a chilling silence. Hat continued, "The plagues that have tried to steal our soul are not from another god!" Her proclamation was drowned in mumbled responses. "My Majesty has brought from the Temple of Amun-Ra in Waset the greatest magus in Egypt!"

Cheftu felt his guts twist. It was true, then: he was no longer an Egyptian in the eyes of the throne. He was startled to discover that after the initial shock, he felt no sadness.

"I present to you Iri, my magus!"

A faint spattering of applause broke out. Cheftu heard muttering in the back of the chamber and the scrape of a moving chair at the front.

"My Majesty, my nobles," Iri began.

Cheftu racked his brain, trying to associate a face with the voice, and came up blank. The comments of the audience had become a low roar, and Hat inquired coldly what the problem was.

"It is the priestesses you have requested," the chamberlain answered. "The Israelite prophets have also arrived."

"Send them both in, chamberlain," Hat said, her voice ringing throughout the room. Cheftu heard the scrape of metal doors and then the faint pattering of footsteps walk up and past him. Cheftu smelled the faint odor of ashes.

"Apiru!" Hat's voice was loud.

"Aye, Hatshepset." The court sat in dumbfounded silence at the familiarity of the address: *Hatshepset* was Pharaoh's name when she was only second daughter with no hopes of the throne. Hat was silent, and Cheftu could almost hear the pounding of the hearts around him.

"Ramoses?" Her voice was incredulous.

"Aye, sister. Though I am called Moshe now." The gasp of shock was as tangible as a wave, buffeting the room. Hat's footsteps were audible as she walked down the steps to the floor.

"Sister?" Her voice was shaking. "First you betray my father, who loved you above all sons, and you were not even his spawn! Then you side with a slave against the growth of Egypt, by murdering our cousin, my betrothed! Now you devastate our land with plagues and you dare call me *sister!*" Her voice had risen in livid fury. "Go and worship your 'el,' your god! Take your families and your children! But you will leave your flocks and herds!"

Hat's fury was like another presence, and Cheftu felt the people around him shrinking from her anger. So this was how the pieces fit together, he thought. Not only did Moses murder an Egyptian in defense of an Israelite, not only had he killed one whose blood was royal. *A cousin.* He had killed Hatshepset's betrothed!

Moshe had stood quietly listening to her demands. "Nay, we cannot. You must allow us to have sacrifices and burnt offerings to present to Elohim. Our livestock too must go with us; not a hoof is to be left behind. We have to use some of them in our worship of Elohim, and until we get there, we will not know what our God requires of us."

Hat's labored breath was audible. "You walk on sinking sand, traitor. When will this darkness leave?"

Silence enveloped the room, as complete as the darkness.

Moshe said, "Now."

Like a cloak being drawn away from the window, the room was once more alight. Sun glinted off the gold of the nobles' garments and warmed the alabaster of wall and floor. The huge painting of a vanquishing pharaoh glowed with returned life. A gasp of awe rose as the day grew brighter and brighter, the turquoise sky visible through the clerestory windows and the sound of birdsong filling the air with a prayer of thanksgiving.

Cheftu recoiled at the sudden brightness until his eyes adjusted. Pharaoh stood three cubits from Moshe, the gold of her costume warming in the sun, glinting off the jeweled eyes of the cobra and vulture in the tall double crown gracing her head.

Her eyes widened as she saw her half-brother Ramoses, once the inheritor to the throne. His mother had so desperately wanted a child that when, despite prayers and building a temple to HatHor, her babe was stillborn, she had taken a child from the Nile and passed him off as her own. Ramoses was twice Hat's age, yet he glowed with health, belying the white-streaked hair and sun lines around his eyes and mouth.

Black gaze met black, and held.

Cheftu saw Hat's hands tremble as she doubled them into fists, having left the crook and flail on her throne. She turned on her heel and remounted the steps, seating herself on the gold-and-enameled chair, her hands grasping the symbols of her power.

"Stay, slave, while my magus reveals you as the charlatan you are! First you played at being a prince, now you play at being a savior?" Skepticism and disgust mingled in her voice. "Speak, Iri!"

Iri paled. "For many years a devastating eruption has been predicted in the Great Green. There have been two such disasters since Chaos. Along with each catastrophic explosion are omens I think you will find very interesting. Listen to how they have affected Egypt." As he warmed to his topic, the nervousness faded from his voice. "A red plant was brought in with the current that stained the water and killed the fish. As the water became more deadly, the frogs left it and wandered up onto our land. The more poisoned the water, the more frogs. They have short lives, and there was not enough food for them, so they died in masses, both generating insects and adding to the many flies, fleas, and gnats in our country."

Cheftu looked at Thut's darkened face and saw a growing anger there. Iri continued, "The bugs infected the cattle, which died. The winds shifted far out at sea and brought some uncommon weather. In this case, a cloud of locusts who wrought a very natural damage on the land. Then hail came, as a precursor of the disaster to strike in the Great Green. The volcano belched up black smoke, ash, fire, and hot earth. This mixed with hail, and when it fell here, it caused rashes, illness, and even some deaths."

The chamber was silent, each soldier, priest, noble, and servant listening to the analysis of the past few months. It could all happen that way, it was true. For a people whose lives were as integrated with religion as a sailor's with the sea, however, the explanation lacked the divine spark to make it believable. The heavens did not alter without a sacred presence to make it happen. One by one the people listened, weighed, and rejected the theory.

Since the gods were in control, this could not have happened without their consent or interference. Cheftu stood, watching Hat's face. The religiosity of her people would be her downfall. Life did not happen without a purpose and a hand behind it. They would believe nothing else. That's the difference between the Greek and the Oriental minds, the scholar in Cheftu thought. That is the key.

Iri bowed to Hat and backed toward his seat.

"Magus!" someone hailed him from the crowd. "If indeed all these things have happened as you said, which god commanded that they happen now? Their god or ours?" Twenty voices joined in, searching for a comprehensible answer in the confusion.

Iri held up his hands. "It is not the hand of any god, but just the reactions of nature," he said, and was drowned out in the disbelief of the Egyptians.

One of the soldiers, at Hat's command, banged his shield with his sword. The sound reverberated throughout the room, bringing silence. Hat sat on the throne, glittering and angry, her black eyes focused on Moshe. Without dropping her gaze, she called for the priestesses. They had been huddled together, their graying robes hidden in the brilliance of the first light.

They walked forward, and Cheftu watched in horror as Pharaoh recognized Chloe the same moment he did. Hat sent a questioning look Thutmosis' way, and Cheftu remembered she thought Thut had wed Chloe. She stood in the front of the group, tall and proud, despite the ash in her black hair and the smudges and creases of her clothing.

"What does the goddess say, Lady RaEmhetepet?" Hat asked. "Since you are still before me, I assume that the darkness was broken before this"—she motioned with her flail to Moshe—"this slave pulled his great illusion and revealed Ra." She turned to Thutmosis. "What say you, nephew; did your bride bring aid?"

Thut looked at Hat steadily. "When I left the temple this morning, I took the life of the priestess, as I am commanded to. This lady was not that priestess, and is not my bride."

Hat whirled on Chloe. "My lady . . ." Her tone was lethal. "Did you send another to die in your place? The right and responsibility were yours! You sacrificed someone before you? Who is dead?"

Cheftu felt cold sweat run down his back. Chloe had been in the temple. In these direst of times it was her duty to dance and plead before the goddess, then meet either Pharaoh or Horus-in-the-Nest, who were the physical manifestations of Ra. She was to please them, in a parody of seeking the god's pleasure. If the spell was not broken, it was the royal male's job to sacrifice the priestess in order to save Egypt. Instead Thut spent the night with someone else and plunged the sacred dagger into her breast while she was still warm from their union.

Chloe was responsible for the dead priestess! He closed his eyes in a brief and heartfelt prayer. She stood like a statue. Cheftu had the hideous fear that she didn't have the memory to know what she was supposed to do. She'd said she had no emotional memory. That was where this information would have been.

"ReShera. I sent ReShera," Chloe said, her voice void of emotion.

Hat's steely gaze fixed on Chloe, filled with revulsion and disappointment. "So you have broken your vows, betrayed a holy sister, and ignored my edict that you marry!" Chloe stood silent. Hat took a deep breath, her next words stiff: "Very well, priestess. In honor to your family, Count Makab, and the position you have held in my heart and in my court, you will marry Thut, conceive a new RaEmhetep priest, give birth, and then be turned over to the Sisterhood for execution as befits a soiled priestess. Remove her authority and take her from my sight!"

Cheftu stepped forward in protest, but Thutmosis gained Hat's attention. "Nay, Pharaoh. She is wed. I cannot take another man's wife."

Hat asked in a voice throbbing with hatred, "Whose wife?"

Thut indicated Cheftu, who stepped forward, approaching the throne. "You!" she screeched. "A traitor and a traitor!" Thut looked from Cheftu to Hat, obviously bewildered. "You will not miss your wife! You are banished! May you meet again on the Shores of Night!" Her voice was shrill, and Cheftu looked at Chloe. She was already in the grasp of two soldiers, her broken ankh necklace, symbol of her position, lying in pieces at her feet.

Her green eyes were frightened in her ash-smudged face. He ran toward her, then screamed in pain as one of the Kushite guards lashed out. He fought, anger and fear giving him strength, paying no attention to his bloody back. Chloe was kicking and fighting as they half carried and half dragged her from the chamber. Then he saw nothing but ceiling as he was tripped and a spear pressed against his heaving chest.

He lay there, panting, terrified, replaying the fear in Chloe's look as she was taken from him.

Hat once again took her seat, and her voice was barely controlled as she spoke to Moshe. "Take your cattle. However, you will leave the eldest child of every family as a hostage. A credit on the family's return. Every family who does not return will have murdered their child. I will send scribes throughout the villages and we will have exacting records of every Israelite in Egypt." She laughed, brittle but confident. "I see the fear on your face, Moshe. It is good to be afraid of the throne of Egypt."

"I am not afraid of you, Hatshepsut. I am afraid for you. You have just pronounced a death sentence on your own people."

"Get out of my sight!" she hissed. "Make sure you do not appear before me again! The next day you see my face you will die."

Moshe's voice was powerful as it washed over those present, imbedding itself forever into their consciousness. "Just as you say, I will never appear before you again.

"But hear what Elohim says. 'About midnight I will go throughout Egypt. Every firstborn son in Egypt will die, from the firstborn son of Pharaoh, who sits on the throne, to the firstborn son of the slave girl who is at her hand mill and the firstborn of all the cattle. There will be a loud wailing throughout Egypt—worse than there has ever been before or ever will be again. However, among the Israelites not a dog will bark at any man or animal.' So you will know that our God makes a distinction between Egypt and Israel," Moshe said, "all of your officials will come to me, bowing down before me and saying, 'Go you and all the people who follow you!' After that I will leave."

He turned his back and walked the length of the room, awash in light yet still filled with darkness. Tears ran down Cheftu's face as he heard Moshe's steps fade.

The worst was yet to come.

CHLOE WAS THROWN INTO A DARK ROOM. It stank of urine, and she shivered at the scampering sounds of rodents. Once again she was in the dark, only now it was a dank darkness, all the more terrifying because she knew that somewhere above her the sun shone, bathing Egypt once more in its rays. Cheftu . . . She swallowed her tears and tightened the sash at her waist. The memory of the anguish in his amber eyes haunted her. Had he been hurt? She had thought he was a favorite of Hat's, so why was she so cruel? What had happened?

Now the Sisterhood would get her. She doubted Hat would make Thut marry her, so she'd just lost at least nine months of her life. She had also killed ReShera—unknowingly, but she was still dead.

Chloe wiped away the tears that streamed down her cheeks. She thought back to that fatal decision. When AnkhemNesrt had asked her to go to the White Chamber and Chloe had consulted the "other," the only thought had been that to go to that chamber was state-sanctioned sex. *Nothing* about death or sacrifices. No doubt that knowledge was wherever the real RaEm was.

Had they changed places? Did RaEm have Chloe's cursory memory? Enough to get by in the twentieth century? Not that it mattered. Chloe had no idea how to return and wasn't even sure she wanted to. Oh, Cheftu! she cried. What had happened to him?

Would she ever see him again?

She sank to the floor, reaching for her necklace. But it was gone, broken into pieces and smashed on the audience chamber floor by the soldiers. Oh, Cheftu! she thought. Please forgive me! Because of her, he was going to be banished. To leave forever this land he loved so well and to which he had just returned. Why hadn't Thut defended him? Because to admit Cheftu had sworn fealty to him would probably have gotten them both killed. Chloe buried her head in her hands, letting the tears come.

CHAPTER 13

Cheftu laid down the brush with which he had been committing his staff and his holdings to Count Makab. He would be shocked at the turn of events. Makab was not wise with money, but he was just and would see the slaves emancipated and awarded a fee for their loyalty.

Sun streaked through the open garden door. The light cut through a pitcher of wine next to Cheftu, honeycombing the room in a prism of red. Like blood, Cheftu thought dully.

The slight body of an Egyptian woman had been delivered to him that morning. In exchange for his wife, the guard explained. Her face was covered, but her appearance had jarred Cheftu. He'd met ReShera only a few times, that he was aware of—the woman hadn't seemed to care for him. The corpse had worn a silver ankh with ReShera's name, so it must be she, but he was confused. Without Chloe's green eyes, one black-haired, brown-skinned woman looked much like another. Cheftu and Ehuru had taken her to the local House of the Dead to see that she was buried properly.

Thut had done his job well, killing her quickly and letting her blood drain. Rejoicing that it was not Chloe, Cheftu had covered her lean figure with a linen robe. At least not Chloe yet.

RaEm. Chloe. He felt tears in his throat. What he felt was so much more than love. She was the woman he trusted, the woman he respected, the woman formed from his own *ka*. Who was now the gods only knew where.

He turned back to his letter. He must gather their belongings and book passage, then he must find Chloe and rescue her.

Ehuru entered the room. "My lord, you have a visitor." Cheftu looked at him. Ehuru had aged overnight. Company was Cheftu's last desire, but it was necessary. He gave a ghost of a smile. "Show him in."

Lord Makab entered the room, his linen gleaming white, but his face drawn and gaunt. Cheftu got to his feet, extending both arms.

Makab embraced him. "My friend, life, health, prosperity."

"To yourself also. Please, be seated. Have you eaten?"

"I have no desire to. . . ." Makab's voice was low. "How is my sister, Cheftu? What matter of dark magic is this?" Ehuru appeared in the doorway, and Cheftu requested wine and whatever food could be found.

"You know, then?"

Makab sank into a chair. "Know what?"

"How is it that you are here?" Cheftu asked, trying to ease his friend's feelings.

"I received a missive that RaEm was going to marry Thut, so I began to travel. First our horses died on the way to the river. We had to walk for several days. I lost several good retainers to a hailstorm of fire—I confess I have never seen the like! We were living off the land when locusts descended. They clogged the streams and ate all the greenery. We survived by eating them. Then we reached the river, only a few days' journey, but this blackness descended and the people were terrified. We had a mutiny and lost most of the crew and the captain. We just arrived. Out of an entourage of twenty, only six of us are left." He sighed, accepting wine from Ehuru. "The torments on the Shores of Night could be no worse."

"Did you come directly to me?"

"Aye, my good friend. I knew you had been assigned to look after . . ." His words stopped. "To look after her when she was banished here. I thought she was going to marry Nesbek, but then she is going to marry Thut. . . . I do not know what is happening here."

"She married me."

Makab laughed. "She despises you!"

Cheftu grinned as he crooked an eyebrow. "As I did her."

Makab rubbed his face hard, then downed the rest of his wine and handed the cup to Ehuru for a refill. "How?"

Cheftu sighed. "It would take days and a lot more wine to explain.

Suffice it to say she is a captive of the state, I have less than a week to leave Egypt and never return, and the worst plague of all is about to strike."

Makab's expression was murderous. "Captive of the state? A hereditary prince banished? Plagues? Explain, Cheftu. Give me facts in quick succession. Why is she a captive?"

"She accidentally sent another priestess in her place for a ritual at the temple. The other girl was killed, as a sacrifice."

"A sacrifice? A human sacrifice? That is a barbarian ritual! We Egyptians haven't practiced such since Chaos!"

"The sun has risen every day, without fail, since Chaos. It did not these past few days."

Makab looked away. "Agreed." He peered over his cup at Cheftu. "So she substituted someone else?"

"Aye. So it seems."

"You sound unsure."

Cheftu scratched his chest. "I am. Something is not adding up. Hat's judgment was too quick. She is pharaoh, but she is acting without the proper religious authorities. She even let *soldiers* strip RaEm of her priestess authority."

"Mere soldiers? Only a high priest can take away religious authority. While Hapuseneb may have turned over a lot of the priesthood to Pharaoh, living forever!, I am sure that he alone holds that power still!"

"Indeed," Cheftu mused. "It is not adding up."

Makab drained another cup of wine. "What is this about your being banished? Surely it is not true?"

"Aye." He handed Makab the letter he had sealed a few moments before. "I have written asking you to take care of my servants and holdings."

Makab looked at him. "Has Hatshepsut, living forever! gone mad? She cannot banish you! You have inherited your position for generations, as have I! What is her reasoning?"

Cheftu dropped his gaze. How to explain to this paragon of ancient Egyptian stability that he was an impostor and had been for fifteen years? That his sister was in reality a woman from the future who could handle a bow and ride a horse bareback?

Makab watched, realization dawning on his face. "This is about RaEm's *ka*, is it not?"

"That is a simple way of looking at it, but accurate."

"She did not understand about the ritual, and that is why the other priestess died, correct?"

"Aye, that is truth enough."

Makab got to his feet and walked to the garden window. "I knew something was incomplete in her when I saw her at Karnak. Never have I seen eyes so green. They were the eyes of a stranger, and we were as alien to her as she was to us. How did this happen?"

Cheftu ran a hand through his hair. "It is something about the Silver Chamber of HatHor. I do not yet know. She does not deserve to die for such an error, though that is hardly something I can tell Pharaoh."

Makab turned back to him. "How is it that you know these things, Cheftu? How could she trust you?"

Cheftu rose to his full height and stared at Makab. "Did you know me as a boy?"

"Aye. We were all *w'rer*-priests, doing our time in the temple as oldest sons until we were called home to tend to our families."

"Aye."

Makab continued to look at him, his dark eyes narrowed with concentration. Minutes passed, then he suddenly took a step back. "Who are you?"

"Why do you ask?"

"You were a sickly boy. You could not run fast, or hunt. You had difficulty reading. Now you are as fast as a cat, a hunter and a scholar who memorized the scrolls in the temple within a few days of reading them." Makab took a deep breath, frowning. "One time you were found on the floor of HatHor's room. You were sick for days." His hand slipped to the amulet on his wrist. "What are you?"

"I am your friend, Cheftu. But"—he paused—"I was also a young man with a brilliant future, and a loving family, who had come to Egypt to decipher the hieroglyphs." Cheftu sighed as he watched fear accumulate in his friend's face. He sat down again. Haft extended, he offered his dagger to Makab. "If I am a *kheft* to you, my friend, then kill me. Without Chloe I have little desire to live anyway. Or you can wait. I am the firstborn, so I will not have long to live." He grinned ruefully.

Makab took the dagger and looked at his friend.

Cheftu watched him, his gaze carefully bland. With a casual movement he reached up and tore the throat of his linen shirt, revealing the brown, hairless chest of a nobleman. "Do it, or join me to help Chloe survive."

"Her name is Klo-e?" Makab stumbled over the syllables, never looking away.

"Aye."

"You are from the same . . . ?" Makab left the question hanging.

"Nay. She is from another country, many years ahead of my time."

"Will you take her back?"

Cheftu sighed, dropping his hands from his shirt. "I do not know how. I do not know if it is possible. However, unless she escapes the Sisterhood, and soon, there will be no more Chloe, and no more RaEm."

Makab stuck the dagger in his belt and seated himself across from Cheftu. "Do you know where she is being kept?"

"Will you help me?"

Makab's brown stare met his. "Aye, my friend. I will help you return to your own worlds, if you so desire. We must make our plans."

Cheftu sighed and grabbed Makab's hand. He felt a slight hesitation, and then his grip was returned. "I will tell you what I know."

THUT FELL ONTO HIS COUCH, his head still ringing with Hat's recriminations and threats. She was returning to Waset but would be back on the next ship once she checked the progress on Senmut's projects and established herself as the savior who had returned Ra's light to the world.

Hat had left RaEm with him. The Sisterhood was sending a representative to escort her out to the western desert, where, if she was lucky, she would die immediately. Like the poor girl I killed, Thut thought miserably. For no purpose. While my seed was just taking root inside her, the blood of her virginity still on my body. For no purpose. All that was needed was a word from Moshe to his god, and life and light returned.

So Moshe was the uncle he'd heard of only in whispers. The one his father had vowed to continue to hunt—to no avail. At midnight some night, the firstborn sons would die. A whole generation of men. Thut closed his eyes, eager to be rid of the thoughts that tormented his mind. Now he and every other thinking Egyptian watched the sun set in panic, wondering if it would fail to rise again. Wondering if this would be the night of death.

Or bring destruction as this darkness had. In three days more than a fifth of the city had been killed, mostly in fear. Old men stabbing into the darkness, killing their family members and neighbors. Young women, trying to protect their children, frightened of the darkness and unable to feed them. Families committing suicide because they believed Amun-Ra dead. He ran a weary hand over his face. The streets were running with blood. The air was filled with the mourning cries of those consumed with guilt. They had killed in terror, ignorant of whom they struck.

Granted, he could punish the people—the Apiru, the Israelites: beat them, enslave them further, even kill them. Then what price would their jealous god extract? If only I could take these consequences on myself, Thut thought. Protect those who serve and love the throne and the gods.

However, a god did not compete with a man. Thut knew now they were dealing with a god. There was no doubt he was powerful; apparently his people didn't know his name, calling him Elohim, "their God." Wasn't the sun god Amun-Ra called the "Hidden One"? Two unknowable deities were fighting each other over the land of Egypt. Apparently Amun-Ra had other things to do and was paying little attention. Thutmosis dared not even think the god was incapacitated or dead. He forced himself to sit up and planted both feet on the floor.

Then there was Cheftu, his newest lord, whose heart had filled his eyes as he'd watched RaEm dragged from the room. Even now Hat's Kushite guards watched RaEm's cell. Lord Cheftu had not endangered Thut by entreating him to intervene. That was a debt Thutmosis would honor someday.

Thut stood; he had not seen his wives or children in what seemed to be weeks. The children whom even tonight he might lose. Fear added speed to his feet, and the prince regent was almost running by the time he reached his harem doors.

THE DARKNESS GATHERED AROUND THEM, Cheftu, Makab, Meneptah, and Commander Ameni, who owed Cheftu his life after a battle in Kush. Cheftu's hand was slick with sweat as he touched the hilt of his dagger. Tonight he would kill if need be, and there would be no absolution, no forgiveness, because he intended it. Just pray God it would restore Chloe to him. His Egyptian heritage was a small loss compared to losing her.

The moon was waxing; it would be full tomorrow. Meneptah warned them tomorrow would be the night of death. He had described how to protect themselves, and Cheftu was disappointed that neither Makab nor Ameni had paid the close attention they should. *Still* they did not believe.

These dark musings would do no good tonight. Tonight—when it was his responsibility to see these men delivered safely to their homes before dawn, when the alarm would sound and he and Chloe would be on a swift ship to the Great Green. He had gold, jewels, food, and clothing. Already he had forwarded a wealth of spices. They would always be financially secure.

Quietly they slipped through the foliage, meeting in the shade of the great abandoned temple. AnkhemNesrt had crept into his garden last night and told him of overhearing RaEm's guards in the temple. She drew a map of the interior and marked several possibilities for underground chambers and rooms. Cheftu memorized it instantly and prayed it was accurate.

The moon outlined everything in black and silver. Echoes of the remaining priestesses resounded from inside the building. There was no sign of any guards. He knew Hat was expecting his response and would be prepared. Not being able to see her preparations made his stomach churn; but there was no choice. He crept forward.

They wore no sandals, preferring to step silently through the stone chambers. Cheftu ducked back as they entered a cross-passage and he saw the distinctive features of a Kushite guard. Several torches flamed around him, and his sword was unsheathed. Light shone off his ebony skin, darker by contrast to the white of his kilt and leather collar. He also wore a knife in his shinguard, another blade on the outside of his upper arm, and a quiver around his chest. The corresponding bow lay on a table behind him.

Cheftu swore silently. The man was as armed as a thief. What could they do? He felt pressure on his arm and looked around. Ameni stood behind him, weighting a small dagger in his hand, trying to get the right balance. It was a one-shot try. Cheftu faded into the shadows. Ameni's aim was true, and the luckless guard sank to his knees before falling on his chest and pushing the dagger in farther.

They waited a few endless seconds. The guard's fall had been silent, but Cheftu was paranoid. Advancing like vultures, they found the guard dead and relieved him of his weaponry. He had been stationed before a branching hallway, one passage leading into a trapdoor, the other winding off through the night. It was not in AnkhemNesrt's map. They split up, Cheftu and Meneptah, Makab and Ameni.

As they crept down the ladder from the trapdoor, Cheftu fought the urge to send Meneptah away. He could die tonight, and it would be another death on Cheftu's head. His thoughts froze as he heard quiet, furtive steps coming up behind him. He jumped off the ladder and twisted to face his opponent. He gasped as he felt the outstretched blade cut into the guard's abdomen but knew nothing else as he wrestled the Kushite, closing off his breath and releasing him only when he felt the body go limp. He checked the pulse: not dead. After a moment's indecision he beckoned Meneptah, and they raced, fleet-footed, down the sloping hallway.

CHLOE STIRRED AWAKE, hearing something beyond the sounds of rats, her stomach growling, and the snore of her guard in the other cube. She shifted, the pull of her restraint waking him up. He grunted at her and settled down again. It was quite a devious arrangement, Chloe thought. She was in a small inner chamber and leashed by her ankles to a guard in the outer chamber, with a door between them. Every move she made, he felt—and usually woke up. She sighed deeply. If anyone looked in, it appeared to be just a solitary cell with one inhabitant—the guard—and looked no further. Certainly not through a seemingly solid wall with only a wedge cut in the bottom for her bindings. She stared at the wall as the sounds came again, metal clashing with metal. Her guard drew to his feet and opened the door to the hallway. She heard his cry and felt the forward motion of his body as he inadvertently pulled her forward by her ankle leash, slamming her into the wall. She called out feebly for Cheftu . . . and slipped into darkness.

THE MAN WAS DEAD, THE ROOM EMPTY, no other doors. Ameni looked at the carnage, the bloodstained walls, the decapitated and maimed bodies of those who had only been doing their job. He felt slightly sick. Meneptah was losing his dinner to the ground, and Cheftu was so full of despair, he could barely stand. Ameni kicked in the body and closed

the door. Wearily he led the group up and out into the breaking dawn.
. . . Their mission had failed.

CHEFTU STARTED AT THE KNOCK, fearing it might be Hat, but then he
reasoned she would break down the door, not knock. He was relieved
when Ehuru came in, Meneptah trailing behind him. Meneptah said
nothing but joined Cheftu at the table, staring at the thin bread and
wine that was available. Cheftu looked away. The ship had sailed without
them. Chloe was lost, somewhere in the depths of that cursed temple,
and Thut had received a representative of the Sisterhood a half decan
before. Grains of sand dropped through an hourglass in his mind. For
the love of God, there had to be a solution!

"Will you join us, my lord?" Meneptah asked when Cheftu returned
to the present. "We could use your skills, and this would provide a way
for you to leave the country. No more boats are leaving the dock; it is a
royal decree."

"I cannot leave until I know RaEm is beyond my reach. I must continue
to try to find her. Perhaps once she is in the desert they will not guard her
so heavily." He was grasping for the wind and knew it, but he dared not
think beyond. "A member of the Sisterhood is here in Avaris. Perhaps one
of us could imitate her. . . ."

Meneptah shook his head. "I do not think members of the
Sisterhood need to shave again at *atmu*. It would give us away."

Cheftu's smile was fleeting. "Aye, of course."

They were sitting in silence when Ehuru entered, his eyebrows raised
to his wig. "A message for you, my lord."

It was terse, written in Makab's clear hand. "The lady is on the boat
Goddess of the Horizon. She is being transported there now and will be there
with only two Sekhmet guard-priestesses until midnight. After that, the
high priestess will return and they will set sail immediately. I wish you
and the lady a safe journey, however far you may go." Wordlessly Cheftu
passed it to Meneptah.

The Israelite read it and turned to him, brown eyes full of warning.
"My lord, my friend! You know the significance of tonight! You must be
inside one of our homes to be safe. You dare not risk it!"

Cheftu looked at him with a sad smile. "I dare do nothing less."

CHLOE WAS JERKED TO HER FEET. Her head pounded, and the fury in the voice of the Kushite guard was palpable. The door between the cells opened, and Chloe slipped in a cool, sticky pool before she stepped outside. Shackles were cut off her ankles, and she was dragged up the sloping hallway. At knife point she climbed a ladder. Once inside the temple proper, she looked around. The guard shoved her toward the light at the end of the passageway, and Chloe almost cried with relief when she saw the sun. It was creeping downward, but for the first time in several days she felt warm, able to forget her losses and hungers. Except for Cheftu.

She ground her teeth.

Roughly she was pushed into a chariot, her hands tied around the guard's massive waist as he tore through the poorer sections of town, heading toward the waterfront. The scent of blood and roasting meat hung in the air, and Chloe thought briefly of all the times she had passed up a steak in favor of pasta or fish. The image of a medium-well-done T-bone, a piping hot baked potato with everything, a fresh green salad, and a tasty merlot filled her for just a second. Then the vision faded away, as unreal as a scene from a movie instead of the life she used to have.

The sun was low, the sky welded into stripes of copper and violet. They came to an abrupt halt before a solitary ship. Chloe knew this was her last chance to run. She tensed her legs, trying to gauge their strength as the guard untied her wrists. As soon as she felt the slack she reared back. Either she would be able to choke him or they would pull free and she could run. Free, she jumped from the chariot.

The safety of trees was a few steps away when the guard's weight crashed against her legs and she went down flat, the breath knocked out of her. He dragged her to her feet. Her legs trembled and she gasped for air. He called to the man on deck for assistance, and Chloe tried again, freedom only steps away. She heard a shout, and then darkness enveloped her.

CHEFTU TASTED BILE as he saw the Kushite knock Chloe out. She had fought bravely, and Cheftu was appalled at how badly she was worn. Even in the dying light he could see the blood on her ankles, bruises on her face, how thin and pale she was. Just a little while longer, he thought. Then you'll be mine again! This time I will protect you with my life.

The brute had gotten her on board and was now burning feathers, using the acrid smell to awaken her. Cheftu saw her shake her head, then hunch over. A figure clad in a hooded robe approached her, and Chloe shrank back from it. Cheftu craned to see more, but the falling darkness was too complete. He watched the full moon rise slowly, thinking of the people he had urged to follow the ritual example of the Israelites that evening. Chloe's screams brought him to his feet. In the quiet of the evening he heard the slap of leather on flesh. Her flesh. Acid danced in his stomach. He would kill the Kushite and the hooded figure. He would kill them both.

The cries stopped, and the torchlight shone on the hooded figure. It was a woman, her voice vaguely familiar as she called to the Sekhmet guards on the boat. Then she and the Kushite were gone, the rattle of their chariot a fading sound.

The moon was rising, flooding the area with light. Cheftu listened intently for voices. He heard nothing, so, after slipping out of his sandals, he stepped into the shadows, creeping toward the boat, his sword in hand and dagger clenched between his teeth. In his blue mourning kilt he blended into the shadows, easily taking the first Sekhmet guard-priestess.

Her body sank quietly to the ground, his jeweled dagger sticking out from between her ribs. He pulled it out, gritting his teeth at the resultant gush of blood, and swallowed the vomitus in his throat. He wiped the blade on her kilt. Once more he merged into the gray shades of night.

The second guard was more difficult, and they had a silent struggle before Cheftu pushed home the blade, holding her body like a lover until she was still. This time he didn't bother to retrieve the knife. When at last he reached Chloe, tied to the mast, he released her wrists. The light showed the raised welts on her back. She had been beaten but was not bleeding. Her pulse was strong.

Covering her mouth with his hand, he wafted a charred feather under her nose. She jumped and filled her lungs to scream, but Cheftu covered her mouth with his own, absorbing the sound.

When she softened into his kiss, he pulled away. "You are well?"

She looked dazed. "Aye. How did you get here?"

"Later, beloved. We must be gone." He looked up at the moon, rising and orange, a harvest moon. A harvest of souls, he thought grimly. "Tonight is the Passover. Can you walk?"

She got to her feet, unsteady but upright. He helped her down the ladder with more haste than grace. Chloe stood for a moment over the still figure of the guard, then looked at her feet. "She's my size," she whispered and knelt, untying the woman's sandals. Cheftu turned to hurry her when he saw what she was doing. They took the shoes and ran into the protective shelter of the trees.

Cheftu grabbed his pack and medicine and hurriedly rubbed salve on Chloe's ankles as she threw off her filthy robe and stepped into the blue one he provided. He crushed her to him, allowing only for the present moment. Cheftu knelt over one sandal as she tied on the other. When she was dressed he handed her a basket and yanked her forward into the streets of the city.

THUT STOOD ON THE PARAPET, watching as the moon rose. Tonight would be the night of death. His elite guard was useless, despite their strong bodies and flashing swords. They would soon be drained as a sacrifice to the pride of Egypt's throne.

The moon reddened as it rose in the sky, painting the city in the colors of death. White for the bodies that would begin their journey to the afterworld tonight. Red for the blood of the children who would die, hardly having lived fully. Blue, blue for the *khaibit* shadows with fangs and talons in those dark streets and for the color all Egypt would wear for seventy days.

He remembered with a bitter joy that Senmut was also a firstborn son.

CHLOE AND CHEFTU RAN QUICKLY through the dark, silent streets. The night was ominous, the stillness a forbidding sound all its own. The moon hung low and full in the sky . . . its orb the color of blood. Chloe stopped for breath, holding a hand to her breast as she gasped, "No one is out? It is the middle of the week, yet these streets are deserted?"

"It is the Passover. Do you have older siblings?" His voice was thick and brusque.

Chloe thought for a moment. "Of course, Camille and Makab." The realization of her words struck her. "Oh, dear God, Makab?"

"I have told him how to prepare. He should be safe." If he listened, Cheftu added to himself.

"Do you?" she asked, her voice the echo of a whisper.

He was silent, their rapid footsteps loud. "I have a brother, Jean-Jacques." He paused again. "However, I am the eldest born here."

His words were fuel to them, and they fled into the Apiru district.

"Cheftu, look!" she whispered, her voice throbbing with emotion.

He knew what they would see. Still he could not believe this was the time; it did not reconcile with what history had thus far reported. Rameses was the pharaoh of the Exodus. Rameses, who made the Children of Israel work on Pi-Ramessa, who made them bake bricks without straw. Apparently what François knew as history was wrong. "There is blood on the lintel and doorpost?"

"Aye." Chloe turned away slowly and stared up at the moon, red and bloated. "Tonight the angel passes over, separating the believer and the unbeliever. Is that not what you said?" Her gaze was still fixed on the moon. "It seems to be growing, deepening in color."

Cheftu felt her trembling beneath the thin cloak. "Aye. We must hurry. Meneptah will be waiting for us. He knew what I was doing tonight, and if we do not show up, he will be concerned." He kissed her quickly on the forehead, and they set off down the street, their pace rapid but careful in the dark.

The narrow streets twisted and turned into midnight blue cul-de-sacs, darkened switchbacks, and total confusion. Suddenly Chloe stopped, her mouth dry. "Where are we, Cheftu? Why are there no lighted houses?" She turned to him, fear in her moonlit eyes. "I do not think we can find it in time. Cheftu," she said, her voice warbling as she looked at the sky, "this mistake could cost . . ."

He laid a finger on her lips. "Do not think about it." The moon was hidden from view by the crooked tenements. Cheftu saw the roof of an abandoned building several houses down. He grabbed Chloe's hand, and they ran toward it. They climbed up the broken stairs and looked up.

"It is getting late," he said. "Soon Thutmosis will call for Moshe and tell him to leave. We must be with the Israelites. It is our only chance of getting safely away." He looked down into the black street.

"Surely someone would give us the safety of their home for the night," Chloe said.

Cheftu turned to her, the blue Egyptian robe, baring one rosy-tipped breast, his wedding bracelet on her arm, her remaining earring in the likeness of HatHor. "To them we are Egyptian."

Chloe nodded sadly in acknowledgment. She looked up at the sky, and Cheftu watched her eyes glaze in horror. He whirled around and felt the blood leave his face.

Like phosphorescent spiderwebs the descending darkness spread, crisscrossing the moon and running down, slowly covering the sky and stars as far as the eye could see. "It is a net of death," Chloe whispered.

He grabbed her hand and they struggled down the steps, fear making their feet uncertain. Heading away from the darkened Apiru section, they crossed the common market square and saw some old stalls, not more than lean-tos, but some form of protection.

Cheftu pushed her inside one, instructing her to stay far to the back.

"Nay! You are the one who is in danger! Let me do this!" After wasting precious moments in argument, Cheftu stepped inside.

Chloe ran to a pile of rubbish just outside the Apiru section. There were many bloodstained branches there, and she grabbed several. She ran back through the abandoned market, losing her sense of direction when she looked up and saw the moon almost covered in the web, its garish red illuminated by the net.

Agonizingly long minutes later she found the shed and tried vainly to brush some of the remaining blood onto the shed. It was dried. Chloe began to panic. Cheftu could die any minute.

"Chloe," Cheftu said, "set them up against the frame." Feverishly they worked, trying to keep the branches from falling, using Chloe's waist sash to tie the rope onto the frame. They ran inside, and Cheftu took both their cloaks, spiking them onto the pegs outside, forming a curtained doorway. They were blocked in as best they could manage. Shaking, they stood holding each other. Chloe smelled Cheftu's fear and heard his heart pounding. He could die tonight.

"Pray God that he overlooks our not following the instructions exactly," Cheftu said. "We have had no lamb, no herbs, no unleavened bread. Pray that he is merciful." They sat down, huddled together in the dark, and listened.

Chloe thought of the many doors she had seen with no blood and began to cry softly on Cheftu's silken chest. He smoothed her hair with an unsteady hand. *"J'aime et j'espère,* Chloe."

I love and I hope.

A nearby scream rent the night. They clutched each other closer. A mournful wail rose up several streets away. Soon the air was filled with sounds of grief, anguish, and deepest fear. Chloe's tears stopped as she listened to the sounds around them.

"All this pain," she whispered. "How can people worship such a cruel God? I never even really thought about God, I mean, in personal terms. During these past few weeks, when even Thut and his priests were covered with boils and were powerless, I started wondering."

Cheftu lifted her chin, his amber gaze meeting hers in the darkness.

"The maliciousness of such a God, to teach a lesson like this . . ." She trailed off.

Solemnly Cheftu looked at her. "God did not do this maliciously. He spoke through Moshe many times, but Thutmosis refused to listen. He was so afraid of Hatshepsut's ire, her scorn, and losing face before her that he kept changing his mind. He made deals with God and broke them, Chloe. Thutmosis himself was going against his better judgment. Furthermore," he said, his tone becoming more intense, "Hat was the one who decided to take the firstborn Israelites as hostage. God simply knew her heart and prepared Moshe for it. So Pharaoh herself brought on this specific plague, not God."

He looked toward their curtained door, musing. "Just as Thut decided when a plague would cease, those many times before, so the Great House decided what the final tragedy would be, by simply parting her gilded lips."

The cries around them grew worse and seemed to be getting louder. Chloe burrowed closer to Cheftu, praying fervently to the God who suddenly seemed the most powerful thing in the universe. The one who could take Cheftu from her in a breath. Tears coursed down her face as she clung to him, daring and fearing the angel who could take him away.

"We are living through Bible history," Cheftu said in a voice thick with amazement. "The greatest miracle is still to come." They sat in silence as the night around them grew still. A shriek painfully close set their hearts pounding again. The hair on Chloe's neck stood on end as the makeshift door fluttered violently in the suddenly shrieking wind. A pain shot through her body, like an interior probe. She stared at the doorway, glimpsing a fearsome specter. Cheftu's body tensed, and Chloe hid her face against his chest in horror. *Surely she had not seen accurately!*

Yet Cheftu was still breathing.

The night quieted again, and they slept in each other's arms. When Cheftu awoke, his muscles were tired and stiff. He stood, then walked to the cloaked door and peeked out.

The sky was fading black, no sign of a moon at all, but he could see the rosy tint of dawn in the east. Chloe joined him, her taut body close and warm in the chill air. No one moved in the streets, yet a gentle peace seemed to have fallen.

He pulled down their cloaks, noticing the gouges in the cloth, and took Chloe's arm to lead her away. They walked into the winding street, each entry lacking bloodstains. They passed through, but at the neck of the street Cheftu turned and looked back.

On each of the unmarked doors was a faintly glowing mark, as if the luminescent claws of a huge rabid beast had scratched at it. Curious, he ran back through to their hut in the marketplace. No marks. He took a few steps into the streets of the Apiru. No marks.

"The Destroyer passed over," he mumbled to himself, and filled with a new strength, he ran to meet Chloe and head to the warm, waiting house of friends.

ALREADY THE STREETS WERE FULL, and people packed their few possessions as Moshe distributed the wealth to them. In the last hour before dawn, before a gathering of praying Apiru, a weeping and broken Thutmosis had come bearing the body of his firstborn son. Thut had handed over his coffers and the donations of many nobles and left to deliver his cold eight-year-old to the arms of Anubis.

Chloe saw D'vorah immediately, and they embraced. Chloe was recruited by Elishava to help load the donkeys and gather the children, and Cheftu joined Meneptah to group the rest of the healers and pool supplies.

Moshe had broken the huge throng into twelve smaller tribes, each represented by a color and standard. Within each tribe were twelve men whose duty it was to keep their tribe in close order and communication.

Groups of Israelites would join them as they moved into the desert: fam-

ilies from the nobles' houses along the river; other families who lived on iso-
lated estates; those scattered throughout villages from Zarub to Aiyat.

It was eerie, leaving in the cool dawn. Egyptians lined the roadway,
dressed in blue, their hair undone, their faces smeared with ashes. A
defeated people offered their gold and jewels to the strangers who
moved through their land; strangers with a powerful, vengeful god;
strangers who in four hundred years still spoke their own language, married their own relatives, and wore the one-shouldered garments of two
dozen monarchies past.

Wailing rose from every street. Periodically an enraged mother was
restrained by her family as they watched those who had been friends and
neighbors leave, death in their wake.

The Israelites walked through the gates of the city, and the sun shone
fully on them. Moshe called a brief halt, and the group milled around.
Chloe felt the strongest sense of destiny. Cheftu looked over her
shoulder with a grin as she pulled out a piece of papyrus, quickly
sketching the faces that had always eluded her as an artist. The lines
seemed to flow unbroken from her eye to her arm, moving effortlessly.

She drew the grandfather, leaning on his staff, the child with the
geese, and her own beloved, the strong lines of his face and the fire in
his eyes as he looked at her, over his shoulder. Trembling, she looked at
the picture . . . that one Camille would eventually find.

What did this mean?

Moshe sounded the horns and they were off, a ragtag group of vic-
tors who had never lifted a weapon aside from their prayers. Chloe and
Cheftu merged with the slow-moving mass of people: old people, children, young mothers, and their shepherd husbands. Chloe shouldered
the basket containing her few extra garments, her palette, a bowl of
unleavened bread, and other necessities, plus the gold they had been
given as they left. The guard station was far behind them now, and Chloe
smiled in stupefaction that she was part of the Exodus from Egypt.

The fountainhead of the Israelite nation—never mentioned by the
Egyptians because it happened only once. Once they were destroyed by
plagues on command. Once they lost their firstborn in a lunar web of
blood. Once their slaves left Egypt behind them in shambles. *Only once.*

Chloe glanced behind them, her vision obscured by the cloud of dust
these six thousand clans were stirring. The din was deafening, the calls
and cries of thousands of animals and children mixing with the chatter
of women and the excited undertone of men.

Moshe kept them moving, acknowledging the psychological importance of being on the other side of the great pylons covered with Hatshepsut's triumphs. They were free for the first time in four hundred years! The excitement around them was a living thing, even in the exhaustion from this first many-*henti* walk.

By noon the next day the sun was high and powerful, slowing down the tribes and quieting them through exhaustion. By dusk they were pressing forward painfully, all straining to hear Pharaoh's chariots on their heels.

Moshe called a halt at noon the following day, and the multitude sank with relief onto the sizzling sand, ate unleavened bread, then collapsed into sleep.

Chloe was so exhausted, she could barely think. Cheftu had formed a lean-to with their baskets and cloaks, and they fell asleep instantly, waking refreshed in the cold night air.

After throwing on cloaks for warmth, they ate dates and raisins that Meneptah's family had shared, then hefted their bags. As the tribes assembled, facing Moshe with the stars of Abraham numbering millions above them, a hush fell.

Moshe prostrated himself, and the tribes followed suit, for behind Moshe was a funnel of fire, spanning into the heavens, twisting and spewing flames yet consuming nothing and giving off no heat.

The former Egyptian prince rose to his feet and cried out over their awed and bent heads, "Hear, O Israel! Elohim is one God! He goes before us! Behold the fire of his power, wisdom, and glory! Arise!" As a body they rose and followed the flame tornado.

Cheftu was rooted to the spot, his face ashen. "Do you realize where we walk, my beloved?" he asked. "We see such wonders, yet shall forget so soon."

"When do we expect Thut?" Chloe asked quietly.

He glanced around and answered, "It has been several days. If they have not come already, then perhaps they will come after the seventy days of preparation. That gives us seventy days to get to the sea."

Chloe nodded, the remembrance of the carnage in Egypt clear in her mind. All those bodies to prepare, bury, and mourn. All those who would never serve Egypt because of the stubbornness of a king and the demands of an omnipotent God. She trudged forward with Cheftu, her mind flitting from one event to another like a psychotic butterfly.

GOSHEN

"PHARAOH, LIVING FOREVER! HAS ARRIVED," Ameni called to Thut.

He sat in his brown and bare gardens, the fountains empty except for dark stains, a reminder of the blood that had filled them, until at his request the Israelite god had removed it.

Thut was unshaven, dressed in his blue mourning robes, his eyes red rimmed with the pain of the people who had come to see him. His magi, holding their children or siblings in their arms, had decried him for the stubbornness that allowed them to die.

He was not ready to meet Pharaoh, not when he would have to admit the Israelites, those ignorant and uncouth slaves, had defeated him. Perhaps he was *not* fit to rule, Thut thought. Indeed, all he wanted for himself and his people was to live and die and worship in total and complete security.

He ran a shaky hand over his face. She would not understand.

Approaching servants warned Thut of the coming battle. Wearily he rose to his feet, his gaze on the ground.

"Holy Osiris!" he heard her say. "Even in the garden of the god, this calamity would strike?" Her voice was filled with outrage and more than a little fear. She did not look well.

Her once lustrous black hair was dull, braided, and hanging down her back. She wore a tunic and kilt, emphasizing her royal standing only by the pectoral resting between her full breasts. The kohl that ringed her eyes highlighted the violet shadows beneath them. She fixed her gaze on Thut, and he inclined his head, not caring at all whether she was satisfied.

She turned to her entourage. "Bring my nephew and me beer and food!" she demanded. "Then leave us." Hat sat on the bench across from him, surveying the empty, twisted grapevines, the trees as bare as winter, without even bark to clothe them. Every blade of grass, every stalk of papyrus, every blossom in this verdant area . . . gone.

Did she feel a tremor in her soul, he wondered, as she looked at her ruined country and her shell of a nephew? He had not bathed in days, and his robe hung loosely. Hat reached out and laid a hennaed hand on his leg. "I feel your grief, Thut. I too have no—" Her voice broke, and she steadied. "I have no one to support me."

He glanced up sharply. "Even at this moment of grief can you think of nothing except power and the succession of Egypt, Hatshepsut?" His voice was rough from tears. "Have you no woman's heart? Your lover is dead! My firstborn son is gone!" His outburst ended, and he stared down at this hands.

"I had that prophet in my court fourteen times," he said. "Fourteen times! When the Nile turned to blood, I was surprised, but not too concerned. Then when the plagues struck as the prophet said, I was filled with fear, but too angry to take back the words the 'mighty Horus-in-the-Nest' had spoken."

She sat, silent.

"Why my own advisers, even Lord Cheftu, pleaded with me to give in and let the slaves go, I could not. My pride was at risk. I did not care for Egypt, just my wounded pride.

"The last time I saw Moshe, I stood before him, a shell of a man, and threatened him. I realize now, death was no threat to him. He had no fear because his desert god knew what I would do.

"Yet until I beheld Count Makab dead, my friend Sennedjm dead, and my firstborn Turankh, lifeless in my arms—my wife Isis actually killed herself from grief—until then, the impact of my decision was not clear to me."

He pointed to the parapet facing the city. "I stood there that night. Ra's weak eye was like blood, and it seemed to pour down over the people. *Haii-aii*, Hatshepsut! The grief I heard that night! The cries of mothers who had entrusted the safety of their children into my care! Me! A god! I am responsible." The grief in his voice was double-edged.

"My pride has murdered a generation."

Thut buried his head in his hands, shoulders braced against tears no god would shed. They sat there for many moments, in that wreck of a garden, one intent on repentance . . . the other on revenge.

CHAPTER 14

THE SINAI

The days and weeks ran together for Chloe. The tribes walked each night, following a pillar of fire, which turned into a gentle cloud that shaded them from the sun during the day while they slept.

Cheftu spent a great deal of time caring for the sprained ankles, pulled muscles, and upset stomachs of a people in transit. Their position in line had changed. They were now bringing up the rear. They were accepted by Meneptah, his mother, and D'vorah. To the majority of the Apiru, however, they were Egyptian, the oppressors of four hundred years. Only because Moshe had spoken to Cheftu and thanked him for pulling Caleb out of the fire were they accepted, Chloe felt.

It wasn't that they weren't Jewish. Hundreds of other Apiru had joined the Exodus, people who had never heard of the Children of Abraham. It was that they were Egyptian, wealthy, and of the priesthood, a thing that plain white clothing could not hide. Bred into Cheftu was an air of command, and Chloe guessed it was recognizable in her as well. So they kept to themselves and Meneptah's small clan.

Her thoughts halted as once again she pulled up their baskets and arranged the cloak over them, affording some privacy and shelter. After digging a shallow pit, she laid several sheets of unleavened dough into it, covered them with sand, and lit a fire on top. She took out a pot and put it into the fire to make the soup that had sustained them so far. Elishava walked into the shade and seated herself on the hot sand, fanning wildly.

"How are you this morning?" she asked pleasantly. "The walk was good, aye?"

The older woman's dialect was difficult to follow, and Chloe smiled and said it had been good. She watched as Elishava poured a small amount of water on her hands and sluiced her face with it. Though Cheftu said the Jewish purity laws had not been written yet, the years of living in Egypt had made them a hygiene-conscious race. People began to arrive at their fire, D'vorah from walking with the little girls, singing songs and memorizing history, then Cheftu and Meneptah, who worked daily in one of the medical wagons. Chloe passed around the water as everyone rinsed, then handed them the soup and bread. As they did before every meal, Meneptah intoned a small prayer to the God of deliverance. "Thank you, O God, who makes bread from the field."

After a murmured agreement people began to share their days. Chloe alone had no task except to attend the tent and food, which was time-consuming and required organization but did not allow interaction with people. Aharon had suggested that the former priestess of HatHor keep a low profile, as there were already problems with the tribes whining about security and trying to worship other gods in this one God camp.

The sun was high and hot, the terrain bare. The locusts had also been here. What would be known as the Gulf of Suez flowed off to their right, patrolled by soldiers protecting Egypt's borders—soldiers who were most likely dead, being the firstborn. Chloe chewed a lip as the others ate around her. To their left was the Sinai desert, whose towering mountaintops were unseen, surrounded by dust and dirt and a terrible dryness that made one's scalp and nostrils bleed.

But the Israelites were free. It had really happened. She drank carefully of the precious sweet water and watched as Meneptah forgot to eat, his gaze fixed on D'vorah. She was recovering well. The terrible burns on her face and hands had faded. She was no longer the fresh beauty she had been, but from Meneptah's dazed expression it didn't really matter. She had slipped into his family, loved by his mother, embraced by his sisters and brothers, and Chloe and Cheftu bet these two would meet under the marriage tent before the Ten Commandments.

He leaned over, as if he could read her thoughts. "If he does not want his soup, do you think he will give it to me? Though I dreamt last night of salmon en croute with new *pommes de terre* and choc—"

Chloe held up a restraining hand, while visions of paella, lobster bisque, and pistachio gelato danced in her head. "Do not talk that way. We have only been eating like this for maybe two months, *haii?*"

Cheftu laughed and said in Egyptian, "Mmmm . . . just think of roasted fowl with pomegranate or fish stuffed with nuts . . ."

Chloe shrugged. "From what I remember hearing, we have about forty years of this left."

"Perhaps, since the Great House has not pursued, the sea will not need to be parted, everything will go well on Mount Sinai, and we will not have to wander for forty years."

Chloe looked at him, setting aside her dish. "Do you think we changed history?" She watched the chattering Apiru.

"I do not know what else to think. Thut is a broken man. I do not believe he would change his mind. He realized this was no stone god, but a living and breathing deity. He desperately wanted us to leave, though of course he threatened Moshe to save face."

"That is why he let us go?"

"He did not care. Meneptah said his boy, Turankh, was in the chariot, the pink of life still in his cheeks, his youthlock braided for playing teams the next day. Nothing was on Thut's mind except his destroyed family and country. I can understand his preoccupation with his family; I cannot imagine his grief."

The sun was dizzyingly bright, and people were gathering their cloaks to sleep. Chloe shielded her eyes until the heavy cloud that covered daily came to darken and cool the day as a fresh breeze blew in from the sea.

She rose, carrying the pottery plates to the sand. There she crouched and scrubbed them with sand, cleaning the porous surface, then packed them again. She was sleepy and lay down in the shelter of her cloak, her cheek against Cheftu's steady heartbeat. "I am so glad you are here with me," he said sleepily. "We belong together. Even time could not separate us."

"If you had to pick a time to return to, Cheftu, when would it be?" she asked, eyes half-open in the shadow.

He sat up a little and reached for the waterskin. "Where do you get these questions, *haii?*" He chuckled. "From Egypt? If it were my choice?" He thought for a moment, drinking sparingly, the mingled sounds of the thousands of people lost in the still daytime. "The time of Solomon. To see the Temple in Jerusalem . . . *aii*, that would be a marvelous, wondrous thing. Where for you, *chérie?*"

Chloe looked across the sands to the rocky cliffs that edged them in.

Mountains on one side, the sea on the other. "To go back in time?" She shook her head. "Given a choice, I would have never done it. History was not an interest to me. Progress and change . . . things moving faster, more technology. I would have gone into the future." She grinned. "I bet they even discover more ice-cream flavors."

"So where would you go?"

Chloe chewed her lip. Nowhere without you, she wanted to say. "I do not know."

They laughed together, their tired bodies entwined. Cheftu spoke after a moment. "I am surprised you are such a woman of the future," he said. "You have adapted to this world so well."

"Offending Pharaoh, murdering a girl—"

"Chloe. *Non*, that was not your fault. You did not know."

She shrugged. "I have made a mess of things." Except my art, she thought. My skills have quadrupled. My memory has sharpened. I am a far better artist than ever before. Somehow Cammy finds my work. I must glue the Exodus panels together and hide them.

"*Le bon Dieu* will bring it about."

"Bring what?"

"Everything."

• • •

A piercing horn jolted them awake, and Chloe, once her heart started beating again, realized it was *atmu* . . . time to move on. She rose to her feet. Cheftu helped her pack their belongings, dispersing the bread and dried fruit they ate daily. As she turned around he pulled her into his arms, standing in the purple smoke of twilight. "We will have a new life, Chloe. Together." His gaze dropped. "Not in the future, not in the past, but living in the present." He kissed her nose. "Remember that when days are rough, *chérie*."

GOSHEN

HATSHEPSUT, LIVING FOREVER! stormed into the room. "This must cease!" she barked at Thut. "You cannot sit there like a corpse before the

Opening of the Mouth! You are Horus-in-the-Nest! You must avenge us!"

He raised blank eyes to her.

"We shall beg Amun-Ra for his guidance! We must bring those slaves back in bondage!"

"I will not go after them, aunt," Thut said in a monotone. "They have a powerful protector. I will not have more Egyptians' blood on my hands. He will surely destroy us all."

"How can you say this?" she cried. "Have you no concern for the effect on our people?"

"I have every concern. However, this god, he is . . . a, an . . . an individual. I will not cross him again."

She paced the room, fists clenched. "I never thought you to be a coward, Thutmosis the Third. We are the Great House! We must prevail! To do otherwise is to disturb Ma'at." She turned and knelt before him, covering his dirty and unkempt hands with her own capable and gloved ones. "We cannot unbalance the forces of the universe. It is unthinkable."

His weary brown stare met her worried gaze. "I will not go."

Frustrated, she stood. "Very well, then, I must return to Waset. I shall bury my high priest, Hapuseneb; my commander of the guards, Nehesi; my grand vizier . . . and my heart—" Her voice broke. A moment passed as she inhaled deeply. "The moment they are safely entombed, I will go after those *khaibits* myself."

He jerked back in surprise.

"You shall be regent until I return in my glory, the Great House leading her troops. Then I shall take back my throne and you shall have to answer for your willingness to hurt the land we are entrusted with! You shall answer to Amun himself!"

She strode from the room, and Thut knew she would not return from her vengeance. "O desert god of the Israelites," he whispered. "Protect Egypt."

THE SINAI

THE SOUND OF THUNDERING HORSE hooves echoed through the hot sand, and Cheftu woke with a pounding headache and churning stomach. He scanned the horizon but could see no signs of anyone . . . yet. He kissed Chloe hurriedly. "Wake up, beloved. That for which we have awaited is upon us."

Her eyes snapped open. "The Great House?"

"Aye. Approaching."

She shook her head to clear it and rose to pack away their belongings. "Shall I wake the others?"

Cheftu nodded. "I will seek out Moshe." He pulled her hard against him. "Be safe, *chérie.*" He scanned the tent city until he saw the pennants denoting the leaders' tent.

The prophet knelt in shadow, his lips moving in prayer. "So, Pharaoh's heart has hardened again?" he said without looking up.

Cheftu nodded, shaking. He was speaking to *Moses.* "I could not yet see the pursuers, but I heard their hoofbeats in the sand."

Moshe's head wagged. "Elohim must rescue us again. We have reached a point where we must again have faith. Perhaps then Israel will truly recognize and turn from following false gods."

"Where will you lead us? My knowledge of the land is great, and we have been walking parallel to the Inland Sea, so we must almost be to the Red Sea."

Moshe's black eyes twinkled. "Elohim will protect us, Egyptian, but you must watch for stragglers. Alert people as you travel to your camp." He turned away and spoke over his shoulder. "Y'shua, my boy, go wake Aharon and tell him to get the tribes up and walking. We shall push hard to the sea."

Cheftu ran through the camp, shouting to wake up and break camp. He did not answer any of the questions thrown at him but raced along to catch Chloe.

• • •

The tribes had managed to put several more *henti* between them and the approaching army when Cheftu finally saw the sand cloud from chariots and horses. He could not find Chloe in this mob of white-clad, black-haired women. Though she was his heart, he did not recognize her. D'vorah, Meneptah, and Elishava were also mingled in, unidentifiable. Cheftu had finally reached the back of the camp, fear of the Great House encouraging the families to walk faster, leaving their belongings strewn behind them in their rush to the sea.

When the front of the lines reached the sea, the words of fear and terror at the imposing body of water washed back like the tide. Suddenly the uncertainty that had nipped at the heels of the tribes was a veritable controlling force.

Frantically Cheftu ran back and forth among the people, searching for Chloe.

Night had fallen. The tribes were captured between the funnel of fire before them and the Red Sea at their backs. Cheftu cringed away, fearing the fire's destructive power, even though it radiated only protection and safety.

They could no longer hear Pharaoh's approaching army, and Cheftu knew they were unseen to the army because of the fire. They were massed on the furthermost point of land. Across eight *henti* of water they could see another desert. The people were crying out, and he saw Moshe, standing high above them on a rock, hands raised in the air. The wind whipped the people, and the roaring rush of waters surrounded them. The howling power of the wind was so fierce, it immobilized Cheftu. He could move neither forward nor back. Crouching, he pulled his linen cloak closer, his eyes tearing as he searched the crowd. Eventually he slept.

When the wind died he raised his head and noted it was sunrise. Before them stood a bridge of land, dry land. It was roughly two miles wide and spanned the distance to the other side. Already the tribes were swarming across it, pulling along their animals and running for safety. Although he had always heard the story, he had never rationally believed it . . . any of it. Even the Bible writers claimed "yam suph," translated into the Sea of Reeds, a marsh on Egypt's northern border, had been the dry land the Hebrews had crossed. Had they, like Cheftu, doubted it was the Red Sea? Cheftu fell to his knees.

Here was the Red Sea, parted.

He panicked as he remembered Chloe. Scrambling down to the rocky shore, he searched for her among those crossing, but from this distance the figures were indistinguishable.

The sky was bright, and those standing close to Cheftu were running down the now dry shoreline toward the path to freedom. Cheftu looked behind him. The cloud was gone, as was the pillar of fire, and he knew Pharaoh's army would be up and following soon. Most of the tribes were in the sea by now, as Cheftu continued to look for Chloe.

Fearing she had fallen, was lying hurt somewhere, he searched the Sinai coastline for her. There was very little area where someone could go unnoticed, and Cheftu began to fear she had crossed the sea without him. Even now she could be on the other side.

Cheftu ran for the shore but halted when he heard the cries of Pharaoh's army behind him. Panicked, he turned and noticed a crevice in some rocks along the shoreline. He had barely reached it before Pharaoh's army thundered down the mountainous slope to rein in at the water's edge.

"We shall pursue!" he heard Hatshepsut's strident tones. "They shall repay in blood for the damage done to our beloved land! Behold! Even the gods of the Red Sea recognize our right of vengeance!"

Cheftu looked out. Hat stood alone in her chariot, the brilliant sun glinting off the gold spokes in its wheels and the gold breastplate she wore. She whipped her steeds and took off at a gallop, her chariot jouncing in the sand as she fought to hold on to both horses.

The soldiers were an elite contingency of Pharaoh's select troops. The *Wadjet* tattoo embraced every arm. He felt sick when he saw Ameni close behind Hat. With battle cries they swept into the sea. Cheftu watched, paralyzed. He *knew* what would happen. It was the reason he could not make it safely across to join Chloe on the other side.

The tribespeople were nearing the end of the pathway. Cheftu saw the army gaining on them, the small figures, jots of color, moving quickly but not fast enough to outrun the finest horses and chariots in the world. Cheftu noted with a twisting gut that the entire force—four thousand soldiers and six hundred chariots—was now in the sea.

The walls of water fell, crashing with such force that his ears rang. Cheftu ran to the edge of the sea, watching vainly as horses reared and screamed, their fear mingling with the terrified shouts of men who stabbed vainly into the water. For a fleeting second his gaze met Hat's; the wild blackness of her eyes embedded itself into his consciousness as he watched her go under the crashing waves.

Within seconds Cheftu was standing knee deep in water. He began to climb back up the rocks, frantically seeking higher ground. The fear in his stomach had become a live thing, twisting and turning, fomenting rebellion against this gracious God of the Hebrews—and of his own true faith. He sat in a crevice overlooking the sea.

The roiling waters were filled with heads and arms and hands, all reaching for salvation. Their cries were lost in the battering waves. He stood, searching for a glimpse of Hatshepsut's chariot—and found it. It was bobbing sideways in the white water, Hat's body thrown across one of the wheels, impaled on a gold-plated finial, her face a mask of hate. No longer living forever . . .

Egypt was dead.

The Egyptian warred with the Frenchman in Cheftu. He felt all the grief the real Cheftu did, but he felt it through a prism. The knowledge that God had indeed rescued the Israelites, just as the parish school books said, competed with the awareness that there was no way to retrieve Hatshepsut's body for a proper burial.

The gods would forget her, she who had brought such prosperity and peace to the two lands. For a moment he remembered the companion he had trusted, respected, and loved from afar for so many years. She'd drawn him: her strength, her commitment to peace, her desire to beautify the land and restore splendor to the gods. Cheftu remembered the banquets when they'd sat together, the songs they had sung while away from Waset, and always, the golden goddess who was merciful to everyone, until her paranoia destroyed her.

He felt empty; an anchor in his life was gone. She had controlled so much of who he was and what he did. He had loved her and followed her loyally, until this. Sand flew in his face as he contemplated his betrayal, necessary but vile. Could he have changed things? Could he have prevented this ignominious death? Guilt burned in his belly.

The path was gone, every trace hidden under *khetu* of water. Faintly he could make out dots on the other side. He stood at the tip of the Sinai, and they were in Arabia. Yet for all the *henti* between them, it could have been the distance of a hundred years.

The Israelites were safe.

He was alone.

Wearily he sat down, his kilt drying in the ferocious winds that blew across the water. I should go pull out those bodies that wash ashore, he thought, yet still he sat unmoving. The sun rose, and the reflection off the turquoise water was blinding. Never before had he felt so alone. The mind that had invaded his at age sixteen also seemed to be gone.

Chloe was gone. Perhaps even now she was walking into the desert, searching for him; she would be a Bible character now. He allowed the loneliness to wash over him in waves as destructive as those that had claimed his friends, foes, and pharaoh. He debated drowning himself, joining his compatriots in the blue water.

He stood and picked his way to the shore, trying not to think beyond the necessity of retrieving bodies. Soon he was on the sandy path that had led to "God's highway." The waters were still now, just the natural tide of the Red Sea. He scrambled over the rocks and looked in the shallows for bodies.

For hours he searched. He felt his skin burn. The searing heat tormented his recently healed scars. He was blinded without kohl. He found not one body. Finally he crawled under a high rock out of the sunlight and fell asleep.

The cooling breeze of evening revived him. For moments he lay with his eyes closed, reliving the feeling of Chloe close to him in sleep. Murmuring her name woke him completely. It awoke him to the realization that she was gone.

For a few minutes he contemplated how he could travel to find her. After all, he knew where the Israelites would settle forty years from now.

Despairing, he rose to his feet. Rage gurgled within him, and he screamed to the sky, slipping into the French of his true heritage. *"Nooooooo!* You are unfair!" He stood, head bent, chest heaving. "You show me heaven in the arms and soul of this woman, only to take her away?" He felt his control slipping. Fists clenched, he continued to yell at his unromantic God. *"Pourquoi, mon Dieu? Pourquoi? Pourquoi?"* His last question was more of a whimper than a protest. Anguish tore the flesh from his bones as he sagged on the beaten sand.

Far behind him on the Sinai beach, the brilliant sunset reflected briefly off the scarab clasp of a beaded bracelet encircling a brown wrist.

PART IV

CHAPTER 15

Cheftu woke on the sand, water lapping his ankles. The tide was coming in, and to the east was the tiniest glimmer of salmon and gold, heralding the sun's entrance. He sat up, moving back from the water. His throat was dry and his eyes sore and scratchy. The utter stillness of the dawn was frightening. The solitude was broken by a rush of birds rising from the water as they called to each other. Another day. Wearily he stood, halfheartedly brushing sand from his kilt and cloak.

He scanned the shoreline again, searching for any sign of life, any debris hinting at the thousands of lives lost the day before.

Nothing.

Too exhausted to care, he shielded his eyes once again and looked across the rough sea. Somewhere he knew Chloe would be searching for him, looking among the hundreds and thousands of men with dark hair. His pain at the thought of her tearstained face, her heavy heart, almost tore him in two. "RaEm," he said in an anguished whisper.

But he was not truly calling for RaEmhetepet, Lady of Silver and priestess to HatHor. His soul longed for a futuristic love who spoke French, handled a bow and arrow as well as any soldier, had eyes that could flame with passion, and possessed a talent that brought life to papyrus.

Angrily he dashed the tears from his eyes, turned away from the sea, and began the long walk toward Egypt. In the back of his mind was the faint hope that he might die in the desert, but the self-preservation that had served him all these years recoiled at the thought of his eyes being pecked out by scavengers and his body shredded by jackals. I *really* am an Egyptian, he thought wryly. I cannot bear the thought of my body destroyed. He reached the sandy rise and looked out a final time toward the water.

Egypt held nothing for him. His position and family were destroyed. He looked east—the turquoise mines on the Red Sea were said to kill a man in a quarter of his lifetime. Beyond that? There were a dozen kingdoms where he could go, resume his life. Why would he? He looked again at the water, at the waves lapping on the shore.

There was a movement—he saw it from the corner of his eye. The sun was rising rapidly, and Cheftu shielded his eyes and squinted. Below him, to his east, just above the incoming tide, was something. . . . He looked harder. Was it a bird? A body? He saw a glitter on it, sparkling in the sunlight, and heard a rushing in his ears as hope surged through his body.

"Chloe," he breathed. Energy coursed through his veins as he ran to her. "Chloe!" Then he had her in his arms. She was *here!* He lifted her and carried her farther away from the tide. He pulled off his cloak and laid it underneath an overhang, then laid her gently upon it. Sitting beside her, he brushed her matted hair away from her face, his hand trembling. She had a nasty cut on her cheek and abrasions on her head.

Instinct took over, and he examined the wounds carefully, checked her eyes. She seemed to be suffering a mild concussion. Here, with no fresh water, no way of taking care of her, this could be deadly. Fear began to overtake the joy he felt.

Even now she could be lost.

Cheftu bowed his head and, for the second time in the last twenty-four decans, wept and prayed. Only this time it was for wisdom and guidance . . . and in repentance.

God had rescued Chloe for him. Of this there was no doubt. Elohim had not taken her away. He watched the fluttering of her eyelashes anxiously as she fought for consciousness. She lost the battle, and Cheftu's fears mounted.

She should not sleep; it could result in death or a waking death that was even worse, for then the physical needs of the body must be met but the *ka* was trapped between two worlds.

He seized the water skin still tied around her waist and ran to the shore. After filling it with the cool morning sea, he raced back to her and threw it full into her face.

She came around—with a vengeance. "What the bloody hell!" she shouted in English, sitting straight up. The sudden movement made her clutch her head with both hands and cry out in pain. But she was alive! She was here! Cheftu didn't care if she damned him to all of Dante's Inferno, one eternity after another. She glared at him, then looked around, her face altered. He knew she had suffered the same terrible loss he had.

She threw herself into his arms, kissing his face, then winced, her hands to her head.

"You were hurt," he said, touching her abrasions. "How do you feel?"

She squinted at him, panting through gritted teeth. "My head is about to break. "

Cheftu took her hand in his, massaging her palm with firm, circling strokes. The tension in her face eased and she lay very still. "Chloe!" His voice was sharp, and she answered with a mumble.

"Chloe!" He slapped her face, bringing her around in an instant.

"What was that for?" she said, holding her cheek where the red pattern of his hand marked her sunburned skin.

He drew her close. "I am sorry I struck you," he said. "But you cannot sleep. You are hurt and must stay awake. I . . . I saw you falling asleep, and I"—his voice cracked—"panicked, I guess. I was afraid you would not wake up." He knew his grip must hurt, pressing all the bruises on her back and rib cage, but the fear inside him was a taloned thing. Bitter bile filled his throat. They sat, uncomfortably close but unwilling to move, to relinquish their holds. Cheftu pulled her to his chest, caressing her hair as he spoke about the night. "What happened to you?"

Chloe grimaced. "Well, you ran off to tell Moshe about Pharaoh . . ." She sat up, her tone changed. "Where are the bodies?"

He traced his finger across her cheekbone and down into her matted black hair, grasping it with his hand. "Gone. The waves drowned them, just as the Bible said."

"But the bodies! There were thousands. . . ." The sun poured into his eyes so that they looked like honey, clear transparent gold. "Gone?" she repeated.

" 'And Israel saw the Egyptians lying dead on the shore.' Apparently they are on the other side."

"That's impossible! Currents do not run like that," Chloe scoffed.

She sat up, looking out at the blue waters brushing peacefully against the shore. The rise above the sea had been almost leveled by the thousands of feet: humans, horses, geese, sheep, and finally Pharaoh and her soldiers. A gull cried sharply as it raced off across the water. The other side was visible, and in the quiet of dawn they could hear a faint jingle, like a sistrum or tambourine.

In her mind she placed the tribes in a biblical illustration, a Doré or an Alma-Tadema. Occasionally laughter drifted across the waves. Aside from that, they were frozen in time: no longer Meneptah, D'vorah, and Elishava—instead *The Children of Israel on the Shores of the Red Sea.* Flat, almost a caricature, lacking the life and passion and intrigues of reality.

The water caressed the shore gently, smoothing over the rocks that jutted out now, but in Chloe's time would be sand. Where were the bodies? The armor? All the gold of collars, bridles, and swords? Had God taken even that proof? Or was it only on the other shore, where it couldn't be retrieved and honored? A final slap to the Egyptians?

"A bead for your thoughts?" Cheftu said.

"I saw it."

"What?"

"The parting. It was as though a spell fell across everyone but me. Thousands of people were standing up, dead asleep. I could see the waters churning, boiling as it built into walls. Then the wind changed and blew directly between the walls, all the way across the sea. I could not feel the slightest breeze, but I watched the sand dry, the remaining crustaceans blown to Arabia. It was like a funnel of air, parallel to the ground. It took all night; the stars came out, the moon shone, and the wind kept blowing." She looked back at him. "It was so loud, I still can barely hear." She looked at the calm waters.

"Before dawn came, people started awakening. Conveniently, those closest to the water awoke first. They were astounded!" She smiled at the memory of the families gathering their things and descending to shore, then walking onto the sand—one guy had even picked up a handful and thrown it into the wind, where it had scattered like dust. Children had been fascinated by the wealth of coral along the sides, but mostly people had run. The walls of water were towering high, shrouding the highway in shade. "I watched for you," she said. "Everyone was traveling in families, so it should have been easy to find you. As the day went on, and more people crossed, I did not see you." She looked down. "Meneptah's clan crossed, and I began to get scared. I couldn't believe this was really happening, and it seemed that every picture was etched into my memory, every face, every detail. Then I heard the army." Cheftu sat beside her, drawing her close, bracing them against the overhang.

"I caught sight of you as Hat's troops came down the rise. Pandemonium. A lot of the chariots got stuck in the sand, and the soldiers were shaken when they saw the walls of water. I heard one voice call out, 'Pharaoh, their god fights for them!' However, they were disciplined and followed her in." Cheftu's fingers ran through her hair, calming, reassuring.

"There must have been thousands of men, most of them in chariots. I started screaming when I saw the last ones step onto the sand, but it was too late. Their chariots were falling apart, their horses panicking. I heard a loud crack, and suddenly all I could see was white water and arms and legs and heads bobbing in it like broken dolls. And the noise! The rushing filled my head, almost, but not quite, drowning out their cries, their entreaties, and their curses." She touched the cut on her cheek. "I went a little berserk and ran down to the shore, determined to help out. That is when I fell, I guess. I remember nothing else." She paused. "Except praying that you would stay here," she finished, her voice barely a breath.

"*Haii*, Chloe," Cheftu said, burying his face in her neck. "My love, my darling, my *ab*. Oh, thank God you are here!"

"I am here, beloved," she whispered. "I hope I will always be here."

He laid her down, looking into her eyes, probing her sore head, and finally pulling her body against him. "Now you can sleep. It has been long enough," he murmured into her hair. "We must rest. Then we must flee."

⋯

Her eyes felt welded shut and her tongue was the consistency of a washrag. Every bone was bruised and every muscle ached. She smelled, and sand was stuck in every crevice of her body. But the will to get up was gone. Cheftu snored beside her. He didn't snore unless he was exhausted—an understatement for them both.

The heat was already intense, scorching her skin. She opened her eyes. They'd have to find some shade. Birds wheeled above them, calling and crying as they dove into the waters for fish. Fish. Food. Chloe was suddenly ravenous. Tired, gross, and starving to death. "Cheftu . . ." She nudged him. "Get up."

He groaned and turned. "Put out the torch and come to the couch."

She shook him. "The torch is the sun. Cheftu, wake up."

This rough beginning was an omen for the day. They could barely move, and it required the greatest will to retrieve their luggage, which Chloe had hidden carefully. A swim was cleansing, but the salt burned their wounds and dried them further. Strict rationing of water followed an almost raw fish dinner, and they fell asleep in the sand.

Two days later—two days that Chloe could scarcely recall—they woke up actually alert.

"What are we going to do?"

"It is too early to sound so panicked," Cheftu groused.

"Should we go back to Egypt?"

His eyes opened and he rubbed his face, scratching at his beard. "We cannot."

"Haii." She looked out across the sea. "I want to go home." Cheftu stiffened instantly. Chloe felt raw sobs building inside her. "I want television and hot showers and pizza delivery. I want underwear and Macintosh and Hershey's Kisses." She took a shaky breath. Cheftu hadn't moved. "I am sick of being hot and chased and hungry and tired. I miss Juan."

"Juan?" he asked coldly.

"My spokes-iguana. He made me a small fortune. I should have changed his costume at least three times by now. A new costume with every new dish," she explained. Cheftu frowned. He put a hand to her forehead. "I am not sick," she said. "I just want to go home." He gathered her to his chest, but Chloe pushed away. It was too hot for hugs.

"I have thought about our position," he said, changing the topic. "Egypt is impossible. There are other courts; as an Egyptian physician I would be welcome. Indeed, I am known in many of them. But . . . Thutmosis knows them as well."

"We are still running from him? How is he going to respond to all this?"

Cheftu sighed. "That it is a boon from Amun-Ra. Thut has waited to rule Egypt; now there is no one else. Even his sons are dead, and Hat's daughter, Neferurra, is not the woman her mother was." They walked in silence, heading toward the pile of rocks just barely visible on the horizon. Cheftu kept looking toward the plains, as if expecting to see a cloud of dust heralding the arrival of more soldiers.

"*Assst,* so we are just walking off into the sunrise?"

"Thut will send soldiers. We are the only ones who know what happened. This knowledge is power; we can barter with it."

"How? She is dead."

"There is no body. No proof." Cheftu pointed. "We will stay along the water and walk until we find a place, far enough away, to rest."

"Then?"

He walked in silence, deliberate forceful steps. "Then I will take you home."

"But—"

"Enough!"

▬
• •

The moon had risen, and they donned cloaks to keep out the biting wind. In the distance they heard the heartrending cry of the jackal, its call a haunting reminder that he was the Egyptian god of the dead. Only the dead were here to hear his cries. What *had* happened to all the bodies? Thousands of lives extinguished, yet not a shred of proof. Nothing. The tide was coming in, and they started heading inland from the beach, its rush of waves soothing them into near somnambulism. They stopped periodically to sip the tepid goat-flavored water and chew on duck jerky and raisins from Chloe's bag.

A blazing sunrise woke them up, eyes sticky from the blowing sand, throats dry from the little water they had taken. Cheftu swore as he rolled over, rubbing his face with his hands. "We must get out of the sun," he said, and they picked up their belongings and headed for a nearby rock.

They woke again at the sun's zenith, hot, tired, and cranky. Shouldering their bags, they walked down to the shoreline, letting the waves cover their tracks and cool their bodies. Night fell again, and they drank a few more drops of the precious water before lying down under the canopy of stars.

They rose with the sun and continued to walk in the surf, their feet blistered and sore but pressing eastward. There was very little water left, just enough to coat the tongue, but they trekked on, forcing one foot before the other. About noon they tore at more duck jerky, but without water it was horrible, the salt further drying their mouths and heightening their thirst.

By *atmu* they were asleep, huddled under the overhang of a rock. She felt slightly more human and quite rested when she woke up, except for the parched feeling in her throat and nose. The smoldering remains of a fire were close by, and Cheftu was curled up like a giant pill bug. They were situated in the deep shadow of a towering rock face, facing west, the ocean visible to their left. Chloe stretched and rose.

Creeping from the shade, she was blinded by the light. It had to be almost noon, she guessed as she looked around. There were no signs of habitation around them, and she walked cautiously out to the water. How many days had they been traveling? She couldn't even recall if they'd spoken after Cheftu's offer to take her home. Had he meant the States? Or France? Was home a place or just people? How would they both go? She splashed her face to wake up. A cry. She paused, listening for it again. It sounded like the cry of a child, and Chloe rose to her feet, trying to pinpoint the sound.

The pebbled beach was empty. Farther back from the water was a cliff of maybe twenty feet, planted with a windbreak of acacia trees, the cool wind rustling their squat and twisted bare branches. The locusts had also been here, it would seem.

The cry seemed to be coming from that direction. Chloe started to jog, but her screaming muscles forced her to settle for a fast walk. She hoisted herself up the small rock face until she was on a level with the trees. The cry was louder now, and she looked around.

A tawny bundle of fur hurled itself at her feet, startling Chloe so she jumped back, grabbing at a tree branch for balance. The little animal was now crying plaintively as it rubbed itself against her bare leg. Every word of Chloe's upbringing regarding not petting strange animals flew out of her head as she knelt next to the animal. It seemed to be some kind of cat, purring like a small motorboat. It raised inquisitive eyes to her, and Chloe realized with a jolt that they looked like Cheftu's, all gold and amber. The cat had darker honey-colored streaks in his fur (she could see he was male), and his ears were large and pointed, with an aureole of golden fur around them. His tail was long and smooth, the end covered in long, darker honey-colored fur. He rolled over on his back, wiggling against her sandaled foot, and Chloe saw the reason for his cries.

There was a bracelet-size patch of dark brown on his fur, dried blood matting the wound with sand and dirt. He reached down to lick it, and she saw that his pink tongue was also cut. She picked him up, taking care not to touch the wound.

"*Aii!* You are heavy," she said as she used all her remaining energy to hold on to the pounds of squirming fur. "What have you got here, little guy?" she murmured, looking closely at the wound. His purring stopped, but he stayed still in her arms as she gently poked and prodded. A large thorn was stuck in his side. It had broken off, but the edge sticking out was also sharp—probably how he'd cut his tongue. The cat watched her with a knowing stare, and Chloe looked back at him. "We are going to have to see Cheftu for this," she said, and bundled him into her cloak.

He was impossible to carry, but once he saw she was going down, he went before her, waiting. With a few scrapes and scratches, she managed it. When they arrived back at the rock, Cheftu was still asleep, the encroaching golden sunlight just cubits away. Chloe watched the animal wander up to Cheftu and sit beside him. He watched, yawned, and then mewed peremptorily.

Cheftu jackknifed with a curse. Chloe giggled at the expression on his face, until she realized he was holding his knife. The cat, who had wisely leapt away a moment before, now walked up to him as if interviewing a candidate.

Cheftu flopped back onto the sand. "By the gods, Chloe! Are you trying to gray me before my time?" The cat seated himself beside Cheftu and stared into his face. "What is this?" Cheftu croaked as the cat arranged himself like a sphinx, his outstretched paws flexing in the air.

"It appears to be a cat of some kind. He is wounded, Cheftu."

Gingerly he petted the beast, fingers sensitive to his movements. "Where is his mother?"

"I do not know, why?"

Cheftu rubbed his face hard, trying to wake up. "Because lionesses have a problem when their cubs are stolen away! Where did you find him?"

Chloe looked down at the furball on the sand. "He is a lion?"

"Aye, one from the mountains." Cheftu drew to his feet, straightening his kilt as he shoved their few belongings in his basket. "We will walk away quickly." He was glancing around them fearfully. "That way we will still be able to walk!"

"He is hurt, Cheftu! Can we at least pull the thorn?"

The cat seated himself before Cheftu, and he began to probe the animal's body, speaking softly.

"Can you help him?" Chloe asked.

Cheftu raised an eyebrow. "I can do brain surgery, so I think I can get a thorn out." He opened his medical kit and began to search for tweezers. He settled for pincers. "He is not going to like this at all. Please wrap him in some cloths and hold him down." He handed her a medicinal fat to rub in, to make the extraction easier.

Despite the creature's struggles, they wrapped him and proceeded to pull not one, but three thorns from his side. His yowls were deafening, and more than once Chloe was reminded he had sharp little teeth as he sank them into various parts of her anatomy.

Cheftu bathed the wound with salt water, and they both cringed at the cat's cries of pain. Then Cheftu rubbed ointment in the sore and put a clean linen bandage over it. Chloe released the cat and he raced away, almost out of sight . . . and proceeded to rip off the bandage.

"So much for patient appreciation," he said. Chloe laughed, then sobered as Cheftu grimaced while drinking from the waterskin. "We have to find water today." They got to their feet and gathered their gear.

"How far do you think we have come?" she asked.

"Not far enough," Cheftu grunted. "They might be able to trail us, I do not know. We walked along the water's edge, which should provide us with an element of protection, but we should not depend on it."

He pulled a cloth from his basket and wrapped it around his head as he spoke, and Chloe watched his long, elegant fingers twist and turn the fabric until he was wearing a turban. With the rest of the fabric swathed across his bronzed face, nothing was visible except his amber eyes.

Chloe also wrapped her head and face; the wind had picked up, and stinging sand blew into her eyes, nose, and mouth. He helped her with her trunk and strapped on his own. Movement in the sky caught his eye, and he pointed inland.

"What?" Chloe asked.

"Vultures." He looked at the cat. "Maybe he has no mother after all." He pointed again. "They are circling. Either prey is dining or whatever it is, is dying. We must go."

An indignant yowl stopped them in their tracks. The cat strode from behind them to several feet in front of them and then turned, the brilliant sun narrowing his pupils to tiny black slits in his luminescent eyes. His fur was matted with dirt, and they could see his bones under the flesh, but with his tail waving like a standard he set off, glancing over his shoulder, a drill sergeant prompting recruits. Cheftu and Chloe looked at each other in amusement and set off to the east, led by their new pet.

Said pet did not lead for long. He played. Every step they took, he took five—up an incline, down the incline, swatting and pouncing, playing in the surf. Then he would sit and they would keep walking. Just when they imagined he'd stayed, he bound out from behind a rock or off the cliff.

They tried to walk along the sea's edge as much as possible, letting the waves wash away the tenuous proof of their persistence. By nightfall they were both ravenous, and Chloe found herself sobbing dryly out of frustration and exhaustion. Once again they camped near the rocky wall that faced the sea. Too tired to set up their tent and with no water for soup, they chewed on the last jerky and wet their lips with the warm, brackish water. Rolling into each other for additional warmth, they fell into semiconscious sleep.

• • •

Chloe couldn't open her eyes. They were glued shut. She tried to lift a hand and wipe the glue away, but they were pressed to the earth by a heavy weight. Her mind flitted from reality to reality. She could hear her name being called; was that Cammy? She strained forward and could see faint images.

It *was* Cammy. She was seated in the temple at Karnak. A lean, bespectacled man stood beside her, patting her shoulder and back with gentle, comforting strokes. Cammy's face was buried in her hands, her shoulders shaking . . . and her beautiful chestnut hair had a white streak. White? Chloe heard nothing, but the grief Cammy displayed tore at Chloe's heart. The lean man, who looked familiar, paled beneath his tanned skin.

A gurney was wheeled in from somewhere out of Chloe's vision. It stopped before the lean man. He lifted the sheet, and Chloe screamed when she saw the face.

It was her own.

I can't be dead! she thought frantically.

Then she was wet. Tears? Her own? No. The water was all around her, pouring down her face, her neck, collecting in the space beneath her. Someone was bathing her face with sandpaper, rubbing at the cut on her cheek, rubbing it again and again. The pain brought her fully awake. She slapped away the cloth, only to discover it was the tawny cub. She blinked. Two pairs of golden eyes gazed at her. Cheftu clasped her wet head to his chest. "I thought I had nearly lost you," he whispered. She pulled back and looked at him.

His face was gray, his eyes abnormally large. He spoke through gritted teeth. "What happened, Chloe?"

The images flew back and forth before her eyes like some cosmic remote gone awry. "I saw myself," she said tremulously. "I was dead—I think."

The words came out in a squeak, and Cheftu crushed her to him. "It was horrible!" he said in his accented English. "It seemed that beneath your features was another face, peering through. Worse than anything was the inlaid knife that appeared and disappeared between your ribs. I would reach for it and it would be gone. Then there again." He covered her hair with kisses. "You were so pale, so still."

With a shaking hand he lifted her face to his. "Although most frightening were your eyes. They were closed and you would not awaken." He pressed a kiss to her lips. "You were leaving me, Chloe."

She clung to him, her breath coming in short rasps. "Don't let me go, Cheftu! Please!" Then the tears came. They were few and far between, but Chloe shook as if there were an oceanful. She could not forget the pain in Cammy's face. She had looked all of her years and then some. "If only I could tell her I am all right! That the redhead is no longer me! She's the only reason I need to go home!" Chloe broke down again.

"Here, *ma chérie*," Cheftu said, handing her the waterskin. "Drink it so you can cry and rid yourself of these poisonous humors." Chloe lifted it with both hands and drank the sweet, cool water. Cheftu warned, "Do not take so much. With nothing to eat, it will make you ill." She handed the skin back to Cheftu and allowed him to lay her carefully back on the ground.

Some of the color had come back into his face, but he still looked awful. The ponytail and beard he'd grown while they were with the Israelites were matted and dirty. A multitude of scrapes and bruises covered his face and torso. His nose was peeling, his lips cracked and bleeding, his eyes bloodshot, and his linen filthy. However, he was alive.

Despite the abrasions, bruises, matted hair, and BO, she was, too. "Where did we get the water?"

Cheftu's lean, dirty face broke into a wide, white grin. "The cat."

"The cat?" Chloe repeated, confused.

"Aye. He apparently did some exploring while we were asleep, and when I awoke he grabbed my hand with his teeth and would not let go until I followed him. I was mostly asleep still. Otherwise we might not have a cat." Cheftu's glare shifted to the feline one that was so similar, as if delivering a threat. "He found a well just around that promontory." He pointed. "Actually, it is a congenial spot. There is room for living quarters and lots of animal tracks, so I know we can get fresh food." He glanced at the cat. "All of us can. There is even a large, empty cave for storage within stone-throwing distance."

Cheftu looked excited, she thought. "Is it far enough away from Egypt?" she asked with a frown.

"I believe it is. We will be between the gates of Egypt and the valleys of Canaan. I have not seen any other signs of habitation."

Chloe sat up; the water was revitalizing. "Then let's go."

She was still weak from her strange dehydration experience, and Cheftu half carried her as they walked around the edge of the promontory. The cat frolicked in the sunlight, chasing real and imaginary creatures. The Red Sea stretched out northeast and southwest of them, sunlight glinting in its clear depths, reflecting the turquoise, green, and lapis waters.

Cheftu took his knife and stood in the water, the gentle waves caressing his shins as he waited, still as a statue. The cat curled up by Chloe's leg and stretched out, the lighter-colored fur of his belly exposed to her soft petting. His purring grew so loud that Cheftu looked over his shoulder in dismay. When Chloe pulled her hand away, the cat pranced off to the water's edge, running back in fright from the oncoming waves and shaking off the water drops that sprinkled him. Cheftu remained motionless, and Chloe watched the line of shade change as the sun passed toward the west.

Then, in a splashing fury, Cheftu stepped out of the water, a wide grin on his face and the palpitating body of a large, beautiful fish in his hands. The cat, smelling dinner, ran to his side, and they walked toward

Chloe, both beaming with pride. She looked up in horror as Cheftu handed it to her.

She sat back, hands behind her.

"Prepare our dinner."

Chloe looked at him, stung by the imperious tone of his voice. "Why should I?"

"Because you are a woman. The man catches the dinner, the woman cleans and prepares it."

"Not this woman," she said with a wrinkled nose. "It smells and it is gross."

Cheftu crooked an eyebrow at her. "So I am to provide us fully with food? Will you allow me to serve you?" His voice was heavy with sarcasm, and Chloe could tell he was rapidly losing patience. But suddenly it was too much—too much change, too much stress, too different. She just couldn't take it.

"I did not ask for you to serve me! I can look after myself! I do not want your stinky fish!"

He stared at her, his already dark skin deepening with anger. "As you wish, madame." He sketched a bow and walked back to the shoreline. After a confused backward glance at Chloe, the cub scampered after Cheftu, following the food.

"Traitor," Chloe muttered, getting to her feet. She grabbed her basket and walked away, rounding the jutting land, until she saw the place Cheftu had found. It did look perfect. She looked at the surrounding low cliffs. The trees were still decked in green growth—apparently the locusts had not made it here. The small beach was crescent shaped, the sandstone cliffs providing a windbreak and hiding places. She already saw that the area was honeycombed with caves. Several palm trees clumped together marked the high tide. With the azure sky, the clear sea, and miles of golden sand, this was paradise.

Seeing it alone and in a funk took some of the glow of discovery away. She stepped into one of the caves facing the water and set down her stuff, looking carefully for animal tracks and scat. There didn't seem to be any, so she pulled out her cloak and lay down. Sleep came quickly.

* * *

Her first thought was that she must have died and gone to the Grand Sunday Brunch. The aromas were heavenly! With effort she opened her eyes in the darkened cave. Outside, the sun painted the water in pink and orange; already a cooler breeze blew.

She smelled a fire and heard Cheftu singing . . . not the Egyptian songs she knew all the words to, but "Frère Jacques." Chloe laughed and rose to her feet, wrapping the linen around her as she stepped outside. The man must have been a Boy Scout, she thought, amazed.

He'd built a fire and was broiling the fish. If the cat got any closer, he was going to be a fireball, Chloe thought. His little eyes were narrowed against the flame but unmoving from his objective. She could see the edges of the flame, where the bread was cooking, and saw a parcel of papyrus, close to the edge of the fire. "This is a masterpiece," she whispered.

Cheftu looked at her, across the fire, his face unsmiling. He broke off singing. "Thank you. Where is yours?"

Chloe looked at him in surprise. She'd been temperamental earlier. Not very nice. Okay, a witch on wheels, as Mimi would have said. However, pride reared its ugly head. "I have yet to catch it."

"You are welcome to share our"—he indicated the cat—"dinner. The oysters are chilling in that pool over there—" He pointed toward the tidal pools south.

Haughtily she stepped away. "Nay, but I thank you. I will do my own." She walked toward the shore, trying frantically to remember how to catch crabs. She'd done it only once, but it had been pretty easy. All she needed was bacon. She stopped.

Unfortunately they were fresh out, so what would substitute?

Cheftu called her for dinner, but Chloe refused to turn. She was being immature, she was being ridiculous. Unfortunately she just couldn't stop. She whirled around when he touched her. His eyes were dark, almost brown in the fading light. His voice was low, velvety, and caressing. "Come, *ma chère*. Let us dine together in our new home, *haii?*"

She ground her teeth. "Nay."

He licked his lips and looked away. "Why not?"

"Because you think I am a burden. I can take care of myself." Her tone of voice was ludicrously defensive, but she didn't care.

Cheftu's words were measured. "I apologize for . . ." He looked away and then back. "Damn it, I do not apologize! There is nothing wrong with asking you to participate! I hunt and you clean and cook, or the other way. I do not mind cooking, but we must work together! Now quit this childish, infantile, ridiculous behavior and come eat dinner before the cat . . ." His expression froze, and he repeated, "The cat," before he ran back to the fire. Chloe heard his shouts across the beach and saw him in pursuit of his dinner, now fleeing on golden paws. His frustrated curses rose in the air, and she saw him throw up his hands.

A few minutes later she walked toward him. He was seated on the ground, back to her, face against his braced arms. "Cheftu?" He didn't move or acknowledge her. She laid a hand on his neck, feeling the muscles bunched and tightened in knots. She dropped to her knees and began to massage out the kinks. They sat there as the darkness became complete, Chloe gently ridding his body of its tension, Cheftu turned away and closed off. She could feel the slight ridges of his burn scars and the muscles and tendons that had carried her, ministered to her, rescued her so many times. She should be grateful.

Instead it rankled.

She didn't want to be the weaker partner! All her life she had been able to compete on almost any ground with any male. It had been hard, yes, but she'd earned their respect, even from the hotshots in her class, and it made her stronger. Cheftu had never seen anything other than her weeping and fainting and being sick and weak. She dropped her hands. She couldn't handle an unequal relationship. She'd had too good of an example of an equal one growing up. Her parents were so in love and so equally dedicated to each other that she sometimes felt they hadn't needed children. Father worked in obscure Middle Eastern countries, and Mom excavated them and threw fabulous alcohol- and pork-free parties.

Chloe loved Cheftu body, soul, and mind but could not and would not live with him without his respect. How could she win that from a nineteenth-century man? Even ancient Egyptian women had more power and freedom than the women he had known in his own time. No matter how long he had lived here, those first sixteen years were French. She knew well enough that you could take the child out of the country and its customs but never fully take the customs and country out of the child.

She sighed and turned her back to Cheftu, hunkered down, and stared out at the approaching tide. She heard a loud rumbling and realized with embarrassment that it was her stomach.

"We still have the oysters," Cheftu said tiredly. Apparently he'd heard it, too.

"I will get them. Which tidal pool?" Chloe asked as she got to her feet.

"The third on the right."

She crossed the rocks, counting the tidal pools. The moon was rising, a sliver in the sky but enough to show her the large pile of oysters. Cheftu must have been diving to get this many, Chloe thought as she placed them in her shredded gown. She stumbled back to the fire.

It was a roaring blaze, and Cheftu had uncovered the bread. The papyrus packet was open, and Chloe saw that the herbs and wild onions within it were steamed and crunchy. With the knife she began to pry open the oysters, jabbing herself several times and swallowing her curses.

The oysters were delicious, the taste far different from that of the chemically engorged ones Chloe had eaten in her own time. They wrapped the herbs, mostly a wild garlic chive, into unleavened bread and ate with gusto, passing the water skin back and forth in silence.

Chloe's stomach felt as tight as a drum when they finished, seated among the empty oyster shells and the dying fire. They had not spoken a word, and the cub had not dared to show his face. Cheftu was distant, avoiding her gaze, sitting with his shoulders hunched, staring out to sea. Chloe yawned for the seventh time and got to her feet, taking handfuls of shells with her. Cheftu noted her movement and looked away again. In three trips she had thrown all the shells away and come back for her blanket. "Will you put out the fire?" she asked.

"Aye."

She stood a moment, seeing the wreck her temper had made of the evening. He'd tried so hard. "Good night."

"Aye."

"I am sorry," she said.

He glared at her for a moment and answered again, his voice heavy and tired. "Aye." Chloe stared at the fire a moment longer, then walked toward her cold and lonely cave. She lay for hours, shivering, while Cheftu sat beside the fire. After a while the overpowering smell of fish surrounded her, and she heard a sandy tongue cleaning fur. After an exceptionally long bath, the cat curled up in the crook of her knees and fell asleep. She caressed his head with her fingers, delighted that his purrs could soothe her soul so well. Finally she slept.

•••

Unfortunately, nothing had changed in the morning. They were still distant. They ate stale bread, and Chloe again craved a cup of coffee. Even instant would have been appreciated. The cat had been gone when she awoke, cold and stiff. The sun rose rapidly, sending much needed warmth through Chloe's body, but still her heart was cold. Cheftu didn't even look at her.

He'd washed at some point, she noticed. His hair was neatly tied back from his face, his beard and mustache clean. He'd scrubbed out his kilt and tied it in place with a narrow leather thong. His legs and arms were scratched and nicked, but he was still sexy. Chloe had the uncomfortable feeling that he'd done this last night and felt horrible all over again. He rose to his feet, staring across the water, his words clipped. "I will make us some bricks for a dwelling and will catch a bird for our noon meal."

"Agreed," Chloe said meekly. "However, I will fix dinner."

"As you wish," he said, and walked off toward another cave where he'd stored his gear.

She got up and doused the fire, wishing she had a clue what to do. Tears inched down her face, and she buried it in her hands, sobbing. Moments passed, then she felt Cheftu embrace her, his strong arms holding her close and tight. "Do not cry, beloved. We will survive. I will take care of you."

She pushed him away. "I do not want you to take care of me! I am acting like a child, and I am disgusted with myself! But I cannot stop!" Tears ran down her cheeks. "I want to be your equal! I cannot stand it that you think I am weak and useless! I am not RaEmhetepet!" He reached for her again, and she turned away, crying into her hands. The cat brushed against her ankle, his purring a balm. Still crying, she picked him up and held him close, her tears falling into his fishy fur.

Cheftu said slowly, "I am confused, Chloe. I have never had this sort of responsibility. Your life is a gift, and I must guard it carefully." He snorted in derision. "I have never lived without servants—not here and not in France. I only know how to provide for myself because of hunting trips and the army."

He turned her, lifting her chin with his finger. "Unfortunately, I do not know how to give you security. We are living on the edge of the desert; I have no idea where. We dare not go to an Egyptian because I am banished and you should be dead. If we go to the tribespeople in the desert, they will kill me to marry you. Anywhere we go to trade, we will be noticed"— he smiled grimly—"because of our eyes, if nothing else. My only thought is to hide you, protect you, try to form some type of life for us. Then take you back to Egypt and get you to your own time," he said wearily.

"I am not your responsibility, Cheftu," Chloe said. "I am my own."

He looked at her, fully, for the first time that morning. "I know very well that you can provide for yourself, but you are my responsibility because you are my heart. I cannot eat unless I know you also receive nourishment. I cannot sleep without your body next to mine. You are a gift to me because I love you. For no other reason. No other commitment or tie. Because you are my soul."

He looked away. "You do not understand. You think I see you as a possession, as a belonging, or a pet, to take care of because I 'own' you—" His voice broke. "I can never own you, Chloe. You are free to leave me any time you wish. You are free to make whatever decisions you will. I will see that you are safe to make those choices." His look met hers, tormented. "Allow me this, Chloe."

She turned away, ashamed and humbled by his words. She wanted to hold him to her, but the gap seemed so wide. They were all each of them had. Her head throbbed with unanswered and painful questions. After a while Cheftu touched her hair in a soft caress. "Be safe, my precious one," he said, and left. The cat bolted from her lap and followed, leaving Chloe alone under the soaring blue tent of the sky.

She worked all day, first clearing the fire area, then cleaning the largest cave with a palm-frond broom. When a large group of birds settled on the beach and on the acacia trees above them, she took her painted throwing stick and went hunting. After two hours she had two birds and an unlucky brown furry thing that had run through the grass by the trees. She'd leave that for Cheftu to skin. With mixed pride and revulsion she hacked the heads off the birds, pulled out their feathers, and cut them open.

Then she barfed up breakfast.

Uncertain as to her next step, she threaded them onto a stick and suspended them above the fire. Blood sizzled as it hit the rocks below. Chloe guessed they would take a while, so she went for a swim. The water was glorious, warm, and cleansing, washing the days of grime from her body. When she got back on shore her fire was surrounded by big, ugly birds, who were tearing at the flesh on the spit. Shouting, Chloe ran toward them, angry that they would ruin her hard-won dinner.

By the time she reached them they had flown away, taking the dead brown furry thing as well. Chloe looked into the sky: the sun was on its westward journey, probably about three hours to dusk. Determined, she grabbed her throwing stick, kohled her eyes, put on her kilt, and set off to kill dinner.

The sun was setting by the time she was seated next to the fire, three birds now stuffed with sea scallops, twisting merrily over the heat. She'd been sick again when she'd cleaned them, but the growling of her stomach had helped her get a grip on her queasiness much more quickly.

Keeping an eye on the fire, she went into the largest cave, taking some of the palm fronds and laying a bed dais that was softer and more cushiony. She'd found a squarish rock and set it by one side of the bed, then lit some incense to clean out the room's previous owner's smells. In the small cave where she'd slept the night before, she stored the food, or the little that was left, hanging the bags on broken branches to protect them from predators.

She'd even woven some fronds together for rather large and unwieldy plates. Then she waited. And waited, hunched in her cloak, as the moon rose. The cub came back first. She turned to see the sketchy outline of Cheftu's body scrambling down the cliff side. He walked to within range of the firelight, his body and clothing covered in muck. Handing her a fistful of speckled brown eggs, he looked approvingly at the fire, then went to wash.

The plates made him smile and they gave thanks quickly as they had done since joining the Apiru, then tore into the stringy, overdone bird. There was more than one cooked feather, but Chloe thought that all in all, it was edible food. Cheftu must have agreed—he sucked the bones dry and broke them open for the cat to eat the marrow.

"We need to name the cat," Chloe said conversationally.

"Given his eating habits, 'Thief' would be a good name, and appropriate," Cheftu answered as he pulled one of the unsucked bones away from the bundle of fur.

Chloe grinned. "I was thinking of something more petlike, since he seems to want to stay around."

"How about 'Miuw'?"

"I am not going to name a cat 'Cat'! He deserves more, don't you, my precious," she crooned at the purring animal.

"Bast?"

"That's almost as bad as 'Cat.' "

"How about Ankh? I mean, he did show us the fresh water and saved our lives."

"Just like an angel," Chloe mused.

Cheftu scoffed. "If he is an angel, the rules are quite different than they were in my time!"

"Because he stole your fish?"

"Exactly. He also stole my noon meal. It is his way of life." They looked toward the cat as he sat on his hindquarters, licking his belly clean, limp as a rag and more closely resembling a panda than a cat.

"Then he will be 'Thief.' "

"Good choice," Cheftu said, and took a long drink.

Chloe got up and gave the rest of the birds to the cat. Cheftu watched her. "Are you going to sit here by the fire?" she asked him.

He stood, facing her, his body limned in red. "Should I?"

Chloe's breath caught in her throat, and heat rushed through her body. "Nay, Cheftu. Take me to bed . . . please."

He stood silently for a moment. "We are still angry with each other."

"I do not care. I want you." She reached out, touching his warm skin. "Please." She grabbed his belt and pulled him closer. He smelled like earth, and Chloe realized that he was covered in dried mud. She kissed a patch of clean skin just above his collarbone.

"To want me is not enough," he said, grabbing her shoulders and holding her back. "I have given everything for and to you, Chloe. Still you want. Always it is what *you* want."

"Cheftu?" Chloe was appalled. Was that the way he saw her? Grasping and greedy?

"Tonight I am not bending. I love you. I would die for you. However, I will not suffer to be your convenience." He stepped away. "I realize you do not want to be with me forever." His glare impaled her. "Although it is what I want. Tonight, whether it is petty or not, I cannot bear to be close to you."

Chloe stood still as a cenotaph, then sank slowly to the ground.

"I will find a way home for you," he said, and walked away.

Tears burned furrows through the dust and sand that covered her face like a mask. Home for her had never been a place; it was people. Now home was Cheftu. Too bad she hadn't realized it in time.

CHAPTER 16

Morning dawned, and Chloe stretched luxuriously in the blanketing. Cheftu lay on his stomach beneath her, his upper back her pillow. A soft kiss was rewarded with a sleepy grunt. Out of the doorway, she saw the beach. The tide was going out, the sky barely tinged with violet, pink, and orange in the early morning clouds. Birdsong drifted in the wind, and Chloe smiled. Thief was curled up on them both, his head resting on Chloe's leg, his body curled into the space supported by Cheftu's calves. Chloe ran her hand down the sloping planes of Cheftu's body, relaxed in sleep.

He murmured, but he didn't move when she kissed his back and neck, so she turned onto her stomach and looked out at the rosy morning. The sky was silver lined, the air dense with the call of birds.

Cheftu's hot hand traveled across her back to her shoulder. Chloe turned to face him, her body welcoming his sleepy passion. Silently they moved together, Cheftu awakening more with every movement, his stamina wearing Chloe down. He drew back, pressing one of her feet to his chest, kissing it, intensifying his movements.

"Look at me!" he commanded hoarsely. Chloe opened her eyes, dazed. "I want to see you . . . I want you to know it is me. *I* am making you burn; *my* body moves inside you—and for all the years you live *I* will have been the first. I have marked your soul. Give me you, Chloe."

His words were guttural and hardly discernible, but Chloe saw the ferocious intensity of his dark features. She felt a breaking inside, a melting of all that was her, a loosening of herself—her identity, her goals, her life. With it came a laser-bright awareness of this man, of who he was. Of what he meant to her.

Cheftu gasped as he tried to maintain control, piercing her innermost being with his anger, his love, and his frustration. "When you leave you will remember me . . . *seulement!*"

She clung to him, panting and sweating, the climax twisting like wire inside her, emotion and sensation binding her to him. Cheftu took all she offered and gave himself—his hopes, dreams, and disappointments—his soul. As the wires finally tore loose and Chloe was released, she stared into his eyes, and felt his brokenness meet hers, felt their melting, their completion. Just as she thought it was over, Cheftu drove her to delirium. "Join me!"

Waves of pleasure engulfed her, jolting her body as she clung to Cheftu. With a final groan he sagged, his crouched legs shaking. He fell beside her, brushing her sticky hair from her face as their breathing returned to normal.

The awkwardness returned.

Cheftu pulled away first. "I must get to the mud pit," he said, reaching for his kilt. "In a few more days we will have a mud-brick house."

Chloe wanted to reach to him, tease and laugh, but he was withdrawn, uncomfortable. She scrambled after him, tying on the ragged remains of her dress. He grabbed his pouch, then halted and drew out a handful of seeds.

"What are these?" Chloe asked.

His skin colored as he looked beyond her. "Giant fennel. A preventative; so I do not get you with child." His expression was solemn. "I would not have you return to your time with the disgrace of a baby in your belly. Swallow one . . . after . . . after . . ." He inhaled and focused beyond her shoulder for a long, silent moment. "It should keep you safe. Make sure they are taken with plenty of liquid and after you have eaten something."

Now was the time to tell him she didn't want to return. Instead she stood silently, watching as he walked away, back up the cliff, leaving her alone under the blue bowl of sky.

She took the seed as she contemplated what to do. How could

they have come through so much and now, when it was all over, fall apart?

Her grandmother Mimi had always been her anchor . . . the string to her kite, allowing her to safely fly and explore and be free, with no fears of getting lost. When Mimi died Chloe felt the string had been cut. No one else had been closer, known her more intimately, accepted her as totally.

When she traveled back to Egypt, it suddenly made sense, Mimi's death. It had been the final bond holding her to that time. She loved Cammy, but the loss wasn't nearly so great. She knew Cammy was consumed with guilt, and she wanted to ease that but couldn't. Her parents, as long as they had each other, would survive. They would understand. *Here* she had discovered love. It was messy and painful, but with the grit and tears and sex and blood was the realization that this was real life. Not observing others and sketching down what they did or wore or where they lived, but living and doing and wearing and loving herself.

She was alive, gloriously alive. Why did she want to return to an existence of malls, McDonald's, and machine guns, if only to stand on the side? Cheftu was here; he loved her, she loved him. All her life, all her experiences, it all had prepared her for this.

She got to her feet. He wanted a helpmate who would stay for always. She would.

THE SUN SCORCHED HIS BODY as Cheftu shifted another mud brick. His inventory now stretched from the east side of the mud pit all the way to the windbreak before the desert began in earnest—probably a hundred bricks in all. His skin prickled and he spun around, scanning the trees close by. He could barely hear the sounds of someone moving at the mud hole.

Carefully he laid down his brick, grabbed his dagger, and crept stealthily through the trees. Thief lay undisturbed, so Cheftu relaxed and looked around, pausing to wipe the sweat that dripped down his brow. Apparently nothing was amiss. He walked back to his bricks, gathering brush along the way.

Minutes later, while shaping another brick, he heard Chloe's voice. A shiver went through his body . . . even her voice intoxicated him. She was speaking loudly and in English. "Oh, don't you give me flack!" she shouted. "I'll be out in a second. . . ."

Curious, Cheftu walked back. The mud hole was somewhat shaded, and he saw the white remnants of her dress hanging from one of the trees. Then he saw her in the bog, mired up to her waist. Thief, his paws muddy, was sitting on the side, a speculative expression on his face. Her black hair just touched her shoulders, which were dark brown from the sun. She bit into her lower lip as the muscles of her arms flexed and struggled against the sucking mud. As Cheftu watched silently, he felt himself hardening. She looked like a woodland nymph, earthy, sensual, yet innocent. What *flavor* would this be?

As she wriggled in the mud, it gradually sucked her lower. She was struggling with all of her might, stubbornly refusing to admit defeat to the patient, passive bog; but obviously the mud was winning. Cheftu continued to watch as she worked her way up slightly, only to sink back in a bit farther with each additional movement. This continued until the mud had engulfed her to her chest and she stopped sinking, the smooth, shiny muck supporting her weight and cushioning her breasts. Desire flared through him at her little cries and squeals. So this was the woman who did not want to be rescued? The way she looked, trapped, defenseless, and unspeakably erotic, he thought she just *might not be* rescued, at least for a while.

"I lost my probing stick there," he shouted out. "Are you fetching it for me? You did probe the depth before stepping out, didn't you?"

She spun her head around. "It seemed solid and then . . . *whoosh!*"

"I did not know you liked mud," he teased. "In some cultures it is considered quite sensual. Were you going to seduce me?"

"Nay, I was trying to get the cursed cat unstuck," she fumed. He looked at her hanging clothes. "I was not about to ruin the only linen I had." She wiped her brow with a mud-caked forearm and, realizing the mistake, shook her head, sending brown speckles flying. "*Assst!*"

Cheftu glanced back toward Thief, noting his hindquarters were encrusted with mud. He looked back at the helpless woman before him. She was a beautiful, brown, living statue.

"Just sit still and I will pull you out," he called, picking up his muddy staff.

"I . . . ugh . . . don't need . . . errr . . . your help!" Chloe said, resuming her struggles, now determined to free herself. As Thief made his way to

Cheftu's side, the two of them sat on the packed earth to watch her demonstration. Her sleek, slippery body repeatedly emerged about a cubit, then sank in the relentless bog. Cheftu felt his heart pound as she writhed against the mud, twisting and turning, each graceful muscle and sinew active.

"Are you sure that you don't want me to rescue you?" he called.

Chloe was exhausted but making slow progress—one leg was halfway to the surface. Cautiously she spread her weight evenly across the surface. Her other leg was still firmly in the wet vacuum of the bog. After a few moments of trying to free it, she was back to the beginning. In frustration she slapped her hands into the mud, spattering it everywhere.

"Haii-aii, beloved," Cheftu said consolingly, almost concealing the amusement in his voice. "Wait for me, and I will help you out."

Realizing that she was firmly stuck, Chloe didn't refuse his offer this time as he stripped off his kilt and stepped into the mud. The sight of him fully aroused sent an answering heat through her. He walked toward her carefully, his staff in his hand, plumbing the depths for solid footing. His skin, tanned mercilessly by the sun, merged into the mud, so that he looked like an otherworldly creature rising from the depths. Cautiously he made his way closer to her suspended body. Finally he extended the stick to her. Exhausted and beaten, she slowly and laboriously extracted her arms from the goo and grabbed the sturdy branch. She watched the muscles in Cheftu's arms ripple with the effort of pulling her slowly through the reluctant clay. When she was a few cubits away, he stopped.

"Chloe . . ." His voice was low, husky, and Chloe felt her own moisture melt into the mud. "Do you really want me to help you free?"

She nodded, panting from exertion.

"Do you like the way it feels?" His voice was like melted butter . . . decadent and delicious. "Tell me." His eyes were dark, almost opaque, passion etching lines of tension around his mouth.

She gasped. "Mud . . . what did you think?"

He arched an eyebrow. "I know you are more descriptive than that. If it were a *glace*," he said with a wicked, muddy smile, "which flavor would it be?" He pulled her again. The texture was smooth as lotion, caressing every inch of her body, sucking softly at her thighs, massaging and stroking her. "Ch-chocolate cappuccino gelato," she stammered.

"What is gelato?"

"A creamier, thicker, more sinful ice cream," she murmured, watching his eyes flame. "It is so rich, you think you're going to die if you eat more, but you cannot resist it. It is slick on your tongue until it melts, spreading the taste throughout your mouth—" Her words ended with a soft gasp as she felt his grip on her wrists.

His eyes were slitted as he pulled her to him. Clinging to him as he stepped backward, she was amazed at how soft yet solid he felt. She felt his every straining muscle coated with mud, and she stared into his eyes, directing him as they walked backward. He pulled her to her feet once they were both only knee deep.

"Are you safe now?"

"Am I?" She felt his hands clench against her back. "I came here for a reason, Cheftu."

He withdrew without moving a muscle. A shutter fell behind his eyes, and she suddenly was scared. Too late? Change of heart? "I want to stay."

He blinked.

She ran a mud-covered hand up his slick torso. "With you. Wherever. Whenever. I am yours." She began to wonder if he'd had a stroke, as he just stood there, blinking. "Are you breathing?" she finally asked.

He kissed her, hard. All the energy, anger, and passion that had been leashed was free. He was rough and clumsy as they toppled backward onto the muddy shore. Holding her close, he kissed her forehead and crooned to her. It was minutes before she realized he too was crying.

The mud was drying in the heat and becoming as thick and sticky as paste. They struggled, laughing and crying, out and away from the bog. Cheftu's strong arms held Chloe close to his side. Hand in hand they climbed down the cliff and ran to the ocean, laughing like children as they bobbed in the shallows, had water fights, and tried to catch minnows with their hands. The sun was low when they stepped out and lay on the beach, letting the last of the day's heat dry them.

Cheftu boiled the eggs, and they ate them with leftover bread in the early darkness. He drew Chloe to him, and they stayed in the receding waves, connected, until the quiet intensity grew too much and they finished in fury what had begun in calm.

• • •

The days blended together, like beads on a necklace. Each different, each precious, and together they made a whole. For the first days they worked in the mud pit, shaping the bricks that would make their home and cooling themselves in the afternoon by soaking in the mud. At *atmu* they carried down the day's worth of bricks and laid them on the scratched-out plan for a two-room house with solid roof (for storage and hot nights) and alcove for cooking. One side was planned so the door looked toward the palm trees. One day, Chloe said, she would make a hammock, and they could swing and talk and make love in it.

They'd awoken one morning to a family of scorpions sleeping on their mat, inches from Cheftu's leg. Bleary with sleep and her heart pounding in her throat, Chloe had smashed the closest one with a dagger and they'd both run, naked, into the cool morning.

Five days after the scorpions, the house was standing. It had taken some real work to create the large window, bracing it with more branches, but with the addition of palm fronds and rigged with torn linen to form a movable window shade, it was quite habitable—if you didn't mind not having a front door.

Cuisine improved. Cheftu explained that the brown furry thing she'd found before was a type of rabbit. He showed her how to split it, clean it, add fresh herbs that grew close by, and then roast it, skin and all. Amazingly enough, the skin peeled off when it was done, providing enough fat so that the meat was not dry and stringy.

They dined on oysters and caught more fish. They had run out of flour, so there was neither bread nor the beer that was made from it.

"You have never told me about your family. I know you are the oldest," she said one night. They'd spent the day farming the one arable strip of land, carefully tending the small shoots that had grown up in the past weeks. Sex, their main recreation, was out for the moment. The good news was that the giant fennel seeds were working. Cheftu was relieved.

"They are from the Oryx—"

"No, no," she interrupted in English. "Your French family."

Cheftu grew ominously silent. "It matters not," he said stiffly.

"Sure it does. You said you have a brother, but he is older, right? What does he, did he, do?"

Cheftu got up. "I am going to hunt with Thief tonight, I think."

"You can't just walk away! I did not ask about former lovers, just your family! What is wrong?"

He gripped her forearms. "It does not matter. Do not ask. I was betrayed, and I have no desire to recall it."

"Betrayed? By whom?"

"My brother. Good night."

Chloe stared, openmouthed, as he and Thief hiked up the trail and disappeared over the ridge. Would she ever know this man? "So much for no secrets and no boundaries," she whispered.

•••

With no warning their just blossoming life came to an end.

The day repeated the pattern of the previous ones. Cheftu was hacking away at the earth with a makeshift hoe of shell and branch, and Chloe had just caught fish for lunch and cleaned it before setting it on their rocky grill. Suddenly Thief, who had been focused solely on the fish, flattened his ears and began alternately creeping and running toward the cliff face. Away from the pounding surf, Chloe could hear the sounds of struggle. She wasted precious seconds debating, then scrambled up the cliff side. Peering over the edge, she saw Cheftu pulled flat between two soldiers. They were speaking, but she couldn't hear them. The smell of roasting fish was carrying on the wind to them, and she ran back down, racing into the cave for the bow and quiver. She tore through the basket, panic rising as she heard Thief's growling and saw his tawny fur ruff rise.

Then she heard Cheftu calling out in English, "Hide yourself! They do not know you are here!" He masked his words with other screams and curses, and Chloe cowered in the back of the cave. The soldiers might not know she was around this very second, but it wouldn't take a temple education to figure out that cooking food and one working man didn't add up. She nocked the arrow carefully. Three men were visible, though there were possibly more, but they were out of range. The soldiers had bundled Cheftu into the house and were now grouped by the fire to the rear of the mud-brick building. She poked her head out; one man had his back to her, urinating into the sea. Chloe released the arrow and ran to the house when she saw him fall to his knees, his dying groan drowned out by the roar of waves, his hands reaching frantically around to his back.

The darkness of the hut was refreshing, but she needed Cheftu to be silent. "Beloved?" she whispered in English. He moaned in response, and she ran to his side, almost tripping on the mostly finished hammock. He was bound, but steady enough on his feet. Chloe grabbed her belt, cloak, and waist pouch, then cut the flax ropes. They could hear the three soldiers wondering what was taking their compatriot so long.

Halting, they listened as the soldiers joked about their diet of unleavened bread and dried meats. "Some date wine would ease him!" one of them offered, and they all laughed. Creeping to the doorway, Chloe tried to plan a route. Thief had disappeared, the unfamiliar smells of the soldiers increasing his fear of predators. Chloe's eyes searched over their little bay . . . where could they go? It didn't matter—she grabbed Cheftu's basket trunk and shoved in their food and belongings.

She caught Cheftu's gaze in the shadows, and they kissed briefly. They ran out across the beach, by the dying man in a pool of his drying blood, and around the promontory, back toward Egypt. Reaching the other side of the cliff, they listened, trying to hear beyond the rhythm of the waves. The breeze dried her nervous sweat as Chloe shifted the basket. Cheftu looked upward and motioned her first. They began to climb.

Cries of discovery floated up to them. Their tracks would be easy to follow. Chloe bit back a scream as Thief brushed against her leg. They began running inland to the well. They could plan from there.

Chloe filled their bottles with shaking hands at the well while Cheftu kept watch. Still on dry ground, they headed northwest, desperate to escape yet uncertain *where* to escape.

They ran through a grove of trees that grew parallel to the cliff's edge, crashing heedlessly through the undergrowth, and right into another well area, where six soldiers, three chariots, and six horses were resting. There was a moment of mutual shock before Cheftu and Chloe split up, each running around the small encampment. The commanding sergeant sent four men after Chloe. They tackled her, and her cries halted Cheftu. Two other soldiers restrained him from running toward her as she was set on her feet.

Chloe considered fighting until she saw the knife held at Cheftu's neck. Sweat poured off him, his hair slick with it, his kilt torn, and his arms and legs crisscrossed with scratches. Her eyes filled with tears as she looked into his raging countenance. But when he saw the resignation in hers, his eyes melted. "Do not tell them we are Egyptian," he said in English. "Our penalty will be death."

Speaking in another language to each other was a good idea, but still a barrage of questions from the soldiers hit them. Cheftu stared stonily at the captain, his head high. "Why do you trap us?"

"Are you an Israelite?" the man demanded.

Cheftu shook his head. "Nay. We are free."

The captain whipped his flail across Cheftu's face, and Chloe gritted her teeth. "Did you see what happened to the Pharaoh and soldiers, slave?" he asked.

"Nay. We saw nothing." Chloe flinched as Cheftu was slapped on the opposite cheek. The hands that held her shoulders were as resistant as granite, though she squirmed in their grasp. The marks on Cheftu's face glowed red against his burnished skin, and his eyes were hungry gold, like Thief's.

The commander stared at Cheftu. "Take them to Avaris," he said. "Between here and there we will get the truth from them." He touched the finely crafted bracelet on Chloe's wrist. "Why would an Egyptian deny his heritage unless he had rebelled with the Apiru?" he mused, staring into her face. Chloe bit the inside of her cheek. Why had Cheftu said their penalty was death? Their wrists were bound, and for a few seconds they stood together.

"I am sorry," Cheftu whispered before the soldiers on either side of him drew his hands to the front and tied him to the chariot.

The soldiers set up a tent to rest in, and Chloe and Cheftu found themselves sitting against acacia trees, cubits apart. Cheftu's eyes were closed, and welts were rising along his cheekbones. She saw the tension in his body and knew he was awake. The soldiers took the water supply into their tents and left their captives to the abandonment of the scorching afternoon heat. There was no need for a guard, since without water they wouldn't last two hours.

"What is our plan?" Chloe whispered, her eyes on the soldier lying before the tent.

"Rest. We can do nothing until nightfall. After that . . ." Cheftu's voice trailed off. They sat in silence, the droning of the cicadas a music in this desert glen. He swallowed, his tongue darting out to moisten his lips. "I love you, Chloe. They do not need you. If you can get away, they'll take me and be gone. Thief is nearby. He can guide you to water."

She kept her eyes focused on his hands. Such mobile, long fingered, lovely hands. She'd never drawn them.

"Where is the quiver?" he asked, his voice no louder than the buzz of an insect.

"By our basket and my bow, over there." She gestured with her chin. She rested her head against the wood, closing her eyes against the afternoon glare. Thank God for kohl.

"You cannot leave without them."

"What is it?"

"Drawings. Silence: they are awakening." They both slumped in a parody of sleep, but a few moments later they heard the even breathing of the guard.

"Whose?" Chloe barely breathed.

"A fourteenth-century friend. I knew him as Alemelek. I did not know he was a traveler until his deathbed."

"What made it obvious then?"

"He began to pray . . . in Latin." The corner of Cheftu's mouth turned up. "You could say it was a dead giveaway."

Chloe digested this. "What should be done with them?"

"Hide them. They are a clue for those who would study Egypt after us."

"I love you, Cheftu," she murmured through the heat and exhaustion.

"*Je vous aime*, Chloe," he whispered back. He stretched one sandaled foot to her, caressing the side of her leg with the edge of his foot. Chloe closed her eyes as she felt his callused toes, the amazingly soft top of his foot, and the wiry hair of his ankle and calf. She looked up and saw Cheftu's half smile. "We will survive. Rest now."

The creaking of chariot wheels brought them around, and Chloe noticed that the sun's fingers of light were coming from the west. The guards gave them each a few swallows of water, then the two chariots were hitched up and Chloe was walked behind one, Cheftu behind the other. They started off at a strong pace, and Chloe felt her arms ripped from their sockets as her feet sought the rhythm of the horses. A breeze whistled across the sandy dirt as Chloe kept pace. They were headed due west, into the rocky mountains of the Sinai.

The soldiers were tired, wanting to get home to their families. Chloe knew that she and Cheftu were considered insignificant prisoners and that each chariot held only two people. As the sun set and the *henti* unraveled, the journey became a wad of pain in her chest and abdomen, and Chloe cursed them. She glanced around once and saw the other chariot parallel, Cheftu lurching behind it, his arms outstretched.

Fortunately, at night the horses had to step carefully in the pock-marked dirt, wary of snakes, scorpions, wadis, and stones, so Chloe could walk more slowly in the cold night air, feeling it burn in her chest. The moon was waning, casting a sickly glow across the desert night, deceiving her about its rocks and ridges. Chloe heard the heart-wrenching cries of jackals in the hills about them. The soldiers heard too and decided to camp for the night. The other chariot grew near, and Chloe saw that Cheftu was as exhausted as she.

There was some debate as to how the guards would keep watch. The captain concluded that if Chloe were held, Cheftu would stay. So she was gathered into the overzealous embrace of a young soldier, one hand on her breast, the other holding a knife to her throat. He couldn't have been more than seventeen, but in the twentieth century he would have been the starting fullback of any championship football team. Cheftu was shackled to the spoke of one of the chariots, directly opposite Chloe.

His face was expressionless as he watched her twist away from the obnoxious advances of the young soldier, who did it for sport. He embraced Chloe like a snake, his blade reflecting the moon, and Cheftu had to force his eyes closed. To be falling down exhausted on the morrow would not help them much. To see Chloe cowed by the soldiers tore at his heart. He knew if she were alone, she would fight, the same as he would, but together they were too vulnerable. He tensed the muscles in his arms, aching to stretch, when he felt a presence behind him. He glanced over his shoulder and swallowed in fear at the reflected gold eyes. Then he choked back a cry of delight when he recognized the rumbling purr from the cat's throat.

Thief butted his head against Cheftu's shoulder. Though he was still a cub, he was growing larger every day. *"Va t'en,"* Cheftu whispered, afraid the monumental purring would waken the soldiers. Thief butted his head on Cheftu's thigh, his big paws outstretched as he nuzzled like an overdeveloped kitten. "Go away," Cheftu said again, pushing away the cat with his tied hands.

Thief stretched and lay back, waiting for his adoptive father to scratch his belly. Sighing, Cheftu did. "I will do this, then you must leave. Agreed, Thief?" He looked up and saw Chloe's eyes were open and glassy with tears. Cheftu petted Thief absently as he tried to speak across the distance to his wife, captured in a death embrace by another man.

She was beautiful, carved in moonlight. All the world was faded to gray, except her eyes, Cheftu through. They blazed with a green fire, alive and defiant of the position they were in. They trusted him, despite his ineptitude this afternoon. Despite the danger he had put her in. His eyes burned with tears his body had no moisture to shed, and he felt Thief settle down to sleep.

Chloe's eyes also closed, and Cheftu rolled to his side, careful not to make any noise, then rested his head on the lion cub's sturdy rib cage and slept.

• • •

Chloe lost all sense of time. They traveled sometimes in the day and sometimes at night. She was guarded by a different soldier each night, and only dehydration and exhaustion had prevented rape. She'd not had another chance to speak to Cheftu, but when their eyes would meet before she was assigned her guard for the night, he would speak of his love for her with a quick wink and smile. Once he'd written a note for her in the sand, words she'd found the next morning as they were breaking camp. *"Je vous aime et je espère."* I love you and I hope.

They both were haggard. Cheftu's beard was unkempt and his hair lank and greasy. His broad shoulders were blistered and peeling, and Chloe could count the ribs in his back. They were fed enough water; Pharaoh wanted any survivors kept alive, he just hadn't specified how close to dead alive was. Fortunately everyone was too tired at day's end to try to prod answers from them.

Chloe felt sand in every ridge and hollow of her body. Her breasts and buttocks were bruised from rough handling, and her shirt and kilt were in tatters, affording little protection. They stumbled on. Cheftu watched their meager belongings, and Chloe knew in her heart they would get a chance to run; they just had to be ready.

The sun was scorching. Chloe felt her skin sizzling in the arid air. Her nose had been bleeding from dryness, and even the soldiers, with their healing oils and fatty diet, had been showing wear. The water supply was running short, and so were tempers. Then the wheel of Cheftu's chariot cracked. It would take at least two soldiers to fix it, so Chloe's group was to head through the deep canyons, toward the oasis with the horses, and meet up with another band of soldiers, then send them back—no more than a day and a half in travel.

Cheftu was tied beside her to the sole chariot, and the soldiers also walked because the horses were dying. Suddenly the bay collapsed with a pitiful cry and the whole chariot lurched to a halt, leaving one horse.

Chloe and Cheftu stared at each other; this was their chance! The sergeant and his soldier ran forward, swearing in common Egyptian. For a few moments Cheftu and Chloe were forgotten. The slack rope allowed Cheftu to slip free and wound a soldier with a spear.

The sergeant yelled: Chloe looked over her shoulder as the other two soldiers stumbled toward them, clumsy in the rock-strewn wadi. Cheftu handed her a knife and she knelt, cutting herself free. She heard sounds of struggle as she took their gear and the soldiers' remaining water. With Cheftu's quiver and her bow strapped across her breast she crept behind the horse, who was nervous, shying away from her dead companion. The sounds of snapping bone and impacted flesh surrounded her.

Cheftu and the sergeant were rolling on the sand, punches flying. The other soldiers had started running to the rescue. She nocked her arrow, aimed, and released. One fell, dead, the other dropped for safety. Cheftu screamed, and Chloe saw the sergeant had stabbed him in the thigh and blood was staining them both. Cheftu was losing, the days of near star-vation and forced marching having eaten away his strength. She shrieked, distracting the sergeant for just a moment, allowing Cheftu to put all his remaining energy into a knockout blow. Chloe cut the horse's traces and pulled herself up. The horse reared, trampling the wounded soldier. Cheftu was pale as he ran toward them. With a groan he pulled himself up behind her, and they rode through the twisting, rocky valley, west toward the sun.

••••

The sun sapped the color from the Sinai, and the horse stumbled. They had no food and little water, and their only advantage would be riding the horse until she died. Mountains rose to their west, towering thou-sands upon thousands of feet into the sky. Soon they would cast a shadow stretching *henti* across the desert. Shadow, Chloe thought, and we'll be in it.

They dozed as the horse panted, her steps slower and slower. At dawn the next day she fell, collapsing in on herself almost like a camel. They had to move quickly to avoid being pinned. Vultures circled above them, and Cheftu, pale and sweating, made quick work of butchering her. A scroungy bush provided flame, and they tore at the tough meat.

"Where are we?" Chloe asked, slightly more coherent with protein flowing through her veins.

Cheftu indicated the huge mountain. "Gebel Musa."

"It's not Moses' mountain, though. We didn't even go through the desert." She thought for a moment. "Where does he get the Ten Commandments?"

"On a mountain across the sea, I would suppose," Cheftu said, his voice slurred.

"That's the Arabian peninsula . . . and that is major irony," she said with a scratchy laugh.

"We must walk while we have food," he said, rising. "These birds aren't going to wait much longer . . . and you don't want to see that."

They strapped on their baskets, winding their cloaks tightly for protection.

"Where do we go?"

"Oasis. Ahead." Cheftu stumbled, and they walked on.

Chloe's lungs felt as if they were on fire. She'd been walking since she was born, and she hated it. Heat made her vision wobbly. She saw spots. Cheftu, his sweaty hand in hers, wrenched her up when she stumbled. They walked farther into the searing, rocky wasteland. Chloe fell again and Cheftu stopped beside her, resting his hands on his bare knees, gasping for air. The silence around them was immense. No other sounds marred the heated afternoon. Cheftu raised his head, the reflected glare of kohl protecting his vision. "Need a cave. Rest."

Chloe looked up; the dark holes in the surrounding mountains promised cool shelter. She licked a few drops of water off the end of her waterskin. It evaporated almost before it touched her lips. Hands shaking, she tucked it into her sash. Cheftu was gray under his mahogany skin. The wound in his thigh was black with flies: a living bandage.

"We rest. Then head northwest."

How far? How many days? She knew that if they were off even so much as a half mile, they could be lost forever. They slept in the shade of an overhang, and Cheftu grilled a snake for dinner. They walked under a canopy of stars. Silent.

The next day merged into decades for Chloe. Her throat was so dry, it seemed to crack when she swallowed. Her tongue was swollen with thirst. When she rubbed her nose her hand came away bloody from the cracked skin inside. She pulled her ragged white robe closer around her, trying to deflect some of the numbing sun.

Cheftu's wound was angry, swelling. He limped and staggered, plodding forward, his head nodding as he walked in a semiconscious sleep. Chloe could feel the sun's claws tear at her skin, heavy on her eyelids, even as she moved her feet from scorching, rocky sand to more of the same.

Her body had become a prison of heat and pain, and she felt a draw upward, as if she could fly skyward and be free of the broken, battered flesh with which she was cloaked. Cheftu dropped to his knees, dragging her down. Chloe panicked when she felt his burning flesh; his eyes were closed and his pulse thready. Another rest; another cave. They needed a cave.

She stood and looked around. The terrain was changing, the towering, rocky cliffs becoming softer, the ground sandier. She saw an overhang and grasped Cheftu around his waist, dragging him up what looked like a goat path. She laid him against the stone, shading his body, fanning his face halfheartedly with the edge of her cloak.

They needed water—not just the little bit that was left in her waterskin, but much more, to soak his burning flesh in. And his leg . . . the stench was stomach churning. She put her head in her hands. Please God, help! Her eyelids closed over her burning orbs, and she felt the gentlest breeze stir her clothing.

White rock, a voice whispered in her consciousness. She jerked awake. White Rock? It was a lake in Dallas, but why would she think of it now?

Remember Moses. Not the man, but the stories. White rock.

Chloe pressed trembling fingers to her temples. Was she going insane? Suddenly, in her mind's eye, she saw Joseph seated at a table, arguing about the Tanakh. Moses wasn't allowed into the Promised Land because he *struck the rock!* Joseph had said there was no need for Moses to strike the rock. Dig below limestone and one could find water.

Dazedly she pulled herself to her feet. Cheftu slept on in the heat-saturated afternoon, his leg a bloody mess, his skin scratched, bruised, and blistered. Chloe looked out from her perch in the hills, shading her eyes to see any white rocks. After tucking both waterskins in her belt and grabbing her cloak, she crept down from their overhang, sliding the last few feet. Oh, God, she thought, help me to recognize the right white rock.

BLESSED COOLNESS SURROUNDED HIM, enveloped him. It smelled like goat. Cheftu stirred, shivered, and relaxed as he felt long-fingered hands touching his body. They soothed, petted, relieved. The blackness around him intensified, and he collapsed into it.

CHLOE TIGHTENED THE WET CLOAK AROUND Cheftu, though the evening wind was beginning to blow through the wadi and she needed to take it off him soon in case he became chilled. He was scorched with fever, his body heat drying the cloth within minutes. He'd flinched when she'd tried to clean the skin around his leg wound and then had fallen unconscious. The wound was rotting; something would have to be done immediately or blood poisoning would set in. She had no antiseptic, no tools, no antibiotics. The only other thing she could think of was barbaric.

She had no choice.

Praying for more strength, she gathered a handful of tinder, some of Cheftu's dried herbs, and one of her papyrus drawings. Hands shaking, she shredded everything into a pile and pulled out the flint. Then, with mounting impatience and a twisting stomach, she started a fire.

She pierced the scab, pressuring it. Vile pus poured out, carrying with it the infection, she hoped. With water and his herbs she purified the gash, rinsing it again and again until the overflow ran pink. Just blood.

With a piece of her torn cloak wrapped around its handle, Chloe held the knife into the fire, watching it turn black and then red hot. Tears streaming down her face, yet hands steady, she laid the scalding edge on the freshly cleaned wound. Cheftu screamed, sitting bolt upright, then fainted. Chloe smelled the stench of burning flesh as she moved the knife to another part of the wound, cauterizing the length of it with heat and melting the flesh in healing.

She spent the next hour dry heaving into the sand at the bottom of their cliff. He had opened his eyes for a moment and then collapsed again as pain engulfed him. Chloe prayed she had made the right decision. She had packed some of Cheftu's healing herbs on the angry red mark. It needed to stay dry. Shouldn't be a problem—in a desert.

He'd lost a lot of weight in the past couple of weeks, but she could still see the lines of muscle and sinew beneath his skin. Unfortunately she could also count his ribs, see his hipbones and the underlying works of his joints. She traced those lines, feeling the body she had loved so well and so often . . . the arms that had cradled her, provided for her, protected her, and taken her in passion again and again. Her eyes burned, desperate for tears yet not having the moisture to give. All the things they had never done, the places they'd never seen. The things they'd never talked about.

"Oh, Cheftu," she whispered, bathing his hot forehead in water. She sniffed, wishing for his voice, his low chuckle and raised eyebrow. "I never told you about my family," she said. "You probably would laugh at my father. He's got dark hair and a twang. It's not bad, just different. Oh, and my Mimi. She gave me my red hair. . . . Oh, Cheftu, Mimi would love you." Chloe choked on a dry sob. "Please stay with me, darling. Please don't go to Mimi before me!" Tears scalded her eyes. "I wish we could have all had Christmas together once. Christmas in Reglim. That's where she lives . . . lived. A big house, a wraparound porch, and a peach orchard out back." Chloe sniffed. "At Christmas she bakes up a storm." Her mouth moistened at the memory. "She's a southern belle and doesn't believe any meal is complete without at least five pies, three meats, and, as she would say, a whole slew of vegetables from the yard."

Chloe looked at the silvery expanse of Egyptian desert. It looked almost white, like snow. "I remember once when it was so cold, it snowed. Snow is so rare in East Texas. It piled up deep along the street and against the house. Icicles hung from the porch, and the swing was so cold that your fingers almost stuck to it." She closed her eyes, telling him about the cold. The ice. The snow. She bathed his body as she sang Christmas carols. She described her attempt at sledding, in which she wound up in the hospital. She told him how she saw each snowflake and how when she was a kid she had cut up a whole box of construction paper, making snowflakes. Chloe put her head on her arms, swaying to the chords of the music, shivering in her corduroy dress. She needed gloves. Maybe she'd get some for Christmas?

CHEFTU SHIVERED. An icy wind cut through his clothes, and he heard the faintest whispering of "Adeste Fideles" around him. It had been a long time since he'd been sung to, tucked before a roaring fire against the cold, wintry outdoors. He opened his eyes suddenly . . . to night. Across the sky, from horizon to horizon, stretched stars: welcome light instead of the sun. He knew he was burning with fever, but his head had cleared some with the coolness darkness brought. He twisted and saw Chloe, knees pulled up to her chest with her head resting on them, swaying to and fro as she sang fragments of Christmas songs.

He felt the cold around him, the comfort of blankets and cider. He saw her world with peach orchards and icicles. She'd entranced him, the litany of her words pulling his mind from his pain-ravaged body into her world. Now he wanted water. "Chloe?"

Her head jerked up, her eyes as wide and black as the sky. "You must rest." She spoke automatically, and Cheftu realized with a pang that she was a walking corpse herself. Searing pain gripped his leg. Chloe dribbled water—fresh, cool water—into his mouth, and Cheftu swallowed convulsively . . . then unconsciousness claimed him.

CHLOE CREPT DOWN THE CLIFF, her legs shaking, her mind foggy. She must find some food. Cheftu needed food. A plaintive call stopped her in her tracks, clearing her head for a moment. Wild animals! How could she defend against them?

The sound came again.

She didn't have the strength left to run, yet if something happened to her, Cheftu would surely die. She felt eyes on her back and looked behind her into the darkness. She saw nothing.

Then she heard another different sound—stealthy slithering. The stars lit the night brilliantly, and Chloe felt the hair on her neck stand up. Slowly she turned and saw it: a snake, slithering along on the warm sand, easily within striking distance. She couldn't think what kind it was or what it could do. The black eyes held her as it rose in the air, weaving back and forth, casting a spell of death. Chloe could hear nothing; her blood pounded in her ears, every cell in her body begging for a few more nights, a few more days, to live, even like this. Her eyes were half-closed when a flurry of fur jumped through the night, muffled growls and yowls echoing through the canyon. Chloe scrambled halfway up the cliff; the night was suddenly alive and dangerous. They didn't even need soldiers. Another predator would be more than willing to kill them.

Padded paws crossed the rocky sand to her, and Thief threw down the body of the snake, looking up at her for approval.

He got it. Chloe crouched before him, her back muscles protesting against picking up the growing ball of fangs and fur. He began to purr, rumbling in the darkness. Like them, he didn't look so good. His fur was matted, and he seemed to be favoring his right rear paw. He followed her up to Cheftu and licked his face with a sandpaper tongue as he inquired with growls what was wrong.

Chloe sat down by the smoldering remains of the fire and took Thief's paw in her hand. She found the cut, filled with sand. With a little water, both on his paw and in his tummy, Thief settled down for the night, protectively curling around her and Cheftu, facing the dark night. She lay back beside Cheftu, tangling her fingers in Thief's fur, and thanked God for surviving another day.

• • •

The creeping patterns of sun brought Chloe around. She lay in the overhang, looking out across the wadi. In the morning cleanness she was surprised at how pretty these cliffs and stones were. Each was striated with myriad colors, some bright and some pale, but giving a life to the dismal deadliness around them. Then she noticed the plants, little flowers and weeds, growing up high, anywhere she supposed there was a dribble of water. She heard scrabbling and saw Thief returning from his hunting, a small furry creature in his mouth. Chloe looked at Cheftu.

He needed more medical attention. She had to get him out of this canyon. His breathing was shallow, rough, and way too rapid. She rose and crawled up from their overhang, clinging to the cliff's face and scarcely wincing as she felt stones cut through her sandals.

Breathing heavily, she finally hauled herself up onto the pinnacle. The Sinai desert, or at least part of it, spread before her. She drank deeply of the water, soaked her torn cloak, and then tied it around her head. Just a few cliffs beyond, sand stretched for miles. There, at the very edge of the horizon, was a smudge of green. The oasis? She drank again and headed back down the mountain. She had no choice but to try.

She could almost hear Mimi's sweet southern voice: "Kingsleys do not give up."

• • •

Hours later Chloe surveyed her handiwork. Cheftu looked bloody uncomfortable, that was for sure, but she couldn't carry him. She couldn't saddle him on Thief. So this was the compromise.

He was stretched out on his cloak, which managed to protect most of his body, tightly wrapped inside it. His arms were stretched above him, his wrists tied firmly to a thong that led up to and around Thief. Chloe carried their scanty supplies, her own tattered cloak wrapped around her head, the waterskins crossing her chest like bandoliers. She would carry Cheftu's ankles.

As the crow flew she imagined they had eight or so miles to travel. As the wadi curved, it could be more than that. She doubted it would be less. Everyone was filled with water, and Thief had eaten. Now there was nothing but to do it. Praying God would keep them safe, she reached down, pulled Cheftu's legs to her waist, and called for Thief to go.

・・・

Chloe stumbled in the darkness. Although they had traveled only for several hours, it felt like eternity. Thief had fiercely objected to being used as a donkey, but after a few aborted attempts to chase after the small wildlife, he plodded faithfully ahead. Chloe's back was wrenched. You wouldn't think a bag of bones like Cheftu could weigh so much. His fever was worse, and Chloe felt reality fading in and out. She ate some of the grass they found in crevices in the rock, then heaved it up again. They were still doing okay on the water supply—she'd found more limestone.

Falling to her knees, she released Cheftu's legs and collapsed close to him. Thief snuffled around her face, mewling and crying, but Chloe didn't care. Sleep. Blessed sleep and to feel nothing. Sleep . . .

・・・

By the third day Chloe was dragging Cheftu. He hadn't awakened once. He was either dead or comatose, and she was too scared to check which. Chloe had freed Thief, and she alone pulled Cheftu, his wrists tied around her waist, cutting the spare flesh above her hipbones. She'd broken a finger getting more water from another rock and had been momentarily terrified when her deeply burned skin tore off at her wrist as she brushed against the wadi wall.

This time when she fell, it was for good.

CHAPTER 17

The wizened old man tapped on one of his litter bearer's shoulders. His gaze was fixed, not on the approaching mountainous cliffs, but on the bowl of entrails he was holding. Waving a fan in front of his face, he commanded them to stop.

Stepping down from the litter, he was surrounded by his guard, their sun-browned bodies strong and wiry, a contrast to his stooped and slow one. However, they kept his pace as he walked into the mouth of the wadi, his still-keen eyes searching for the vision he had seen the night before, the vision he'd been awaiting. The entrails were his map, and he moved to the left, as they indicated he should. According to the stars, and the histories, this was the right day.

Then he saw them. A lion cub got to his feet, the fur on his ruff rising. The old man spoke a few words, and the cub sat down and proceeded to wash his paw but kept a watchful gaze on the party.

"They are alive, but barely, my liege."

"Bring them."

He looked in amazement at the tangle of dirty, blackened limbs, the skeletons that were just barely covered in flesh. They hardly looked important enough to bury, much less rescue. Summons from the unknown God were so rare, however, that when they came, they were never denied. The man turned and made his way back to his litter.

CHLOE COULDN'T SAY WHEN the pain ebbed and she became aware of life around her. It was several more days after that that she even remembered Cheftu and Thief. Even then the strength to open her eyes and discover their welfare eluded her. Through the gentle ministrations of an anonymous and silent helper, she felt nourishment flood her body and rich oils soak through her skin.

She opened her eyes to a white room and closed them again.

They were back in Egypt—ancient Egypt with all of its foreign gods and garish colors. Egypt, where if Cheftu were not already dead, he would be.

Cheftu!

Chloe lurched to her feet, drawing the linen shift more closely around her. Maybe they could escape? If it wasn't already too late? She slipped from her couch and caught herself on the edge of it as a debilitating wave of dizziness engulfed her. It passed, and she crept toward the curtained door. She looked out. No one was around. Stepping gingerly, she walked into the corridor.

"Child, do you seek the Egyptian?"

She whirled around at the sound of the voice, her position immediately defensive. A wizened old man stood before her, torchlight playing across his painted face. Chloe gasped. True, she'd seen old, but this guy was *really* old. Antique. Ancient. Decrepit.

His head was shaved, tattooed with symbols she couldn't identify. A priest? Huge gold earrings hung from his lengthened lobes, and the harsh black kohl lines around his eyes and brows only emphasized the network of wrinkles on his face. He was the color and texture of fine paneling, and he wore the elaborate kilt of the previous dynasty. He smiled broadly, straining the muscles in his wrinkled neck and around his mouth. He had amazingly strong, white teeth and healthy pink gums. Big teeth.

She met his gaze and was startled to see it full of laughter. "I see you are surprised to meet one of the golden god's own in this land bereft of lotus?" He smiled again, sticking his head forward, his teeth in her face. "Has Bastet got your tongue, my child?" His frail limbs moved with a grace that belied the age around his eyes.

Chloe pulled back, confused.

"Please, have a seat with me." He turned and walked into another room.

Chloe followed, her instincts telling her he was to be trusted. A gilded chair stood to one side of a huge brass brazier. The walls were lined with white painted linen, portraying the weighing of the heart by Ma'at. In the corner stood a wooden couch, and blood surged through Chloe's veins when she recognized the pain-racked body on it. Cheftu!

She ran to him, kneeling between the carved leopards that decorated each corner of the couch. He was flushed, his skin on fire, but he'd been bathed and his bandage changed. She looked over her shoulder. The man was seated on the chair, facing away as he fanned himself in the afternoon heat. Chloe placed a kiss on Cheftu's brow and walked back to their host.

Her voice trembled with tears. "I thank you, priest, for all you have done for him. Is he going to recover fully?"

The old man turned his wily gaze on her. "Aye, priestess. Your care of him was quite skilled. A simple scar that should heal quickly, if there is no fever or rot. Now, go and clean up, then we shall eat. You must heal and return to Egypt. You have destinies to fulfill."

Chloe froze in her tracks. "We're not in Egypt?"

"Nay, child. This is the Mirna Oasis in the Sinai. You are safe. Go." He smiled again. Really big teeth.

A black slave touched her elbow and led her beyond another curtain into a bathing room. Already the low bath was filled, and Chloe saw a tray with wine, bread, and fruit. The slave indicated some towels and a trunk of linens and bowed himself out. Enthusiastically Chloe threw aside her rags and stepped into the bath, reveling in the scented sand bar provided and opening the various fragrance bottles that lined the adjoining table. She sank into the water, wedging her body, breasts to knees, in the tub. It was glorious to wash the dirt and sand and grime from her body and to smell clean again.

She shaved, plucked, and oiled her scrawny body, feeling vaguely human again. Rising, she dried off and then rummaged through the trunk for clothing. Seated on the edge of the bath, she saw another room, dark but full of scrolls and equipment. She stepped toward it and then admonished herself for intruding on her host's hospitality.

A short while later she emerged from the bath, groomed enough for an Egyptian dinner party. Her dress was beautiful, if outdated. Her hair floated free, clean and oiled as it hung from the crown of her head to her neck. She wore an ornamental silver lotus to hold it back from her face and had lined her eyes and extended her eyebrows with the kohl provided. None of the sandals had fit, and she had dared not loofah the protective calluses off her feet, but she had put on faience anklets. She felt, for the first time in weeks, as though she might survive.

The old priest was still seated in his chair, but Chloe noticed with a smile that his eyes were closed and the tent was filled with his sonorous snoring. She walked to Cheftu. He had stopped thrashing around and seemed to be a little cooler. Thank God!

• • •

It was a seamless night. Her startled awakening gasp was rewarded with a chuckle. "You slept like the dead, my child." Chloe recognized the voice of the old priest. "Would you care to eat this night with me?"

Chloe got off the couch and stumbled toward the voice. A curtain had been drawn between the main room and the sleeping chamber.

"How is my patient?" the old man asked.

"Still feverish," Chloe said, "but sleeping well."

"That is good. The night is a healer of many illnesses. Please," he said, indicating another chair, "be seated. Would you care for wine?"

"Nay." Chloe grinned. "I fear I had too much already."

He chuckled. "I see you are a woman with moderate tastes. That is well."

Chloe accepted the cup of juice that the black slave brought and settled into the carved and gilded chair. "Please, forgive me for not asking earlier, but to whom do we owe our lives?"

"You do not owe me your lives. Only the gods are worthy of such sacrifice, but I would know what brings a noble couple to living like jackals in the desert? Forgive me for my manners!" he exclaimed. "I am called Imhotep."

"I am . . ." She paused.

"RaEmhetepet," he finished. "Though you are, in truth, not."

Chloe stared at him. "How do you know?"

He chuckled again, the lines of his face deep cuts in the torchlight. "There is much I know beyond the pale of these five senses. Still," he said, "there is much hidden in a veil of otherworldliness. I know that you and

Cheftu are not who you seem to be, and for that reason have had to flee for your lives. I also know you have been privileged to see things that most mortals have not. The unknown God has blessed you."

Chloe's mouth hung open during this impossible speech. "I . . . we . . . can we . . . ," she spluttered.

He laughed, the sound filling the chamber, bouncing off the woven rugs and fabric-lined walls. "I can understand your confusion, though I confess I do not know how I know. When your heart awakes," he said with a nod of his tattooed head toward the sleeping chamber, "we can sort how all of this came about. Now"—he leaned forward—"are you hungry? During dinner we shall discuss how I came to be here. I am certain we have two sides of the same throwing stick."

He motioned for the black man and moved his hands in the air, forming signs. The slave bowed and exited. "Khaku is deaf and mute," Imhotep said. "These signs are our conversation."

They sat in silence, Chloe looking beyond the open tent flap to the darkening horizon, while Imhotep focused somewhere inside himself. Khaku came back in, his arms wide to support the tray resting on them. He set it on the small table between the two chairs, and the smell of roasted lamb drifted to Chloe's nose. Her mouth watered. She was handed a glass bowl, and Imhotep reached forward, pulling the meat off the bone and taking a handful of the oiled corn mixed with sultanas and pistachios. It was a feast. The lamb melted in Chloe's mouth. They ate in silence, pausing only to drink fresh water.

Khaku moved around, lighting more of the lamps until the room glowed with the sun's brightness. Finally Chloe and Imhotep sat back, satiated, and ate the candied orange peel that Khaku presented. It was chewy, like gum, and once again she wished for coffee. Imhotep looked at her fleetingly, a crease of confusion between his brows, then turned away. "Shall we play hounds and jackals?"

Chloe nodded. "Should we check on Cheftu?"

"Certainly, but I am sure he sleeps well. Khaku shall feed him," Imhotep said as they rose and drew back the separating curtain.

Amazingly, Cheftu was resting, his skin much cooler. Khaku sat in the darkness, bathing his brow with cooling water, and Cheftu snored gently. Chloe realized Khaku must have been the one who had forced her to take broth and soaked her burned and peeling flesh in oil those days before she even woke.

Imhotep drew back the linen and touched the wound, leaning forward to smell if it was putrefying. The cauterizing had healed well, though there would always be a vicious scar. Chloe shuddered and brushed Cheftu's hair away from his face. He smiled faintly and murmured, falling back into deep sleep. Imhotep, satisfied with the progress of the wound, took Chloe's elbow and guided her into the other room. The remains of dinner were gone; now a game board rested on the small table.

Chloe seated herself, twisting the beads of her overdress so that they were not in the most uncomfortable position possible. They began to play. After even scores at the end of three games, Imhotep turned away from the game and looked at Chloe . . . not just a cursory glance, but as if he were trying to see her soul beyond the outside artifice of black hair and ringed eyes.

"Have you heard the name Imhotep before, my child?" he asked, smiling broadly, his teeth glinting in the light.

"Of course," Chloe said. "He was a great philosopher, an adviser to Pharaoh Cheops."

"Aye. He was also my several-times-removed grandfather." He watched her carefully.

"Only several times? That would make you hundreds of years old."

He laughed. "I do not look a day over two hundred, correct? I have very nice teeth for one so old, aye?"

She smiled, though slightly disturbed. If this old man were mad, what help would he be? "That is impossible," she said, ignoring the teeth comment.

"Is it? Is not traveling through the years of millions of lives also impossible? That is what you have done, though, is it not?"

She was silent. He knew a lot about her and didn't seem disturbed. Who was she to say that someone couldn't live for hundred of years? The Bible talked about some man who lived to be eight hundred something. The Bible was turning out to be a lot more accurate than she'd originally given it credit for.

"Are you immortal?"

The expression on his face was truly appalled. "The gods forbid! I am not immortal, just long-lived. It is both gift and curse. Still, I have dynasties before I land on the Shores of Night."

"So with all the time in the world, do you just travel around?" Chloe asked. He spoke so calmly, as if this were the truth. Maybe she should play along.

He sighed. "Not by choice. I was last in the court of Thutmosis the

First. A great pharaoh, founder of what is proving to be the highest point in Egyptian civilization so far. Such an improvement over the Hyksos." He shuddered. "They had no appreciation for the delicacy of Egyptian religion or custom. Only their damned horses." He shook his head at the memory.

"But I digress. I was a trusted physician in the court of Thutmosis the First. He was a great man, though a bit short-tempered. Always costive. Why he didn't eat more dates, I cannot understand. *Haii!* His favorite wife, Aset, became pregnant, and like most great men, he hoped it would be a son to carry on his name and lineage.

"He called upon me to cast a horoscope for the future of the child. The omens told me this child would be usurped by a prince of slaves." He paused, looking down at the forgotten game board. "I was a weak man. I knew Pharaoh would be displeased with that reading, so I lied. I told him the prince would rise to be the greatest leader Egypt had ever known. Thutmosis believed me because I dared to say his son would do better than he would. The months passed. Aset grew rounder, and one night she gave birth. Egyptian physicians do not attend births; normally that is for the midwives. I went to the chamber anyway, and was barred admittance. Pharaoh was on one of his many campaigns.

"Aset's child was born dead.

"She had erected a great chamber to HatHor, and now it appeared as if she were betrayed by the great lady. To avoid any questions and to regroup, she took the fastest boat and sailed to the former capital of Avaris. The Hyksos palace was still there, and Aset decided it would be a safe place to recover and decide what to tell Pharaoh." He paused again, looking at his wrinkled hands. "I followed her, on another boat. By the time I arrived, Aset was bouncing a healthy boy on her knee. Pharaoh arrived, and he proclaimed that Ramoses was a perfect child and would be Horus-in-the-Nest."

Chloe leaned forward.

"I fear," Imhotep said with a wry smile, displaying his teeth, "that I was overcome with guilt. I was to examine the child in the presence of Pharaoh, and it became obvious to me that the child was actually older than he should have been. The warning I had seen in the stars made me momentarily brave, and I denounced the queen, stating that the child was too developed and consequently could not have come from her body. I said she had given birth to a stillborn.

"I was not certain who this child was, but I guessed it was an Apiru baby, since their children were the ones in danger. Pharaoh was sick of the fomenting rebellion and had decreed that all male babies be killed before they were weaned. He saw the children as little rebellions waiting to happen, and after just ridding Egypt of the Hyksos, he had no desire for another foreigner on the red and black throne." Imhotep took a sip of water before he continued.

"I almost lost my head." He chuckled faintly. "Pharaoh flew at me, in a violent rage. Of course his son would be superior. How dare I defame the queen? I was sent back to Waset immediately. For years I served in the temple at Karnak. Though I had little actual power, I spent my time in the god's presence and studied the sacred writings. I began to read the night sky, like a map of instructions and clues. I was never asked to cast another horoscope, and did not see the young prince until he came to be inducted.

"The rite took two years. He was a strapping boy—strong featured, well built, a son any man would want. His eyes were black as Aset's, and he had all of Thut's prowess with bow, knife, and horse. He was courageous, even tempered, and wise. Even I had begun to doubt what my memory told me was true."

His gaze met hers, the reflected lights dancing in his black irises. "There are sacred services performed only on those of the royal house. Since Pharaoh is god on earth, he is the highest priest of all. He embodies more magic and power than any other being. In the fourth degree of priesthood, the initiate is in solitary confinement for a year and a half. In this time he practices the things he has learned, namely, the astrological, medical, architectural, and Osirian aspects of the previous degrees. He is forbidden certain foods, sexual release, and alcohol.

"Ramoses was placed in a tunnel underneath my part of the temple. The words I said those many years ago had become nothing but intriguing rumor, and Egypt loved her young prince, and prayed for him as he progressed through the seven stages of the priesthood. I would go by the room in which he was a prisoner, and oftentimes heard him speaking. It was a language unknown to me, which piqued my interest, since I spoke all the known languages of the countries with which Egypt traded.

"I began to inquire, and learned that Ramoses had been weaned by an Apiru, but more important, an Israelite. Through a network of channels, I managed to get one of their precious scrolls and taught myself their words. I began to listen to Ramoses as he worked during the day.

"He was praying to another god. Praying like a child, singing songs with great emotional and spiritual impact, but without understanding." The old man took another drink, running his tongue over his lips. "The time came, and he was released from the Days of Wrath and moved into the Battle of the *Khaibits*. He passed through all the remaining levels of induction and was received with joy by his father at the age of fourteen.

"Though he was but a boy, Thut took him campaigning and encouraged him in all manner of education. I bided my time, wondering what price my cowardice would extract from Egypt. Ramoses grew, married, but was unable to father children. Thut was embarrassed for him, so kept him out of the country, fighting wars. Ramoses spent a lot of time in the Sinai, and when he returned, he would visit Avaris. I was uncertain as to whether that was because he visited his old nurse—in great secrecy, mind you—or his dear cousin, the Vizier of the Ostrich Nome, Nefer-Nebeku.

"Thut the First continued to have children. His first wife gave birth to one lovely daughter, then another, whom they named Hatshepset. About the time Hatshepset was in the schoolroom, but was yet a child, Ramoses killed Nefer-Nebeku; he was Hatshepset's betrothed. By the time the news reached Thut, Ramoses had already escaped into the desert.

"Thut sacrificed many men searching for his errant son. He was willing to forgive, until an Israelite slave named Do'Tan came forward, claiming that Ramoses had killed his royal cousin in a fury over a slave." Imhotep chuckled, but this time his laughter held no humor. "Thut was enraged. His eldest daughter had just died under mysterious circumstances, his younger son had died in the cradle, and his middle son was a weakling from a common slave. Hatshepset was his only successor.

"He called back the soldiers from the desert and set the whole country about the task of removing Ramoses' cartouche from everything and replacing it with Hatshepset's, whose name he changed to Hatshepsut, living forever!"

Of course, Chloe thought. Changing her name from that of a noblewoman to first among the favored noblewomen. "Living forever!" was a phrase each pharaoh inherited and that Moshe had ignored in his dealings with her.

"Possibly because she was to be the crown prince, she continued to wear the clothes of a young man, though it was scandalous by the time she was sixteen Inundations." He paused and licked his lips. "I thought I was safe, that Thut had forgotten me. Unfortunately I was wrong. One day while I was reading the sacred scrolls of Ptah, soldiers entered the temple and took me. Pharaoh told me that because of my family's prior contributions to Egypt, I would be given two choices. I could serve in the temple at Noph for seven Inundations, then be killed as a traitor, or I could be banished immediately and made to wander outside of Egypt's glory for the rest of my life."

"So you chose banishment," Chloe said.

"Nay. I chose the temple."

Chloe frowned in confusion.

"Pharaoh ascended to Osiris before my term was up. Hatshepsut was forced to marry Thutmosis the Second, living forever!, and the torch-light was off me for a while," he explained.

"So, when did you begin your life as an *anu?*"

Imhotep shivered and blanched. "When I saw something so terri-fying in the Temple-of-the-Ka-of-Ptah in Noph that I knew human eyes should not view it."

Chloe's pulse leapt. "What? What did you see?"

His black stare bored into her. "Do you realize that if I tell you, I will be releasing this power again?"

"Tell me," she pleaded.

"Very well, but may the fear be on your soul. I saw a *kheft.*"

Chloe sat back, surprised.

"A *sem*-priest stepped into one of the smaller rooms and, crossing his breast in obeisance, knelt. A fire seemed to consume him, changing his hair and his eyes before he disappeared."

Chloe could scarcely hear, blood pounded so loudly in her ears. "Then," Imhotep said, "he reappeared. Only not as before. He was wearing the guise of a man, but he was in great pain. I ran to him, kneeling by his side. Blood poured from his nose, mouth, and ears; I knew he would not live. He was gasping to say something, and I leaned closer, trying to hear what his last words were."

Chloe leaned closer, her body covered in a cold sweat. "What did he say?" she choked out.

"It was a foreign tongue I do not know. He died. Then he changed back to a *kheft*, with pale hair and skin." Imhotep looked down as if ashamed. "I knew if someone asked who he was, there would be a great investigation, so I weighted his body and took it to the Nile, leaving it as an offering to Sobek." He warded off the Evil Eye with a gesture. "That night I took my belongings and all the gold I had saved from selling things before my disgrace, and crept out of Egypt." He stared past Chloe at the painted hieroglyphs on the wall, and Chloe stared at her café au lait-colored hands.

GOSHEN

THUT III LOOKED ACROSS THE CITY. Already others had moved into the houses abandoned by the escaping Israelites. At last count, several other tribes had joined their exodus. No one had been heard from.

Just like Hatshepsut. Thut swallowed. He knew she was dead; though they had been blood enemies, they were also blood relatives, and he sensed she was no longer in this world. The soldiers he'd sent after her had found nothing except tracks leading into the Red Sea. No bodies, no horses, no chariots. Surely if she had gone to another country, she would have at least sent a courier to let him know. He very much doubted she had gone anywhere willingly. She was dead. Perhaps the final justice of the desert god who'd laid Egypt to waste was that even the bodies were gone, a snub to Egypt's afterlife rituals.

Thut began pacing, the heavy fringe of his blue kilt brushing his muscled thighs. What harm would come for Egypt to know that Pharaoh had been killed and nothing remained of her? To a country whose self-esteem and personal pride were based on the actions of the royal godhead, it would wreak even more havoc in this already lost and distraught land! What could he do? The people did not even know she was dead. His pretense was running out of time. It had been almost seventy days since her departure. For how long could he rule as Hatshepsut, living forever! before she was declared dead? He'd wanted the double crown, but not at the price of Egypt's pride.

He turned at the sound of approaching footsteps. Two soldiers entered the room, their kilts dusty and travel stained. They saluted sharply, their eyes straight ahead. He saw the younger one's thigh was bandaged. "Life, health, and prosperity. What happened?" he asked, gesturing to the wound.

"It is nothing, My Majesty."

Thut raised his brows but motioned for them to be seated and called for beer. "What is your report?"

The older man leaned forward. His wig was askew, and Thut could see his peeling scalp. They had been in the sun a long time. "We found none of the soldiers, My Majesty. But we did follow some tracks. They led toward the copper and turquoise mines, but then were lost. There were two sets, one man and a young boy or . . ."

Thut's hand tightened around his goblet. It could not be! "Did you find them?"

"Aye, My Majesty. A man and woman were living on the edge of the sea. They had set up a house and were farming a small patch of land. We took them by surprise."

"You captured them?" Thut asked, setting aside the goblet. "They are here?"

The soldier swallowed and squared his shoulders. "Aye, My Majesty, we did capture them, but they escaped a few days into our travel. During a skirmish a mountain cat killed two of the soldiers. The male captive was wounded. The woman took advantage of the situation and stole a horse. Majesty"—the man's eyes were wide—"she rode on its back!"

It must be they, Thut thought. "Then?"

"She and the man rode into the heart of the desert mountains."

"Did you search for them?"

"Aye. For several days. The mountain cat was trailing them, so I doubt they survived. We had little water left and began to walk west to the Inland Sea. Two of the soldiers volunteered to stay and continue the search."

Thut's muddy gaze rested on the soldier, who looked down. "The woman's eyes were green." It was a statement.

The soldier nodded. "Aye, My Majesty."

"The man moved like a cat and had eyes of gold?"

"Aye."

Thut sighed. Of course, he knew they had escaped Hat's justice and wondered fleetingly in the past weeks if they had fled with the Israelites or had just left at the same time. He'd been informed that Cheftu had booked passage on a ship for the Great Green, but with the confusion of a third of the population dying and another fifth disappearing, he had not found out if they had made the ship. It was obvious Cheftu had stolen RaEm away from her rightful punishment; Thut had seen the dead guardswomen with their wounds of medical precision. Only one man could kill so cleanly.

He sighed again. They would have to be found. They knew, and as far as he could tell, they were the only ones who knew what had happened to Hatshepsut and her select guard.

The soldier stood before him. "Go. Refresh yourself for two days. As Ra rises on the third you shall be leading fresh soldiers out to resume the hunt. They must be found. Alive." Thut moved his hand and they bowed, backing toward the doors. He walked onto his balcony.

The swollen river ran like a band of silver, hammered out into a hundred filigreed ribbons, weaving through the black soil. Most of the workmen's houses were flooded, and Thut knew that behind him was a rough town of temporary dwellings from which the *rekkit* watched the waters recede, leaving the thick, black mud that was life in this land. His kilt stuck to his legs in the humid heat, and for the first time since the suicide of his wife, Thut felt a tremble of desire.

Also he felt a rumble of unease. Something pricked his memory, and he called for guards. The last time he had been with a woman . . .

Decans later Thut walked through the quiet, predawn streets, looking for that one path. Two bumbling soldiers followed him, and he forced himself not to run and lose them. The firstborn . . . how long would Egypt mourn their loss? He reached the river and realized that once again he had gone too far. He turned and walked back, looking carefully each way, searching for the narrow path to the old hidden temple.

He was staring at the ground abstractedly, when he seemed to see, darkly drawn in the sand, the outline of horns and a disk. He looked up in the direction the horns pointed and could see the trail, hidden by branches and ostraca. Stepping over and moving shards of rock, he walked down it, winding through the ragged undergrowth. The path dipped, he remembered, then ended flush against a door.

Thut remembered the door, left a crack open in that unforgiving darkness of months past. He pushed it, and it yielded. Stepping into the small stone chamber, he saw the bloodied stone couch. That poor girl, he thought. She had been so young, so innocent. Drugged, he realized now. She had never known a man, but he'd wager she'd had sensual encounters. Her reactions had testified to it.

May it please the gods, they would never have to resort to such archaic religious ritual again! The gods were not bloodthirsty, and Thut still felt unclean from the sacrifice he had made. ReShera had been her name, and he was certain he had seen her before.

He walked through the room, his sandals echoing faintly. Why had he come here? Why?

Because something was not right. Hatshepsut had passed judgment too quickly, and Cheftu had been startled at the sight of the girl. Hadn't he even said he'd thought she was older? Even the Sisterhood had not pursued RaEm as they should have, but let her go, preferring to worship HatHor without two priestesses. Actually the new RaEmhetep priestess had taken her place, but she was four years old. Thut, a royal prince of Egypt, inducted to the Seven Degrees of the Priesthood of Waset and the Three Degrees of the Temple-of-the-Ka-of-Ptah, knew that such worship was unwise.

Thut sat on the stone couch, staring at the first rays of morning that picked through the clerestory windows. The room, brightening in the sun, had not been opened since that dark day. Debris was piled in the corners, a testimony to the ferocity of the plagues. In this room built of pristine white Old Kingdom stone, unused for dynasties, the bloodstain was a deep scar.

He kicked at the debris, angered and uncertain as to why. A clink of metal on stone drew his attention. Kneeling on the floor, his bare hands mindless of the dead and decaying refuse, he pushed back the rotting foliage, feeling for whatever made the noise. He scrabbled in the pile for many moments, and then his fingers brushed it . . . a chain.

The inscription on the tiny gold scarab was easy enough to read even in the weak light. The implication was astounding. He looked around the room again, a room that he alone and another priestess had ever entered. He himself had carried her drained body to the door. Thutmosis swallowed. A gold scarab lay in his hand.

Gold, the one thing never to be worn by a priestess of HatHor. It was inscribed with a name far different from the one the priestess had given.

"Basha."

Thut left the room, almost running up the hill in his haste to reach the temple. He wanted some answers.

CHEFTU AWOKE IN EGYPT. IT SEEMED LIKE EGYPT. He smelled the myrrh of temple ritual, his body was supported by the tightly woven bands of an Egyptian bed, and he felt the complex linen bandage around his leg—Egyptian design. Strange that his last memories were of heat, cold, rocks, sand, and raging pain as they ran on and on, fearing even to spend a second of turning to see their pursuers.

Where was Chloe? He murmured her name and felt a cool hand on his forehead, but it was not hers. A voice spoke, sexless and authoritative. "Your time together is limited, my lord." What did that mean? The fear engendered by the statement was powerless against the exhaustion in his half-dead body. He slept.

CHLOE WAS SEATED NEXT TO A SLEEPING CHEFTU; he'd been resting for a week since she'd woken up, waking only to eat. How long had they been here? Time seemed to stand still between meals and naps and board games.

Khaku came in, beckoning to her, and Chloe followed him through her room and the bathing chamber into the room at the back of the tent that she had observed earlier.

It looked like Merlin's cavern, Chloe thought. Star charts were scattered about, and against one wall were baskets of all shapes and sizes holding labeled and sealed containers. She cried out when she saw Imhotep.

He was facedown. Khaku bent and cradled the old man, clicking his tongue in grief. Chloe counted his pulse; it was strong. Kahku carried him to the couch and laid a feather in the torches. The singed smell brought Imhotep around. He was weak, but fine. He sat up on shaking arms and looked around, frantically, as if he'd misplaced something.

He peered at Chloe, an expression somewhere between fear and admiration. "Leave us, Khaku. Bring the young man; we must talk now."

Khaku fussed over him for a few more seconds and then left, doing as his master commanded.

"Go, my child." Imhotep gestured to Chloe. "Take the bowl from that table; do not look into it, but bring it to me."

Chloe found the bowl. Concentrating on a spot above Imhotep's head, she walked to him, setting it carefully on a small table. Cheftu came in, supported by Khaku. His color was good, and he winked at Chloe. They sat on the couch, and Khaku pulled a stool forward so they all could see the small table. Then he bowed and left.

Imhotep seemed improved. "This morning I thought I would cast your horoscopes," he said a little breathlessly. "I had some sacred oil from Midian and some of the healing waters from Ptah's temple." He swallowed, his gaze flitting from Cheftu's still features to Chloe's curious ones, noting the strong-fingered grasp that held them together, a human chain. "I poured them in the divining bowl, and then, *haii*, I cannot describe what happened. It was like a khamsim blew through, not disturbing anything else, but stirring the water." He leaned over and stared into the bowl. "When at last I could see, this was what I beheld."

Chloe met Cheftu's gaze, and with a reassuring squeeze he released her hand. She leaned over the bowl and had to steady herself on the edge of the table. It was a map.

Cheftu scooted forward and saw it also. "Egypt," he murmured in English.

"It is a map of the Sinai and the two Egypts," Imhotep said. "It is as clear as a scribe's drawing. But look more closely, children." Chloe angled her head for a better view. From somewhere along the eastern edge of the Inland Sea, a path led across the water and into the desert between the sea and Waset. There it stopped.

"What does it mean?" she whispered, looking up into Cheftu's eyes. She was so close, she could see the circles of bronze that encircled his pupils.

He turned to Imhotep. "Was there anything else?"

The old man paled and sat back. "Aye, son. There was." He looked from face to face, then spoke in a monotone. " 'You must leave that which you carry in this place, then you must return to your lives.' "

Chloe looked at Cheftu. What did they carry?

Cheftu looked aghast. "Why?"

"Because you share a destiny. A destiny so vital, it will transform people's lives, their thoughts. It will tear your flesh from your bones, because of its demand."

"Demand?"

"A sacrifice."

Chloe raised an eyebrow at Imhotep. "How can we carry anything when . . . Wait a moment." She turned to Cheftu. "Those scrolls."

"The scrolls! Alemelek's scrolls!" He struggled to rise, but Imhotep laid a restraining hand on him and called for Khaku.

A few tense moments later, Cheftu pulled the scrolls from the quiver and unrolled them. There were about fifteen, all fine papyrus, covered with drawings of fruits, trees, and flowers, others of villages, and several of a family. And Meneptah.

Chloe choked when she found the one of the village. "I'll be damned," she said in distinct English. She felt Cheftu's stare, but her gaze was tracing the lines of the figures. She rolled it up and saw the botanical drawings. Her hands were cold and shaking as she slumped forward on the stool, staring at the map.

" 'A dig in the eastern desert,' " she quoted. She opened the basket that Khaku had also brought while Cheftu looked on in surprise. She removed a false bottom and pulled out several notepads and two well-wrapped scrolls. With trembling hands she opened them. Cheftu had on his doctor's face, watching Imhotep. However, the old man's gaze was steady as Chloe unrolled a long scroll.

Cheftu flinched when he saw his own countenance looking back at him as they sat watching the Exodus prepare to go forth. Chloe felt the blood leave her head.

"What is it?" he asked. "What do you see?"

She put a hand to her face. "The future."

"What!?"

"In 1994, my sister, who studies Egypt, will be part of a dig that discovers these papyri. I did not recognize the one of the Exodus as my own, because I had never before drawn faces." She looked at Cheftu. "Before you I never knew . . ." She bit her lip and looked down. "However, this village, and these fruit, I remember them clearly. The discovery was so amazing because it dated from the time of Thutmosis and was not in two-dimensional Egyptian style. Camille said there were about fifty of them, but they had not all been unwrapped."

Cheftu and Imhotep both looked confused. There were no direct translations for a lot of what she had said, but apparently they got the impression she knew what she was talking about.

"Where were they found?" Imhotep asked.

Chloe looked at the water and oil map. "In the eastern desert outside of Luxor . . . Waset."

"Hatshepsut's secret chamber," Cheftu said.

"What?"

"Assst! She had it built so that she and Senmut could be together as man and wife throughout time—an action forbidden to Pharaoh, but not if kept hidden!" His voice rose in sudden comprehension. "That must be where these are found! Hat said the reason she chose that location was because the land was barren. Nothing out there at all!"

Imhotep looked from one to the other. "You are to place them there," he said, gesturing to the wealth of papyri. "You have about forty scrolls here, if you take all. What do they depict?" he asked. "Are fruit and trees so important in the future?"

Chloe frowned. His point was good; what was their purpose? Cheftu began to flip through them. The plague of blood, several of the different stages of locusts, a street in Avaris during the hail, the hallway with sick servants, a recalled rendition of when Hat and Moses met face-to-face and the sun came out at his God's command. "They are just illustrations from the Bible," Cheftu said. "Interesting, but hardly worth the complexities of time and space we have experienced."

Chloe began pacing. "Aye, just illustrations. Everyone knows the stories," she said, then stopped. "But they do not believe them!"

Cheftu looked up, frowning. "Do not believe the Bible?"

"Nay. Nor did I before"—she paused—"before this. Did you?"

"Aye. Why would the Jews use a fabricated story on which to base their entire existence as a people?" Cheftu asked. "It is humiliating enough for them to admit to being slaves, but then the desert? The many times they disobeyed and God punished? Why would someone falsify that?"

"Aye." Imhotep chuckled. "You will never read of an Egyptian battle lost or a pharaoh falling short of his duties."

"That is it!" Chloe cried. "There is no other validation of the existence of Israel, or the Passover, or even who the pharaoh was! Even my sister thinks it was Rameses the Great, if anyone at all. This is proof! Cold, hard facts written on paper from the right period." She sat down, flipping quickly through the drawings. Several of Alemelek's were Egyptian style—one actually telling the story of Ramoses! With a shaking hand she passed it to Cheftu and Imhotep, who leaned over it, reading quickly.

Chloe sat down. This was bloody unbelievable!

She began to shake. They were responsible for delivering the scrolls to the tomb. Then to go back to their lives? The room was quiet now, the puzzle solved.

Cheftu laughed in amazement. "Alemelek was so afraid he had not been used by God. He felt guilty for marrying and not confessing to a priest. The night he died, I was shocked out of my wits to hear Latin. We hardly spoke, he was so ill. He asked me to administer last rites, which I did, but poorly. Then he made me swear on the Host that I would give him a Christian burial."

"Did you?"

"Aye. The night before we left. Meneptah and I traded his body for another, and I broke an ankh to make a cross."

"Where did you bury him?"

"In the caves behind the City of the Dead."

Chloe chuckled. "That is sure going to mess with a lot of Egyptologists' minds!"

"Children," Imhotep said with authority, "now that you know your task, your destiny demands it be done. Soon. I have laid false trails, but the voice warns me that they will not gain you the time I had hoped. You need to leave soon." He glanced at Cheftu's leg. "Is there any way I can aide you?"

"Water, food, clothing," Cheftu said. "What was the second part of . . . what you heard? How do we go back, and what is the demand, the sacrifice?"

"I do not know how you got here. Obviously, it was necessary for your world. I regret to say I do not know how to get you back."

"The man you saw 'disappear,' the one who was so pale . . . where exactly in the temple was he?" Chloe asked.

Imhotep pursed his lips. "I will think on it and draw you a map. I will also"—he shuddered—"cast individual horoscopes for you. Tell me your birth dates."

"December twenty-third, 1970," Chloe said unhesitatingly. The old man's hands faltered as he wrote down the date.

Cheftu was pale. "December twenty-third, 1790," he whispered.

The old man dropped the quill and stared at them. "When?" he breathed. "When during the night?"

"Twenty-three minutes after twenty-three hundred hours," Chloe said, freezing at the sound of her own words. Realizing she had spoken in English, she translated into Egyptian, but Cheftu had understood.

"That is my birth, exactly," he said.

"You are both of the house of RaEmhetep," the old man said. "It is the unluckiest day of all births in our year. The lintel in the room was inscribed with '*RaEmhetepet, RaEmHetp-Ra mes-hru mesut Hru Naur, RaEmPhamenoth, Aab-tPtah.*'"

Chloe gasped, hardly able to choke out the words. "What did you say? Repeat it!"

"'*RaEmhetepet, RaEmHetp-Ra, mes-hru mesut Hru Naur, RaEmPhamenoth, Aab-tPtah.*'"

"Add on the phrase . . ." She concentrated, trying to remember the symbols that had haunted her for days in their incomprehensibility. "'*Tehen erta-pa-her Reat RaEmhetep EmRaHetep.*' 'Prayer in the twenty-third doorway at twenty-three of RaEm.'"

The old man frowned. "Prayer in the twenty-third doorway? Are you certain?"

"I think I am," she said.

"The other part is easy," Cheftu said. "The twenty-third of the month of Phamenoth, which more or less corresponds to December."

Imhotep shook his head. "I do not know what this other could refer to. I will look through my library."

They all froze then at the words drifting in from the front room: "We demand shelter in the name of Thutmosis the Third, Pharaoh of Egypt, living forever!"

They wasted no time.

"Head west to the shore. Caravans pass there. Join as brother and sister," Imhotep hissed as they stripped and dressed, accepting packets of food and rewrapping the papyri, while Khaku stalled the soldiers.

"Take the donkey outside. Be careful—there have been mountain cat tracks in the last week."

Chloe chuckled. Cheftu stared hard at the map, imprinting it on his flawless memory.

Imhotep pressed an ink palette into her hands. "For more," he said. "There are only forty scrolls. Search your memory for the rest."

In minutes they were equipped, and Imhotep slashed the back of the tent for an escape route. With luck there would be too few soldiers to surround the tent. Tears streaming down his face, Imhotep said, "May your God lead you and protect you," he said.

Then they were gone, ducking from shadow to shadow, weaving through to the other side of the oasis. They traveled through the heat of the day, though the wind through the wadi kept them cool. Imhotep had warned it was flood season, so they walked on the wadi's edge. Any sound could foretell a rush of water that could submerge them instantly.

"Why do we have to travel as brother and sister?" Chloe asked at *atmu*.

Cheftu sighed; though he rode the donkey to ease his leg, he was still weak. "It's protection. As your brother, if someone harms you, I have recourse. Either they have hurt my family's standing and future, or they have insulted my forefathers." He groaned, shifting on the gray animal. "Unfortunately, as your husband, they have simply hurt my feelings. I have no greater claim on you."

"So it is better to be my brother than my husband?"

"*Absolument.*"

"That makes no sense to me."

"Why not?" Cheftu asked. "Doesn't your brother carry the responsibility for your family name? Makab does."

"Since my only brother is a black sheep and hasn't been mentioned by name in many years, it is up to Cammy and me to 'carry on' our names. Cammy is, was, so much like Mom with her love of archaeology, it was obvious she would follow in her footsteps," Chloe said. "That is why I joined the military, like Father. There's a long-standing tradition of Bennets and Kingsleys serving—from every generation. Someone had to maintain our heritage—it was not going to be Caius—so it was me."

"You have a brother named Caius?"

"My mother is *really* into history. At least it's not Caligula."

He chuckled weakly. "So you are a woman of the future. It makes sense now."

Chloe wiped sweat out of her eyes. "A strange form of rebellion?"

"There is so much about you that I do not know," he muttered. "I do not even know what to ask."

• • •

It was dark. After the business of setting up camp, eating, and feeding the donkey, they leaned against each other, with Cheftu's leg stretched out.

The braying of the little gray animal woke him, and Cheftu jerked awake, his knife close to his body. Growling, an animal pounced from the rushes, landing beside Chloe. Poised to stab the attacker with his knife, Cheftu recognized Thief just in time. He hobbled over to the donkey, who was straining at her ties, her eyes rolling in fear, and tried to calm her. By that time Chloe had convinced the cub to get off her, and he was sniffing the bones from dinner.

Cheftu rubbed his face, sore with mosquito bites. He could see the tint of dawn sneaking up on them. They had made such a noise that any moment he expected arrows to rain down on them. Thief butted his leg, and he groaned from the pain shooting through it. Multicolored spots rose before his eyes, and he realized in surprise that he was sitting again; Thief, who had been soundly admonished, was his cushion. Chloe handed Cheftu water and dates. The Perfuming, he supposed.

"What now?" she asked.

"We walk."

"Aye." They rose to their feet, Cheftu wincing.

"Does that need to be rewrapped?"

"Nay. Just keep that overgrown house cat on my other side. Agreed?"

PART V

CHAPTER 18

The moon was a crescent above them, and Chloe shivered, drawing her cloak closer. Thief skulked in the dunes, and Cheftu traced the map from his memory onto the sand. Staring up at the sky, he was a picture of every woman's fantasy: the lean, muscular lines of his body etched in silver light, his long lashes casting angled shadows across his cheekbones. His hair was still long and was tied back, but he was clean shaven.

Chloe sighed. They hadn't touched each other for more than thirty days—but who was counting? They'd been lucky; the caravan they'd hooked up with was going to Waset, then south into Kush. Unfortunately it was some strange religious sect where the women and men lived completely apart, and they expected the same from Chloe and Cheftu in exchange for the journey. The walking had been good for Cheftu's leg; his limp was now almost unnoticeable. In Waset they had finally stopped, and Cheftu had gotten them a donkey ride out to one of the *rekkit*'s fields. From there on they'd walked.

The caravan had been strange, not speaking to anyone for a month. No one spoke the high Egyptian she did. Chloe had never produced so much work in such a short period of time. The other women spent a great deal of time with their children. She had caught their pitying looks, for, she guessed, they thought she was an old maid. Worst of all was that the distance between her and Cheftu had grown to be more than physical. They could have been strangers. Thief, who had terrified all of the animals initially, lived at a distance. Out of kindness they had left the donkey behind.

For a month Cheftu had barely spoken, and she had lost the ability to read his eyes. No practice, she thought. So she had drawn . . . putting in ink those memories that haunted her days and filled her nights: the sea, the soldiers, the camps, the fire, the cloud, and the Passover.

She had even managed to capture an accurate rendition of the specter of death. Eerily enough, the drawing had blown into the fire and burst into flame. This experience greatly spooked Chloe, so she stuck to pictures of the streets and the sky. Altogether she had done fifteen . . . which was more than she remembered Cammy mentioning, but she'd allowed for rats and dust and damage. The best work would survive; she was certain of that.

Camille—she seemed little more than a dream. Chloe couldn't remember even one tag line or commercial, how to get to her house from the Tollway or even, distinctly, what the Tollway was. Little by little the twentieth century had faded, so much so that when she did get home— who knew?

Had RaEm traded places with her? It seemed likely. Cheftu had told a similar story of "merging" into someone else. If RaEm had, what had she done to Chloe's life?

"It is nearby," Cheftu growled in frustration, looking at the sea of silver sand around them. "I cannot mark it exactly, but we are here, southeast between Waset and the sea."

Chloe looked around, jerked back to the present. "Did Hatshepsut mention what kind of marker she set up?"

"Nay. She only mentioned the place once. I had never thought to come here, so I didn't ask for directions!" He was tense and snappish, but so was she.

"There is no need to take out your anger on me. We just have to think like Hatshepsut. Did she know the desert well enough to pinpoint her location by the stars?"

Cheftu snorted. "Nay."

"There must be something around here. A cenotaph, an obelisk, something." She started walking.

Cheftu kicked over his drawing and walked toward her. He touched her gingerly on the arms. "I apologize for my anger. It just seems we have come so far, to have achieved nothing."

"We just got here," Chloe said. "Let us get some sleep, then we will look things over tomorrow."

"Seal it with a kiss?" he asked, tilting her head back. He looked into her face with a faint smile. Then the humor faded from his features, and his eyes glowed with emotion. "I want so badly to hold myself away from you," he whispered. "I do not want the agony of our separation." He swallowed, his gaze dropping to her lips. "However, if we are going to be separate for always, I want to live now."

Chloe traced the lines of his face, gasping as his eyes closed in pleasure. He pulled her closer so that she felt his body beneath his kilt, smelled the earth and sun in his skin. He caught her hand and held it. "Have I told you how beautiful I think you are?"

"Never," Chloe said. "You have never told me."

"I have been a fool." His fingers trembled as they moved across her face, and his voice thickened. "I think the beauty of your *ka* far outshines the perfection of your face and figure. I love to see you straighten your shoulders to face a task. Your courage far outweighs the feel of your skin or the melody of your voice; I wept those days, though I had no tears, when they forced you to run behind the chariot.

"The nights you slept with a knife at your throat, yet you never let it truly frighten you." He looked up to the sky, speaking to the Unknown in which he believed. "Thank you for this woman! Her spirit holds me, her heart heals me! Thank you for giving her to me, if even for a little while." He choked and pulled her close, running his hands up and down her back as they stood in the hazy silver glow. "Please forgive me for wasting even one precious moment," he whispered against her shoulder.

He held her away, looking into her face, the words bubbling out of him. "*Je vous aime,* Chloe. I have missed you. You are my compatriot." He kissed her hands, and she was startled to feel his face wet. "You excite my body, entice my spirit. Your eyes shine with a life and enthusiasm in living that makes me awaken joyfully every day." He ran a finger over her lips. "From here I take the breath to sustain me, body and soul. I can live without food, endure without water, but only your kisses and words give my life color and flavor. These past weeks have been cold and tasteless." He bent to her, coaxing her heart into his body through lips, tongue, and hands. "You hold my heart, *chérie,*" he whispered.

Chloe was amazed at how much she desired him, dirty and exhausted as they were.

"*Je t'aime*, Chloe. *Je t'adore*," he whispered over and over, his hands seeking her body beneath her voluminous robe. Drunk on adrenaline, hungry for each other after weeks of nothing, he gathered her up and stumbled into the shadow of a sandstone cliff.

Frantically they tore at each other's clothes, murmuring endearments and taking the life from each other, their bodies asking and answering age-old questions, their hearts and souls intermingling with every whispered word and impassioned confession.

Thief stood guard in the moonlight, high up on the cliff's edge, his fuzzy bottom resting on a cartouche etched slightly into the stone.

WASET

THUT PACED THE SILENT ROOM, FUMING. How could there be no funds? "What about the priesthood of Amun-Ra?" he asked. "They were well provided for by my aunt. Surely they can donate a little for the sake of Egypt's protection?"

Ipuwer, his newest advisor, raised his scrawny arm for permission to speak, placating the new pharaoh. Thut grunted his consent. Ipuwer was a weasel, but he was somewhat meticulous.

Thut glowered; when the desert god had taken all of the firstborn sons, he had crippled Egypt for generations. The firstborn were the ones whom parents spared no expense in educating. They were the brightest because they received the most attention, the best of everything.

Now Egypt was being managed by idiots. Hardly a friend or confidant remained. Now that he thought about it, he was lucky to be alive. If his older brother had not died as an infant, then . . . then what? He would be in the same position, just now taking the throne and crown that had belonged to him for so long.

Ipuwer had stopped speaking several moments earlier, and the whole cabinet was watching Thut, waiting for a response to the half-witted second son's comments. Thut put hand to his head. Where could they get more gold? Egypt was destroyed. He must revive her and make her an empire. Empires feasted on gold, but one had to have it to get it.

He walked to the open balcony, staring onto the beauty of Karnak.

Gold-hammered doors, gold-covered floors, obelisks covered in electrum. To take any of it would be blasphemy, and with all the discontent in the land, that would be suicide. Not that the *rekkit* would be upset, but the priesthood and the nobles—they were the power in the country and had yet to accept Hat's death.

No body, no proof. So he was acting regent; everything would be done in her name for the next five Inundations, until she was declared dead. Unless he could find that cursed magus and wily priestess! He clenched his fists. They knew! They had seen something and had vanished into the wastelands of the Sinai.

He walked back into the chamber. "You are all dismissed," he growled.

Ipuwer raised his hand in supplication. "Does My Majesty desire to hear my poetry?" he asked. "Would it soothe you?"

Thut glanced down at the papyrus before the scrawny man. "What have you written?

Ipuwer smiled and began reading: *"The land spins as though on a potter's wheel. The towns are destroyed. Upper Egypt is a ruin. All lies wasted. Mourning does not cease, wailing will not be still. Plague reigns in Egypt and the Nile is blood. Every tree has been smote with hail. Nothing green lives, from the delta to the cataracts. The stones, columns, and walls of the cities are ash. Egypt dwells in a cloak of darkness."*

Thut felt his blood vessels bulge through his shoulders, chest, and abdomen as he clenched his fists. "What drivel is that?" he shouted.

Ipuwer took one look at the acting pharaoh and grabbed his papyrus, backing wildly toward the door. "Just a record of past days, Majesty," he warbled.

"Destroy it!" Thut bellowed. "Tear it, burn it, then bury the ashes!"

Ipuwer shuddered and left.

Forcing himself to calm down, Thut sprawled on a chair. He needed to go to his pottery room, maybe even take a dancer with him. Either sex or ceramics should calm and replenish his soul.

A pity they could not replenish his coffers.

Night had fallen. Thut wondered if he would ever feel safe again, watching the sun go down. Deep inside was a fluttering fear that it wouldn't rise and he would spend the rest of his days like a jackal, scouring the earth under the moon. He looked down into the garden . . . Hatshepsut's garden.

The men, the second and third and fourth sons, had tried to restore some of its beauty, clearing the pools and refilling them, training new vines to grow as the old had done, sweeping the porticos and replastering the walls. It retained a haunted feel, waiting for a mistress who would never return. Thut turned into the rooms—his rooms as pharaoh.

He hated them, the overdone decor and everywhere, everywhere, Hatshepsut's face! They would be torn down soon and melted, probably into plating for his new chariot.

Suddenly overwhelmed with all he had to do to restore Egypt, he put his head in his hands. He had to rule in her name unless someone testified to the priesthood and nobles that she was dead. The fools were still waiting, along with the families of her soldiers, for a communication to tell them where she had chased the Israelites. It was unfathomable that so many people would just disappear—that there would be nothing left.

Unfathomable, just like the past seasons. Ipuwer's words came to mind: *All lies wasted. . . . Plague reigns in Egypt and the Nile is blood.* It would be five years before he became Thutmosis III, living forever!, wearing the double crown he had coveted for so long. Five years before he would have the authority to start healing his bleeding, bludgeoned land. Yearning rose within him. His gods were dead, but there was one who lived on . . . triumphant. Unbidden, a prayer spilled from his lips: "Just let me rule . . . be a worthy pharaoh . . . restore my people . . . please."

MY LEG! CHLOE WOKE UP FRIGHTENED. Where is it? It's gone! She tried to move, but it was numb, dead. Genuine fear woke her fully. Then, when she saw the reason for her alarm, she exhaled so forcefully that Cheftu woke. Thief had curled up on her legs, as he used to do as a cub. However, unlike the two of them, he had gained weight and size in the intervening months, and his raw muscle and bone were deadening her circulation.

When Cheftu stopped laughing and actually helped, they were able to push Thief off, despite his unhappy cries. "Overgrown house cat?" she asked Cheftu, breathing hard after freeing herself. He smiled and shook his head.

Chloe opened her seed package and took one with the water from her water skin. "I am glad there is this cliff for shade," she said. "Ra is already punishing this morning."

"Aye," he agreed, drinking after her.

The thought struck them at the same time. This was the only cliff for *henti* and *henti*. A natural marker.

• • •

The sun was setting by the time they found the passageway. A deep well had been sunk into the ground, and after some finagling they had refilled their skins and washed off a little of the sand. After walking around and searching almost every square cubit of the rock, they found the steps. As they shoveled the sand with their hands, Chloe finally understood the all-consuming thrill of knowing you were about to discover something incredible. No wonder Cammy loved this!

The steps led under the rock, the last few actually a ladder of sorts, carved into the wall. It was a narrow passageway, and Cheftu grunted as his shoulders scraped, squeezing through it. Once below, they lit torches. It was a plain, dark room, the ceiling low. They crouched, moving the torch to find the other exit. They searched the floor, the walls.

Chloe called Cheftu to her side, and they saw a faintly carved ladder leading up, through a small crevice, into the ceiling. Chloe went first, grateful for the weight loss that made it slightly less painful to squeeze through. She took the torch from Cheftu and held it out. "Oh, Cheftu!" she gasped.

"What? What do you see?"

Then, like a discoverer before her, she said, "Gold. Everywhere the glint of gold."

• • •

With some extra chipping at the ceiling, they got Cheftu through. They sat there, struck mute by all they saw. A few more torches showed them they were in a long corridor: the corridor of a great pharaoh's tomb.

It was haphazardly done, though, not intended for use any time soon. The walls were drawn, but only half painted. The sky that stretched the length of the ceiling was painted blue, but only in one corner were the gold stars picked out. Carved into the sandstone were columns, one-sided versions of the HatHor-headed columns at Hatshepsut's mortuary temple in Deir El-Bahri, the-Most-Splendid. The same graceful sweep of ramp, building up into the rock above, proclaimed Senmut as architect.

Gold was everywhere, a pharaoh's ransom. It looked as though someone had dumped off her belongings: gilded chairs and small tables, heaped with painted and enameled trunks, filled with the clothes Hat had worn since birth.

They continued up the passageway, stopping before an enormous wall painting, fully finished and beautiful in its longing. A man and wife stood in their garden, his arm around her waist, holding a lotus to her nose. They looked out at gamboling children playing with geese and monkeys, their youthlocks swinging in the breeze of the garden. A huge sycamore wrapped all the way around the garden, from the waterfowl in flight to the delicately painted fish swimming in the pool, protecting and embracing. It was from the heart of a man who had had everything except a family life with the woman he loved. Hat was dressed in a fluted, transparent linen sheath; only the ankh in her long fingers and the vulture headdress atop her finely braided black hair gave clues to her position.

Senmut had painted himself with enormous modesty, allowing for the age around his eyes and the slightly peasant features of his face and ears. He was dressed finely, but it was his jewelry that was the most detailed. He wore a long pectoral, and by holding the torch high, Chloe and Cheftu could read the words painted by the side of the Eye of Horus: "Protect my brother from harm; save his soul on the Shores of Night; that which he did wrong, he did for me. Weigh his heart and find it pure."

"She took eternal responsibility for his transgressions," Cheftu whispered. "She loved him for all time, into the hereafter."

"I bet that necklace is here," Chloe whispered, her throat choked with tears.

"Aye," Cheftu said, drawing her close. Breaking away from the enchantment of the painting, they followed a short flight of stairs up to the burial antechamber. It was mostly empty; a lot of the drawings were done but still unpainted. Cheftu estimated they were slightly above-ground, inside the rock. "This is incredible," he said. "I knew Senmut was brilliant, but this is genius, pure genius."

They hit the jackpot.

Turning away from several still uncut false trails, they entered the burial chamber. For the first time in her life, Chloe understood the madness of gold. Her pulse increased, her eyes burned, and for a few minutes all she thought was about how much she could *take*. Cheftu positioned the torches, and they stared. Life-size statues stood in each corner. One was Anubis, his collar a mass of precious stones and his body carved from obsidian with such delicacy that the tendons in the jackal's shoulders were visible. Amun, HatHor, and Hapi stood in the other corners— Amun golden, HatHor in granite, Hapi of greenstone. Each was draped with jewelry and linen so fine that it looked spun from cobwebs.

At the opposite end of the room stood the gold-plated sarcophagi covers, each waiting for the granite one that would carry the body, before it was sealed inside the other and sealed inside again and again, like Chinese boxes for giants. There were at leave twelve full-size ushabti, their bodies covered in gold, their eyes onyx. There were altars covered in enamel, gold, and electrum. The dressing table that had been Hat's when she was a princess stood to one side, covered with makeup pots and dolls, flanked by matching stools.

Then they saw *it*, the object that if found, could set the modern world twirling like a gyroscope. Cheftu sat down, suddenly, in one of the many chairs. "She must have hidden it away from Thutmosis the First in his great anger and purge," he murmured, stunned.

Chloe knelt before it, reading the deeply etched cartouche at the base: "Hail, Horus-in-the-Nest, Prince Ramoses, Makepre, Mighty Bull of Ma'at, He-Who-Brings-Light, Favored Son of Aa-kheper-Ra Tehutimes, Thutmosis the First, Pharaoh, Living Forever! Life! Health! Prosperity!"

She looked into the face of Moshe, prince of Egypt, deliverer of Israel. She touched the gold arm, each muscle hammered in carefully, the dark eyes rimmed in black, the collar of turquoise, lapis, and gold resting, a separate piece, on the broad golden shoulders.

He was life-size, taller than most men, stepping forward with his left leg in perfect pharaonic style, his left hand grasping the Ankh of Life, his right holding the Feather of Truth. He wore the blue helmet of the army, the cobra and vulture jutting forward proudly, defending the body of the Hope of Egypt.

The artist had been true to Moses' form; his nose was sharper than most Egyptian sculptures, the chin more pointed, the eyes deep-set.

Since the statue itself was gold, the kilt was inlaid lapis lazuli, each piece fitting exactly with its partners, laid at varying degrees and angles to give the illusion of pleats. The sash was an actual gold leather strip, its edges embroidered and beaded. The tassels on the ends were uneven, but the cartouche of his name was beautifully stitched. Chloe touched it and, marveling at its softness, turned it over. She gave a shocked squeak. Cheftu joined her, and together they stared at the childish hieratic note embroidered inside: "To my half-brother, Ramoses. May the gods bless you and please remember to feed my pony." And then, meticulously written out in full hieroglyphs: "Hatshepset, Second Princess of the Great House."

"She must have almost died when she saw him in Avaris," Chloe whispered, unable to take her eyes off the statue.

Cheftu led her away, and they walked through an aisle between heaping piles of treasure: throwing sticks, arrows, and bows; quivers inlaid with precious stones; game boards with faces painted on the pieces, some ridiculous, some endearing; fans, flails, whisks, sandals, makeup boxes, trunks of linens; baskets filled with dried foods; dates, raisins, waterfowl jerky; cases of beer and wine, the cartouche and date from Senmut's house.

Before them was an enormous bed, with graceful lotus cut into the feet and posts, draped in linens so soft that they felt like tissue. Two headrests lay on it, one in ebony, engraved with the cartouche of Hat, one in simple wood, unadorned but well used.

It was like a honeymoon after a plane crash—the lovers were gone. The things were beautiful but unused, full of futile hopes. For hours they wandered through, picking up things, admiring the handiwork, and then laying them down. The bodies, for which Hat and Senmut had so carefully prepared, were gone. Their souls might still wander, but this artistry was pointless.

It was too much, too poignant.

She met Cheftu's teary gaze. "Out?"

Taking torches, they walked back the way they'd come, squeezing through the tight holes barring their return. At last they stood in the bare chamber, clean and empty except for the extra rock on the floor and the empty water jugs. They crawled back up the ladder, breathing deeply of the clean air, and were more than a little surprised to see the sun up and blazing.

Cheftu was last out, and he doused the torches with sand, then threw them back down, closing the passage behind them. The sun was hot, but the heat brought sweat, and with a stab Chloe realized it felt good—after being in a place of pointless death, it was a comfort to feel moisture on her skin . . . the dead didn't sweat. They retreated in silence to the shade, content to hold and caress each other as they watched the life of the desert. Thief rolled in the sand, chased the few birds, and then ran to the nearby grasslands, seeking his supper.

Chloe leaned against Cheftu's chest, feeling the cement of their skin together, watching the brilliant blue of the sky, listening to the seven-toned cry of a hawk as he plunged to the earth, grabbed some small animal in his talons, and wheeled away, higher and higher into the blue. The days were much cooler, the colors sharper, than a month ago.

"What day do you suppose it is?" Chloe asked, laying her head against Cheftu.

"I do not suppose, I know. I have kept count since the day we left Imhotep. It is Tybi, about October the eighth or ninth. Time for planting."

"So we leave the drawings here and go to Noph?" she asked, hoping not to get an answer.

"*Exactement,*" he said, kissing her hair. "We must be careful; the *rekkit* are returning to rebuild after the Inundation, and there will be a lot of scribes counting to ascertain what the people will pay for taxes."

"How do they know before the harvest?"

"By the level of the Nile. There are elaborate charts that detail how much yield from each field in each province, and also what they will plant next season."

"Do you miss your home?"

He kissed her head again. "What? Miss sleeping on a couch, clean kilts, a steam shave, bathing, and fresh food? Whatever for?"

She joined his rueful laughter. "Nay, I meant working with the grapes, or with medicine, those kinds of things."

He sighed. "I have not thought about it. It would be torture to long for that which you cannot have, *haii?*"

They sat silently, watching the day come to a close, the sky darken to a deep lapis, the calls of the animals as they either woke for the night or settled into sleep.

"What will you do when you return?" he asked quietly.

Chloe tensed. She didn't want to return, not anymore, not without

Cheftu. However, she had been told clearly *to* return, and Cheftu had not volunteered to join her. "I . . . do not know. My sister must have been so upset this past year; I am afraid it will even be more disturbing to have me back. I wonder how I will change back to the way I really look."

"You do not look like this?" Cheftu asked, startled.

"Nay. I look about as different as HatHor from Sekhmet."

"*Haii?* Like what?" His words were casual, but he was tense with curiosity.

Chloe responded as if automatically. "Oh, you know. Long gray hair, hook nose, little piggy eyes, and a hunchback. Not bad for an eighty-four-year-old woman." She spoke in English, and laughed aloud when Cheftu's mental translation was complete. Poor man, he was trying to decide whether or not she was serious.

"This is a farce, correct? Besides, you cannot be older than mid-twenties, which is still pretty old." He sounded nervous.

She laughed in indignation and turned to him. "Twenty-four is not old. You, however, are what, thirty-one?"

"Aye, but I am a man. What did you look like?" he said, dismissing her huff at his sexist comment.

"My coloring is different, that is all. I have the same features, the same body . . ."

"*Assst,* well, I am very glad about the body," he said, touching his more favorite parts. "Were you a blonde, a brunette?" he whispered as he nuzzled her neck.

Chloe gasped out, "A redhead, actually. . . ."

"With skin like ivory. . . ."

"White, definitely white." More like a dead chicken, she thought.

"May I introduce a new flavor?" he whispered into her ear.

Blood pounded through her as she turned in his arms to kiss him. "I think we might go for a sundae."

"A Sunday?"

She nipped his earlobe. "Not the day of the week. It is an ice-cream special."

"What makes it special?"

She gasped at the feel of his hands, rough against her bare skin. "Three flavors, syrups, and nuts."

"Three?" He pulled back, startled.

"Of course if you cannot——?"

"Of course I can," he commented, folding her legs. "I just clarified. I can do three."

"Cheftu? I, oh, I want them all to be . . . different."

• • •

The days at Hatshepsut's empty mausoleum were like a honeymoon. They sat in the sun in the morning, holding hands and enjoying the peace of life, no one pursuing them, no wounds, not starving. It was a nice change, to put it mildly. They made love in the heat of the day and slept away the afternoon. At dusk one or both of them went hunting with Thief, then shared their dinner over the fire. There was a nearby pride, and sometimes Thief hunted with them, trailing behind the lioness and her cubs.

Lost weight was regained, energies restored; and then the day came. They had to leave. Together they walked through the tomb once more, marveling at Hatshepsut's beautiful things, standing in awe before the statue of Moses, then down and into the entry room. They sealed over the opening, and Cheftu pressed his private seal as an *erpa-ha* of Egypt into the wet plaster. Chloe tried to remember what Cammy had said about how the scrolls were found, and when they walked past two enormous water jars in the hallway, she knew that the final piece was in place.

They looked through all the drawings again, and Chloe wondered if, or under what circumstances, she would see them again. With silent prayers they rolled up the scrolls, leaving the largest wrapped around the back, making it the easiest to unroll. The Exodus scroll. They leaned the jars up, brushed away their footprints, and ascended into the light once more.

As Cheftu disappeared over the top of the makeshift ladder, Chloe told him to wait a moment. Taking the last torch, she went to the opposite wall, the passageway up to where Hatshepsut's treasure house was. Kneeling in the dust, she painted her fingertip with kohl and drew her cat logo and a ladder. Ladders on tomb walls were common; they symbolized climbing to Osiris. They also meant "to move upward." Maybe it would be the proof she'd need in the twentieth century. "Look up, Cammy," she murmured.

Once she was out, Cheftu moved the rocks back to hide the opening, and they took their lightened baskets and began the walk toward Waset.

Cheftu would not let Thief go with them. They had argued for days. Cheftu said Thief was not afraid of humans, and that would get him killed. Chloe suggested a zoo. Cheftu said the nearby pride had no male lions; he could have a family. Chloe said he was a kitten and wasn't interested in females yet. Cheftu said they couldn't protect him.

Chloe burst into tears. "He saved our lives! We cannot just leave him here, alone and forsaken!"

"So we take him into Waset? What then, Chloe?"

"Nay . . ." She rubbed her eyes, sore from her tears. Deep inside she knew Cheftu spoke the truth. She also knew what he wasn't saying. *They wouldn't be here.* He would be in nineteenth-century France, and she would be in twentieth-century America, and Thief would be a memory. Would they become only memories for each other? Was she also mourning Cheftu?

"I just cannot bear to watch."

"Chloe . . ." Cheftu pulled her close. "Thief has guided us, rescued us, and helped us."

"He has saved our lives," she repeated, tears streaming down her cheeks.

"Aye. It is time to do the same for him."

She bit her lip and nodded. "I know. It just hurts so bad. I do not want him to feel unloved." She looked at the cat, sitting a few feet away, engrossed in the process of his hourly bath. As though he felt her gaze, he trotted over and butted his head against her leg. "Do you understand, boy?" she whispered brokenly. "We would not leave you, but we cannot take you with us."

He settled on the ground, his heavy head lying on her thigh. His eyes were closing, and he purred as she stroked his fur. Cheftu, in the process of petting Thief's neck, slipped a flax rope around it, then staked him to the stone. Thief would be able to get free, but only after they were long gone. Then the smell of people and towns would mask them.

"Why do we have to do this?" Chloe said. "It is horrible!"

"He's followed us from the Sinai, *chérie.* Do you think telling him 'no' would make him stay? If he gets any closer, he will be hunted. This is the only safe place, which is why the pride is here."

"He will be lonely."

Cheftu petted the lion, who was rolling on the earth, delighted with the attention, seemingly unaware of his fate. "He will mate from the pride. He is a lion, not an overgrown house cat."

Chloe cried harder, and they sat in the dirt, playing with Thief until he fell asleep, warm in the sun. Then Chloe rose, unable to bear any more. Thief didn't move. She put her hand on Cheftu's arm, pulling him up quietly. They stepped away, but Chloe halted after a few steps and looked back. The cat was free and alert, the end of the rope in his mouth, his furry bottom planted on the cartouche. He watched her with tawny eyes, and Chloe knew that he understood he was loved. She knew that he forgave her and he understood. A frisson ran up her back. *Generations of lions,* she remembered. He won't be alone. "Cheftu?"

Her husband turned, his golden eyes filled with tears. "He knows to stay, beloved. He knows to stay."

So the lion, guardian angel of them and the scrolls since the beginning, now heeded a higher call to stay and continue protecting: a golden sentinel to the secrets of God. The noble fuzzy knight of a hidden crusade. The first of many. . . .

•••

After three days of walking, they reached the outskirts of Waset. Choosing a poorer section of town, they rented a small room. Only Cheftu went out, seeking information on a ride downriver. They ate what he bought on the street. One night after dinner, when the waterfront taverns were filling with customers, Cheftu decided to contact Ehuru.

"You cannot! Are you insane? Thut has probably had your house under surveillance for weeks!" Chloe said.

He put on his cloak. "Do you think they will notice a man with a beard, and hair like a woman, to be a prince of Egypt? I cannot stay here—inactivity is driving me mad!"

"What if you get caught?"

He froze, then turned to her slowly, his amber gaze devoid of emotion. "It is no matter. From here you just wait three more days, take up passage on the *Flying Oryx,* and sail to Noph. Imhotep helped us piece together most of the formula, so you can return to your own life. And leave me."

She got up and walked across the small room to him. "Do you think I want to go?"

Quiet breathing filled the room. "Nay. You vowed to stay with me. I know only God could make you break your vow."

Chloe bit her lip. "It is not my fault!"

"Nay, I know. I do not understand, but I know you would have stayed if you could have." He held her close. "I just cannot imagine life without you, Chloe," he said, touching his finger to her chin. "It is too much to ask for me to take you to Noph, to send you away. That is a love too pure for my soul. Do not make me take you there, please. . . ." His voice trailed off, a plea for mercy.

She couldn't yield. "I will not miss these days with you, beloved," she said softly. "They are all I will live with. Give me golden days, Cheftu, please."

Chloe felt him trembling as he hugged her. "You ask for life, but to give you my death would be easier," he whispered. Chloe stiffened, and he felt it and held her more fiercely. "You know I would never deny you anything. If it is in my power to make you happy"—he looked at her— "I will do it. However, you must allow me the peace of mind to check my home here, those I have loved who deserved better than my forgetfulness." He was determined.

She sat on the flea-ridden couch, listening to his steps retreat. "Oh, Cheftu!" she whispered before the tears came, drowning her halved heart.

THE WATCHER STOOD IN THE DARKNESS of this street of sycamores. The beauty that had once belonged to it was gone. The trees had been eaten by the locusts, though several were striving to bring forth new leaves. The gardens that were hidden behind mud-brick walls were dried and dusty, the water having been used in the fields. Egypt was destroyed. Famine was certain this year and probably for years to come.

The watcher ran a hand over his face, trying to blot out the picture of his young son, stricken, despite the amulets and entreaties to the gods his father served so well. He took a drink from the flagon at his side.

It was wine. He would never have drunk wine while on duty before, but his job was pointless. As was his life. He thought of the grieving woman he lived with, her outbursts of manic energy, her despairing wails that lifted from the courtyard up to his room. He'd offered to make another child, and she had thrown a bottle at him. He touched the still-healing cut on his brow. Glowering, he took another drink.

The sliver of a moon was setting; it was only an hour or so until morning. The wind sang through the bare branches, cooling his nervous sweat. The watcher saw the old man Ehuru take his light and go into the small quarters adjoining the main house. It had been like this for weeks. Ehuru shopped the sparse market stalls and prepared every day as if he expected the return of the *hemu neter*, Cheftu. The watcher rubbed his face, feeling the warmth of the wine lick at his senses. His eyes were almost closed.

Then he heard a sound and was alert, his black stare searching the darkness. Down the street came an Apiru. He was wearing the brief kilt of a slave and had long hair and a skimpy beard. He walked like a young man, and his body was fit, but his beard and hair were gray, his skin dry like papyrus. The watcher clung to the shadows, observing with interest. The slave carried two jugs of beer, and although the watcher did not recognize his face as that of a slave in this area, the weary, plodding steps were something he did recognize.

No doubt one of the fine young lords had sent him out to fetch beer for guests to have with the Perfuming. The watcher was just turning, until he saw the man look into the light.

Eyes like a cat. Gold.

Thutmosis' words seared into his mind. This was Cheftu! He was returning under the guise of an Apiru! Praise Amun! The watcher waited until Cheftu had passed and then ran on fleet feet to the palace, the wine diluted with his enthusiasm. Thank the gods he had not looked away!

THE DISTURBANCE WAS SLIGHT, but Cheftu felt it. No doubt the many soldiers camped out around his home had also. Hefting the jars onto his shoulder, he looked around, as though he were reluctant to go back to his duties inside. His eyes focused on the tree shadow, and he saw a flask beneath it. So that was where the spy had hidden.

Cheftu walked around the gates, back to the slave quarters of his own estate. He climbed over the crumbling fence, taking in the ruined gardens. It was worse than the destruction at Gebtu. Silently he crept across the dusty path and up to Ehuru's door. The sounds of the old man's snoring came back, loud and clear.

Cheftu lowered the jugs and listened carefully. He had not seen the soldiers, but he was almost positive they were there. He stepped inside and crossed the small rooms quickly. Laying a hand on Ehuru's mouth, he called in a loud whisper for the man. Ehuru struggled briefly before he recognized the hand covering his mouth.

"My lord!" the old man harumphed. "Why are you here? Soldiers ask for you daily!"

Cheftu held up a hand for silence; then, barely breathing the words, he spoke of the last few months. The old man sat, absorbed, and listened to his lord tell of the actions of the desert god and of the soldiers. "I wanted to be certain you were taken care of. There is gold there." He handed the old man a scroll. "Hidden beneath the altar in my parents' mortuary temple is a large urn. It is filled with gold. Take that which you need, Ehuru. I have also taken some. When you have memorized this map, destroy it. I bid you the gods' blessings."

He embraced the old man, not mentioning that the deed to the house was made out to him and that Makab's steward had his emancipation papers. The letter in the tomb would explain all. He kissed the worn, leathery cheeks. "You must begin to snore again, my friend," he said with a smile as he crawled out the high window.

Cheftu landed on the ground and rolled into the bedraggled bushes. For moments he lay, listening for the shout of soldiers and the sound of running feet. Nothing. Getting to his feet but still keeping to the shadows, he crept down the street, jogging lightly when he reached the main road. Dawn was just breaking. He ran to the waterfront and awakened the old man who'd rowed him across the Nile twice tonight. With a toothless smile the old man picked up one oar and Cheftu the other as they cast off into the chilly light of morning.

One more stop.

THUTMOSIS WALKED ALONG THE DOCK, watching the ships load. He was dressed like any other soldier, his eyes peeled for the former magus and his heartless priestess-wife. He knew they were in Waset. He'd not bothered pulling Ehuru out of his couch; Thut knew he would never say a word. At this point he had no desire to kill more Egyptians. But he knew Ehuru knew.

He wished he knew where the priestess and magus were going. They had come back, probably for some more funds and a chance for . . . what?

Thirteen ships were leaving for Noph today, six of those going on to Zarub and Avaris, one to the Great Green. The tales he had heard verified that Kallistae and Keftiu had been swallowed by the sea overnight. So even there would be no escape; they would have to return. Thut smiled to himself. He had stationed five soldiers at each ship. They were to check eye color and pull aside any who matched the description his watcher had given.

CHEFTU AND CHLOE STOOD IN THE SHADOWS, watching the soldiers swarm on the docks. They were checking every man and woman. How many more days was Thut going to do this? He'd also assigned soldiers to those caravans that went west. Even the little skiffs that commuted from east to west banks were searched every trip. He had drawn a net tightly, and Cheftu had no idea how they could escape. Not honorably.

The days were running out . . . it was more than a two-week trip to Noph in the best of conditions. Cheftu couldn't promise they would have them. He pulled Chloe away, and they began to walk back to their boarding house. The landlady was becoming suspicious, and Cheftu knew they would have to leave her soon . . . or start bribing her with jewelry, which bore his name and nome.

"Go back to the room," he whispered. "I am going to ask around the docks for someone who would do a short jaunt to Gesy or Nubt, the next towns on the river."

She raised her green eyes to him. "You are not going to do anything stupid, are you, Cheftu?"

He smiled, his eyes hidden by the drape of his headcloth. "*Assst*, Chloe. Be safe and I will bring you a treat tonight."

"You do not have to bribe me, I am not a child. But if you are volunteering could you get me some more paint? I am out of red for my painting."

Cheftu stood silently for a moment, watching the soldiers over her shoulder. "Of course. Go now."

Chloe slipped away from the dock and stepped into a shaded street, the sun blazing overhead. Though taller than most everyone, she blended in with her brown skin, black hair, and rough white clothing. As she felt an iron grasp around her rib cage and over her mouth, she realized she must not have blended in enough. She struggled briefly before her oxygen supply faded and the black spots before her eyes engulfed her.

THUT LOOKED UP FROM HIS NOON MEAL, his soldier's senses warning him of danger. Dismissing the fan boy, he reached for his dagger, then walked toward the balcony of his room.

An Apiru slave knelt on it. The man raised his eyes, and Thut had to bite back the startled comment that rose in his throat. Cheftu's eyes glittered, and Thut saw he had a blade positioned over his chest—ready to plunge it in. "You challenge a lot to come here, Cheftu," Thut said. "Do not bother to kill yourself. I will see that it is done for you."

"If you do, my secrets will die with me."

"Which secrets, Cheftu? The ones about Alemelek? Or the languages in which you write? Or how you can disappear into a desert wasteland and reappear in Waset?"

Cheftu watched him, body tensed like a cat. "Nay, Prince. Or should I call you 'Pharaoh, living forever!' now? I know what happened at the Red Sea. I also know with no body and no witness that Hatshepsut, living forever's position as pharaoh is solid as the Pyramids. It will be five Inundations before you can wear the double crown you have coveted for so long."

"It is my crown!" Thut hissed. "I have served Egypt, and even the desert God of the Israelites has seen fit to give it to me! I do not need anyone's approval. I will crown myself!"

"To do that, you will need gold."

Thut's eyes narrowed. "Do you know of such gold?"

"Aye. A pharaoh's coffers."

Thut's body stiffened. "I will not rob the dead."

Cheftu quirked an eyebrow. "Even the unburied dead?"

"You saw what happened and did not have the decency to bury her?" Thut's voice rose incredulously. "What gods do you serve?"

Cheftu's face froze. "I serve the one God."

His comment fell into an echoing wadi between the two men. Thut stared at him with black, wary eyes. Thut stepped toward him, and

Cheftu pressed the blade tip into his skin. It was not cutting, but the pressure was there. "Do not move closer, Thutmosis. I will destroy myself rather than tell you my secrets before my desires are accomplished."

Thut stopped.

Cheftu's hand was steady.

"What do you want? I doubt a wily magus would step into my chambers unless there was another motive."

"I want RaEm back."

"Back?" Thut asked, surprised. "Are you saying she left you for some other fool? Really, Cheftu, how many times will you let this woman unman you?"

Cheftu's jaw clenched, the muscles working, "Are you claiming you do not have her? That you did not take her hostage so I would reveal myself?"

Thut straightened his shoulders. "I am a soldier. I do not take women hostage. I fight men, like a man. There is no honor in taking your woman. I had almost caught you anyway. Now, back to this gold—despite my not having RaEm, do not think you can leave here without telling me where it is."

Cheftu's eyes narrowed, his gaze intent. "Here is my bargain: In exchange for my witnessing to Hatshepsut's death, RaEm is to be allowed to travel to Noph and live there in safety and unknowing peace."

Thut stepped back, watching Cheftu, wondering about other things the man had said. "More."

"What?"

"It will take more. I need gold and you know where it is." Thut smiled coldly. "Give it to me and you can both go and live anywhere beyond the red and black lands, so long as I never hear from you again."

Cheftu swallowed. "Gold. Gold you want and gold you shall have, but not unless you help me find RaEm *today* and let us go free until after the twenty-third of Phamenoth. RaEm will be allowed to pass safely up the Nile, to Noph, and live there until after the twenty-third of Phamenoth. You will not stop us or hinder us in any way?"

"I let you stay together in this time?"

"Together."

"Then, after this date, you will be mine? Your magic, your power . . . your knowledge? The gold?"

Cheftu watched him steadily. "Aye. It will all be yours, all that is mine to give."

Thut looked at the man, threatening to kill himself for what was apparently the love of a women. "I wonder if this tarnished priestess is worth it, Cheftu? To bring an *erpa-ha* of Egypt so low?"

Cheftu ground his teeth. "Safety until after the twenty-third?"

"Agreed."

"You swear by . . . ?"

"By Amun-Ra and the seven stages of the sacred priesthood of Amun!" Thut spat out angrily.

Cheftu smiled coolly. "I vow that if you do not keep your promises, the one God will destroy you." His voice was soft but deadly. "You have been allowed to go on with your life, but these are again things you should not change. Swear on your crown, Thut! That is what you hold most dear!"

"I swear, curse you, I swear! I also swear that if you are lying to me, I will torture you and your slattern of a wife, for pleasure! I will paint a tomb of those scenes, and you will both live through them for eternity!" Thut's face burned with his rage, and his fists were clenched. "Now, get out, Cheftu, while I still think I need your information. But before you go, give me proof of Ha . . . her tomb. I want to see the gold! I want to be sure you are not lying!"

Cheftu stood and walked within a cubit of Thut. "I have nothing to give you, but this I did see. There is a statue of a fallen prince, his cartouche that of Horus-in-the-Nest during the time of your grandfather. It is perfection: gold and precious jewels, an exacting likeness of the man."

Thut's face paled as he stepped back, stunned. "Hatshepsut and my father argued over that statue once. My aunt-mother had hidden it behind an altar, and my father had it moved. The statue was there." His voice was monotonous, his eyes seeing his father, Thut II, and his reluctant consort, Hatshepsut, as they fought over the statue of a handsome young prince, whose cartouche young Thutmosis could barely decipher." He blinked rapidly. "You tell the truth in this." He stared off for a moment, coming to grips with the reality. "Now, come sit and we can discuss like civilized men who could have your wife." Thut took a chair. "I owe you a debt of honor. I want to repay it."

Cheftu was wary but confident that Thut would keep his word. He was also desperately anxious for aid. Gambling Hat's gold was the only thing he could think to do. Of course, he would kill himself before he showed Thut the location, for the scrolls could not be endangered. He would return to France, and they would stay safe in Egypt. If he did not return to France, Thut still would never get the location out of him. Lying was without honor, but Chloe's life was worth more than honor to him.

"No one even knows we are alive," Cheftu said. "Most of the people we knew are no longer living, either. RaEm had no gold, but a few witnesses on the street recalled a . . . a woman taken by another woman. A huge woman, with tattoos." He looked at Thutmosis. "It sounds like a Sekhmet priestess, though I did not know they had a temple here in Waset."

Thut's expression was blank. He walked toward one of the few enameled boxes containing his clothes and jewelry. He rummaged through it impatiently and then turned, a gold necklace in his hand. "Cheftu, when I . . ." He sighed. "That priestess who was sacrificed during the plague of darkness, you were surprised to see her. My guards reported you said she was much younger than you had thought."

Cheftu pursed his lips. "Aye. She had been a sister-priestess to RaEm since birth. She was twenty-four Inundations, but . . . she looked younger."

"Haii," Thut said, pacing. "Do you know the name 'Basha'?"

Cheftu rose to his feet. "Aye. She was RaEm's handmaiden most of her life. She was raised in the temple, but had an insignificant birth date, so could not serve as a priestess." He didn't add that she was also the one who had likely poisoned RaEm. "She disappeared one night."

"I doubt she did," Thut said, holding out his hand.

Cheftu took the necklace, then handed it back. "Where did you find this?" he asked.

"The Temple of HatHor in Avaris."

Cheftu's eyes automatically went back to the gold. "But it is . . ."

"I know. This Basha was the wrong priestess, yet ReShera is gone."

"ReShera stood to inherit RaEm's position and power. She was born a few hours too early," Cheftu mused. "She hated RaEm and thought she was poisoning the priesstesshood. Not to mention RaEm's relationship with Phaemon."

Thut looked at him. "I could never get her to speak to me. How do you know these things?"

Cheftu looked away. "Another priestess talked. Not RaEm. . . ." He stood, embarrassed.

Thut's mouth curved in a sly grin. "When did you speak to another priestess? They are usually sequestered away with duties."

"The fowling party," Cheftu said. "She was very, um, willing to share, under the right circumstances. I knew RaEm was in serious danger. I had to know from whom." His gaze held Thut's. "Do you think ReShera has her?"

Thut shrugged. "What of it? It is within her right as a fellow priestess." He held up a hand at Cheftu's darkening anger. "I have made a promise to you and will keep it. We shall go see."

"ReShera follows Sekhmet, I think. Do you know where the temple is?"

"I am Pharaoh. But do not forget the price, Cheftu. Your life, your knowledge, and the gold."

"Aye, My Majesty."

CHAPTER 19

Chloe threw away the braided grass, and it landed in a pile with the other hundred pieces she had picked out of the darkness and laced together to keep her sanity. She had woken up in a dark, dank cell, and after a few hours of almost total fear, she had calmed down. It had taken hours to get the bindings off her wrists and ankles and another to untie the vicious knot holding on the gag. They had tied it into her hair! At least now she had freedom of movement. She touched her raw and bloody wrists. Her mouth still felt stretched from the gag. Chloe swallowed the last drop of spit she was able to muster, savoring the moisture against her dry tongue. Had it been days, or did it just feel that way?

She was so thirsty. Her tongue felt as swollen and dry as the cloth she'd had in her mouth. She sat still in the darkness, wondering what would come, what was the purpose to being here. The "other" was almost gone, the thoughts and traditions so embedded in Chloe's own mind that she didn't need the constant consultation. Still, she could have used the company. . . .

Chloe reached for more grass, automatically breaking it into three sections. Cheftu, oh God, she thought, please help me!

A noise in the corridor stopped her. Her only chance of escape would be to rush the jailer. The door opened slowly and Chloe crouched, her muscles protesting. An enormous Kushite woman held out a long spear, training it on Chloe's breast. She motioned forward and

Chloe rose, a cubit from impalement. Once outside Chloe was thrown against the wall and her wrists refastened. She moaned in pain as the new leather bit into the open wounds. Her eyes smarted as she was pushed forward, up the main hall of the temple.

Help me, she thought.

CHEFTU, THUTMOSIS, AND A SMALL CONTINGENCY of guards pushed through the sparse undergrowth to the side of the temple. It was mostly underground, the crumbling lioness statue half-hidden by vegetation.

Leaving the guards placed strategically, Cheftu and Thut walked through the dark hallways. Cheftu's perfect memory recalled the map he had once seen as a *sem*-priest, and he led them through the hypostyle hall, with its crumbling pillars, to the cross-passageway. Voices were audible behind them, and they stepped into the shadows moments before two huge women, pulling Chloe, came around the corner.

Thut's insistent hand on his arm was the only thing that kept Cheftu from leaping out and taking Chloe. Her face was creased with pain, and he saw her arms were behind her, tied at both the elbow and wrist, the way Pharaoh tied foreigners. The men followed at a distance. The sound of voices grew louder, and Cheftu realized with a start that they were singing about the glory of vengeance and blood. It was a horrible, archaic song, quite unlike the music he had heard during his years in Egypt.

Thut pulled Cheftu's arm and prevented him from walking into the main chamber openly. They crept around the edge, in the shadows of the columns. The singing had quieted down, and one of the priestesses was seated on a silver chair. She was dressed in a white robe and a Sekhmet headdress. Cheftu realized he had seen it and her before—at the Temple-of-the-Ka-of-Ptah, in Noph. She had been the incarnation of Sekhmet and had bitten RaEm's wrist, a bizarre ritual, he'd thought. This was why: she's mad.

They cut the bindings from Chloe's arms, and Chloe gasped as they pulled off the leather. Cheftu saw nothing but red for a few moments as he heard the priestess's chilling laughter—a response to Chloe's pain. Thut's hand was like rock on his forearm, and Cheftu knew they needed to listen. If there was corruption in the priesthood, Thut needed to clean it out. Cheftu ground his teeth in the darkness.

The figure on the chair stood up and walked forward. "My murdering priestess-sister," she said.

Cheftu and Thut exchanged glances; no one had prepared Chloe for ReShera's face when she pulled off the mask.

Chloe stepped back with a cry. "You live!"

ReShera laughed. "And you shall not, dear sister."

Chloe's face was white in the moonlight. "I do not understand."

"I doubt you do, RaEmhetepet," she said. "Until recently you never understood me. So I shall explain—it gives me such pleasure to watch you quiver before my eyes."

"Then who died?" Chloe asked.

ReShera stared. "What?"

"Someone died. I sent someone to her death. Who was it?"

ReShera's face became another mask, one bleached with hate whose black eyes brimmed with madness. "My beloved Basha."

It took a moment for ReShera's words to penetrate all those minds present, hidden and unhidden. "Beloved?" Chloe repeated.

"Aye. She had been mine since she was a girl! I shaped her, molded her, created her to be a creature to serve Sekhmet. I protected her from your violence!" ReShera hissed. "Only because of you is she gone. You, who would sleep with any rutting beast, except the prince! You, who stole my brother and took his life! You think yourself so much more valuable than any other! As did the goddess HatHor—but she is also weak. Better to serve the goddess Sekhmet. She devours her enemies! Takes their power that way! As I shall yours, priestess."

"How did you do it?"

ReShera looked confused, and Chloe repeated the question. "You were worshiping with us, yet Basha was sent? How did you do it?"

"I did not kill her," ReShera said stonily. "You murdered my beloved Basha. You did!"

"I did," Chloe agreed soothingly, in hopes of getting the truth. "How did I do it?"

"You slipped out of the temple and got her from the tunnels where she was staying. She was weak and hungry, and it was easy to get her to eat drugged food and change clothes. You walked her to the White Chamber and sat her down, then snapped the name necklace off her and put on your own. Then you heard the prince and ducked. Once he was violating Basha and you saw that she liked it, you were filled with anger and left. I have been playing dead all this time. Hatshepsut, living forever! was seeking a reason to eliminate you. She knew I was well."

ReShera smiled, an eerily beautiful woman who had stepped over the chasm into madness.

ReShera reached into her sash, then put her hand into her mouth, adjusting the silver extended-incisor mouthpiece. "So now I must take your power, RaEm, and give it to Basha. Do you know from what we gain power, RaEm?" ReShera asked conversationally, not waiting for an answer. "There are two ways. The contemporary way is to learn your secret name, then erase it." She smiled, a wide, predatory grin. "The other, more ancient way, is to drink your blood. Life flows through us in our blood. A permanent Inundation, if you will."

Chloe trembled. The revulsion she felt for the insanity in this room coursed through her veins. Bile filled her mouth, and with a grimace she pushed it back down. She must find ReShera's weakness, work from that. "So, you are going to kill me because you hold me responsible for the death of your lover? How can that be? Basha should not have even been there. She was not a priestess. I did not send her into Thutmosis, you did."

ReShera ignored her and continued her tirade. "You are responsible!" she shrieked. "For Basha's death and the destruction of Egypt! We needed a strong woman on the throne, but you worked behind her back, plotting her downfall, to put a man on the throne." Her words were venomous, ridiculing. "Then you murdered two guards of Sekhmet and entered into an unholy liaison with that man."

"What man?"

"The magus."

"Why did you make me miscarry?" Chloe asked calmly.

ReShera stepped close, her smile poisonous, wicked, and exquisite. "For my brother, Phaemon."

"Phaemon? Your brother?" The face from her nightmares flashed before her. A man, his eyes changing from passion to terror as a blade was pushed into his belly. Chloe almost felt the rush of hot blood over her hands. The smell... by the gods! She looked up at ReShera's face. The same cheekbones and wide winging eyebrows. The counterpart perfection of form.

"Aye. Phaemon, the soldier you seduced during one of your debauched revels with Nesbek. You killed him. You destroyed him so fully that night that he will never walk in the West!" ReShera's voice filled with tears, almost pitiful. "So it was fair you lose someone, too."

Chloe, overwhelmed by the revelation, shook her head as though to clear it. If she did not move quickly, her chance to jump ReShera would be gone. "When?" she asked ReShera.

"When? The night he met you in HatHor's chamber here in Waset! It was your assignation spot; in your depravity you defiled your role and your goddess by mating when you should have been praying! You are the reason the desert god won! You weakened Amun-Ra! I have the small satisfaction that Phaemon wounded you, because you were ill for days afterward."

Chloe stood in shock. The night she came through—the red on her hands, the familiar acrid smell, which even then was associated with fear. She had been covered in blood! Had RaEm killed the soldier before she switched places with Chloe? Assuming they had traded? Then where was the weapon? The body? If RaEm had gone into the future as Chloe, where was the missing soldier? Had he, or rather his body, gone into the future also? He was ReShera's twin . . . born on the twenty-third of Phamenoth. Was it possible?

"Because of the death you gave to Phaemon, you also will never walk in the West! I will pluck out your eyes! Sever your limbs! Scar that face and body you value so highly! I will drink your blood and feast on your heart! Do you know what I will do to your seat of pleasure? That ultimate vanity that has led you so far astray . . . ?"

ReShera was in Chloe's face, describing with unholy glee the future that awaited her, but Chloe dismissed the vitriol the woman was throwing at her, ignoring the spittle that landed in her hair and on her face. ReShera had a knife in her belt but nothing else, and she was so angry that she paid little heed to Chloe.

Chloe leapt, grabbing the perfect little body, snatching for the knife in the woman's sash. She held it to ReShera's throat, calling out to the guards. "You have heard the accusations of this priestess," she said. "I would not dare any of you to step forward and defend this woman." She twisted her hostage's arm behind her body, holding the knife at ReShera's throat. She called out, "Be wary. If indeed this story is true and I killed the brother of a fellow priestess with whom I shared my body, and in the Silver Chamber, on the most fearful night of the year, what other blasphemies could I commit?" Chloe smiled, hoping she looked at least half-mad.

"Drop your weapons." They did. "Lie down."

Cheftu and Thut sat in stunned, admiring silence, watching the battered woman take her hostage out. "I had no idea such abominations existed within the priesthood," Thut said slowly. "Cheftu, where is

Phaemon? Where is the body? Did your lover kill this man?" he asked quietly as they watched Chloe cross the room.

Cheftu thought rapidly; how could he explain? What had happened? "If they cannot find a body, how can she be accused of murder?" he whispered. "ReShera is mad. She drinks *blood.* She might have killed him and now wants to lay the crime at Ch . . . uh, RaEm's feet just as she tried to blame her for Basha's death."

As soon as Chloe left the chamber there was a stifled clatter of weaponry as the women followed her . . . and ran into Thut's guards. "I join my troops," Thutmosis told Cheftu. "Until the twenty-third, *neter.* And then I will have my answers."

Cheftu stalked Chloe into the dark rooms below. She opened one of the doors and threw in her struggling hostage, then slammed the door. There was no lock, so she wedged the knife through the latch and raced past him, up and out of the temple. He followed her, noting the soldiers who merged into the shadows as she passed. "The prince needs your assistance," he commanded them, and pointed to the chamber that held ReShera.

He wanted to speak, to embrace her, yet what could he say? He'd not helped her, but only watched as she'd fought bravely for her life. *She did not need him.* If he arrived at the boardinghouse before her, she need never know how he'd failed. He could say he'd hidden away from the soldiers and was unable to return home at night. After all, as a male priest it would be his death if anyone knew he'd been here. That was a feeble excuse. Cheftu knew he would never forget Chloe's courage as she'd accepted blow after physical and mental blow, then had rescued herself.

God had indeed chosen well.

THE SHIP PULLED AWAY FROM THE DOCK, heading to Noph. Chloe stretched as she reclined on the couch, facing the water. Thut had finally given up. Cheftu said he was nervous about the timing, uncertain whether they would get to Noph. But here they were, on the way, a night sailing, an impossibility without Cheftu's bribery.

Chloe looked across at him. They had settled for hiding in the open. Cheftu was shaved and trimmed, and though his clothes were not those of an *erpa-ha* any longer, they did fit the profile of a tradesman and his wife. He was talking to the garrulous old captain, and occasionally a snatch of their conversation drifted over to Chloe. She looked at the ghost white city as they glided by. Waset.

She would not see it in this time again.

How did she get there? What did she know? Apparently Luxor was the doorway in, and somewhere in the Temple-of-the-Ka-of-Ptah was the doorway out. One could not go "in" through the "out" door.

Would Cheftu go with her or try to return to France? Did anything still live there for him, or was it over and he eternally displaced? How could she travel to twentieth-century America and he to nineteenth-century France at the same time? Imhotep hadn't said there was a window of opportunity, though it stood to reason that with twenty-three of everything else, they would also need to be there in the twenty-third minute. Was that *only* the twenty-third minute, though? Chloe didn't know, but in less than a month she would find out.

She'd see Cammy again. Watch TV. Read papers.

And mourn. Deeper and harsher than even Mimi's passing would be the loss of Cheftu. The vision before her blurred. Cheftu . . . Perhaps he would tell her his full name and she could find his gravesite. A chill enveloped her. She didn't want to find his gravesite. She wanted him beside her. She wasn't cut out to be a tragic figure, to be part of a doomed love affair. So why was she here . . . preparing to be separated forever?

At least there was *something* she could take. She pushed away from the rail and walked over to her couch. She would provide Cammy with some more drawings and herself with a more lively memory.

The days would pass quickly now; pray God the nights would be slow.

CHEFTU WATCHED HER IN THE MOONLIGHT and for a moment just drank in the features and physique he knew and loved so well. Chloe glanced over her shoulder, then reached into the pouch at her waist and scattered something in the water. He moved closer as she methodically emptied the pouch. Stepping forward, he touched her shoulders, and after the initial surprise, she sank back against his chest. He nuzzled her neck, smiling at her mews of pleasure.

"What are you doing?"

"Watching the world go by."

Lips on her neck, he grabbed her fist and caressed it with his long fingers. "What are you throwing out to Sobek?" he whispered, his fingers gently prying hers apart. His attention sharpened when he felt the tiny seeds in her palm. He spun her around, looking at her in shock. "What are you doing? Why do you throw these away?"

"I no longer want to prevent a pregnancy," she said, meeting him face on. "Damn you, memories will be all I have! Why can I not have your child? Our child?" Her defiance turned into tears, and Cheftu looked up into the black sky. Once, this was all he'd wished for: this woman, better than any dream, and the days to watch their children grow.

He pulled her close. "It is not to be, *chérie.*"

"Why not?" she cried. "Why is this sacrifice necessary? Why can we not be together?"

"Haii-aii! Beloved, I wish I knew the answers, but I don't. However, you cannot make a child and raise it without two parents. It will be *un batârd,* a horrible future . . . no education, no decent marriage. I will not do this." He tilted her head back. "I am surprised you would."

"The world is different now," she said sulkily. "A bastard is your boss, not the child of an unmarried mother. Still . . . my family would be shamed. They are never going to believe this wild tale of an ancient world and the love we share." She began to cry again. "Why me? Why were we chosen to live this? I never asked to be wantonly used by God . . . I am not like you. I am not a puppet on a string."

Cheftu blanched in the moonlight. "You are not being wantonly used by God; you and I are tools, not puppets. You have made choices that led to this path. This may be your destiny, but like anyone else, you can turn away. God selected you because he knew your heart, your courage, and your tenacity." He dropped her hands and turned to the water gliding by, molten silver threads catching light and reflecting it, urging the ship forward.

"I do not know whether I even believe in God," Chloe said angrily. "He is cruel to give and take indiscriminately. I may not even fulfill this 'destiny.' " She watched Cheftu as if expecting and fearing his rejection.

At length he spoke, his heavy French accent almost obscuring the English words. "I have been in this land and time for fifteen years. I will turn thirty-two when you leave, and I will live the rest of my life . . . um . . . who knows how. I have sacrificed to idols, I have been inducted into five degrees of the seven in the priesthood of Waset. I have heard demons, I have seen people die from fear. I have absolved sins as if it were my right." He turned to her. "Once have I complained to God. Then I discovered that his plan was better. I did not understand at that moment, but time proved it true. Not because I am a good or righteous man, but because *le Dieu c'est bon.* He has given me life, friends, family in two centuries, health, my mind. Granted, it has not always been easy, but he has guarded me. Always, though, the choice of my reaction was mine alone.

"Our decisions create us, Chloe.

"I could have stepped back into time and traveled again. We have found most of the clues in these short days—I could have done the same earlier! I could have chosen madness or to kill myself or to rape, pillage, and murder. These are all things that are and were choices for me. Somehow God specifically picked me, Jean . . ." He stopped himself, then went on:

"Who I was is no matter. He knew how my heart would behave and placed me here. Why? To be, like any other time, a tool for him to use. A method of loving people with my arms, of serving people with my skills, of sharing with my heart. It matters little where I live—" He choked. "I would that it were with you, but that is not to be, not any way we can imagine." He sighed. "Still, that is no excuse for us to blame God."

He turned, his eyes shining. "We have had the most, Chloe! We have climbed the Pyramids, talked with pharaohs, seen the deliverance of God! He spared our lives, specifically, again and again and again! Think of it: we were not hit by the killing hail, we survived the desert, the soldiers, starvation, and thirst. If this is the price we pay, then so be it!"

"I—I do not understand your faith," she stuttered out. "I have never understood God that way." She swallowed. "I know the things we have seen, but I cannot truly believe in the hand you claim is behind it."

Cheftu took her clenched fist. "Do you believe in the sun?"

"Amun-Ra?"

He chuckled. "How Egyptian you have become, *ma chérie. Non.* The power of the sun. The rays, what they do."

"Of course. I can see the results."

"Haii! But if you did not . . . ?"

"It would not change things." They stood in silence for a moment. "I hate it when you do that," Chloe said tightly. "What were you a professor of, at age sixteen?"

"Of nothing specific. I taught about everything. Mostly languages."

"Were you as arrogantly correct then as now?"

"One cannot argue with truth. It alone gives freedom to dream and know. Though, aye, I was an arrogant brat!" He pulled her close. "I love you. I know you will let his work be done through you." He kissed her shoulder.

"Is that not emotional blackmail?" Chloe asked dryly.

He turned her face to his. He was perfectly serious. *"Non.* It is because I know the beauty of your soul. It is because I believe the best of you. It is because I know your God."

She turned in to his body, her voice choked with tears. "Then take me to bed, Cheftu."

"Do you have the seeds?"

She opened the pouch and sniffed. "Enough for ice cream five times a day from now till Christmas."

"Une provocation, ma chère?"

She kissed him, leaving him reaching for her as she walked to their pallet at the prow. "Aye. A challenge I trust you are up to?"

Cheftu grinned wryly and swung her into his arms. "Shall I let you judge that contest?"

•••

At Noph, the boat docked parallel to the other seven boats docked beside it. Chloe and Cheftu picked up their basket-woven trunks and followed through and over the many boats, a jumble of voices around them. They stepped onto the dock and turned immediately to the market.

A cacophony of sounds surrounded them: peddlers and vendors. As they walked through the marketplace, Chloe tripped on a package. She bent down and picked it up as she saw an old woman reaching for it—obviously the owner. Chloe extended it. When the crone raised her black eyes, Chloe felt an icy finger trace her spine. "This is yours, old mother?" The woman shook her head violently, denying it. "Please, is this yours?" Her bright gaze held Chloe's, and she heard in her head, *Take it, it is the future.*

"Chloe, come on," Cheftu said, tugging on her arm.

A sense of déjà vu flooded through Chloe as she turned to follow Cheftu, the air around them filled with the old woman's laughter.

They walked to the shabbier part of town, the mud-brick town homes leaning against each other like weary old people. The whitewash was chipped, and the shouts of children in the streets reached their ears. Despite its economic and social destruction, life in Egypt continued. Chloe saw a wooden hanging of a scorpion, and Cheftu pushed open the door. They stepped into a small courtyard. A lime tree at one time had shaded the courtyard; now it stood, bare branched, waving slightly in the breeze.

A middle-aged woman came forward, wiping floured hands on her striped *shenti*. She looked sharply at them, then laughed out through toothless gums. "My Lord Cheftu!" she cried, and hugged his neck. Chloe looked from the frumpy woman to Cheftu in surprise.

"Mara!" he greeted her. "Life, health, prosperity! This is my wife, Chloe."

The woman crossed her breast, one hand fiddling with her amulet against *khefts*. "Your servant, my lady," she wheezed. Mara looked back to Cheftu. "I see my lord and lady need a room." She bustled around to the staircase. "Just follow me."

They creaked up the stairs into a surprisingly bright room with a wide, curtained couch and a low table and stools. The window opened onto a small balcony from which they could see the Sacred Lake of the temple. Chloe heard the chink of gold, and then Cheftu was behind her, his arms tight around her waist.

"Former girlfriend?" she asked, basking in the sunshine streaming across the whitewashed buildings.

"The old girl is a goddess of a cook and silent as the grave. She was with us on the expedition to Punt. When she opened this boarding-house, Commander Ameni and I would come visit her, just for her lentil stew." He stood silent.

"What?"

"I was wondering if I would ever recall an incident or a memory not peopled with those who died in the plagues." His grip tightened around Chloe.

"You are crushing me," Chloe gasped out, and he loosened his hold. "I do not want to play this role, Cheftu . . . I do not want to go back." She turned in his arms and raised his face with her hand, touching the lines of cheek and jaw, nose and brow . . . memorizing it. His eyes were purest gold in the sunshine, and Chloe knew he was hiding his pain so she would not have to bear it. "What is today?" she said fearfully.

"The twentieth," he said. "We have three days, two nights."

"So we have today?"

"Until dinnertime," he said with an attempted smile. "Mara's cooking is not to be missed."

To Chloe, there was not enough time. She had loved Cheftu a hundred times, yet there were not enough hours left to absorb him into her flesh, to feel the satiny length of his skin and his power, to hear his throaty words against her skin. Not enough time.

• • •

Cheftu sensed her withdrawal and couldn't fault her for it, though he longed to tear into her and force her to share all with him. The resiliency he so admired and the strength of her that made him weak with longing were pulling her away, preparing her to return. She didn't want to go, but she knew she must—he loved her all the more for it. A memory fluttered at the edge of his consciousness. What if she was *not* returned to her time? What if she traveled somewhere else?

"Chloe," he said, "in your own time, you are red haired, correct?"

"Aye."

"Remember that dream you had? The dream when you thought you saw your sister and I thought I saw other features, hazily?"

"Aye," she said, moving away. "I was rolled out on a gurney, dead, I guess."

Cheftu didn't know exactly what a gurney was, but he could tell from her total motionless silence that the same idea had come to her. "If that was not a dream, but rather a glimpse of the future . . ."

"RaEm could be dead."

She turned to him, and Cheftu saw fear in her eyes. "I cannot go back like this! I will never fit in, never be able to explain." She looked out the window again. "I could step into someone else's body! Then what will I have? What will I be? How will I prove what I know?" She turned anguished eyes to him. "I will be so alone without you. . . ."

Cheftu put his hands on her arms. "If it is possible, I will follow you."

"Follow?"

"Aye. We have the same birthday. We got here the same way, even if from different times. I am going to study this while we are apart, see if there is more than this doorway, and if I can, I will follow you to your time."

"What about the sacrifice? What about that?"

Cheftu shrugged. "If I cannot follow, then apparently that will be the sacrifice. I can only try; if God does not allow it, I have no choice, do I?"

She ran her hands over his hard body. "Will we recognize each other, even in the same time? There are billions of people in my time. Billions . . . with a 'b.' Besides, how do I know you will not become a woman?"

Cheftu threw back his head and laughed. "A woman? You are afraid I could be a female?"

She furrowed her brow, hands on her hips. "It is not any crazier than the rest of this trip! Why not?"

"I have a male soul, beloved!" He kissed her hungrily. "I will always be a man, you a woman. This is the only way it can be. Now, enough of this foolish talk." He drew her to him, molding her warm body to his as he caressed the bones, muscle, and sinew he loved so well. How could he still want her when they had been together so many times? Almost to the extent of Chloe's "Baskin-Robbins" store . . . yet there was always more.

•••

Cheftu left the boardinghouse, the scent of Chloe still on his skin. Mara had fed him the Perfuming, and he walked into the bright sunshine. Heading toward the docks, he knew he would not buy passage to the Great Green as he had told Chloe, but he should stay gone a convincingly long time. He wandered across the main residential square, then walked up the Street of Goldsmiths.

The bracelet he'd given her as a wedding present was sadly worn, the silver soft and bending, the beads breaking. He would buy something for her. Though she had not brought any jewelry through with her, Cheftu prayed God that he would let her take back this small memento. He stepped into the courtyard of one Menfe, his heart breaking but his mind intent.

THE PLAINLY DRESSED BOY sloughed along after Cheftu. Even though the great lord was dressed in tradesmen's clothes, generations of command and power made him easy to identify. That was all he was supposed to do until the twenty-third of Phamenoth. Two more days, and the lord would be delivered to Thutmosis. The boy would have completed his first duty as Pharaoh's elite bodyguard.

CHLOE BIT INTO THE FLAKY PASTRY as she moved her marker. She caressed the top of Cheftu's foot. "Your move, beloved."

He rolled the throwing sticks, then counted up the points halfheartedly. "Cheftu?"

He raised his gaze from the board.

"What if we had managed to stay here, together? What would it have been like?"

He tossed throwing sticks, the clatter of them falling the only noise. "You enjoy slow torture, *haii*, beloved?"

She caressed the top of his foot with hers. "Nay . . . I just . . . well, was curious."

He smiled weakly. "Always curious Chloe." He ran a tongue over his dry lips. "We could have lived anywhere. My medical skills are very useful." He fingered the scar on his leg. "So are yours." He met her gaze. "Thank you for caring for me in the desert, beloved."

She looked away. "If we had stayed in Egypt?"

"If we had not offended Pharaoh, living forever? We would have dined at *atmu*, fowled with the court, and sent our children to the House of Life for education."

"Boys and girls?"

"*Absolument.*" He moved his piece. "You could have done anything. Manage, sell, paint."

"Even my artwork style?"

"Nay. Egypt is a rigid world, you know this. However, I have seen your traditional work, and you are without parallel." He watched dull red rise in her cheeks. "You could have painted our tomb . . . painting us eternally peaceful and joined. . . ." His voice trailed off.

Dear God—only one more day. He looked at Chloe, wrapped in a linen sheet, since they had hardly left the couch in the past twenty-four decans. His body was exhausted, pushed to the limits of endurance. He was trying desperately to store the experience of her to relive for a lifetime, if he managed to live. He moved his pointed blue marker. There was so much he wanted to say, such useless words to describe the unending pain he felt. Oddly enough, he felt no anger, just hurt—hurt so intense, he was tempted to wound himself physically just to counteract it. Yet there was a peace, a peace he couldn't explain.

Chloe rolled. Cheftu narrowed his eyes, trying to envision her with red hair and pale skin. His imagination failed him. He didn't care what she looked like, and that was the irony. He wanted her so much, so badly, needed her so, that the physical aspects of love were secondary to learning her soul and mind.

She lifted her foot to his kilt, caressing his abdomen and lower. She kicked aside the game board and crawled on him, a sleek cat. *"Fraise?"*

"Holy Osiris . . . !"

She was relentless, and all thought left Cheftu as feeling submerged him completely. He turned on his side, her muscular legs tempting him, and with a wicked laugh proceeded to teach Chloe about losing control.

•••

When Cheftu awoke he saw the sun, and his heart fell. The twenty-third. In twenty-four decans, where would she be? His heart contracted at the thought. Gently he turned over, dislodging Chloe, and the cool air touched his body. He realized how cold he was without her. She was deeply asleep and made no protest as he drew her to his chest, pushing her hair off her face as he murmured silly love words he could never say to her face and made promises to her sleeping form he couldn't keep once she was awake.

Then, holding her close to him, he wept. Silently the tears streamed from the corners of his eyes; his head pounded with despairing prayers. He breathed, open-mouthed, trying not to wake her, unwilling for this day to begin. She was not his. Despite his attempts to bind her and brand her, in the end she was free. It had been a blessing to know her and love her. *Le Dieu c'est bon.* He ground his teeth. A blessing; what a pathetic understatement. His body tensed with repressed emotions, and he pulled away from Chloe, tucking the blanket around her, afraid to awaken her. Standing at the window, he took gasping breaths. She must not see this. He had to be strong—for her, to make it easier.

When she was safely gone, he could wail like an infant.

When she was *safely* gone.

• • •

Cheftu was seated at the small table, writing. He looked up as she yawned. "Sleep well, beloved?" he asked with a soft smile. He poured a cup of milk and brought over the tray of pastries.

Chloe kissed him and accepted the Perfuming. "Aye," she said. "I had hoped to awaken earlier."

"You needed your rest." He kissed her, swallowing the words that said wherever she awoke tomorrow she would need to be at her best. "How do you feel?"

"Saddle sore," she said with a wicked grin, "but I'll be fine." Because I'll be in the twentieth century, home of antibiotics, shots, and hospitals, she thought. Will all of this be a dream then? She looked into Cheftu's eyes: golden. Never had she seen such eyes.

Cheftu dropped his gaze. "I bought you a gift," he said, stepping back to the table.

"I did not get you anything," she said. "I . . ."

He laid a finger on her lips. "I wanted to get you this. I want to say these words to you." He fumbled with the string around the small package, finally tearing it away. A ring lay inside, a perfect round of silver and gold, twisted together. He reached forward with a trembling hand and held it up to the light. In the center of each joining was a stone chip, the exact color of Cheftu's eyes.

"Aii!" Chloe cried out when she saw the sun streaming through the stones. "Assst, Cheftu!" Tears fell down her cheeks, and she looked up to his eyes, reddened and filled.

His voice was harsh with tears. "As unbreakable as is this circle, so is my love for you, Chloe. As pure as the metal, so do I love you. Like the silver and gold, our lives are woven together, forever binding us, even though we now take separate paths." He raised her hand and placed the ring on her middle finger, the finger most closely associated with the heart. He kissed it and held his mouth there, exhaling loudly as he fought for control.

"Cheftu!" she murmured through her tears, through her kisses. "Oh, God, how can I leave you? Come with me, please, come with me. Do not make me be without you—" Her voice broke, and they held each other, tears and passion mingling . . . the hours drifting away.

• • •

Mara knocked on the door. "Those patients you mentioned are here, Cheftu," she said in a low voice.

They were up immediately, dressing frantically. Chloe tied her sheath with shaking fingers as Cheftu slipped into his kilt and went to the window. "I cannot see the soldiers, but I hear them. Thank God for Mara's loyalty," he said. Chloe tied her bag around her waist and took his hand, the ring he gave her pressing into their joined flesh.

With a swing and some deft steps they landed on the street, hiding in the darkness. Cheftu took her hand and they ran through the night streets of Noph, dodging the *rekkit* and racing through alleyways to avoid the soldiers.

Here we go again, Chloe thought as they pounded up the deserted street to the Temple-of-the-Ka-of-Ptah, home of the twenty-third doorway. Peace filled her. She was doing the right thing. It didn't feel good—actually it hurt damnably—but she knew it was right. Focus on facts, not feelings, she told herself.

The temple was empty, the superstitious cowering at home on this day, considered the unluckiest in the ancient Egyptian calendar. No wonder there had been no more births on this day—the women born were destined to serve the goddess and die. Chloe shivered. A year ago it had all been different. She'd been alone, looking forward to new things in life, and almost an agnostic. Now she stood with the man who was her soul, praying to a God she'd met, while soldiers swarmed through the city searching for them.

They huddled in the shadows, Cheftu with one hand on his short sword, a torch in the other. Chloe held the hieroglyphic note in her hand, the last legacy from Imhotep.

They must find the twenty-third doorway. She looked at the map, as she had done a hundred times or more, searching through the passageways for something that would clue them into the twenty-third doorway. "Any luck?" Cheftu breathed over her shoulder.

"Nay. I suggest we go to the room where I first saw the clues. Maybe there is more of a description there."

"The sacred pools, *haii?*"

"Aye."

He released his sword and doused the torch as they wove back and forth through the columned courtyard, listening for others. None. Cheftu led her down a short corridor, and they stepped into the cross-passageway. Clinging to the shadows, they crept down, freezing when they heard the cry of a cat. They stood, not breathing, waiting for the footsteps they feared. Nothing. Creeping, they stepped into the cavernous blackness that was the Chamber of Sacred Cleansing.

It was pitch dark; Chloe couldn't see the white of her dress, never mind the ceiling. She heard the scrape of tinder and then the torch flared, accentuating the strong lines of Cheftu's face. He looked at her, and she wondered if he could hear the pulse pounding in her throat. He walked around the mud pool and stood beneath part of the ceiling. He held the torch high, but the room was still shadowed.

Chloe's hands shook. "Can you read it?"

"Aye," he said heavily. "In order to step through the doorway to the otherworld it says we have to be a priest or priestess of the order of RaEmhetep, on the twenty-third day, natal day twenty-three times three."

"We have guessed that means not only the twenty-third day, but also the twenty-third hour and twenty-third minute," Chloe said, excitement churning her insides.

"In the course of Ptah in the east," he murmured. "The depiction above is what the night sky should look like."

"Does it tonight?"

"Exactly," he said, his voice thick. "The 'prayerful obeisance in the twenty-third doorway,' that I do not understand."

"Obeisance?" Chloe said. "I thought it read 'prayer.' "

"Nay. This is an older dialect. The symbols are slightly different from those of today." He squinted up at the ceiling. "This is also a different glyph from those usually used."

"Cheftu!" Chloe squealed. "When you were in the chamber, in 1806, did you bow or anything before you crossed through?"

"Of course not. It was a pagan place, why would I . . . ?" He fell silent. "Wait. There was a piece of silver on the floor. . . ."

"Did you kneel to get it?"

"Aye. I put my hand to my heart. It was pounding with the thought of having found something."

"That is it!" Chloe crowed. "I tried to keep my backpack from slipping as I knelt!" They both looked at the ceiling, at the stick-figure drawing of a man, kneeling on one knee, his arm crossing his breast, and his left hand outstretched. "That is exactly how I was positioned," Chloe said breathlessly.

"As was I."

Chloe felt the hair rising on the back of her neck. "So where is the twenty-third doorway?"

"I need to get closer," Cheftu said. "The drawing up there has more details on the lintel of the door. Can you boost me?"

"I'll try," Chloe said, lacing her fingers together.

He stepped out of his sandals, and Chloe braced herself in the corner, groaning as his weight pressed down, while she pressed upward as hard as she could. He found a niche for his knee and leaned back to look up, holding the torch above his head. "I cannot hold you much longer," Chloe said through gritted teeth as she felt her back muscles straining. She groaned in relief when he jumped down. "Anything?"

"Aye. The doorway has the horns and disk of HatHor and is painted red. I do not know if it is an actual doorway, but maybe there is a wall painted like that around here. Where did Imhotep say he saw the priest change?"

Chloe thought furiously. "In an underground room, close to the papyrus storage." She looked at the map, wishing for a red tag reading "You are Here."

In his perfect memory Cheftu was already holding the map; he looked at the floor. "The picture shows obeisance. Looking at the floor and reaching for something." He knelt.

"A trapdoor?"

"I am not certain, but it is worth a search." They scrabbled on the floor, fingers running around the edges of the stones, searching for a ridge. Chloe skimmed her fingertips across one of the stones and then, with a small cry, drew it back.

"Are you hurt?"

"Just a cut."

"From what?"

"Holy Osiris! I think it is here!" Chloe said. "Hand me the torch!"

She took the torch in her trembling hands and searched. The metallic gleam was dim. Cheftu rubbed away the dirt; it was a flat lever of thinly hammered electrum, obviously not used for many, many years. "How does it work?" Chloe asked.

"Let us see," he said, and pushed it, hard. Nothing happened.

They waited a moment, and then a great creaking echoed through the room, and Chloe felt the ground begin to shake. She leapt onto another stone and watched as the floor directly underneath the drawing moved back, revealing a stale darkness that made the chamber above seem light. The creaking stopped, and Chloe jumped at Cheftu's touch on her arm. "Shall we?" he said, and they shuffled forward, holding the torch over the edge. They could see the first two steps, spiraling downward. Nothing else.

Gritting her teeth to keep them from chattering with fear, Chloe began to walk downstairs, Cheftu's warm hand on her shoulder, the other holding the torch high above them. "Is it going to stay open if we need to get out?" Chloe asked in a small voice, into the total darkness.

Cheftu paused. "I have no idea. Maybe you should wait above, while I search down here. That way, we're safe on both accounts."

"Nay," Chloe said firmly. "We do this together or not at all."

Cheftu was silent above her. "Then wait a moment while I try to rig it so that we are not trapped down there, *haii?*"

"Five minutes, Cheftu." She stood still as he walked up the steps. It was the plague of darkness all over. The stairs had spiraled so that the chamber above was hidden from view. She swallowed, hard. She had a feeling that something was not right. Cheftu had been odd, alternating between affectionate and withdrawn. They had managed too easily to elude Thut's best soldiers. As Cheftu would say, it didn't add up.

She heard footsteps above her.

"Chloe?"

"Still waiting," she said as he walked down to her, the torch keeping her dark fears at bay. Then his hand was on her shoulder, and they descended. And descended, farther and farther into the darkness. The steps were slippery, with nothing to hold on to except each other. Then Chloe couldn't go down any farther; they had reached the bottom. A gust of air extinguished the torch.

Cheftu stopped next to her and drew her into an embrace, burying his face in her neck. "I love you, *ma chérie!*" he whispered. She reached around him, feeling the granite muscles that held her tight, the skin that was sticky with cold sweat. Something beyond what she had expected was wrong. In the darkness she could almost hear shuffling.

He pulled away, glancing over his shoulder at the staircase. "Let us go," he said, thrusting her behind him as they walked across the chamber. It felt very small. She heard Cheftu fumbling around and then gasped as the torch illuminated the darkness.

The room was small but exquisite. They had come down the south wall, and to Chloe's right was a wall painted with the night sky, its constellations clearly marked. To the left was a wall covered in hieroglyphic writing, and Cheftu already moved alongside it, his lips moving as he read the message.

Directly across from Chloe was the doorway.

In actuality it was a large alcove, the paintings outside it identifying it clearly. She walked toward it, her heart in her mouth, and began to read the signs. It told a story, a story of a priestess who was blessed by an unnamed god who brought her from the otherworld to view his *neter* power and send her . . . hmm . . . somewhere? . . . to describe what she had seen. The design was typical two-dimensional Egyptian, but Chloe's skin crawled when she saw that the dark-skinned, black-haired priestess had green eyes.

Peace engulfed her . . . the same peace that had drawn her here, to be used yes, but as a tool, with every freedom to refuse. *Destiny*, a voice breathed through her consciousness.

Cheftu now stood behind her, and she could hear his strangled gasp. "It is you. All of this speaks of you," he said.

The goose bumps on her body were the size of peas. "Yes," she said in English. "I am supposed to return." She heard it again, the stealthy steps somewhere above them. "Come with me," she said. "I know you believe you have nothing, but in the twentieth century we can be together. Maybe you have a new destiny!"

"*Non*, I cannot go back. Jean-François Champollion *le jeune* faded with me in the nineteenth century."

Chloe spun around, choking. "Jean-François Champollion!" For a moment she stared incredulously at his bronze features. "That . . . that . . . that is not your name, is it? Are you, were you, Jean-François Champollion?"

"*Je suis*," he said with a credible bow. "My brother betrayed me. He discovered the key to the hieroglyphs, as you said."

"*No!*" Chloe screeched. "I told you *a* Champollion did it! Jean-François! *He* is the father of Egyptology. You!"

Cheftu's face was gray, even in the blazing torchlight. "It is not possible," he whispered. "How do you know these things?"

"I read a book the day before I crossed through! It was about Napoleon's coming to Egypt. It mentioned the older Champollion, and how he brought his little brother," *who was already a linguist in his own right,* she recalled Cheftu's own words. "He became very ill on the trip, right after Karnak. He was sent home with Jean-Jacques, and it was a while before he was healthy again." Her voice dropped to a hoarse whisper, the words she had read now scorched into her mind's eye. "After that, everyone who met him said he seemed like an ancient Egyptian, he was so in tune with the culture!" She continued, staring. "He spent his life deciphering the hieroglyphs! He claimed they were not just religious pictures, but that they also represented sounds and an alphabet. He wrote books outlining the pharaohs and how they lived. He spent his whole life on Egypt."

Cheftu sagged against the wall. "You are serious? He accomplished this in my name? I did not fade into disgrace?"

Her mind fumbled to believe this. "Dead serious," she said. "The boy you saw . . . you must have changed places, and he . . . well, was Champollion." She stared at her husband. "He must have been, because you look only vaguely like Champollion's picture."

"Mon Dieu," Cheftu said, sinking to the floor.

She knelt beside him. "Champollion?" she whispered, laying an icy hand on the knees she knew so well. "I don't know what to say," she said. "It's odd to discover your husband is a . . . a historical figure!"

"Aii, history," he said, his cold hand over hers. Sounds came to them, muffled but definite. *"Haii, mon Dieu,* what have I done?" he whispered as he looked toward the stairs.

"What?" Chloe asked, suddenly aware that Cheftu was listening for someone.

"Go into the doorway, beloved," Cheftu said, rising and pushing her forward. "You must leave."

Chloe walked over and stood in the alcove, her knees knocking. "I cannot leave without you," she said.

"Go with God, beloved," he replied, his voice cracking.

She swallowed as soldiers stepped out of the darkness, their bows trained on Cheftu. "What is this?" she cried.

"Go!" Cheftu yelled.

"Aye, *kheft,"* Thut said, stepping forward. "Leave before more evils are heaped on Egypt. Do not cheapen the gift of life your lover has bought you."

Chloe looked at Cheftu, stunned. "Bought me?"

Cheftu stared at her, his eyes bright with tears.

"Once you leave," Thut said, "which was the former *erpa-ha*'s request, this room will be dismantled. Then Cheftu will lead me to the golden glory *that woman* stole. With the gold she took from Egypt I will rebuild, and become the greatest pharaoh Egypt has ever known. Then I shall conquer. After I have finished reclaiming Egypt's resources, I shall eradicate memory of her dishonorable rule. Not even one cartouche of her shall remain!"

"Why?" Chloe asked, tears streaming down her cheeks. "Why now? She is beyond you."

"Someone must take the blame for the Apiru god's works!" he hissed. "Someone must have bloodied hands from the death of thousands! It will not be me! Since those things happened, *technically*, while she was on the throne, her accepting blame for them is natural, and we can purge Egypt. This destruction was due to the unnatural state of affairs: a woman on the throne. I will erase her name from the King's List, and it will be a lesson to not interfere with the laws of Ma'at."

Chloe looked at Cheftu. His face was like parchment, tears streaking his kohl into black-and-gray stripes down his face. He dropped to one knee, as if too weak to stand. Soldiers moved around him, and Chloe cried aloud when she saw the spears pressing red points into his neck and chest. Cheftu reached up, holding one away from his jugular.

In the end there was no time for tears, no last words, no lingering touch. She knelt, her eyes fixed on his, not speaking, just drinking in the last sight of him, her *ka*. Already a wind whipped around her. She crossed her breast with a trembling hand, and they stretched left hands toward each other as Cheftu closed his eyes in anguish. *There is no greater love than to lay down your life for a friend. . . .* The words floated through her brain.

Time snapped.

Cheftu's agonized cry faded into the roar of jumbled sound, tearing, separating, dividing her soul and body. Painful currents leapt through her scrambled senses until, at last, blissful, peaceful darkness enveloped her, warming, comforting . . . like a beloved embrace.

EPILOGUE

Thutmosis, Egypt's Mighty Bull of Ma'at, Lord of the Two Lands, Lord of the Horizon, Horus Hakarty, Men-kheper-Ra Tehuti-mes III, Ruler of Upper and Lower Egypt, Beloved of Buto, Son of the Sun, Living Forever! Life! Health! Prosperity! stormed through his chambers, restless in the hours of night. When he slept, dreams came to him— dreams based on reality yet tinged with horrors from the *Book of the Dead*. He stepped onto his balcony, inhaling the fresh air and listening to the chink of chisel and hammer that floated up on every breeze in these days. The removal of Hatshepsut was almost complete. The council had finally declared her dead after he had ruled in her name for five Inundations. The *rekkit* were no longer fearful of the gods' wrath; his enemies inside Egypt were dead or gone.

"Gone," he said out loud. His mind moved back, involuntarily, to the Nophite chamber. He'd been so glib, so certain he had the key in his hand. Not only would he get all that Hat had secreted away, but he would have the satisfaction of a broken and willing Cheftu. Vengeance on the man who had sworn fealty and then broken it would be restorative. Cheftu had been held tightly, a dare to move toward the woman in the alcove.

Then, in a shorter time than an eyeblink, they were gone. The torches were extinguished as if a mighty, rushing wind had blown through. Both were gone. Even as the soldiers dismantled the room, finding a dozen secret passageways, not a clue to their whereabouts had ever shown up. Still, a guard stood watch, waiting, hopelessly, Thut thought, for RaEm and Cheftu to resurface.

He stepped inside and lay on his couch. He needed to rest. Before dawn he and the new might of Egypt would set forth across the desert, purging the sands of those who did not worship Egyptian gods or follow Egyptian customs. A tribe would either assimilate or die. In their dying, Egypt would take their gold and spices, and gain. He would build an empire, a mighty empire that stretched far beyond the Egypt of his forefathers. Thut knew without a doubt that from this moment on he would be successful in all he did. He smiled grimly, thinking of the Presence that gave him such confidence. He had served his time as a tool of the Unknowable and was now free to live as he would.

He closed his eyes as exhaustion shook him.

Tomorrow would begin a new life for the land of Egypt.

DARKNESS ENGULFED ME. It was pitch, like night. I sat up slowly, my hand to my pounding head where it felt slightly disconnected. My sense of direction was shot; I had no clue as to where I might be. The silence was consuming as the last images from the temple played back in my mind . . . and with their viewing came searing pain. *Haii*, Cheftu! Oh, God, Cheftu!

Then I froze as the ghost of a voice echoed, rich and velvety, in the blackness around me.

"Chloe?"

AUTHOR'S AFTERWORD

There are as many theories about the Exodus, the path the Children of Israel took through the desert, the pharaoh at the time, and the number of people who went as there are archaeologists and theologians. According to the Bible, Solomon built his temple 480 years after the Exodus from Egypt. This places the Exodus in the eighteenth dynasty during the lifetime and reign of Hatshepsut.

Pharaoh Hatshepsut ruled as a man, though she was a woman. She co-reigned with her half-brother, and after he died she entered a co-regency with the child Thutmosis III, whom she quickly usurped, crowning herself Hatshepsu I. She historically brought a period of peace and prosperity, restoring old monuments and establishing new ties with other countries. Apparently she had the priesthood and the nobles behind her, a powerful political statement in any day and age.

Factually, no one knows what happened at the end of her reign. There is no body, and her tomb is empty. All that is known is that Thutmosis, for whatever reason, during his reign sought to eliminate her from the King's List and to erase every good thing she did. Why? Jealousy is an easy answer, but for the type of ritual destruction Thutmosis—and probably other kings—endorsed, it is too shallow.

A reasonable explanation is that something happened during her reign that was such anathema, the only way to rebuild and restore Egypt was to repudiate her and her reign completely. Only under those conditions would the accepted and systematic destruction of her monuments occur. Combining this with the Exodus timeline . . . and the reported miraculous or just frighteningly fierce and prompt plagues that destroyed the countryside . . . we have a possible explanation.

Yes, the plagues are easily explained by science. Bloody water is red algae; fish die, and frogs go on land. Lack of food leads to their deaths, generating flies and gnats and lice. They infect the cattle; the cattle infect the people. An eclipse, a locust plague—common enough in Africa—hail, then fear make the Egyptians sacrifice their own children, trying to win the favor of their gods. The slaves get to leave. But even with a rational, scientific explanation . . . the timing mystifies. The duration and control of the plagues is something Pharaoh and all his court could not explain, and neither can we.

Senmut is also lost in history. Five years before the end of Hatshepsut's reign, he vanishes. No comments. No body. His pets, of which there were many, were mummified and buried. His family was buried in the tombs he had built for them. But of the grand vizier, architect, and *erpa-ha* we know nothing. Was he murdered in a palace coup? Or was he, a firstborn son, caught in the final plague?

Moses is known from the Bible and revered as a prophet in all three monotheistic religions. As a former prince through adoption, he alone of the Israelites had the position, authority, and ability to negotiate with Pharaoh. Certainly he understood and spoke the high, flowery Egyptian of the court, something few Israelites could claim. But whom did he kill that he fled his adopted father's wrath? My supposition is certainly one possibility, but who knows?

Very little is known about the religious practices of ancient Egypt, though it stands to reason that eating a calf in its mother's milk, so strongly forbidden by the Hebrew God, could have been a religious ritual. Was HatHor, seen as a cow and the goddess of dancing, music, and love, the "golden calf" that caused Moses' great wrath when he smashed the first copy of the Ten Commandments?

To my knowledge human sacrifice was not an Egyptian concept, though I am certain that, as in every culture, darker cults existed. Of all the ancient world the Egyptians were by far the most hygienic, the happiest natured, and the least bloodthirsty. Their gods liked beer and bread, and everyone in both this world and the afterworld sought to live peaceably with their family in a tree-laden garden.

Egyptian medicine, from the papyri we have, is exactly as portrayed. The Egyptian mind was so interrelated with magic and religion that taking "medicine" or undergoing surgery alone would not suffice. For every physical action there was a concurrent spiritual one. The Egyptian equivalent of "take two aspirin and call me in the morning" was "have an enema, get an amulet, and call me in the morning." The Egyptians were also known for their sophisticated techniques. Brain surgery and cataract surgery were both done—though no one knows how the patients fared.

The land bridge between the Sinai peninsula and the Arabian coastline exists, and in the passage of seventy days, it would be possible for a group moving at seven to ten miles a day to reach the coastline from Avaris. Unleavened bread baked in the sand beneath a fire, limestone as an indicator of water, the mountains, and scarce wildlife are all as true today in the Sinai desert and of its dwellers as in Moses' time.

Chloe's military background and reservist assignment are possible. In Denton, Texas, a mere thirty miles from Dallas, the Federal Emergency Management Agency guards, watches, and reacts to national disasters. Though the military aspects of the agency are confined to terrorism alone, the "uniforms" may volunteer to assist in any disaster. The air force group based there is minuscule, but as an air force brat myself, I couldn't place Chloe in another branch of the military.

Like many of the other characters in *Reflections in the Nile*, Jean-François Champollion *le jeune*, the father of Egyptology, actually existed. He was born December 23, 1790, although, in contrast with my book, he did not travel to Egypt until 1828. It is documented that he had a strikingly Oriental appearance, with dark skin and "yellow" eyes. It is also documented that speaking to him was like "speaking to an ancient Egyptian come back to life." After learning more than twenty languages, he discovered the key to the hieroglyphs through the Rosetta stone.

A note on sources and spellings. Having "grown up" in the British Museum, I used E. A. W. Budge's *Egyptian Hieroglyphic Dictionaries* for many of the ancient words in *Reflections*. As this book is a culmination of a lifetime of study, I cannot possibly give a full listing of the articles, books, maps, stories, illustrations, and other materials I have used.

However, my constant guides during the writing of this book were John Anthony West's *Traveler's Key to Ancient Egypt*, a wonderful guidebook and insight to all things Egyptian; Ian Wilson's *Exodus: The True Story*, which inspired and instructed me; Peter Clayton's *The Rediscovery of Ancient Egypt*; and, most important, the original story of the Exodus from the Bible in three different translations, including Hebrew.

Did the Exodus actually happen? Though there is no "accepted" proof for it outside of the Bible, something similar must have happened for it to become the bedrock of Judaism and the foundation of the nation of Israel: "Hear O Israel: the LORD our God, the LORD is one . . . be careful that you do not forget the LORD who brought you out of Egypt, out of the land of slavery." (Dt. 6:4,12)

So, the journey continues.

J. SUZANNE FRANK
Denton, Texas, June 1996

ACKNOWLEDGMENTS

A word of thanks to a group of people whom I cannot thank enough. To Melanie and Dwayne, who unfailingly read through countless versions and gave their critiques and enthusiasm; to Joe, Laura, and Rene, who proofed and polished; to Dr. Phillipe A. Dubé for verifying how to cauterize; to Dr. Diane Boyd for the French translations; to Anne Henehan and Pat Sprinkle for the last minute Latin; to Lynn Job for insight into the military; to Dr. Barbara Wedgwood and SMU Continuing Education, who gave me a chance; to Mary Ann Eckels for believing in me and referring me; to my "kids" and Carrie and Donna, who prayed that I would get published. May I never forget this lesson: God listens and answers. Great thanks to my friends and writing group for the encouragement. And thanks, Mel, for the title.

Forever will I be indebted to and enamored of my editor at Warner Books, Susan Sandler, who was willing to take a risk on an unknown. In every writer's fantasy, would they be so lucky to get a "Susan" of their own. She saw my vision and loved this world of the senses and adventure as much as I. Thanks so very much, Susan—you are the best!

Most profoundly I thank my family. For a decade's worth of *Writer's Digest*, the conferences, and always knowing my words would be in print someday, thank you, Daddy. Mom, for all the bits and pieces of biblical lore, cutting-edge discoveries, human insight, and artistic vision, thank you. To my Baba for the zest of life, Chloe's background, and a thousand other things—words cannot say enough. To Granny, for the gift that changed my life forever.

Finally, to my partner in crime—who gave me Egypt and Israel in the flesh, the understanding of soul mates, a Mac notebook, and liberal helpings of Diet Coke and M&M's: Rob, bless you. I love you.

My thanks and love to you all!